THE DISTANCE BETWEEN US

GEORGIE CAPRON lives in South West London with her husband and daughter. Alongside her writing she works as a primary school teacher and she particularly enjoys teaching English. She studied Italian and History of Art at the University of Edinburgh and did a PGCE in primary education at the University of London.

THE DISTANCE BETWEEN US

Georgie Capron

An Aria Book

First published in the UK in 2018 by Aria, Head of Zeus
part of Bloomsbury Publishing Plc

Copyright © Georgie Capron, 2018

The moral right of Georgie Capron to be identified
as the author of this work has been asserted in accordance with
the Copyright, Designs and Patents Act of 1988.

All rights reserved. No part of this publication may be reproduced,
stored in a retrieval system, or transmitted in any form or by any means,
electronic, mechanical, photocopying, recording, or otherwise,
without the prior permission of both the copyright owner
and the above publisher of this book.

This is a work of fiction. All characters, organizations, and events
portrayed in this novel are either products of the author's
imagination or are used fictitiously.

A catalogue record for this book is available from the British Library.

ISBN: 9781035916825

Printed and bound in Great Britain by
CPI Group (UK) Ltd, Croydon CR0 4YY

Head of Zeus
First Floor East
5–8 Hardwick Street
London EC1R 4RG

WWW.HEADOFZEUS.COM

About *The Distance Between Us*

Happy children, happy husband, happily ever after?

Tasha knows that she should count her blessings: married for eleven years, mother to three healthy children, she should be content with her lot. However, feelings of frustration have settled over her like a dark cloud. Despite living under the same roof and sharing the same bed, Tasha has never felt so distant from her husband, Charlie. She feels worn down by the mental load of motherhood, drowning in the never-ending chores that keep the family and household afloat. Most of all she worries that her once happy marriage is slipping away from her.

Tasha longs for something to change, but when change comes calling will it really be the answer she was hoping for? And is it possible to fall in love with the same person twice?

Also by Georgie Capron

Just the Two of Us
One Summer in Positano

For my family

Chapter One

Tasha stooped to slip on her black suede heels, trying not to trip on a pile of abandoned sports kit. She picked up the offending articles, swiftly identifying which of her three children was the culprit, walked down the corridor and shoved them in the laundry basket.

'Bella, is that your games kit I've just nearly fallen over in the hall?' she yelled up the stairs. The house seemed to be permanently awash with possessions, with Tasha fighting an endless one-woman battle to restore order.

'Oops! Sorry, Mum!' Bella replied through a mouthful of toothpaste as her younger brother, Max, came scampering down the stairs rosy cheeked from the bath.

Flora was sitting at the kitchen table trying to finish her homework. 'What are you doing, Max?' Tasha asked, noticing a mischievous giggle. She suspected he had been up to no good, hoping it wasn't a repeat of last week's antics, involving a can of shaving foam and an attempt at graffiti on the bathroom wallpaper. Max's burst of creativity had left an oily residue in the apparent shape of his favourite animal, a giraffe, which, to the untutored eye, was hard to interpret as anything other than an oversized drawing of male genitalia.

'Just getting a drink of water,' he replied, the picture of innocence.

Tasha didn't have time to suss out any potential mayhem that may or may not have occurred upstairs. She was about to go out and she hadn't finished putting on her make-up.

'Where can Daddy be?' she asked no one in particular, mentally cursing Charlie for being late on the one night of the year she had dared to make plans of her own.

Tonight was the celebratory dinner of her last school friend to get engaged and, as always, the gang had pounced on the opportunity to ditch their children and get glammed up for a night. Tasha was desperate for a few glasses of prosecco and a good gossip. She hit speed dial on her mobile, clenching it between her shoulder and her right ear as she fastened an earring with her spare hand. Straight to voicemail again. She hung up. He must still be on the Tube.

'Right, Flora, you need to start thinking about finishing up or you'll be in bed far too late.' Tasha grabbed a few dirty plates from the counter and loaded them into the dishwasher.

'It's too hard!' Flora moaned, rubbing her head with her hands.

'Then just tell Mrs Edmundson that you couldn't do

it and I'm sure she'll help you!'

'It doesn't *work* like that, Mum.' Flora sighed. 'I've got to get it right or I'll get in trouble. You *never* understand.'

Tasha took a deep breath; when it came to Flora she couldn't seem to say anything right these days.

'But surely it's OK to make mistakes, darling!' Tasha reassured her. 'It'll just show Mrs Edmundson that you need more practice. I'm sure you're not the only one finding it tricky…' Tasha knew her daughter would be awake all night beating herself up if she thought she was letting herself down. 'Daddy can have a look when he gets home… which should be any second.'

She surveyed the scene in front of her. For some unknown reason the contents of her handbag were strewn all over the floor. Last weekend's papers and piles of unopened mail were stacked on one end of the table. Abandoned school bags, PE kits and coats lay slumped against the wall instead of hanging on their designated pegs by the front door. The bins were overflowing and the floor was desperately dirty and long overdue a sweep. Tasha took a deep breath. There was no time to tackle the kitchen – maybe Charlie would do some tidying when he got home? She doubted it, not after such a 'busy' day at the office. 'Right, you little rascal, up to bed,' she said, ruffling Max's sandy-blond hair as he rushed past her and back upstairs, still giggling.

She chased after him, pulling her black stretchy skirt down as she went, trying to feel whether her pants might be visible through the material. She had excavated a pretty black top with a lace trim from the bottom of her chest of drawers, which, though crumpled, at least made her look as though she'd made an effort.

Tasha arrived in Max's room to find him tucked up in bed, for once. 'What story would you like, little mischief maker?'

'*Aliens Love Underpants,*' Max pleaded.

'Not again?' Tasha laughed half-heartedly. It must be the millionth time she had read it. She knew every word off by heart.

'It's the best!' he squealed as he wriggled over to make room for her. She chided herself for being so unenthusiastic.

Tasha checked her phone once again – still nothing from Charlie. Trying to put her mounting impatience to one side, she read Max the story and then kissed his pale forehead and turned off his light. Whilst she was grateful he seemed to have gone to bed without protest for once, she noted that Max never seemed to have one of his full-blown temper tantrums when Charlie was in sole charge. A petty part of Tasha would rather he was climbing the walls and kicking off at the exact moment her other half walked through the door. Bella was already in her room next door, reading a Harry Potter book. She was obsessed with the young wizard and his motley crew.

Every night Bella needed persuading to put down whichever well-thumbed book she held and to go to sleep. She was a classic bookworm. Tasha could always tell if she'd been up in the middle of the night reading from the extent of the bags under her eyes the following morning. She frequently received phone calls from Bella's school enquiring whether she was getting enough sleep. They clearly thought Tasha was too lax to enforce the regulatory 7.30 p.m. bedtime. How right they were! No matter how early she tried to start their bedtime routine she was lucky if she managed to get them down by eight o'clock.

'Right, darling, time to turn your light off,' Tasha said as she kissed her goodnight.

'Night, Mum.' Bella reached to switch off the bedside table lamp.

'No sneaky reading in the dark...'

'I won't!' Bella smiled, resting her head on the pillow and closing her eyes in a bid to convince her mother that she meant what she said.

Tasha pulled the door to before heading back downstairs to try and encourage Flora to part with her homework. Her mind boggled at the complexity of the algebraic equations a ten-year-old was expected to solve these days.

Just as she was peering quizzically at number eight the landline rang.

She picked up the receiver. 'Hello?'

'Tasha, it's me,' came the ever-so-familiar voice of her husband, Charlie.

'Where are you? I'm so late!' she moaned, expecting the reply to be that he was just about to walk through the door at any second.

He paused. 'I'm afraid I'm stuck here,' he said, awkwardly.

Tasha's heart sank, swiftly replaced by a flush of anger. '*What?* But it's Steph's engagement dinner. I'm all dressed up and ready to go…'

'I know. And I'm sorry.'

'God, why didn't you tell me earlier? Then at least I might have found someone else to help. I'll never find anyone now…' Tasha was aware she was whining but she couldn't help herself.

'I was stuck in a meeting room with no signal.' Charlie sounded somewhat sheepish. 'I'm really sorry. I'll be home as soon as I can…' He tailed off.

Tasha slammed the phone into its holder, misjudging her aim and causing the phone to ping up and fly down the back of the table. This did nothing to calm her nerves. She dragged the side table out with a screech and extracted the handset from a coating of dust so thick it had congregated into giant, spidery clumps. It was clearly a very long time since she had pulled out the furniture to clean the harder-to-reach gaps. She tried to quell the tide of burning resentment that welled up inside her. Her eyes smarted with tears. She knew

Charlie's job in asset management was all-consuming but she still felt unbelievably let down. She had been *so* looking forward to this evening. It was yet another disappointment to add to the never-ending list that seemed to be accumulating under Charlie's name.

'Dad's not coming home?' Flora said with a sigh. 'Great. So *you're* the only one who can help me?'

Tasha took a calming breath. 'Sorry, darling, I'm afraid he's stuck at work.' She fixed a false smile on her cheeks and said with a sort of crazed enthusiasm, 'Don't worry! I'm sure we can figure it out. Let's have another look!' She pulled up a chair and sat next to Flora. Together they puzzled through the remaining questions so that Flora could get herself upstairs and ready for bed. To add insult to injury, Tasha's phone vibrated with messages on her school friends' WhatsApp group – a bottle of champagne and lots of brimming glasses, a photo of Steph with her sparkling diamond ring, and a third saying 'Hurry up and get here!' undoubtedly aimed at her.

Kicking off her heels despondently, she made a few phone calls to her trusty friends with au pairs and her usual babysitters, but as she had suspected no one was free last minute to come and look after her children. She picked up the phone and called Flo, her closest friend from the group.

'Tash!' she said, already sounding as if she'd had a couple of drinks. 'Where are you?'

'I'm so sorry, Flo... I'm going to have to bail. Bloody Charlie is stuck at work. I'm so gutted...' Tasha felt her eyes fill with tears, which she furiously bit back.

'Oh, no! What a shame!' Flo replied. Tasha could hear all the hyperactive chatter coming from the rest of the group. She felt even more upset not to be there.

'Look, send my love to Steph and apologise for me. I'll arrange to see her soon...' Tasha hung up and sighed loudly.

After a few minutes staring blankly at the peeling paint on the wall, in desperate need of redecorating, she dragged herself upstairs to check on Flora, who was in bed reading. 'Lights out soon, darling,' she said.

'I'm just going to get to the end of my chapter.'

'OK, sleep tight!'

'Mum?' Flora said, peering over the edge of her book. 'Thanks for your help earlier...'

'*You* did really well – but I'm not sure how much use I was!' She laughed as she closed the door.

Tasha popped in to check on Max and Bella who both seemed to be sleeping peacefully. Lacking any enthusiasm, she went into the kitchen and slopped the rest of the children's dinner into a bowl. Pasta and a tomato sauce, not very exciting. She whacked it into the microwave and pressed the timer, finishing the washing-up while it turned around. She grated some cheese over the top in a bid to make it a little more appetising before carrying her meal through to the sitting room and plonking herself on the sofa. What a surprise – there was nothing to watch. For the second time that evening she felt absurdly close to tears. How come all of her friends had managed to sort out childcare except for her? It was Charlie's fault. She hoped that he would be feeling guilty.

Chapter Two

When Charlie finally got home later that evening he found Tasha sitting on the sofa watching *One Born Every Minute*.

'Hi,' he said, bending down to give her a kiss. She kept her eyes fixed on the television, cradling a large glass of red wine close to her chest. She tried to suppress the disproportionate anger that raged in her chest.

'Hi,' she replied, keeping her voice flat and her tone curt, trying to communicate just how unimpressed she was.

'Sorry about this evening,' Charlie said.

She glanced at him. The sight of his dishevelled brown hair, his kind blue eyes crinkled and apologetic, almost softened her resolve but she couldn't help herself. Instead of telling him not to worry about it, that it wasn't his fault that he had got stuck in a meeting, she shrugged her shoulders. 'It's OK,' she said.

Charlie knew her well enough after eleven years of marriage to realise that there wasn't an awful lot of point in talking to her when she had gone into quiet mode. She would answer him with as few syllables as possible. If he forced the matter things would undoubtedly escalate into a full-blown argument, which he was clearly keen to avoid. Knowing that it was better to leave her in peace, he went upstairs to have a shower.

Tasha remained on the sofa, simmering quietly. She didn't know at what point she had stopped feeling as though she could talk to Charlie about her emotions. There would have been a time where she would have tackled her disappointment straight away, talking it out, arguing even, but then making peace and laughing it off, possibly even ending up in bed to kiss and make up. The worst thing was that she wasn't even sure if Charlie noticed. Was he upstairs worrying that she was annoyed with him? She doubted it.

Charlie had always been the most happy-go-lucky of guys. In fact, it was that particular character trait that had attracted her to him in the first place, fourteen years ago at the tender age of twenty-three. She remembered the first second she had seen him, across a crowded party. Tall, dark and good-looking, with those huge, warm blue eyes. She had thought he looked perfect and had repositioned herself next to him to place her order at the bar, striking up conversation as she'd waited for her drinks. It had turned out he had been single for several years, not even looking for a girlfriend until he met Tasha. He had sworn off women completely following a nasty breakup. But when he had met Tasha it had been love at first sight. She had helped him move on from his heartbreak and they had never looked back.

She still loved him to the end of the earth, and she knew how much he loved her, but somewhere along the way, amidst the sleepless nights, the school runs, the endless piles of laundry and the humdrum of daily life, it was safe to say their relationship had lost some of its initial spark. The all-consuming lust she had felt for him in the beginning had dissipated. She supposed most marriages were the same... well, at least she hoped theirs wasn't unusual in that respect; it seemed inevitable really.

*

Friday morning dawned bright and breezy. Tasha felt a lot better as she stepped from the open-plan kitchen into the garden and took in a deep breath of fresh air. She sipped her coffee, admiring an intricate cobweb that had appeared overnight, spun silver in the morning light. The grass was heavy with dew. Fat droplets of water clung to glossy leaves and dangled from branches like miniature crystal baubles. It was her morning ritual, a moment's peace to herself before she got the children up and ready for school. Charlie had already left at some ungodly hour to go to work leaving Tasha to relish this time alone at the start of each day before chaos inevitably broke out. Having finished her coffee, she tipped some porridge oats into a pan and poured milk over the top, setting it to simmer while she went to rouse the children.

Once they were all up, dressed and full of breakfast

Tasha helped them gather their bookbags, homework diaries and coats, ruing the fact that she had yet again failed to ensure each child's bags were ready to go the night before. It had been her over-optimistic new year's resolution, picturing the calm morning routine that her excellent organisational skills could create with a bit of forward planning. Tasha accompanied the children to school before setting about her household chores, fighting the overwhelming sense of boredom that had grown steadily heavier over the years. As she loaded yet another wash into the machine she received a text from Charlie to remind her that he wouldn't be home for dinner. He was meant to be going out for drinks with a few of his friends from university. She had known this was in the diary so had arranged for a friend to come over for a catch-up dinner, she was grateful that she had made plans so she wouldn't be spending yet another evening drinking alone in front of the television.

While she cooked moussaka for dinner her thoughts returned to the previous night. Irritation and resentment simmered away in the pit of her stomach. They had gone to sleep after reading their books side by side in virtual silence. In a way she wished Charlie had taken her passive-aggressive bait and that things had escalated into a full-blown argument. At least then she could have aired her grievances. Anything was better than the current lack of communication that seemed to be building a gulf between them that at times felt insurmountable. It occurred to Tasha that last night's disappointment would never have happened the other way around. Charlie would never miss a night out due to childcare arrangements. He was always out already so he never needed to cancel his plans last minute because she couldn't get home in time. It was so unfair.

At half past three Tasha was waiting at the school gates as first Max and then Bella came barrelling out of the door and into the playground in a flurry of grins, school bags and blazers. She scooped up as many belongings as she could, taking one grubby hand in each of hers to walk home. Flora, who was playing hockey, was being dropped off by another mum later on. Tasha couldn't help but laugh as they chattered all the way home, full of energy and ready for the weekend. She tried to muster matching levels of enthusiasm when, really, all she longed for was a weekend of peace and quiet, to read a book uninterrupted, or something equally unheard of.

'Are we still going to Richmond Park tomorrow, Mum?' Bella asked.

'That's the plan,' Tasha replied. 'I'm hoping it'll stay dry so we can have a nice picnic.'

'Yum!' cried Max. 'Can we make sausage rolls?'

'And take tomato ketchup?' Bella asked.

'We'll see what we can do!' Tasha laughed.

They continued to plan their picnic all the way home. They were clearly children after her own heart: food was often their favourite topic of conversation.

As they entered the kitchen Tasha screeched in dismay. 'Oh, *sh...ugar*!'

'What's happened, Mum?'

'Why is there water everywhere?'

'It's the machine,' Tasha said. 'It must have flooded.'

'Oh, no!' the children gasped, enjoying the drama.

'Right! You go into the sitting room while I try and clean this mess up...' Cursing under her breath, she took off her shoes and socks, rolled up her jeans and waded through the water to locate the mop. *Bloody typical,* she thought. All their appliances were conking out; some were as ancient as the house itself and in desperate need of replacing. This was going to be another expensive purchase if she couldn't figure out a way to repair it herself.

At eight o'clock the doorbell rang. Tasha opened the door and threw her arms around Rosie, one of her oldest friends.

'It's been too long!' she said as she hugged her, taking the bottle of wine Rosie proffered and leading her into the kitchen. 'Excuse my bedraggled appearance, I haven't had time to change. The sodding washing machine broke...'

'Oh, God! Any idea why?'

'There was a blockage. After unscrewing the plug and draining it I found three of Charlie's cufflinks, a hair tie and a safety pin... fingers crossed that's all that was wrong and we won't have to buy a new one.'

'What a nightmare! But well done for fixing it. And how are my favourite little angels?' Rosie asked, peering up the stairs.

'Asleep, thankfully,' replied Tasha, crossing her fingers.

'What, even my goddaughter?'

'She's reading – I told her you'd go up and say goodnight.' Rosie disappeared upstairs to have a chat with Flora while Tasha opened a bottle of wine and poured them both large glasses. Rosie had proved to be the most wonderful godmother. She was single and had no children of her own so was free to give due time and attention to Flora and her numerous other godchildren.

Sometimes Tasha envied Rosie her freedom. She was a long-term singleton, by choice rather than through circumstance. She was a journalist who wrote a very successful blog about her single lifestyle in her free time: an extremely entertaining read, which had won her thousands upon thousands of followers and some lucrative advertising contracts. Tasha suspected her popularity was also partly down to her huge doe eyes and pouting lips – she looked as if she had had collagen implants but it was all annoyingly natural.

'Flora seems well,' Rosie said as she joined Tasha in the kitchen. 'Is she still acting like a moody teenager?' She took off her jacket and slung it on the back of one of the mismatched wooden chairs. Tasha's furniture collection mainly consisted of hand-me-downs from both her and Charlie's parents, as well as an assortment of junk-shop pieces and freebies she had picked up from Freecycle or even, in the case of their chest of drawers, the side of the road. Having spent every penny they owned on the house, they had never had much spare cash for its interior design.

'Is she ever! She can be a serious handful. You wouldn't believe the attitude! Especially at the moment. She's a bit stressed about maths and she really struggled with her homework last night. I think I might ring her teacher and see what we can do to help...'

'Poor Flora.' Rosie frowned, taking the glass of wine Tasha offered her. 'I always hated maths.'

'So did I, so I'm not much use. Charlie was meant to help but he didn't get home in time.'

Tasha told Rosie about her cancelled plans the night before, knowing she would get a sympathetic response from her old friend. She had known Rosie since the age of eight, when her parents had moved into the farm down the road in Surrey and Rosie's mum had shown up on the doorstep with a big shepherd's pie. Tasha and Rosie had been heartbroken when Rosie's family moved away a few years later, but they had remained the closest of friends through lengthy phone calls and regular visits during their school holidays.

'How annoying. Why didn't you just book a babysitter?'

'It was too late at the last minute.'

'Well, next time you should to avoid disappointment.'

'That's exactly what I promised myself last night. There aren't many opportunities for me to go out and have fun so when they come up I need to make sure I am not relying on Charlie. It was actually the fact that he didn't ring me earlier and give me time to sort something out that made me most cross.'

'Why didn't he?'

'He said he was stuck in a meeting – but surely he could have slipped out for a minute or two?'

'Mmmm, I'm sure he could have found a way. But he's not an arsehole, Tash, you know he wouldn't have done it on purpose.'

'I know,' Tasha said as she topped up their glasses. 'I'm just feeling a bit frustrated at the moment…' 'Did you discuss it when he got home?' Rosie asked.

'No. I wasn't in the mood.'

'You know, you probably should have tackled it then and there.'

'You're right. I definitely feel worse having bottled it up. I'd almost rather have had a row with him to clear the air.'

'It might not have ended up in an argument. And isn't it always best to explain why you are annoyed so he can prevent the same thing happening again?'

'I do know that. It sounds childish but I guess I want

him to know without me having to explain it. He should realise how important these evenings with my friends are to me, to have a much-needed break. He should have had the foresight to realise he was going to get stuck and call me with enough notice.'

'Men aren't exactly renowned for their intuition.'

'Sadly. Anyway, enough about me and Charlie, tell me everything about you.'

'Let me just pop to the loo and then I'll tell you all about the new features editor – he is so divine!' Rosie sighed as she disappeared into the downstairs bathroom.

Tasha laughed. She thought about Rosie's advice and knew she was right. Sometimes she wondered whether she enjoyed the bubbling of resentment that seemed to well up inside her with surprising regularity. It was a mixture of self-pity and martyrdom, both of which she disliked intensely but which she realised were fast becoming old friends. She knew that all the marriage books and relationship advice would agree with Rosie, that she should air her feelings in a simple, non-accusatory manner, stating the facts and the corresponding emotions. But she never seemed to manage to do so. She wanted Charlie to know what to do without her having to tell him. She wanted him to just 'get' things, to be more in tune with her needs and her feelings.

Rosie and Tasha polished off the bottle of wine over dinner. They caught up on each other's news, marvelling at how different their lives were and laughing at the more hilarious aspects of family versus single life.

'I admire you, you know,' Tasha said.

'Why?'

'You are so confident. How did you become so independent? So self-reliant? What happened to the little geek with train tracks that I used to know and love so well?'

'Good riddance to her. I suppose I needed to learn how to handle myself! My train tracks and bushy eyebrows were never going to get me far in life, were they?' They collapsed laughing as they recalled Rosie's headgear, reminiscing over the first time they had plucked each other's eyebrows, leaving nothing more than a thinly tweezed line.

'I need to get some of my confidence back,' Tasha sighed.

'You're still an incredibly gorgeous woman,' Rosie assured her. 'You just can't see it. All you see is a busy, exhausted mother of three!'

'Perhaps we should go and have a day of pampering, just the two of us... leave Charlie in charge of the kids?'

'I'd love that!' Rosie said as she drained her glass. 'Right, I'm afraid I've got to make a move... I'm off to a leaving do.'

'God, your life!'

'It's fun, if a little exhausting,' admitted Rosie.

'I'm so jealous. Call me in the morning if there's any

gossip?'

'I will,' Rosie promised as she pulled on her jacket. Her blonde hair fell in a silky cascade onto her shoulders. It made Tasha green with envy. Her wavy hair needed constant taming and would only look that sleek after a good session with her trusty straighteners. Tasha was determined to get herself to the hairdressers before long for a much-needed cut. She tried to remember when she had last had a trim; it must have been almost a year ago.

She waved Rosie off and went upstairs to check on the children. They were all asleep, Bella with a torch and her Harry Potter book on her chest. Tasha smiled as her heart burst with love for her daughter. She crept into her room and removed the book and torch, watching Bella's chest rise and fall with each breath. Her dark brown hair curled softly on her pillow. She looked so peaceful.

Tasha went back downstairs to tidy up before making her way up to bed. She brushed her teeth and took her make-up off, putting on her pyjamas and slipping under the covers. She spread out like a starfish, taking advantage of having the bed to herself, the sheets cool and crisp against her skin. She woke as Charlie nudged her to move across onto her side of the bed. He felt cold and smelt of beer as he pulled her towards him, spooning the back of her body as he wrapped his arm around her and nuzzled her neck. He was so familiar, so comforting, she fell back asleep in the crook of his arm, a smile on her face. Rosie might have the exciting, glamorous life Tasha often dreamed of, but she didn't have this: a family. Tasha reminded herself just how lucky she was.

An hour or so later Tasha felt rather noticeably less lucky having woken Charlie countless times in a futile attempt at stopping his alcohol-induced pneumatic drill impersonation. Finally accepting defeat, she got out of bed and made her way into the spare room, which doubled up as a storage unit. The bed was unmade and covered in towering piles of paperwork and clothes waiting to be filed, sorted and put away in the loft. Tasha cleared the mountain of debris onto the floor and snuck under the musty-smelling duvet to try and go back to sleep.

Chapter Three

On Monday morning Tasha found herself alone in the house once again, ploughing through a mountain of ironing that she had let build up for far too long. She lost herself in the monotony of the task, listening to Radio 4 as she worked. Her mind wondered back to the weekend. It had flown by in record timing, as they always did. Luckily the May sun had come out in force for their visit to Richmond Park. The children had run off exploring as they walked the winding paths that led through the Isabella Plantation, the deep reds and shocking pinks of the azaleas resplendent against the dark green foliage. They had stopped to admire their reflections in the Still Pond, posing for a photograph taken by a kindly stranger – the image of happiness as they smiled against the picturesque backdrop, the children beaming as they struck comedic poses for the camera. They had even cranked open the barbecue for the first time that year, Max doing his best to help as he turned the sausages. Tasha loved seeing Charlie and Max next to each other; they were so similar in so many ways. Max absolutely hero-worshipped his father – at the weekends he was rarely far from his side.

Tasha, on the other hand, had spent most of the weekend feeling annoyed with Charlie. She didn't even really know why any more. She was repressing an anger that seemed irrational. At times she wasn't sure what the anger was even about. Frustration, yes, but at what? She found herself reminiscing obsessively about her former life as a GP, before Flora, before motherhood. Despite her frustration at the endless paperwork, the bureaucracy, the short appointment times and the exhausting hours, she missed the reward, the satisfaction of an accurate diagnosis, the challenge and the unlimited variety.

Tasha continuously ruminated over her decision not to return to work after having had Flora. She had failed to anticipate just what a mammoth task it would be to retrain, to catch up on the medical advances that had been made in her absence. If she had returned to work part-time between each child she would not have allowed such an enormous chasm to open up in her knowledge; she could have kept a foot in the door. At the time she had thought that being a mum would be all she would ever want. She'd never anticipated the desire to have something more, something for herself, her own salary even. She'd never expected to feel so lonely, so cut off and so bored. She was embarrassed to admit it even to herself. Surely many women would be envious of her position? Charlie was just about able to support them; she had the privilege and joy of being there for her children no matter what, to watch assemblies and attend sports days and hear about the minutiae of their daily lives. She felt awful for feeling dissatisfied with her lot. She should be counting her blessings, not indulging herself with regrets and wishful thinking.

Later that afternoon Tasha traipsed up to her bedroom to have a good clear-out. It was a job she had been meaning to get around to for months. Rummaging around for a top to wear last Thursday had been a near impossible task: her drawers were overflowing with clothes. She couldn't remember the last time she had even worn half of them. Many of them didn't even fit her now that she'd put on a few extra pounds. She decided to make a pile for charity and a pile to keep and was soon immersed in the process of sorting.

Realising it was far too warm in the room, she threw open the windows and looked out. Their neighbour, Javier, who lived in the house opposite, was downstairs playing the saxophone. He did this most days when he wasn't at work. Sometimes Tasha could hear the music, soulful jazz or blues, as it lifted on the breeze from an open window. She paused and listened, watching him for a minute or two. Suddenly he turned his head and looked directly up at her, as if he could sense her watching him. She blushed and quickly looked away, returning to her chest of drawers. She felt embarrassed, worried he would think she was a desperate housewife, stalking him from across the street.

Tasha turned her attention back to the task in hand. As she pulled open the top drawer it occurred to her just how rarely she ever wore the sets of matching lingerie that lay abandoned at the back. In fact, she couldn't recall the last time she had put one on. It seemed like a lifetime ago when Charlie used to surprise her with gifts of underwear, beautifully wrapped in layers of tissue paper, delicate lace and silk. She remembered him ripping the buttons off her shirt during one particularly passionate encounter in his enthusiasm to take off her clothes. She longed to experience that level of desire again. She still enjoyed making love to Charlie; it was comforting and familiar, easy even. They knew what worked and how to please each other, but the voracious appetite for one another that they had experienced at the start of their relationship had disappeared.

Her thoughts turned back to Javier. When she and Charlie had moved into their house on Havers Street there had been an old lady called Barbara living there. She had been Flora's first babysitter. She had moved out of London a year or so ago and Javier had moved in shortly afterwards. Tasha and Charlie had introduced themselves as they returned home from the park one day to find him unloading some boxes from his car. He was dark and softly spoken, with a thick Spanish accent and an air of old-fashioned charm. He had warm brown eyes and greying stubble that covered his face and matched the hair that sprouted from his chest, visible through the gap in his shirt.

She remembered joking to Rosie on the phone that a good-looking doctor had moved in opposite, that she thought he might be a bachelor and ready for a set-up, not that Rosie needed any help in that department. She hadn't enquired further but, through her covert observation – she wouldn't go as far as to confess to actual spying – she had surmised that he was indeed single. She had fallen into the habit of tuning into his presence across the road, noticing if the lights were on, glancing over as he fixed his motorbike out on the street and saying hello as she walked past. He was always ready with a smile, a kind word for the girls or a joke for Max when they crossed paths. Maybe she should try to set him up with Rosie, after all?

Chapter Four

Tasha had been having nervous palpitations at the thought of the extended family coming together. It was Max's sixth birthday and the whole family were gathering in Putney for a barbecue in Tasha and Charlie's garden. Both the Nelsons and the Hargreaves were descending en masse for the occasion: Tasha's parents Lizzie and Bertie and her younger sister Chloe had all come from Surrey whilst Charlie's parents, Stephen and Caroline, had driven from Norfolk. Tasha and Charlie's sister-in-law, Becca, was also there along with her two children Daisy and Fergus. The only members of the two families who were notable by their absence were Tasha's youngest sister Ella, who was away travelling, and Charlie's older brother Andrew, who was in the army and currently on tour.

Tasha knew it was going to be extremely noisy and chaotic. Her fear of being judged ensured that she had broken her back cleaning and tidying the house in preparation for her mother-in-law's somewhat unforgiving eye. Luckily, Charlie was at his best as the host – generous to a fault and always charming no matter who he was entertaining. He had a lovely self-deprecating sense of humour and was wonderful with children of all ages. He was also extremely good at barbecuing whatever Tasha threw his way. Tasha had been up since the crack of dawn rustling up vast bowls of Ottolenghi-style salads to go with the meat, already marinated overnight and ready to go. She had made a huge pavlova covered in fresh berries and a Spiderman cake for Max, covered in red icing with a carefully drawn web dragged across it. She had positioned Max's favourite Spiderman toy in the centre as if suspended from dental floss webbing. Despite having been perilously close to throwing the entire work of art in the bin whilst trying to attach the floss to Spiderman's wrists, she was glad she had persevered and felt pleased with her efforts.

'Wow, sis, I'm impressed!' Chloe said as she peered at the cake. 'Where did you get that idea?'

'Pinterest. I bloody hope Max likes it!'

'He'll love it! I don't know how you can be so amazing at baking when I am so crap.'

They went out into the garden with a huge jug of freshly-refilled Pimm's and joined the gaggle of people sprawled out on rugs across the grass. Tasha and Charlie had bought the house when they were first married. They had been lucky to find somewhere with such an enormous garden, despite the fact that it had resembled an overgrown jungle, completely neglected by the previous owners. It was extremely rare in London to have so much outdoor space and it had become Tasha's pride and joy. She hadn't realised just how much she would come to enjoy gardening as she had lovingly cleared, dug, sowed and planted every square inch of soil. In fact, she had lavished far more attention on her plants than she had on the house itself. It gave her immense pleasure to watch the garden bloom and unfurl, especially at this time of year, and she loved involving the children with it too. They all had a patch of earth to plant and she had helped them choose their own seeds. The fruit on the apple tree at the end of her garden was beginning to ripen and the roses were out in abundance – proudly displaying their shocking pink petals to the world.

'Thank goodness the forecast was wrong,' Charlie said as she gave him the jug of Pimm's. He added it to the makeshift drinks table they had erected next to the barbecue.

Tasha had had minor heart failure the previous day when the forecast had shown rain all day long. She couldn't cope with the thought of everyone cooped up inside the house. It was spacious enough for a family of five at a push, but that was about it. Tasha looked up at the sky as a cloud flitted across the sun. 'I think we're going to be lucky,' she said, telling herself off for worrying so much about today. It was going perfectly well so far; everyone appeared to be on their best behaviour.

Soon the garden was filled with the smoky smell of sizzling meat: sausages, burgers and marinated chicken. Tasha's mum, Lizzie, came bustling over. 'Darling, I've just been inside – those salads look to die for! And don't even get me started on that incredible cake!' Lizzie had never been much of a cook herself. She always marvelled at Tash's culinary ability.

'Thanks, Mum. I think we're just about ready to eat actually. Right, everyone, help yourselves!' Tasha called as she carried through a large dish piled high with meat off the barbecue. They all traipsed into the kitchen to load their plates.

After tea and birthday cake, the various family members piled into cars to drive back home. Max had been absolutely delighted with his cake. His beaming grin covered in chocolate was all the reward Tasha needed to feel that her *Bake-Off*-worthy endeavours had been worth the effort. It had been a lovely day, but she was exhausted. There was a mountain of tidying, cleaning and washing-up to do, not to mention getting the children ready for the following day at school. Sticking to her resolution, she was determined to get them to pack their bags in advance, identifying possessions and ensuring homework and reading had been duly completed. Charlie had left her in charge of it all whilst he went upstairs to work. She couldn't help the sneaking suspicion that whatever it was that was so urgent could probably have waited until after the children were asleep.

Determined to snatch at least a quarter of an hour for herself, she left Charlie in charge of sorting out their dinner while she indulged in a relaxing bath.

When she got out of the water she could smell the bacon sizzling; he had clearly decided on bacon and eggs, his speciality. Inspired by her recent sort-out, Tasha went into the bedroom and selected a particularly pretty set of aquamarine lingerie. She almost felt nervous to put it on. As she pulled on her dressing gown she felt worried about Charlie's reaction. Would he think she was trying too hard? Might he laugh at her and make fun of her for wearing it? She knew it was extremely unlikely but she couldn't help the thoughts entering her mind. She got halfway down the stairs before she turned around and went back into the bedroom. She took off the lingerie and put her pyjamas on instead, her heart pounding strangely fast. What was she thinking? They just weren't that kind of couple any more – seducing each other was a thing of the past. She was cringing slightly and glad that she had saved herself the potential embarrassment of Charlie's reaction.

Later that night, as they lay in bed, she tried to remember the last time they had made love. It had been so long, she could hardly recall it. She snuggled over to Charlie and said goodnight. He kissed her and she moved a little closer, pressing herself up against him, giving him the cue. He ignored her, moving away and turning onto his front, as far away from her in the bed as it was possible to get. 'Night, babe,' he said. Within minutes he was snoring lightly while she was left feeling miserable and rejected. Her eyes filled with tears as she tried to go to sleep, a sinking feeling churning at the bottom of her stomach.

Chapter Five

Tasha turned up at her Pilates class slightly breathless. She had forgotten that Max's class were meant to be dressing up as Romans and so had run back home to rustle up a toga with a bed sheet and a belt before dropping it off at school in a flurry of apologies. Tasha found her spot, kindly reserved by Flo, and joined in the warm-up. She had started Pilates after Flora was born, knowing how often she had recommended it to patients as part of their post-partum recovery and keen to try it out for herself. A friend of hers had told her about a community class run by a volunteer and open to the public, with particular support for new mothers. Realising that her core could do with some serious strengthening, not to mention her pelvic floor, Tasha had dragged Flo along, grumbling and complaining to begin with, but to her credit she kept going with the classes each week. As a reward they treated themselves to a sandwich afterwards, or a salad if they were feeling virtuous, and more often than not a glass of wine. It had become a ritual that Tasha relied on to stay sane, and a perfect opportunity to catch up and have a good old chat with her friend. Tasha and Flo were both part of a big group of friends from school. They were all in touch regularly on their WhatsApp group, sharing pictures and videos of their kids' more hilarious moments and generally keeping everyone up to date with the various goings-on in each other's lives.

'Is it just me or is the class getting harder?' Flo asked as they rolled up their mats.

'I think Jodie might well be upping the ante!' Tasha laughed. Jodie's micro hot pants had proved to be a source of endless fascination for Flo and Tasha.

'Can she bloody not? It was difficult enough in the first place. I can't hold a plank for three minutes – is she joking?'

'Me neither! I face planted on the mat after about twenty seconds…' Tasha chuckled at Flo's outraged expression. 'Now where shall we go today? Joe's?'

'Let's try the new place. Has it been a wine kind of week?' Flo asked.

'Absolutely,' Tasha replied. 'You?'

'Afraid so.'

*

As they sat down Flo summoned the waiter and ordered two large glasses of rosé. It was a beautiful day so they had chosen a small table on the pavement in front of the restaurant, both keen to catch the sun at any opportunity. This was the one moment in the week

Tasha always made the effort to carve out for herself: Pilates and a quick bite of lunch. The rest of the week always seemed to pass by in the blink of an eye, lost in the frantic struggle to keep things ticking over, to ensure all members of the household were fed, clean and in the right place at the right time. Tasha never knew what happened to her time, all she knew was that there was never enough of it. It seemed as though the moment she got home from the school run she had to leave again, rushing around like a headless chicken in between.

'Ah, I needed this.' Flo sighed as she took a big gulp of wine. 'Mark has been away with work all week – there's nothing like full-time parental responsibility to drive me to drink. Hats off to all the single parents out there. I don't know how they do it.'

'Hear, hear. I forgot it was Roman day for Max and had to race home to rustle up a toga – hence my late arrival. Poor Max was in floods of tears. He was the only one who arrived in school uniform. I felt like such a bad mother...'

'Not bad, just busy.'

'I suppose... Do you ever imagine what life would be like without them?' Tasha asked wistfully.

'Do I ever? All the bloody time!'

'I saw Rosie on Friday.'

Flo and Rosie had been bridesmaids at Charlie and Tasha's wedding. 'How is she?'

'She's really well. Her life is just *so* different from

ours... It's bizarre to think how life would be without children. Imagine being single even. You literally would have no one else to think about apart from yourself. It's crazy!'

Flo laughed at the thought. '"Yourself" is the very last person we think about. There's just no time!'

'I read a brilliant article on Facebook last night about the "mental load" of a mother. It summed it up perfectly. It explained how even if your kids are at school, or you are at work, the inner monologue of thoughts your mind processes as a mother is incessant. Have the children grown out of their school shoes? Did you remember to let the school know about the playdate? When was the last time they went to the dentist? Have you ordered more washing powder in the weekly shop? Did you send a birthday card to your father-in-law? Try as you might to tune it out or even switch it off, it's impossible to ignore. The mental state of a mother is constantly on alert. No wonder we are all so bloody knackered!'

'I love that! It's so true!' Flo nodded in agreement as she warmed to the theme. 'Men are totally different. Get up, eat breakfast, leave the house, work, get home, eat, go to bed. They only think about the task in hand.'

'Even if a woman goes back to work full-time, she is usually still the one "in charge". Basically, whoever shoulders the responsibility of running the household never escapes the mental workload. It's exhausting!'

'Thank God for wine,' Flo said, chinking her glass against Tasha's. 'At least we have wine.'

'I know!' Tasha laughed. 'It's terrible how much I look forward to a glass of wine each evening. By about half five I start thinking about it, and by the time the children have gone to bed I am actually desperate for my first sip. I'm making myself have at least one night off every week just to make sure I don't become too dependent.'

'That's not a bad idea. Perhaps I should do the same.' As their Cobb salads arrived Flo announced, 'So... Mrs Perfect has been at it again...' Flo's children were roughly the same age as Tasha's. One of their favourite pastimes involved comparing stories about all the different mums they came across in their respective schools.

'Oh, God!' Tasha said. 'What's she done now?'

'She hand decorated thirty cupcakes with portraits of each child in the class. *Personalised* portraits. She even got Megan's freckles and glasses in, for Christ's sake! Megan saved her cupcake to bring home so that she could show me. She thought it was so beautiful she couldn't even bear to eat it. All iced by hand.'

'No!' Tasha gasped. 'That is the *most* ridiculous thing I have ever heard!'

'Tell me about it!'

'Who has the time?'

'The worst thing is that she works full-time as well. I

saw her in the playground yesterday – she picks them up one day a week. I asked her how she managed it...'

'Go on?'

'She told me she stayed up 'till two a.m. to finish them.'

'That's dedication for you!'

'I swear it's a competitive thing. She just wants the rest of us to feel like shit, to feel like no matter how hard we try we are never going to be as perfect as she is. I mean, iced portraits, for Christ's sake. How am I ever going to match that?'

'You don't need to!' Tasha laughed. 'There's always one. We just need to use them to entertain ourselves, not allow them to make us feel bad.'

'Megan's already asked me if I can do the same for her birthday. I had to explain that even if I could bake there was absolutely no way I would be able to do that. Poor Megan and her shop-bought cupcakes from Waitrose.'

'At least they are from Waitrose!' Tasha laughed.

'I might buy them from Iceland next time – can you imagine the look on the other mums' faces? The number of Es on the back of the packet would make them hyperventilate!'

'Oh, go on, I dare you!'

'Don't encourage me...' Flo laughed.

*

When Tasha got home, having detoured via Sainsbury's for some last-minute groceries, she unloaded the shopping before setting about stripping the beds. It had been at least three weeks since she had got around to changing the sheets. She hoovered as much of the house as she could, keeping an eye on the time. At five past three she grabbed her jacket and her bag, determined to make it in time for the pickup from school. She couldn't help but laugh as she thought of Flo trying to compete with the portrait cupcakes. *What was the world coming to?* she wondered.

As she closed the front door behind her she noticed Javier on his doorstep across the road. He had clearly just got back from work. He was a senior registrar in an Accident and Emergency department and, unsurprisingly, he looked exhausted.

'Hi!' she called, giving him a cheery wave as she locked up.

'Hi, Tasha,' he said, pausing and turning to look at her. She loved the way he said her name – his Spanish accent added a lyrical touch. 'How are you?'

'Great, thanks!' she replied. 'You?'

'Shattered!'

'Busy shift?'

'I should have been home hours ago...'

'You poor thing. Staffing issues again?'

'You bet. Overcrowded, not enough staff, ridiculous waiting times, a record number of drunk injuries, and a stabbing to top it all off.'

'Oh my God. Horrific.'

'Are you sure you don't want to retrain?' Javier smiled. They often chatted about the possibility of Tasha re-entering the world of medicine. 'I know... it's tempting, right?'

'Mmmm...' Tasha laughed. 'I hope you manage to get some rest,' she called as she rushed off down the street.

Talking to Javier was often a good reminder of the distinctly unglamorous reality of working for the NHS. She might regret having given it up, but would she really want to re-enter that world? Perhaps there was something else she could do that would give her purpose, independence, her own income... She checked the time and sped up as she realised she was cutting it rather fine.

Chapter Six

Tasha slumped on a mossy tree stump and burst into noisy sobs. Buzz and Bean, her parents' terriers, paused for a moment to look at her quizzically, before resuming their thorough exploration of the surrounding woodland. They were in Surrey for the weekend. The children were busy building a den with Charlie and Bertie, and Lizzie had rushed off to a parish council meeting. Tasha, needing to get away from Charlie and the kids and regroup, had taken advantage of the rare opportunity for solace, offering to walk the dogs.

The journey down had tested her already limited patience to breaking point. It was an unfeasibly warm day and the air-conditioning unit was not working, a job that Charlie had been promising to sort for ages, the car being one of the increasingly few items under his remit. The children had been hot and bothered, the car seeming to magnify the heat of the sun like a miniature greenhouse. They had become increasingly fractious the longer they had been cooped up inside, desperate to escape the minute they'd arrived. Tasha and Charlie had argued about the air-conditioning. 'The car is your *one* job, why can't you just bloody do it?' she had muttered through gritted teeth.

'Actually, I think you will find that I *do* have another job, funnily enough,' Charlie had replied, his sarcasm doing nothing to quell her irritation.

'I've been reminding you for months.'

'And I will do it. I've told you. Now leave it.'

She had been fighting back emotion throughout the course of lunch, absurdly close to tears and unsure why. Now, finally alone, she let the tears roll down her cheeks freely. Taking a deep breath, she looked around her. She tried to stay present, to savour the effect of the dappled light as it sprinkled through the leaves. It was silent apart from the odd chirrup. Alone with her thoughts, Tasha was forced to admit just how unhappy she felt. It had been building up slowly but surely for months now, this feeling of frustration, of dissatisfaction. She swung between moods in the blink of an eye, veering from joyous happiness and love for her three children to feelings of intense claustrophobia, irritation and resentment at the endless monotony of being a full-time mum. She was trying not to begrudge Charlie his freedom, but she could feel herself losing the battle, becoming more short-tempered and less tolerant of his uselessness around the house, his lack of attention.

Pulling herself together, Tasha rummaged in her pocket for a tissue and blew her nose. She wiped her eyes and took a steadying breath, filling her lungs with the smell of damp earth and fresh air. Tasha knew she needed to talk things through with Charlie. She needed to tell him how she was feeling. It was madness that she was sitting here, alone in the middle of a wood, crying her eyes out. Charlie had no idea that she was so mentally unhinged. She vowed that she would address her feelings that evening and talk to him. Rosie had been right, she always felt better when they had discussed whatever was bothering her. She wanted to bring up missing Steph's engagement drinks; she knew she should have dealt with it better at the time but it wasn't too late to do so now. It would give her the perfect opportunity to talk through some of the dissatisfaction she was feeling. Perhaps they could even talk about her going back to work, whether retraining as a GP or to do something new. She just wanted him to listen to her, to support her.

*

That evening they went up to their room after a delicious meal with Lizzie and Bertie; both of them had had a few glasses of wine and she was feeling much more relaxed.

'Charlie?' she said, as they got into bed.

'Yes?'

'Before you go to sleep, there's something I want to talk to you about.'

'Right...' He turned to face her, clearly trying to

work out what she might be about to say.

'I know I should have said something at the time, but I felt too annoyed to talk calmly.' Charlie looked blank. She continued, 'The evening when I was meant to be going to Steph's?'

At this Charlie rolled his eyes and sighed loudly. 'For God's sake! You aren't still going on about that, are you?' Hardly the reaction she had been hoping for. The repressed feelings inside her welled up like a tide and overflowed.

'What the hell is *that* supposed to mean?' Her eyes filled with tears, which she furiously instructed to beat a hasty retreat.

'I told you on the phone at the time that I was sorry. It was not my fault. Do you think I want to be stuck at work for hours on end, Tash? I would much rather have been home drinking wine in front of the TV.'

This incensed Tasha even more. She hadn't meant the conversation to go like this, but he had jumped straight into the deep end. 'How hard would it have been to send me a text? *Surely* that's not too much to ask?'

'Business meetings don't really work like that,' Charlie said. 'I suppose it's hard for you to understand…'

By this point Tasha was smarting. 'Don't patronise me,' she warned through gritted teeth, mindful of Flora and Bella who were sharing a room next door. 'Of course I *understand* what a business meeting is like. I'm trying to talk sensibly about this and you are just making snide remarks. For God's sake, will you just grow up?'

'*I'm* the one that needs to grow up? You have one night where you can't see your friends and you are acting as if it is the end of the world!'

'It's not the end of the world, Charlie. It was important to me. The fact that you can't see that is seriously worrying.'

'Well, I'm not worried. I got stuck in a meeting. Yes, it would have been great if I had been able to call you with enough time to arrange childcare but we both know how unpredictable my job is. I'm sorry you missed out but it's in the past now. You can rearrange another dinner and we can book a babysitter as backup if I can't get home... I don't mind paying for childcare if it keeps us from having this conversation again and again.'

'You are missing the point. It was *that* dinner I wanted to be at – to celebrate with all my friends...'

'There's no use harping on about it, Tasha.'

'I'm not *"harping on"*, Charlie. I am *trying* to explain how I feel and you're not trying to understand. You're just jumping down my throat and treating me as if I am being pathetic.'

'Look, I'm sorry, Tash. It was unfortunate, that's all. Now let's agree to forget about it.'

He pecked her on the cheek and closed his eyes. 'Night, night,' he said. 'Sleep tight.'

That was clearly the end of it.

Tasha felt extremely unsatisfied. That hadn't gone to plan at all. She had meant to have a sensible discussion and explain to Charlie how she was feeling at the moment, not just about that evening but about so much more than that. As she looked at Charlie she realised just how distant she felt from him. She knew that communication was the only way to bridge the gap but conversations like the one they'd just had did nothing but make her feel worse.

She watched Charlie as his breathing became regular and deep, the sound of him sleeping. His face couldn't be more familiar, yet it felt strangely unfamiliar. She suddenly longed for her own space, to have her own bed and some time alone. There were no spare rooms in the cottage. She contemplated going downstairs and sleeping on the sofa but couldn't risk her parents finding her and having to explain why she wasn't in bed. She lay awake once again, staring at the ceiling. Her head was in a spin, her emotions running high. Her heart felt as if it was beating too fast, too heavily. Tears welled in her eyes once again. She took a deep breath and told herself not to be silly. She was fine. Her marriage was fine. She reminded herself that she was blessed to have a husband and three children who she loved more than anything in the world. She tried to quell her thoughts and drift off to sleep but Charlie's words kept replaying over and over again in her head.

Chapter Seven

'So, what do you think? Shall we go for it?' Carlos looked at her expectantly. Tasha had sacrificed Pilates and lunch with Flo to finally get herself to the hairdresser. She had decided to go for a new, blonder look, realising it was high time she treated herself to a little pampering and hoping that a change in hair colour might help lift her spirits. She was still annoyed with Charlie after their irritating conversation on Saturday night and so had no qualms about spending a hefty whack on her card for a cut and highlights.

'Let's do it!' Tasha said, nervous in anticipation of the end result.

Carlos had suggested a mixture of honey and golden tones. 'And I think we might cut some nice long layers in – to give you some volume. Is that OK?'

'Whatever you think is best.'

'And maybe some shaping around the face?'

'Go for it!' Tasha laughed. 'I am entirely in your hands.'

'I promise you, you will look a million dollars by the time I am finished with you!'

Tasha sipped her complimentary coffee and read

Hello magazine while Carlos worked his magic. It was lovely being forced to sit still for an hour or two with no chance of doing any housework. Since having children Tasha had even started enjoying her visits to the dentist, despite the pain, seeing them as an opportunity to lie back and have time out. This was much better.

As Carlos unwrapped each silver foil packet and led her over to the sink she felt a frisson of excitement. Her hair had been the same mousey brown for years – there had been no time for highlights. After her hair had been washed, she watched in the mirror as he combed and snipped then dried her hair, running some delicious-smelling serum through the ends to finish.

'What do you think?' he asked, holding up the mirror to show her the back of her head.

'I love it!' She smiled, genuinely thrilled at the result. 'Thank you so much!'

'You are more than welcome. Enjoy your new colour – you know what they say about blondes, right?' Carlos winked at her, taking her over to the till so that she could pay.

For the first time in years Tasha felt a spring in her step as she walked home. The blonde tones that Carlos had chosen seemed to complement her eyes somehow, making the dark blue stand out more than usual.

As Tasha approached her house she noticed Javier squatting down by his motorbike, which was parked practically outside her front door, fiddling with the back tyre. He seemed to be working a lot of night shifts lately, which meant he was around more during the day. Tasha had to admit she liked bumping into him.

'Hi,' he said, squinting against the sun as he looked up at her. His accent made even the simplest greeting sound exotic. He was wearing a crumpled white shirt with blue jeans. His skin seemed permanently olive brown no matter what the season.

'Hi, Javier,' Tasha said. 'What are you doing down there?'

'Checking the tyre pressure.'

'Oh, right!'

'New hair?' he asked, standing up to look at her properly. She noticed for the first time how tall and broad he was.

Tasha felt herself blush to her roots. 'I've just been to the hairdresser's. I'm not sure... perhaps it's too blonde...?'

'You look beautiful,' he said. He looked at her with such admiration she was almost inclined to believe him.

'I'm not sure...' she repeated. She didn't know why she kept saying that. She loved her new hair but there was something about him that made her feel like a shy teenager.

'I mean it,' he said.

Tasha laughed. 'I felt like it was time for a change.'

'I always say the need for change is a powerful thing. We underestimate it at our peril.'

She looked up at him. His deep brown eyes were kind and honest. There was something very open about him, a sort of compassion perhaps. It made her want to share a bit more of herself with him. 'I've been thinking something along those lines recently,' Tasha admitted. 'Things can feel a bit... repetitive, somehow, without it.'

Javier looked intrigued. Tasha suddenly worried that he might think she was referring to her marriage. She felt the need to assure him that she hadn't been talking about Charlie, though the thought occurred to her that he might not be entirely mistaken if he had jumped to that conclusion. 'I've been thinking about returning to work again,' she added, by way of explanation.

'Really? That's so great!' Javier smiled, showing genuine encouragement. 'A colleague has recently returned after a break to raise her family. I think it's quite a process... but definitely achievable.'

'If I'm honest I'm just not sure that I want to go back to medicine.'

'Why did you leave?'

'For the children, mainly. Charlie and I both felt it was important that one of us was at home, and I was happy for it to be me. But that wasn't the only reason. I had grown disillusioned with general practice. There is a side of me that loved it but a larger side that found it all too frustrating: the long hours, the lack of time. I felt like I was always doing a mediocre job, that I was letting patients down, as well as myself.'

'You certainly aren't alone in that respect.'

'It must be a lot worse in A and E,' Tasha sympathised.

'Overstretched and understaffed, that's our motto!' Javier laughed wryly.

'Full credit to you for persevering.'

'Thank you. It's worth it, at least for me... but then I have much less on my plate. I live alone, I don't have any children...'

'I suppose that makes a bit of a difference.' She smiled at Javier. 'Speaking of which, I'd better get on. I'll leave you to your tyres,' Tasha said, checking the time. She hadn't eaten anything all day. The piece of toast she had intended to eat for breakfast had been abandoned as she'd tried to help Bella locate her recorder. Max had unhelpfully hidden the instrument underneath her bed, 'as a joke' apparently. Her stomach was rumbling. If she was quick she could grab something to eat while she checked her emails and scrutinised the school calendar. After forgetting about the Roman day, she had received a pointed note from Max's teacher reminding her that all school activities were listed well in advance online. She was determined to log them all on her phone calendar to prevent any future mishaps.

Having said goodbye to Javier, she unlocked her front door and closed it behind her with a quick backward glance. He was still standing there, smiling at her.

Tasha looked in the mirror that hung in the hallway. Her navy blue eyes stared back, framed with mascara-covered lashes. Mascara was about the only make-up she got around to applying, if she had time for any at all. She wondered what Javier saw when he looked at her. She scrutinised her reflection. Her new hair fell in a glossy cascade down her back – if only she could always look so glamorous. She was wearing a blue and white wrap dress that she had rediscovered during her recent sort-out. Had he meant it? Was she beautiful? She had really lost her confidence since having children – never quite being able to shift that last stubborn bit of baby weight. Her skin bore the battle wounds of motherhood: stretch marks and the scar of the emergency Caesarean she had had to have when Max was born. Was it really possible that someone like Javier found her attractive? She replayed their conversation in her mind. She realised just how nice it had felt to be listened to. He had treated her as more than just a housewife, more than just a mother. With Charlie, that was all she ever felt like, as if she had lost her true identity somehow.

Chapter Eight

It didn't help that, in direct contrast with Javier, Charlie had failed to even register a change in Tash's appearance. She wouldn't have been too surprised if he hadn't realised that she had had a haircut, but a change in colour? Surely that was enough to at least receive a second glance? He had arrived home having played a game of squash and headed straight for the shower. She had cooked them a nice meal of salmon with chorizo and lentils, trying to make an effort in an attempt to draw a line under their argument on Saturday night. Charlie had sat opposite her at the kitchen table while they ate. Tasha had waited for a reaction... but to no avail. He had chatted away merrily, telling her about his day and asking about the children. She had almost brought it up but decided there was no point. He would tell her it looked lovely, but she would know that he hadn't noticed. Instead she compared him with Javier: he had noticed immediately. How was it possible that a virtual stranger could see her more clearly than her own husband? Her bruised ego took comfort from Javier's compliments.

The following Saturday it was Tasha and Charlie's

wedding anniversary. Tasha couldn't believe how quickly twelve years had flown by. When she thought back to the person she had been when they first met she barely recognised herself. To think how far they had come. So many life-changing things had happened, most dramatically the arrival of their three children and the accompanying shift from married couple to frazzled parents that had followed. In a bid to make amends, still conscious that their relationship had been fraught with tension and irritability of late, Tasha had been planning a gift for Charlie for weeks. She was extremely pleased with her choice. The theme for the twelfth year of marriage was traditionally linen and silk so she had ordered a beautifully tailored linen jacket and a set of silk ties from his favourite shop in Jermyn Street, and she couldn't wait to give them to him. She hoped that their relationship would somehow be restored to its former glory in remembering their wedding day. It had been full of promise, excitement and that feeling of total confidence that no matter what life threw at them, they would conquer it together, that their love would be more than enough to carry them through.

They woke up to Max and Bella bounding into their room at an ungodly hour.

'Wakey, wakey, rise and shine!' Max chirped. Tasha opened a bleary eye and looked at them both standing in front of her. Bella was prodding her toes, her curly hair sticking up at bizarre angles. Max's dimples were deep as he beamed at her; his freckles had really come out in the sun and his little rosebud lips were split into a dazzling smile revealing several missing teeth.

'Come on, then,' she relented, pulling back the cover. They squealed in delight and jumped into the bed.

'Dad, please will you make us boiled eggs and soldiers for breakfast?' Bella asked.

'And then can we go to the cinema?' Max implored as he clambered over Charlie. They chattered away excitedly about what they wanted to do with their weekend.

Soon Flora joined them too, the noise from her siblings having woken her. Tasha loved these rare moments with all of them so cuddly and sweet in their pyjamas – even Flora seemed more childlike and less prematurely adolescent. Remembering the present she had hidden under the bed, she got up and pulled it out, placing it with pride on Charlie's lap. He looked at the parcel with the card attached in confusion. Rather than lighting up, his face fell as the cogs turned. Before he said anything, Tasha knew that he had forgotten. Never before had she needed him to show her just how much he still cared, that, despite the working late and the marital bickering, she was still all he wanted, all he needed. And yet it seemed he had failed to even remember the date. She felt unbelievably hurt. He had never forgotten their anniversary before.

'Oh, my God, babe, I'm so sorry.' Charlie put his face

in his hands.

'What's happened?' Flora asked, scanning her parents' faces. She had an uncanny ability to detect drama.

'Don't worry!' Tasha said breezily, smiling. She didn't want the children to think that he had messed up.

'It's our anniversary,' said Charlie. 'We got married eleven years ago today.'

'Twelve actually,' Tasha said. Insult added to injury.

'Of course, of course, I meant twelve,' Charlie backtracked. 'I forgot to get Mummy a present and I feel awful!'

'Da-ad,' chorused Bella, Max and Flora. 'Poor mum!'

'It really doesn't matter,' she repeated. But it really did. Another opportunity missed, another disappointment.

'Open it!' Bella instructed.

'Can I help you?' Max asked. He loved opening presents. It didn't matter if they weren't for him.

Together they tore open the wrapping paper and Charlie exclaimed in delight at the gifts inside. He tried the jacket on and it fitted perfectly. 'Oh, wow, Tash. These are amazing! And from my favourite shop. You are so thoughtful!'

'Twelve years is silk and linen.'

'Really? Well, this couldn't be more perfect. I feel even worse that I forgot. I'm so sorry. How can I make it up to you?'

'I take it you haven't arranged a babysitter for tonight? Seeing as you forgot? No anniversary dinner?' Tasha twisted the knife. She wanted to make him feel bad.

Charlie looked even more guilty. 'Let me do a ring-around. I'll sort something out. I promise.'

*

Charlie managed to find a local au pair called Nina to come and look after the children. She was a sweet Danish girl whom they had often used in the past. He took Tasha to a restaurant called Cube in Notting Hill. To his obvious relief he had been able to get a table at late notice.

'This place looks all right, doesn't it?' Charlie said as they were shown to their table. The restaurant was dimly lit and full of trendy tattooed hipsters.

'It does,' Tasha said. She still hadn't forgiven him and was determined to make that fact clear.

'Right,' said Charlie. 'Let's have a cocktail to start. What do you fancy?'

Tasha glanced over the bar menu. 'I'll have a White Lady, please,' she said as Charlie placed their order with a passing waitress.

They made what felt like awkward small talk while they waited for their drinks. Tasha knew she wasn't making it easy for him. She was hardly encouraging the conversation to flow.

'To twelve years of marriage,' Charlie said, chinking his glass against Tasha's when their cocktails finally arrived.

'To twelve years,' Tasha repeated, unable to stop the tears that welled up in her eyes.

Charlie looked mortified. He was clearly desperate for her to forgive his thoughtlessness. Taking her hands in his, he said, 'Look, Tash, I'm so sorry I forgot. I feel really, really bad.'

Tasha nodded, swallowing and blinking back the tears. In her heart of hearts, she knew that what he said was true. She was sure he felt as awful as he said he did. But she also knew that she needed to confront the issues in their relationship. Like a pressure cooker, she felt she was going to explode if she didn't. And this cock-up of Charlie's had given her the perfect opportunity to vent some of the tension that was building inside her, threatening to spill out at any moment. Right now, she was in the right, and he was in the wrong. If she was honest with herself she had to admit she quite enjoyed the feeling of having the moral upper hand.

Tasha sipped her cocktail in silence, keeping her eyes fixed on the bowl of nuts in front of her. After several minutes, she lifted her gaze and looked Charlie in the eye.

'It's not good enough,' she said.

'I know.'

'You *have* to start making more effort, Charlie.'

'I know...'

'It's such a cliché, for God's sake, forgetting our anniversary... What next?'

'Look, Tash, I promise it won't happen again. Work has been so busy...'

'Charlie, I've got a million things to remember too. You can't use being busy as an excuse. I single-handedly run our home and keep our three children alive. I am in charge of nearly everything. The one thing you are in charge of, you haven't bloody done...'

Charlie looked blank.

'The car? The air conditioning?' she prompted.

'I do the finances, pay the bills...'

'On direct debit...'

'Look. I know it's a shit excuse. And I promise you, it was a one off. Now, *please*, can you just accept my apology so we can enjoy the rest of the evening?'

There was still so much that Tasha wanted to talk to him about but she just wasn't sure she wanted to get into a full-blown couple's therapy session in the middle of a quiet restaurant. And the waiter was hovering nearby, clearly ready to take their order. She looked at Charlie and at the pleading look in his eyes.

'OK,' she said. 'Your apology is accepted.'

Relief flickered across his face. 'Thank you,' he said, pulling himself up to lean across the table and kiss her. 'And I really *am* sorry.'

They scanned the menus and placed their order, choosing a nice bottle of wine to go with their meal. Charlie had chosen well: the food was delicious. Each course was beautifully presented on pieces of grey slate. Putting their issues to one side, it felt good to be out together, having a few drinks. They both knew that they needed to carve out more time for evenings like this. Opportunities to go out, just the two of them, were few and far between. It had been years since they had been away for a weekend without the children, even longer since they had been on a holiday by themselves.

After dinner they got a taxi back home and made love, as they always did on their anniversary. But as Charlie held her in his arms, unwelcome thoughts of Javier invaded Tasha's mind. To her horror, try as she might to block them out and think of Charlie, they kept flickering back into her imagination. Soon she managed to lose herself in the moment, forgetting anything but the sensations within her. But afterwards, as Charlie kissed her goodnight and told her that he loved her, Tasha felt a crushing sense of disquiet settle over her. What the hell had that been about? Charlie rolled over onto his side of the bed, mercifully oblivious to her deceitful mind as he began to snore quietly. Tasha stared blankly at the wall. A tear trickled down her cheek and onto the pillow.

Chapter Nine

Tasha couldn't shake the feeling of apathy that settled over her as she ploughed through the following few weeks, drowning in the never-ending cycle of the school run, shopping, cooking, cleaning, tidying and generally juggling the numerous tasks that kept the household ticking along. She felt as though she had taken a step back from everything, as if she were watching her life from the outside. She felt despondent and depressed, as though she were at the beginning of a very long tunnel, the light at the end visible but impossibly far to reach.

Flora, Bella and Max were her biggest energy drain and yet her best distraction. When she was with them she veered from crazy adoration to tearing her hair out with frustration, teetering on the edge of tears when fractious moods and short tempers seemed to rule the roost. Luckily, Flora had done well in her recent maths assessment and was over the moon about it. She was being much more pleasant as a result. It was lovely to see her regained confidence and she seemed her age once again – for a while, Tasha had been convinced that she was suffering from the angst one would expect from a teenager, not a ten-year-old. When they weren't bickering as only siblings could, Max and Bella spent hours playing. When Tasha overheard their role play and the imaginary worlds they created for themselves, she marvelled at the pure innocence of childhood. It was moments like these when she truly loved being a mother. Yet while she knew she wouldn't swap life with her children for a childfree, albeit carefree, existence, she just couldn't shake the claustrophobia that had set in.

'Don't you ever feel trapped?' she asked her sister-in-law Becca on the phone as she frantically browsed the aisles of Debenhams looking for a present for their mother-in-law, whose birthday she had completely forgotten. She was hoping to rush to the post office before it shut. If she paid for special delivery it might get there in time for the big day. Stuck for ideas, she had phoned Becca for inspiration.

'Trapped?' Becca asked.

'Yes. By your life.'

'Well, I suppose...'

'You don't, do you? You are such a trooper. And with Andrew away so much... I know I shouldn't complain, really. I mean, in comparison with you, what the *hell* have I got to complain about?' Tasha picked up some rose bath soap and sniffed it, dropping it into the blue string bag.

'We are all entitled to have a good moan,' Becca said. 'It's only natural.'

'Mmmm, and yet I never hear *you* complaining... I

bet you all just love having Andrew back home.' He had returned from his recent deployment a couple of days after Max's birthday.

'It is wonderful. And it certainly makes life a lot easier having two pairs of hands, I must admit.'

'And you can stop worrying about him for once.'

'Exactly.'

'How about lavender bath oil? Caroline loves that, doesn't she?'

'Loves it,' Becca agreed. Tasha threw it on top of the rose soap. 'Have you spoken to Charlie about all this?'

'I tried to a few weeks ago when we were at my parents. It didn't exactly go well. We ended up having an argument.'

'Oh dear.'

'I know. Then he forgot our anniversary, which didn't help matters.'

'Oh, Charlie! How useless.'

'We had a bit of a chat after that too.'

'Did he make up for it?'

'He took me out for a nice meal.'

'That's good. Look, Tash, it's probably just a phase. Now the summer is here I'm sure you will start to feel much better. Everything seems all right when the sun is out.'

'True. It usually does wonders for my mood,' Tasha agreed, though she had a sneaking suspicion a little sun wasn't going to do much to lift her spirits. 'Do you think she'd like a floral nightie?' Tasha asked. She was now in the lingerie department. 'Size 12?'

'Sounds good. Are you and Charlie still on for lunch next weekend?'

'Absolutely. The children are so excited already. I hope the weather's nice. They're dying to get in your swimming pool.' Becca had inherited a large sum of money when her father had passed away, which they had used to buy their dream home in Surrey, making the decision to be close to her mum so that she could get help during Andrew's long stints away.

'Fingers crossed the weather will be good.'

'I doubt it'll be warm enough for me!' Tasha laughed. 'Let me know if I can bring anything,' she said as she ended the call. She took her purchases to the till, picking up some tights for Bella and Flora on the way.

*

As she stood in the interminably long queue at the post office, ready to send the hastily-wrapped parcel to Caroline, she pulled out her phone and replied to a text she'd received earlier from Rosie. They were making a plan for dinner the following evening.

She thought about her conversation with Becca, and her chat with Javier the other day. Once again she contemplated making a return to work. Maybe it was time. The thought of having something that was just hers and hers alone once more was so appealing. She knew she would miss the children, but they were all at school now, they didn't need her as much as they once had. If she did go back to work she knew she needed to decide once and for all whether it would be to medicine or something new. She loaded Safari on her iPhone and looked at the website for the Royal College of General Practitioners, reading through the advice for GPs returning to work after a break. The same questions sprang to mind. Would she still be good at it? Was it easier not to disrupt the status quo? What if she did all that training only to find that she still wasn't happy as a GP? What if the reasons she had had for leaving still applied? She put her phone back in her bag and stared vacantly at the counters, watching the customers come and go as she made her slow progress towards the front of the queue.

Her thoughts returned to her relationship with Charlie. Things weren't quite right between them. There was no denying it. Her fantasising about Javier the last time they had made love showed how disengaged she was from him. Even her subconscious was yearning for change. The fact that he had forgotten their anniversary almost felt like the final nail in the coffin. He clearly wasn't prioritising their relationship enough. She had wanted to confide properly in Becca, to air all her doubts and insecurities, but felt compromised in case she told Andrew and it got back to Charlie. She was as close to her sister-in-law as she was to her real sisters, but she knew she would be better off seeking advice from Rosie or Flo.

*

'I'm worried he's almost given up on us,' Tasha said the next evening as she sipped a large glass of red wine. Rosie was treating her to dinner out at a new sushi place in Mayfair. Tasha had booked Nina again to babysit, unwilling to rely on Charlie and sticking to her resolution to make more plans for herself.

'How so?' asked Rosie as she picked up a sliver of sashimi with her chopsticks.

'It's as if he has decided that I am such a dead cert he doesn't need to make any effort with me any more.'

'After so many years, I can see how that can happen.'

'So can I. That's what worries me. The number of couples you hear of getting divorced...'

'Have you talked to him?' Rosie asked.

'No, not really. The last time I tried, it just turned into an argument.'

'Well, perhaps you should try again? Communication is the key to a happy relationship after all. Charlie probably has absolutely no idea that you are feeling like this, bless him. You owe it to him and to your marriage to explain exactly how you feel.'

Tasha nodded. She took a deep breath and let out a

long sigh. 'You're right. It just all feels so depressing. I long for the days when it was all fresh and exciting. When we didn't have to work at things all the time. Even the word "work" seems wrong – why should it be such hard work?'

'Hey, you're the one who has always loved the idea of being in a long-term relationship! I'm the one who has been happy to be on my own!' Rosie laughed. 'Are the tables turning at long last, I wonder?'

'Why do you say that?' Tasha asked. 'Are you reconsidering your position?'

'Well, there is something about this new features editor, Josh. I think I'm slightly obsessed with him!'

'Oh, yes, Josh!' Tasha clapped her hands together with glee. 'Have you managed to go on a date with him yet?'

'No! Nothing seems to be working. I've tried all my usual tactics but he just politely turns me down every time I suggest something.'

'Are you sure he is straight?'

'Absolutely. He's clearly just not interested in me.'

'That's impossible. Straight and single, there's no way he's not interested. That can't be it.'

'It certainly could be!' Rosie laughed. 'Anyway, I'm running out of ideas…'

'Maybe you should just ask him out, no beating around the bush, like in the good old days?'

'Maybe you're right. I suppose that's one way to find

out once and for all!'

*

Later, as Tasha walked home from the Tube, she noticed that the lights were on across the road. Javier must be home. Letting herself into the house, she thanked Nina for babysitting and paid her. Charlie hadn't got home yet; he was out with Andrew, catching up after all those months apart. Tasha knew how much Charlie missed his older brother when he was away, and how much he worried about his safety. It was a weight off everyone's shoulders now that Andrew was back in the UK.

Tasha climbed the stairs and went to check on the children, kissing each one softly on the forehead, being careful not to wake them. She went into her room. She felt slightly tipsy from the wine she had drunk. As she shut the curtains she looked across the street into Javier's house, suddenly curious to see what he was doing. He was in the sitting room, drinking beer and watching TV as he ate at the little table towards the back of the room. The lower half of the window was covered in shutters, obstructing her view of the rest of the room, but from this angle she could see him clearly. She envied him his bachelor lifestyle. From what she could see his house was tidy and completely clutter-free. The polar opposite of her own home. As she got ready for bed she found herself thinking about Javier once again, about him complimenting her, his attentiveness and genuine interest in her company. She wondered what his story was, whether he had a girlfriend. She had seen women come and go, but no one seemed to stick around for long. She wondered why he chose to be alone.

Chapter Ten

Andrew came out of the house as they pulled into the drive, closely followed by his look-alike daughter, Daisy. 'Welcome!' he called as they clambered out of the car. 'It's so lovely to see you all,' he said, giving Tasha a big bear hug.

'It's so good to have you home!' Tasha said as the children burst into a torrent of noisy chatter, desperate to go and see the swimming pool as soon as possible.

'Charlie!' Andrew gave his brother a playful shove. 'How was the head on Thursday?'

'Pretty dire, thanks to you.' Charlie laughed. 'I'm afraid I just can't keep the pace!' Andrew was tall, broad and built of solid muscle; he could drink his brother under the table. He needed to maintain peak physical fitness at all times for his job – the difference in muscular definition between the two brothers had become a bit of a running joke, particularly in the six-pack department.

'How's my favourite little niece?' Charlie asked, bending down to ruffle Daisy's hair as she sidled up to say hello. 'You're getting so big!' He laughed, picking her up for a cuddle and spinning her around.

Tasha gave Daisy a kiss. 'Hi, darling,' she said. 'Look at your lovely sparkly hairband!' Daisy was dressed head to toe in pink, as usual.

'Hi, Auntie Becca! Hi, Fergus!' Flora, Max and Bella called as Becca came out to join them. She looked sleep-deprived but beautiful in a floral tea dress, her shoulder-length brown hair tied up in a messy bun. The children raced over to see the baby of the family, currently perched happily in his mother's arms, gurgling contentedly.

'Dad, can we show them all my new Wendy house?' Daisy pleaded, tugging on Andrew's sleeve.

'You've got a new Wendy house?' Flora asked.

'Yes, it's next to the pool,' Daisy replied.

'Cool!' Max said.

'Awesome!' Bella cooed.

'Great idea, darling,' Becca added. 'Here, why don't you take Fergus too?' she suggested, passing the baby to Andrew. 'I'll go and get us all some drinks.'

Within moments the children were dragging Charlie and Andrew around the side of the house to visit Daisy's pride and joy.

'You must be so glad he's back!' Tasha said as she helped Becca make a round of squash in the kitchen. 'I know Charlie is.'

'It is lovely. Although it always seems to go by so quickly... Daisy is beside herself with excitement to have him home.'

'I can tell.'

'She'll be heartbroken when he sets off again later in the year. She is just such a daddy's girl.'

'I really don't know how you do it,' Tasha said. 'You're so brave.'

'Sadly I haven't got much choice.' Andrew had been selected for the SAS several years ago and was currently running a training programme in Northern Iraq.

'I can't even begin to imagine what it's like.'

'In a strange way, you do just get used to it,' Becca said. 'You just have to get on with life, I suppose. And the children keep me so busy I don't have time to think too much. Which is a good thing, I can tell you!'

'You are amazing, Becca. Andrew is very lucky to have you. We all are. He must miss you all terribly, poor thing.'

'I think it is really hard on him. But it's his choice to stay in the army. I keep telling him that he can leave if he wants to. He could find work in a new industry. Maybe in finance, like Charlie. I'm sure he could pull some strings...'

'Definitely. Do you think he ever will?' Tasha asked.

'I doubt it.' Becca sighed. 'He's army through and through. It's in his DNA. And it's important to me that he does what he loves...'

Tasha watched through the window as Andrew flew Fergus through the air above his head, eliciting squeals of delight. Her heart went out to Becca. She was grateful that Charlie was not in harm's way. She didn't know how Becca coped as a single parent for such long stretches of time, not to mention the worry of something awful happening. The thought sent shivers down her spine.

After an alfresco lunch the children wasted no time changing into their swimming costumes and jumping into the pool. It was another hot day – it had been one of the hottest Junes on record – and it made a lovely change to escape the sweltering heat of London.

'Watch out!' Charlie shouted as he took a running sprint into the pool, tucking himself into a neat little ball and bombing into the water. A tidal wave exploded over the sides, soaking everyone apart from Fergus, who was having a nap inside.

'Dad!' squealed Flora, Max and Bella as they splashed him back with all their might.

'My hair!' shrieked Flora, making Tasha and Becca chuckle, another sign of the teenager beginning to emerge. Andrew was holding firmly onto Daisy in the shallow end where she was paddling about with her armbands. Tasha and Becca watched from their sunloungers by the side of the pool. Tasha stretched out her legs and sipped her glass of cold rosé.

'God, I'd just love to live in the countryside,' she said, looking at the flower beds bursting with colour as fat honeybees danced from one blossom to another, her gaze drifting across the rolling lawn that led down to the fields below.

'It is pretty hard to beat, isn't it?' agreed Becca. 'Especially on a day like this.'

'Who'd live in London?' asked Andrew. 'Scorching heat, airless, sweaty commutes... not the life for me, thank you very much.'

'Unfortunately some of us are well and truly bound to the daily grind.' Charlie sighed. 'Though coming here always makes me want to sack it all in. Oh, for a quiet, peaceful life. Maybe we should sell up and move down the road?'

'Funny you should say that,' Andrew said. 'The Cunliffes were talking about putting their house on the market the other day. They want to move to Spain when Peter retires.'

'Oh, yes? Which one's that, then?' Charlie asked.

'Hazeldown. You know, the Tudor house with the topiary hedge a couple of miles down the road? You'll pass it on the way home.'

'I know the one,' Charlie said.

'Oh, please can we move here?' begged Flora. 'That'd be so cool.'

'Yes, please, Daddy, ple-e-ease!' chimed Bella and Max.

'Can we get a pool?' Flora asked.

'We *have* to have a pool!' squeaked Max in excitement.

'That's right, children, keep asking.' Tasha laughed.

'Maybe you'll persuade Daddy!'

'We'd love it if you moved here,' said Becca. 'Do you think we could really tempt you?'

'Sadly I'm not sure I could survive the commute,' Charlie said. 'My hours are antisocial enough as it is.'

'True,' said Tasha. 'You'd find it even harder to get home on time.'

'You'd have to get a crash pad in the city,' said Andrew.

'Ha! Very likely.' Charlie laughed. 'With that spare million pounds I've got lying around in a Swiss bank account – no problem.'

'You could always leave?' Tasha suggested. 'Get a local job, less pressure, less hours…'

'Less money,' Charlie added. 'Who'd pay the mortgage?'

'Well, it's a nice idea,' Tasha said. 'Maybe one day…'

'Can we have a race?' Max interrupted, clearly bored of the adults' conversation.

After a series of races and a long and competitive diving competition, Andrew, Charlie and the children played a hilarious game of Marco Polo with some extremely unsubtle cheating from Max. Tasha soaked up the sun and chatted to Becca about the children, about Caroline and Stephen, and Becca and Andrew's plans for a summer holiday in Majorca.

All in all, it was a lovely afternoon. There was nothing like being away from home to truly relax. Tasha had to be physically removed from the possibility of doing housework to even have the chance of a rest. On the way back to London they drove past Hazeldown, the house Andrew had told them was potentially coming on the market.

'Slow down,' Tasha said, spotting the topiary hedge, rather unusually in the shape of a cockerel. 'Let's just have a quick look.' Charlie raised an eyebrow as if to warn her not to get any ideas, before pulling over. There were no cars in the drive, and no lights on in the house.

'The Cunliffes must be out,' she said as she got out of the car and peered through the gate. It was a perfect Tudor house, all sprawling whitewashed walls and dark wooden beams. Rambling roses climbed the walls leading up to the thatched roof. Charlie appeared by her side, clearly unable to resist the temptation.

'It is pretty amazing, isn't it?' he said.

'Gorgeous. And just look at the view!' The house was on the cusp of a hill, with a view for miles looking out over the rolling countryside.

After a few minutes lost in admiration they got back into the car and set off for home, both of them dreaming of a time in the future where a life in the country might become their reality.

'It's so nice to have Andrew back home, isn't it?' Charlie said as he drove down the lanes leading back towards the motorway.

'I was saying to Becca how brave she is coping with

him away for so much of the time.'

'She does cope very well without him.' Charlie nodded, keeping his eyes on the road. 'I may not work the most sociable hours, but at least I am around more than Andrew.'

Even Tasha couldn't disagree with that. 'True. Do you think he will ever leave the army?'

'I don't know. It's a tricky one. A part of me thinks he might. But it's his life, and he's such a natural soldier. It's just in his blood.'

'I know what you mean.'

'Maybe he will leave one day.'

'I wonder...' Tasha looked out of the window as the countryside whizzed by. It occurred to her, not for the first time, just how fragile life was. She turned around and looked at the children. They had all dozed off, exhausted from their energetic activity in the pool. They were breathing peacefully in their sleep. Tasha thanked her lucky stars that they were all healthy and happy. She sent up a prayer that it would always be so.

Chapter Eleven

'Come on, Max!' Tasha pleaded as she tried to persuade him to eat some more stir-fry. He had managed one mouthful then clamped his lips shut and refused to take another bite. This stand-off had been going on for thirty minutes and counting.

'*Mmmmm*!' he shouted angrily through his tightly sealed lips, shaking his head vigorously.

'Please, darling! You need to eat.' Tasha was trying her best to cajole him. She had tried 'bad cop', with zero impact, and was now trying 'good cop'. Unfortunately, neither seemed to be working.

'I've got *so* much homework to do,' Flora groaned. Having finished her dinner, she was pulling books out of her school bag and piling them on the table.

'You poor thing,' Tasha empathised. 'The sooner you get started, the sooner you'll be finished!'

'What do you *think* I'm doing?'

'There's no need for that tone, thank you very much.'

'I've got to practise my recorder, Mum,' Bella said. 'Can I get down, please?' Tasha was grateful that at least one of her children could remember her manners.

'Of course you can. *You* have finished your dinner,'

Tasha said pointedly, looking at Max.

At this point Max clearly decided that he had had enough. He bolted down from his chair, wriggling out of her attempt to catch hold of him and pin him to his seat. He darted into the sitting room.

Tasha chased after him.

'Max! Come back here at once!' she instructed, trying to sound authoritative.

'I don't WANT it!' He spat the words out with as much venom as he could muster. 'It's DISGUSTING!' He crawled into the tiny gap between the wall and the back of the sofa before putting his fingers in his ears and making a series of loud 'bla, bla' noises to drown his mother out.

'Did you even eat any lunch?' she asked, desperate to know whether he had had any sustenance at all that day. He had only managed a couple of spoonfuls of cereal that morning. The 'bla-ing' got louder. Deciding ignoring him might be her best tactic, she went back into the kitchen to help Bella retrieve her recorder music and encourage Flora with her homework. Minutes later she heard the television being switched on. Her spirits plummeted, knowing that a battle to wrestle the remote off him would ensue. Ignoring the temptation to leave him in peace for an easy life, she marched into the sitting room and switched the television off at the socket. Max screeched his disapproval.

'I did *not* say you could watch television. Absolutely

not!' Tasha crossed her arms and attempted to look stern.

'I *hate* you!' Max shouted, his little face puce with outrage.

'Charming!' she replied.

He flung himself onto the floor, thrashing around like a fish out of water, pummelling the carpet with his mini fists. 'UNFAIR!' he shouted at the top of his lungs. Tasha pulled him up and frogmarched him back into the kitchen.

'If you don't eat your dinner then you won't have your reward time watching television. If you want to watch television, you know what you have to do.'

'I don't want to do ANYTHING!' he yelled. 'I want to run away from this STUPID FAMILY!'

Tasha ignored him and concentrated on loading the dishwasher. Before long she could hear him begrudgingly pick up his fork and continue to eat his stir-fry.

'Well done,' she said. 'That is a good decision.' Another battle won, another mini-victory in the never-ending challenge of keeping her children alive and kicking in a semblance of civilisation.

Having simmered down, Max was granted permission to watch television for twenty minutes. His time was up just as Bella finished her recorder practice.

Right. Bath time. Tasha gathered her strength.

'It's time for a bath, let's get you upstairs!' she called

cheerfully, walking back into the sitting room, trying to keep the mood light to prevent any further meltdowns.

'NO!' Max shouted. His eyes were still red from crying earlier. He sat curled up in a little ball, a furious expression back on his face.

'Come on, Max,' Bella said.

'I don't want a stupid bath.'

'You need to wash! Don't be silly!'

'I am *not* being silly,' Max retorted. 'You are.'

Bella rolled her eyes and ignored her brother. Tasha was often amazed at her middle child's mellow nature. She sometimes showed a maturity way beyond her years.

After another stand-off lasting a good ten minutes and requiring what felt like the patience of a saint, she finally managed to get him upstairs and into the bath.

Flora was still drowning in homework at the kitchen table by the time Tasha had finally persuaded Max to go to bed. She helped Flora finish up before sending her upstairs to join her siblings.

At long last Tasha slumped on the sofa in an exhausted heap. The sitting room looked as if it had been struck by a tornado. She felt frazzled and her head was pounding. All she could see ahead of her were endless days with the same battles to be fought, the same routines, the same house to be tidied and cleaned on infinite repeat. She fought the urge to scream. Instead, she hauled herself out of her chair and blitzed the sitting room like a whirling dervish. Charlie was still at work.

She knew she should cook something but she couldn't muster the energy so she took a frozen meal out of the freezer instead, setting it to defrost in the microwave. She poured herself a huge glass of red wine and took a large gulp. It occurred to her that she was drinking rather more than she should be at the moment as she pressed the speed dial for Rosie.

'Please can we swap lives?' she asked as Rosie answered the phone.

'Uh oh! Difficult day with the little rascals?'

'You could say that!' Tasha slouched back into the sofa cushions. 'Max has embarked on a new regime of evening meltdowns, Flora is stressed and struggling with all her homework. She can be a right madam sometimes. God knows what she's going to be like when she starts secondary school. Thank God for Bella. She's such an angel. If she starts too then I don't know what I'll do!'

'Oh, God! You poor thing. Is Charlie home soon at least?'

'Should be at some point. But in the meantime, I need to talk to someone over the age of ten. Tell me something normal… please!'

'Well… I took your advice and asked Josh out.'

'Oh, wow!' Tasha was impressed. 'Well done! What did he say?'

'He turned me down.'

'No! I can't believe it!'

'I love your unwavering faith in my pulling power.

It's not that surprising.'

'Trust me, it is. What was his reason?'

'Well, he's not gay as you had suspected. He actually told me that he would be uncomfortable dating someone who writes a blog about being single.'

'I thought that might have something to do with it.'

'I told him that I wouldn't write about the date, but he said there wouldn't be much point in dating someone who was resolutely single.'

'Well, I can see his point...'

'I said that just because I had been single up until now didn't mean that I always would be, but he just laughed and politely declined. I'm actually quite gutted.'

'I bet!' Rosie had shown her pictures of Josh online and she could see why. He was gorgeous.

'I don't know what I can do to persuade him. I really like him... And the fact that he said "no" just makes me want him even more.'

'Finally a man seems to have got under your skin! I knew the time would come eventually!'

'It's driving me nuts. I can't stop thinking about him!'

'You'll just have to convince him somehow. Do you reckon if it weren't for the blog then he'd have said "yes"?'

'He gave me that impression.'

'Well, you are right, you may not be single forever! Just because you haven't met the right guy yet doesn't mean you never will. I think you'll just have to try a bit harder to persuade him!'

*

As they ate their lunch after Pilates the next day, Tasha filled Flo in on Max's delightful temper tantrums.

Flo was full of sympathy. 'Megan went through the exact same thing last year. I reckon it was the usual "end-of-term-itis" combined with nerves about moving into Key Stage Two. And this heat probably isn't helping either.'

'God, I certainly hope it's just a phase. The thought of Max being like this for the entire summer holidays is enough to make me want to end it all!' Tasha winced, panic welling within her at the thought.

'I'm signing up for every single holiday camp and club I can find. I can't believe we haven't got any holidays planned this summer. What were we thinking? What about you? You're going away, aren't you?'

'We've got the usual week in Dorset. The kids are so excited already!'

'Jeeze, five and a half weeks is a long old time, isn't it?'

'It sure is. I just don't feel like I've got the stamina this year.'

'We're getting older, that's why.'

'That's probably got something to do with it. The thought of being cooped up in the city with a whole load of boisterous children... They have too much energy for their own good sometimes.'

'You can hardly complain with that garden of yours.'

'You're right. We are very lucky. Though I wouldn't mind moving to the countryside and having even more open space. We were at Becca and Andrew's last weekend. Their house is the dream – they even have a pool! If we lived there I wouldn't need to entertain the kids at all – they would happily spend the entire day swimming.'

'That sounds ideal.'

'Maybe one day...' Tasha sighed. 'Anyway, enough of that. Any more Mrs Perfect stories to cheer me up?'

'Funny you should ask!' Flo rolled her eyes, delighted to move onto her favourite subject. 'It was the school fete on Saturday...'

'Of course! How was it?'

'Awful. I got roped in as a volunteer for face painting, not exactly my forte but I thought I'd give it a go... I mean, how hard could it be?'

'Pretty hard, I imagine!' Tasha laughed.

'Well, Mrs Perfect didn't think so. She was the other face painter and oh, my God, the contrast. The queue for her table went around the entire playground. No one wanted me to do theirs. It was like comparing a three-year-old's self-portrait to Rembrandt. I mean, I knew she was arty after the cupcake debacle and I would never *willingly* have pitched myself as her direct competition.

The poor kids who got landed with me! I could only feel sorry for them – I couldn't stop apologising!'

That reminded Tasha that she had better get baking for her children's school fete the following weekend. She had promised to contribute to the cake stall and the mums in charge – both of whom Tasha found more than a little terrifying – undoubtedly frowned upon shop-bought produce.

After lunch she drove to the supermarket, arriving home a short while later armed with the ingredients needed for a huge baking session.

'Let me help you with that,' Javier said, appearing as if from nowhere as she unloaded the boot full of shopping from the back of her car.

'Oh, don't worry. I'll manage.' Tasha smiled. She felt a little flustered and caught off guard, standing in front of him in her leggings and vest top. 'Thanks though,' she added.

'It's no problem,' Javier said. She noticed the spicy smell of his aftershave as he reached across her to lift some bags out of the car. 'My mother always told me I should help a lady carry her shopping.'

'I'm trying to instil some similar manners in my own son, but so far I seem to be failing miserably!' Tasha laughed. 'How are you?'

'Fine, thank you,' Javier said. 'Enjoying this lovely weather.'

'It's gorgeous, isn't it?'

'You look like you've caught the sun. It suits you.'

'I've been doing rather a lot of gardening. Any opportunity to get in the sunshine! Have you got a garden?'

'A small one,' Javier replied. 'Do you want to come and see it?'

Was there a flirtatious edge to his suggestion? *No,* she told herself. *She was being delusional.*

'Maybe another time…' Tasha realised he would shortly be following her into the house. He was her neighbour… surely there was nothing untoward in letting him help her with her shopping? Besides, it would seem churlish to refuse the help he was offering. By the time she had unlocked the door she hadn't thought of a reason for him not to, so he ended up following her inside and through to the kitchen.

'Nice place.' Javier looked around in admiration as he put the bags down. 'Wow! Look at your garden! It's about five times the size of mine!' He moved over to the sliding doors. 'I had no idea the gardens were so much bigger on this side of the road.'

Tasha laughed nervously. Something about him made her feel slightly awkward in his presence. 'Yes, I am lucky,' she said. 'In many ways.'

Javier grinned. 'How are the children? And your husband?'

'Charlie is well, thanks. And so are the children. Somewhat hot and bothered in this heat.'

'I bet! I suppose I'm rather more used to it than you Brits.' At this he laughed, his brown eyes sparkling. Suddenly she found herself wondering what it would feel like to kiss him, what his stubble would feel like against her skin. As soon as the thought entered her mind, her stomach fizzed with a desire so palpable it made her head spin. She tried to suppress it, shocked at herself. She blamed her subconscious. It clearly couldn't stop the salacious train of thought that had started on her wedding anniversary.

'I-I'd better get on,' she said.

'Of course,' Javier said. 'I won't keep you.'

'I've got to bake some cakes for the school fete.'

'Ah – that explains all the shopping! Sounds fun!' Javier raised an eyebrow. 'I've got to get a move on myself... Making the most of a rare day off.'

'Well, thanks for helping me.' Tasha smiled. She wondered where he was going, who he might be meeting.

'Anytime. I'll let myself out,' he called as he walked down the hallway. She noticed she had been holding her breath. She realised she had been half dreading, half waiting for him to make a move and try to kiss her. *Don't be so ridiculous,* she scolded herself. *As if he would be attracted to her!*

Tasha was shaken by the effect he had on her. She felt herself trembling slightly. She poured herself a glass of water. How utterly desperate she must be. She was a happily married woman; she shouldn't be capable of thinking such thoughts about another man. What was wrong with her? Was she really that desperate? Tasha wondered whether Charlie ever felt like this about women he met at work. She hated the thought of it. It was like a mental betrayal. Yet it felt like a lifetime ago since she had had such feelings of attraction towards someone. She knew it was dangerous yet she couldn't help but marvel at the power of desire – how it could lie dormant for so long and then flare up uncontrollably without a moment's notice, taking your breath away.

Chapter Twelve

'What shall we do with the kids this weekend?' Tasha asked, looking up from her book as Charlie came into the bedroom. He had been working non-stop for the past two weeks, missing their school fete and the children's sports day because he couldn't escape the office. Now that things had calmed down a bit Tasha wanted to make sure they had some quality time together as a family to make up for it.

'Not sure,' Charlie said. 'Have you got something in mind?'

'We could have a picnic at Cannizaro Park?'

'Great! I feel like I've hardly seen them all week.'

'You haven't!' Tasha said.

'Don't start,' he said, a note of warning in his voice.

This immediately made Tasha feel defensive. 'I'm not starting. I feel sorry for you, that's all. When you work this hard you must really miss them.'

'I do. I'm bloody knackered, to tell you the truth.' Charlie sighed. 'I'm not sure I've got the energy for all this any more.' Tasha felt like echoing his sentiments. She never got sympathy for the lack of help she received from him when he was busy at work. She was just expected to manage as a virtually single mother of three.

'You can always leave...' she suggested.

'But what about the mortgage? We've got so many financial commitments. It's not as simple as that...'

'I could go back to work. That would take some of the pressure off you in terms of money.'

'Do you want to?'

'I've been thinking about it quite a lot recently.'

'Really? I had no idea.'

'Well, we haven't talked much about stuff like that lately.'

'I suppose not. Well, what would you have to do to requalify?'

'There's a whole induction programme I'd have to go through. It'd be a hell of a lot of work.'

'How would you manage that? What would we do with the kids?'

'I guess I'd have to revise at night and during weekends. And then there'd be placements, which I'd need to arrange childcare for. And eventually we'd have to find some wrap-around care: someone to take them to school in the morning, pick them up, give them tea, do their homework – that kind of thing.'

'It's worth investigating. But you always said you were glad you had left, that you didn't want to be in that world any more... Have you changed your mind?'

'No. Not really. That's the problem. I'm not sure retraining would be the solution. I think I might be better off doing something completely different.'

'Like what?'

'I've got no idea. I keep racking my brains to think what I'd enjoy, what I could use my skills for... but so far nothing obvious jumps out.'

'Well, it's definitely something to think about. If you think you might like to. You are right. Perhaps that would take the pressure off a bit.'

Tasha was pleased with his response. Perhaps she would start looking into her options properly this week. The thought filled her with nerves and anticipation in equal measure.

*

The next morning, they packed the cool boxes with a picnic lunch and set off for Cannizaro Park. 'Can we get an ice cream?' Max pleaded as they passed the ice cream van on the way into the grounds.

'Good idea!' Charlie said.

'No, you can't!' intervened Tasha. 'It'll spoil your appetite. You won't want to eat your sandwiches.'

'Spoilsport!' Charlie laughed.

'Mu-um!' chorused Flora, Max and Bella as they went past the van, their eyes gazing longingly at the garishly bright pictures.

'We can come back later,' she promised.

'But it might have gone by then,' Max moaned.

'I doubt it,' Tasha said. She wished Charlie would be the responsible one sometimes. It was always Tasha that seemed like the killjoy.

Before choosing a suitable picnic spot they went for a walk in the woods. Luckily, thoughts of the ice cream van were soon forgotten as the children navigated their way down hidden paths, searching for abandoned dens and secret hideouts. Charlie had a wonderful imagination and the children loved the stories he made up of little woodland creatures living in the dens and burrows they found. Under the mossy trunk of a tree stump Bella found a little ring of stones carefully arranged in a circle.

'What can this be, Daddy?' Bella asked.

'Oh,' said Charlie, assuming the solemn voice of a wise storyteller. 'Well, this must be none other than a fairy meeting place.'

'Wow!' Bella's voice was full of awe, her eyes widening at the thought. Max crept closer to examine the scene. Charlie went on to explain how all the fairies would gather to listen to stories from the elders, sitting on the stones like miniature chairs. He said that the biggest stone was for the fairy queen, the most important of all the fairies. Tasha laughed as Max and Bella listened, transfixed, to Charlie. It felt so different when she wasn't the only parent in charge. Besides, they were always much better behaved around Charlie. Even Flora seemed more like a normal ten-year-old and less like a hormonal teenager in his presence.

Later they ate their picnic under the shade of a huge oak tree: egg and cress sandwiches, Ribena, chewy bars and yoghurts. When they had finished Charlie bought them all Mr Whippy ice creams with flakes as promised, ensuring that the children were high on sugar and squabbling furiously in the back seats of the car for the journey home. Her interventions fell on deaf ears so Tasha gave up and checked her phone instead, trying to tune out the noise coming from behind her. She had missed several calls from her mother, and her family WhatsApp group showed a hive of activity, numerous notifications flashed up on her screen.

'Oh, God!' Tasha said as she caught up on the messages.

'What's up?' Charlie asked, pulling the car into a space outside their front door.

'It's Ella. The poor thing has caught malaria!' Her youngest sister was working for a charity in Haiti for a month as part of an extensive backpacking trip with her best friend Tammie.

Charlie switched off the ignition and turned to look at Tasha. 'Is she OK?'

Tasha shook her head. 'Apparently she's in a critical condition. I'm going to have to call Mum.' Charlie swiftly took the kids inside, leaving her in peace.

'Darling?' Lizzie answered on the first ring. 'We've been waiting for you to call...'

'Sorry, Mum, I was out with the children. I've only just seen the messages. What's the latest? Is she OK? I can't believe this...'

'She's in hospital in Port-au-Prince,' Lizzie explained. 'The charity organised transport to get her there. Apparently, she was in a critical condition but she's now stabilised a bit. They are monitoring her closely.'

'I can't bear it!' Tasha said. 'Poor Ella.'

'Stupid girl. She didn't take her malaria pills.'

'I did tell her she had to.'

'I bet she just thought it would never happen to her – typical Ella.'

Tasha could understand why her mother was cross. She was clearly extremely worried.

'Well, she's in the best place at least so try not to worry. And malaria is extremely treatable these days.'

'If she was still critical I'd be on the first plane out there, but her condition seems to be improving and Tammie assures me that the doctors think she'll make a quick recovery.'

'OK. Well I'll try calling her and see if I can get any more information. Maybe I can speak to her doctor?'

'Good idea.' Lizzie passed her over to her father next. Having reassured him, she then called Tammie, who was able to get Ella's doctor to speak to her. By the end of the call she felt confident that the situation was as under control as it could be. Apparently, it had started off as a headache and escalated quickly. Luckily, Ella had managed to see a local doctor, who had spotted the symptoms. Her condition had deteriorated rapidly but Tammie had contacted the charity head office and they had arranged a medical evacuation straight to Port-au-Prince.

Tasha felt quite shaken as she hung up the phone. She went into the house and found Charlie and the children watching *Blue Planet* in the sitting room.

'Everything all right?' he asked.

'Is Auntie Ella OK?' Flora said. All eyes were on Tasha as they waited to hear the news.

'Yes, don't worry, darlings,' Tasha said. 'The doctors in Haiti are looking after her very well.' She filled Charlie in on what she knew. It had really taken her by surprise and she felt quite shocked. It occurred to her just how much she took her family's health for granted.

Later that night, as she lay in bed trying to drift off to sleep, she couldn't stop thinking about Ella lying alone in a hospital bed on the other side of the world. She was grateful that Ella had Tammie with her, but she wished one of the family were there too. Childhood memories ran through her mind and she found herself welling up with tears. She wanted Charlie to hold her in his arms and comfort her, but he was still downstairs watching rugby. Tasha prayed that Ella's condition would continue to improve. She was thankful that her symptoms had been diagnosed and treated so quickly. She knew only too well what might have happened had that not been the case.

Chapter Thirteen

Charlie looked up from his laptop the following evening. 'I'm afraid I've got to go to Zurich next weekend.'

'How come?' Tasha asked, holding the steaming iron against a particularly stubborn crease on one of his shirts. The ironing pile was as high as Everest. Every time she thought she was making a dent in it, it seemed to spring back up to full height.

'It's with some prospective clients that we are trying to impress.'

It hadn't been too long since his last weekend away on business.

'The only problem is...' Charlie was hesitant. 'It's Aunt Marigold's ninetieth birthday lunch on Sunday, remember?'

'Oh, *God*. I had completely forgotten about that.'

'You'll have to go without me,' Charlie said, looking apologetic.

'Oh no way! You *cannot* do that to me!' she groaned.

'I'm afraid there isn't much we can do,' Charlie said. 'It would be extremely rude to cancel completely. She'll be upset as it is that I can't make it.'

'But it's such a long drive. Can't you just get out of

the business trip?' Tasha asked, knowing full well the answer would be 'no'.

'It's really important that I go. I need to make sure I'm winning new business to secure my future in the company.' Tasha knew this line off by heart.

'I don't want to go, full stop, but without you it will be a million times worse.'

'It's bad timing... But at least Becca and Andrew will be there.'

Tasha knew that there was no point pursuing the matter. She was going to have to go, no matter how unpleasant the thought. Her good manners alone were enough to stop her pulling out at such late notice, especially knowing Marigold had such a soft spot for Charlie.

Unfortunately, the heat wave had returned with a vengeance by the end of the week. Max, Bella and Flora had all slept badly on Saturday night – their rooms were too hot and stuffy even with fans blowing and all the windows open. Tasha had hardly slept herself. She felt utterly exhausted and the heat didn't help any of their moods. The children had been bickering non-stop all morning, rubbing each other up the wrong way.

'Mum, Max just took my spoon!' Flora yelled.

'Max, go and get one for yourself,' Tasha said. 'You can't take Flora's.'

'FINE!' Max shouted.

He jumped from his stool and ran over to the drawer

with a dramatic sigh. He took a spoon and slammed the drawer shut. Tasha really wasn't in the mood for his temper.

At that moment the phone rang. 'Hello?' Tasha said as she picked up the receiver.

'Darling? It's Mum.'

'Hi, Mum. Any news?'

'We've just spoken to Tammie.'

'Oh...?' Tasha turned to quieten the children.

'Ella still hasn't been discharged. They're saying she's not strong enough yet.'

Flora was now yelling at Max, who had clearly done something else to offend her. Covering the handset Tasha turned back around, shouting, 'I SAID be quiet!' and glaring at the children in an attempt to silence them. 'Sorry, Mum,' she continued. 'What did you say?'

Lizzie repeated herself.

'Look, please don't worry Mum. She will get there, I promise.'

'Apparently she's still being monitored. Her recovery isn't happening quite as quickly as it should be.' Lizzie filled Tasha in on the rest of her conversation with Tammie. Tasha switched into medical mode, reassuring her mother that this was all normal, that it sounded as though the doctors were doing everything that they should be. She had spoken to Ella's doctor again the day before and was still happy with their course of treatment. Despite the reassurances she had given her mother, by the time she hung up, she felt quite tearful. She was overwhelmingly tired, which wasn't helping. She bet Charlie had slept beautifully with no little visitors interrupting him, and in blissful air-conditioning too. Somehow, despite her exhaustion, Tasha summoned the energy to clear up breakfast, get the children dressed, wrap a present for Marigold and load them all into the car.

'How long is it going to take to get there?' moaned Max an hour or so later as he sat in the back of the sweltering car. The air-conditioning unit was still broken and it felt as if they were sitting in a sauna.

It was only supposed to take an hour and a half, but the traffic had been virtually at a standstill the entire way out of London. She predicted it would take at least three hours all in all. Sweat trickled down the back of her neck and she blinked furiously to keep herself focused on the road ahead.

'It shouldn't be too long now,' Tasha lied.

'I'm too hot,' groaned Bella. 'I don't feel well.'

'I don't feel well either,' Flora echoed.

They crawled through traffic at a snail's pace.

'Are we nearly there yet?' Max asked.

'Ow!' shrieked Bella as he leant over and jabbed her in the ribs. 'What did you do that for?'

'I'm bored,' said Max.

'Well, there's no need to hurt me!'

'Max, leave your sister alone!' Tasha instructed,

trying to keep an eye on the two of them in the rear-view mirror.

'*Ow!*' Bella shrieked.

'Max, what did you do?' Tasha glanced over her shoulder.

'He hurt me.' Bella sobbed. 'He pinched my leg!'

'Right, Max, that's it! You're not getting any pocket money this week. And if you hurt Bella again, you won't be getting any next week either.'

'Don't care,' sulked Max.

'Well, you should. Now say sorry.'

'So-*rry*!'

'Say it nicely.'

'SORRY!' shouted Max, crossing his arms bolshily and looking out of the window.

Tasha drummed her fingers on the steering wheel and willed the traffic to clear up. She was going to be extremely late for the lunch at this rate. As soon as they got there they would have to turn around and leave again. At least it was less time making small talk. One thing was for sure, if she didn't get the children out of the car soon, she was going to have a nervous breakdown. Her head was throbbing.

'Flora darling, can you pass me my water? Take one of the cartons of Ribena for yourself and pass one to your brother and sister. It's important we all drink plenty of fluids in weather like this.'

'I'm boiling!' Flora said as she reached into Tasha's

bag. 'Why are we even going to this stupid party?'

'I need the loo,' Max announced.

'Right, well, try and hold it until we get onto the motorway, then we can find a service station to pull in at.'

The bickering intensified as the temperature rose. By the time they arrived at Marigold's house the children were like coiled springs waiting to burst out of the car. They barrelled out at the speed of light and sprinted across the lawn, aiming straight for Daisy and a few other children who were playing in the sprinkler at the bottom of the garden, their cheeks red and their hair stuck to their skin. Within seconds they were wet and cool, leaving Tasha dreading the car journey back even more with no dry clothes to put them in.

'Tasha,' said Andrew. 'You made it!'

'I'm so glad you are here.' Becca wrapped her in a hug. 'I've finally got a wing-man.'

'I'm sorry we're so late. The traffic was absolutely atrocious.'

'Any news from Charlie?' Andrew asked.

'Not a peep... I assume he is having a wonderful time, in comparison to me anyway!' Tasha laughed.

'Well done, you,' said Caroline, coming over to kiss her on the cheek. 'We heard there had been an accident on the M25 from Jeremy. There's nothing worse than a traffic jam. Now come along and say hello to Marigold. She is very upset that Charlie isn't here.'

No rest for the wicked, Tasha thought as she was whisked off into a rather exhausting conversation with Marigold, who was hard of hearing and sadly not quite as with it as she once had been.

'What did you say, dear?' Marigold peered up from her chair like a queen addressing her lady-in-waiting.

'I'm Tasha, Charlie's wife,' Tasha repeated. 'He's so sorry he couldn't make it. He would have loved to have seen you.'

'Charlie?'

'My son,' Caroline added.

'Charlie…?' Marigold repeated, seeming none the wiser.

'Tasha's just arrived from London,' Caroline said.

'London? Oh, how lovely! Have we met?'

'Yes, we have.' Tasha smiled, attempting to move the conversation on. 'What a fantastic party! So many people!'

'Yes…'

'And such a wonderful, sunny day!' Tasha smiled again, full of false cheer. All she wanted was to have a good chinwag with Becca, taking refuge in the quiet shady spot she had found to keep Fergus out of the sun. But no such luck. When she had finished talking to Marigold, Caroline proceeded to make round after round of numerous introductions, each one involving polite enquiries into the health and well-being of her family, and ample discourse about the weather. After several hours of this, sipping sickly sweet elderflower rather than the wine she craved, Tasha felt as if her pounding head was going to explode.

She finally found Becca. 'I think I'm going to have to make a move if I'm going to make it back in time for dinner.'

'But I've hardly seen you!' Becca moaned.

'I know! Our mother-in-law has certainly kept me very busy. I'm not sure how you've got off so lightly!'

'Fergus is a great excuse.' Becca laughed. 'Make your escape while you've got the chance. We'll probably be setting off soon, anyhow.'

'Give me strength for the return journey,' Tasha groaned.

'Good luck! I'll see you on Thursday, anyway.'

Tasha had forgotten they had dinner plans. 'Great. See you then,' she said, kissing her brother and sister-in-law goodbye.

'Right, children, time to go home!' she called, rounding them up like a sheepdog from the mass of children gathered at the end of the garden. They were all soaking wet from the fountain and full of cake, sweets, chocolate and ice cream. Given the sugar high after a single ice cream last weekend, not to mention the car journey that had followed, Tasha was dreading their return to London even more. 'Say goodbye to Daisy,' she said.

'I don't want to get back in the car!' Max cried.

'Neither do I,' chanted Bella.

'It's way too hot,' moaned Flora.

'I know it's hot, darlings, but we can't stay here forever.'

'Well, *I'm* staying here!' Max shouted, stamping his foot.

'Come on now, don't be silly,' Tasha said, trying to keep her cool.

'I mean it. You can't make me!'

Tasha was desperate to get back on the road. She knew she would need all her powers of persuasion to achieve this result without causing an enormous scene. 'Look, I know it's been a long day, but you've had a lovely time playing and at least you'll be nice and cool for the way home. I'll tell you what, you can all strip down to your pants so you don't have to wear your wet things. And when we get home, we can have pizza for dinner. How about that?'

Having finally won the battle, she opened the car door to a flurry of protests. The temperature inside had now reached boiling point. She cursed Charlie for leaving her alone yet again and made a mental note to get the air-conditioning fixed as soon as possible. She never should have left it for Charlie to sort out. She hoped he would be suitably appreciative of all this when he got home. Perhaps he would spoil her and bring back a nice present from Duty Free.

Another argument broke out halfway around the

M25. At one point all the children were crying and Tasha was on the edge of tears herself. As she pulled onto the South Circular, Bella, who had been looking increasingly pale as they neared London, vomited all over herself, the car and Max.

Max screeched, 'Mum! Bella's just been sick on me!'

'Oh, Bella, darling!' Tasha said.

'Poor Bella, are you OK?' Flora asked. 'Mum, what shall I do?'

Bella started to sob, then she retched once again. Tasha tried her best to keep her eyes on the road whilst glancing repeatedly over her shoulder and trying to calm the children down. 'Don't worry, Bella darling, it's all right. It's probably just the hot weather making you feel sick, and all the ice cream. Don't worry, Max, we will clean you up as soon as possible. Flora, here, take these,' she said, reaching into the glove compartment and passing her some wipes. 'See if you can get some of the worst off.'

'Eurgh, Mum, gross!' Flora looked disgusted at the suggestion.

Tasha frantically scanned the road ahead, looking for somewhere to stop. Spying a café, she pulled over.

'Right, let's get you both out and we'll clean you up.'

'But we're only wearing pants.'

'Mum, there is *no way* I'm going anywhere in just my pants,' Flora said, horrified at the thought of doing anything so mortifying.

'OK, well, you can stay in the car, darling.'

'But it stinks of sick.'

'Never mind, with the windows open it'll soon clear up. See if you can use the wipes to clean up a bit. I'll give you double pocket money as a reward.' Flora rolled her eyes. 'Right, you two, at least you'll be easy to clean!' Tasha tried not to care about the curious looks she was receiving as she walked into the café with Max and Bella, who was still crying. She took them both into the toilet and tried her best to wipe them down with soggy paper towels.

The last part of the car journey was even more unpleasant thanks to the accompanying smell of vomit. By the time Tasha finally got them clean, fed and into bed later that evening she felt totally broken. She sat on the sofa with a cold gin and tonic, too exhausted to even turn on the television. Just as she took her first sip, she heard the key in the lock.

'Hi!' Charlie called as he dumped his bag and came through to the sitting room. He seemed in an extremely cheerful mood. 'Are the children all in bed?'

'Yup,' Tasha said.

'Shame! I was hoping to make it home in time for bedtime. What are we having for dinner? I'm starving.'

She couldn't believe he was asking about dinner instead of finding out about the dreaded lunch party.

'I've only just sat down for the first second all weekend. I haven't exactly had time to cook.'

'Do we have anything in the freezer?'

'Go and have a look.'

A short while later Charlie came back into the sitting room. 'I've found a shepherd's pie. How do you defrost in the microwave again?' Tasha explained how to operate the microwave for what felt like the hundredth time. A few minutes later Charlie came back in again.

'I can't seem to get it to work…'

Tasha hauled herself up off the sofa with a sigh. She went into the kitchen. Within seconds the shepherd's pie was defrosting. She returned to the sitting room and collapsed, still waiting for Charlie to ask about her day.

'I actually had a great time in Zurich,' Charlie said, following her back in and flopping on the sofa with a cold beer. 'I think the client was really impressed with us, and it should be good news for me if something comes from it.' He seemed in high spirits: energised and full of beans. The polar opposite of her mood.

'Good.'

'We went to the most incredible Michelin-starred restaurant last night. We had a seven-course tasting menu with matching wines. It was one of the coolest places I've ever been! You'd have loved it!'

'Sounds wonderful,' Tasha said, slightly sarcastically. Charlie wittered on about his weekend as he swigged his beer. She cradled her gin and tonic, taking refreshing sips as she listened to him talk.

'It's all right for some,' she said. 'Sounds like you've

had rather a nice weekend.'

'Of course, I'd rather have been at home, but as business trips go it wasn't a bad one.'

'Of course,' she said, assuming he meant anything but as he disappeared into the kitchen.

As they ate Tasha watched Charlie, waiting for him to ask her about her weekend. Nothing. He couldn't have been less interested, or less grateful. She felt herself bubbling with irritation. How could he be so oblivious? He must have absolutely no intuition if he couldn't pick up on her mood. She had bent over backwards for him today, for his family, and was rewarded with nothing but tales of how he had been wined and dined at vast expense all weekend. There was no word of thanks, even. She felt like laughing at the thought that he might have brought her a present back from the airport. Fat chance! As if he would have been so thoughtful.

As she lay in bed that night she feared that the gap that separated them was far bigger than the mere inches of mattress space between them. The idea of wriggling over to his side of the bed for a cuddle was an impossible thought. After the day she had had part of her wanted to do just that, but she was too annoyed with him. Instead she turned to face her bedside table. She was so tired, yet she couldn't fall asleep. She listened to Charlie turning the pages of his book, eventually switching off his bedside light and finally falling into the deep and rhythmic breathing that told her he was asleep.

She lay there, wide awake, for what felt like hours.

Chapter Fourteen

The weather changed overnight. The heat seemed to have ignited the heavens as dark grey clouds tumbled in, soon crackling with lightning and echoing with deep booms of thunder. The storm had woken both Max and Bella. Tasha had slept with them in the spare room, grateful for the distance from her marital bed, two little bodies curled up against her to keep safe. She cherished these moments when Max was cuddly and sleepy. They were few and far between. Bella was always in the mood for hugs but her little boy was more reticent. She remembered those blissful hours cradling him in her arms when he was a newborn and marvelled at how the time had flown. Despite his tantrums she loved his fierce independence, his feisty little personality. Every time she looked at him, his freckles, his sandy fringe and the pale skin that had rarely seen the light of day that lay beneath, she knew that all his trickier moments were worth putting up with.

As Tasha enjoyed her cup of coffee in the garden the next morning she breathed in deep lungfuls of air. The damp smell of the earth was heavy, the plants bejewelled with raindrops and the grass soaked through. The garden was saturated with water, its thirst quenched by the rainfall over night after a long dry spell. There was a sense of regeneration in the air.

The children rose without protest for once, relieved by the coolness. Arriving in the kitchen, Bella proffered her kilt for Tasha to do up her button. It was too tight for her to manage herself. Tasha made a mental note to dig out the next size up from Flora's hand-me-downs, another item added to her ongoing list. She thought once again about the mental load article that she had discussed with Flo.

'Can we have scrambled eggs today, please?' Bella asked.

'Good idea, darling. We haven't had eggs for ages.'

'Have you seen my skort?' Flora asked, coming into the kitchen pulling on her polo shirt. 'I need it for games today.'

'It's in the pile of clean washing on the stairs, I think,' Tasha replied, clearing a pile of Charlie's papers from the table then fetching eggs and a bowl from the cupboard.

When all three children had located their various belongings, dressed themselves in the requisite parts of their uniform and eaten their breakfast, they set off up the road. Tasha was praying that the rain would hold off; she had forgotten to bring an umbrella and the clouds above looked full to bursting and ripe for another downpour. Luckily the heavens resisted the temptation to open and she managed to get them all safely through the school gate in time for the first bell.

After swapping pleasantries about the weekend with a few of the other mums she headed for home, lost in her thoughts. She was still fuming about Charlie's lack of appreciation yesterday, not to mention his utter failure to read her or her mood. As she rounded the corner she noticed Javier sauntering up the street towards his front door, approaching from the opposite direction. He had the paper and some milk in his hand and was looking up at the sky as if he had just felt a droplet of rain.

'Tasha!' Javier exclaimed as he lowered his eyes, his gaze falling upon her.

'Morning, Javier,' Tasha replied.

'That was quite some storm last night, wasn't it?'

'It certainly was! Were you at work?'

'We were treating a guy who'd been knocked off his bike. There was a power cut but thankfully the generators kicked in. It must have been a big one.'

'Gosh, I hadn't thought about that. Thank God for generators.'

'Indeed.'

'I wonder whether they have them in Haiti...' Tasha said.

'Why Haiti?'

'My sister's in hospital in Port-au-Prince.'

Friendly concern flickered across Javier's face. 'I'm

sorry to hear that. What happened?'

'She has malaria.' Tasha filled him in on all that she knew so far. She was grateful to be able to talk it through with a fellow medical professional.

'It sounds like she is doing well?'

'As far as I can tell. The doctor I've spoken to doesn't speak much English.'

'An old colleague of mine works in Port-au-Prince, I don't think he is at the same hospital, but he might be a good person to contact if things take a turn for the worse? He is French but he speaks fluent English.'

'Oh, wow, thank you, Javier. That would actually be great.'

'Come in and I'll get his details for you.'

He unlocked the door and walked into the hallway. She glanced through the door on her left to the sitting room where she had noticed Javier eating his dinner the other day. It was decorated in neutral tones, simple and uncluttered, just as she had imagined. Beautiful photographic prints hung on the walls. The kitchen had a small island, which was covered in paperwork. It was clearly not in use as a work surface for cooking, as Tasha's was.

Javier rummaged around for an address book. 'I think it should be in here somewhere,' he said. 'Just give me a minute.' As he thumbed through the pages Tasha noticed a trace of his spicy aftershave in the air. The dampness outside had caused his shirt, a pale blue linen, to cling ever so slightly to his back, revealing muscular shoulders that curved down to narrow hips.

Tasha suddenly felt out of her comfort zone. Being in his house felt different somehow. Their previous encounters had always been outside on the street, in the open, with the freedom to walk away and the safety of knowing any passers-by could witness their interactions. In her home, she had been surrounded by all of the evidence of her family. But here she felt strangely vulnerable, as if the power balance had subtly shifted.

'Here you go!' he said, scribbling down a name and number on a piece of paper. 'I'll just write mine underneath,' he added. 'In case there is anything else.' He looked up at her and she held his gaze for a moment.

'Thanks,' she said. 'I really appreciate it.'

'Like I said, it's no problem.'

They stood in the kitchen, somewhat awkwardly. His unsettling effect on her seemed intensified now that she was in his home. She looked around the kitchen, suddenly finding it hard to tear herself away.

'You have so many amazing photographs,' she said, gesturing at a scene of a lake with perfectly reflected snow-capped mountains in its waters. 'That is absolutely stunning. Where is it?'

'I took that one in New Zealand.'

'You took them?' she asked, surprised.

'Yes.' Javier shrugged his shoulders and smiled, his brown eyes twinkling.

'Wow!' she said, taking a closer look. 'A jazz-playing doctor and a photographer – an impressive skill set indeed.'

'Ah, so you've heard my saxophone?'

'Occasionally. It comes through the window from time to time.'

'Do you like jazz?'

'I don't really know much about it. I love the saxophone. And I have enjoyed what I've heard you play, so I suppose I must.'

Javier nodded. He was still smiling at her, almost quizzically now.

'Where did you take this one?' she asked, peering at the face of an old woman, a gap-toothed grin breaking out across her deeply wrinkled skin.

'South America, in a little village in Peru.'

'You are well travelled, aren't you?'

'I don't travel much any more but I spent several years travelling and taking pictures before I began my career in medicine.'

'That's the time to do it,' Tasha said wistfully. 'I wish I had done some more while I still had the chance.'

'There's still time,' Javier said.

'I suppose...' Tasha took a step closer to examine the photograph. Javier was right beside her, looking at the image, seemingly lost in his thoughts. She wondered what he was thinking, who he had travelled with, what his story was. He must be well into his forties; those laughter lines gave his age away. Now that she was so close to him she could see the odd salt and pepper strand of grey in his thick, dark hair.

As she stood there she felt the energy between them slowly intensify. Tasha kept her eyes fixed on the photograph. Once again, she knew she should break this dangerous intimacy and leave but she just couldn't seem to tear herself away. Adrenaline flooded her body. She couldn't even turn her head. Her whole body tingled at his proximity to her. He was mere inches away.

After a while she could bear it no longer. She glanced up at him and found him looking at her. No doubt he was wondering why she was hanging around. He smiled at her and she blushed, feeling her neck flush with colour. She couldn't deny it: she wanted him. He seemed to have an intoxicating effect on her.

'Would you like a coffee, Tasha?' he asked, softly.

'No. Thank you,' she replied. She swallowed. Her mouth was dry. Her heart was pounding. She seemed unable to break the lock his eyes had on hers. Her breath was shallow and she felt a little light-headed. Her mind was screaming warning bells as loud as claxons but her body seemed utterly determined to ignore each one. The rational part of her brain was sending a checklist of reasons to leave through her in rapid succession: Charlie, the children, it went on and on. Yet her primal instincts were overpowering all logical thinking. She was standing in front of this man, who had listened to her, complimented her, noticed her. She knew she was not in a good place with Charlie but that was not an excuse. It wasn't the right thing to do but she was almost daring him to make a move, to see what her reaction would be. Surely she would bat him away and walk past him? Wouldn't she?

Time seemed to slow down. She was aware of his breathing. She could see each piece of stubble on his chin, the caramel-coloured flecks in his deep brown eyes. Tentatively he reached out and touched her hand. At his touch the tingling she had experienced was intensified, as though someone had turned up the voltage. Her whole body thrummed with electric energy. Slowly, maintaining eye contact, he took a final step towards her, closing the gap between them. She shut her eyes. She knew it was wrong but she didn't want it to stop. In that moment, all she wanted was for him to kiss her. She could hear nothing apart from her pounding heart. It overtook every thought. As his lips slowly touched hers every cell in her body seemed to come to life. Parts of her that had lain dormant for years and years kicked into gear. She felt a deep, primal awakening within her. The overwhelming power of lust punched her in the gut with its force. She knew it was hopeless. She knew in that moment she would surrender. As he kissed her she felt herself disappear into the longing that he created inside her. He led her upstairs to his bedroom and she followed blindly, collapsing onto his bed and succumbing to each mesmerising kiss as he made love to her, powerless to stop it.

Chapter Fifteen

'That was amazing!' Javier said as he rolled onto his side. He leant over and kissed her before collapsing back onto the pillows. 'You are amazing.'

Tasha lay there, catching her breath, dazed and unable to process what she had done.

'It was,' she said. And it had been. Passionate, explosive, completely overwhelming. But it hadn't been with Charlie. She hadn't slept with anyone else since first meeting him, fourteen years ago. The second it was over she had felt a disturbing feeling of discomfort seep in, replacing the all-consuming lust she had felt mere moments before.

'Are you OK?' he asked.

'I'm fine. Sorry. I just... I have never done anything like this before.'

Tasha's mind was reeling. Her body felt entirely sated, but the floodgates had opened and the rational voice that had been trying to get her attention in the kitchen was now at the forefront of all the conflicting voices in her head.

'Hey, I promise, you have nothing to worry about. I'm not going to tell your husband.' Javier smiled reassuringly. He was so relaxed, so comfortable in his own skin. She envied him in a way.

'Oh, God, don't say that word.' Tasha clamped her hands over her eyes. 'I feel terrible.'

'We are all human. Programmed to love, to lust, to desire. There is no harm in what we have done. It's simple enjoyment, good for the soul... I respect that you are married. There is absolutely no need for you to feel ashamed.' Javier leant over and kissed her again. He seemed as if he wanted a repeat performance, but now that the spell had been broken there was no way Tasha was going to relent.

'I think I had better go,' Tasha said, pushing him away. 'I'm sorry.'

'Stop apologising!' Javier laughed. 'I think you are an extremely beautiful woman, and today I got to make love to you. It felt amazing. I promise you, you have absolutely nothing to be sorry for.'

Tasha laughed nervously as she got out of the bed. In contrast to Javier, who was lying there in all his naked splendour seemingly without a care in the world, she suddenly felt very self-conscious. Lost in the moment, she hadn't stopped to think about her body, what he might think of those extra pounds, her cellulite. But in the harsh morning light she knew that it would all be on full display.

Javier watched her as she pulled on her clothes. He yawned. 'I'm going to jump in the shower. Are you sure

I can't tempt you to join me?'

'No, thanks. I must get going. Thanks again for the number...' She didn't know what else to say. This was so awkward. What had she been thinking?

'No problem. Are you happy to see yourself out?' Javier stood up and walked towards her. He reached behind her and grabbed a towel from the back of the door, slinging it around his hips. Her pulse raced from adrenaline; she felt quite faint again, this time for entirely different reasons.

'Yes, absolutely.'

He leant forward and kissed her. 'I meant what I said. Please, don't worry. This was just for us, a stolen moment, to be enjoyed, relished, perhaps.'

She nodded. 'Goodbye, Javier.'

'Have a wonderful day,' he called as she turned on her heel, opening the door and walking down the stairs.

She let herself out, trying not to look suspicious, nonchalantly looking from left to right to see whether she had been spotted by anyone. Thankfully there was no one in sight. She exhaled a sigh of relief and crossed the road. Her hands were trembling as she opened her front door.

Closing it behind her, Tasha turned and pressed her forehead into the wood. What had she done? Tears filled her eyes as she thought of Charlie. How could she have betrayed him like that? How could she have been so weak-willed, so desperate for sexual gratification that she would consider looking elsewhere? She had cheated on him, something she had sworn blind she would never have been able to do. She was no better than his ex... She knew all too well just how heartbroken he had been. Now history appeared to be repeating itself. There had been nothing glamorous about it, nothing romantic. It had been a moment's release and nothing more. She was already filled with regret and she had a sneaking suspicion that the feeling would never leave her.

Suddenly desperate to have a shower, to wash off all traces of Javier, Tasha stripped off all her clothes and scrubbed at her skin under the hot water. Her mind had gone into overdrive, immediately jumping ahead to all the worst-case scenarios in which Charlie might find out what she had done. She tried to tell herself there was no way he could, Javier wasn't going to tell him; he had already told her that. He was a decent man and she felt sure he had meant what he said. Despite his assurance she felt panic set in. She felt so stupid. What had she gained from that? What had been the point? She wasn't going to start a relationship with Javier. She had no interest in him other than a deep attraction; he had a mysterious air that intrigued her but that was worth nothing. She was happy with Charlie. There was no way she would jeopardise her marriage. Except that she just had. It was no good, she would just have to cope with the guilt. She had made her bed and she would now have to lie in it. She wouldn't tell Charlie what she had done.

She would just have to pretend it had never happened and mentally strike it out, if that was even possible.

Back in the kitchen, as she put her clothes into the wash, she remembered in horror that she had left the Post-it with the contact details at Javier's house. She wasn't going back to get it, that much was for sure. She thought of Ella and her eyes filled up once again. *Enough,* she told herself. She had to pull herself together.

Tasha went up to the loft to pull out Flora's old school uniform in the hope of locating a kilt for Bella. She tried to stop the vivid flashbacks from slipping into her consciousness. Each one made her stomach lurch in a mixture of lust and regret. Try as she might, she couldn't get the images out of her mind. She considered calling Rosie to discuss what she had done; if there was one person she could confide in it would be her. Even so, she knew she wouldn't tell her. It was better if no one knew.

Later, as Tasha was ironing Charlie's shirts she found tears in her eyes again. Suddenly she seemed only too aware of just how wonderful he was. Memories flooded back of thousands of happy times together: the first dance at their wedding, eating ice creams on the beach in Dorset with the children, taking Flora home from the hospital for the very first time. She pictured his kind blue eyes, his smile lines, him telling stories to the children, and she thought she might be physically sick with guilt.

She desperately hoped that he would never find out just how selfish and foolish she had been.

Chapter Sixteen

As Tasha walked to school that afternoon to pick up Max and Bella it seemed as though she was seeing the world through a newly-acquired veil of guilt. She was no longer the same person who had traced those exact steps that morning.

Max was first out. 'My tooth fell out!' he cried, proudly showing her a labelled envelope. 'It was dangling on one thread of gum. Mikey pulled it out for me at lunch.'

'Eurgh! How disgusting!' Tasha grimaced, pocketing the package carefully, ready for the tooth fairy later that night.

'It was awesome!' Max beamed. He was definitely not as squeamish as his mother.

Bella arrived in the playground moments later. 'I had the *best* day ever!' she squealed, completely oblivious to her mother's turmoil as she jumped into Tasha's arms for a hug.

'Oh, great!' Tasha fixed a smile to her face. 'What happened? Tell me all about it!'

'We had a special visitor who came in to show us his owl.'

'His owl?'

'Cool!' said Max, his eyes rounding with intrigue.

'We've been learning about them all term and today we got to see one for ourselves! It was so fun. It was just like Hedwig in *Harry Potter*...' As Tasha listened to Bella's joyous ramblings her heart pounded. She was still flushed with shame that she could have jeopardised her precious family's happiness so readily.

'What can we have for tea?' Max asked. 'I'm starving.'

'I've got crumpets for tea and then it's fish pie for dinner.'

'Crumpets!' Max pirouetted with excitement. 'Thanks, Mum, you're the best!'

Only Tasha knew how completely untrue this was. She had to keep fighting back tears. She was dreading seeing Charlie. What if he took one look at her and knew what she had done? Maybe the betrayal was written all over her face.

'Let's cross here,' Tasha said at the top of the road, determined not to go anywhere near Javier's house. 'We'll have crumpets and jam then get your homework over and done with, shall we?'

Flora came home an hour and a half later, following netball club, buzzing with excitement, which made a change. 'Guess what, Mum? I've been moved up to the B team!' She grinned proudly.

'Oh, Flora, well done, darling! That's so exciting!'

Flora munched her way through a crumpet and recounted to her younger siblings exactly what had happened, who listened with grave admiration. Even the mountainous maths homework she had been set could do nothing to dampen her spirits. Tasha sat beside her, doing her best to help her whenever she got stuck. She kept half an eye on the door, waiting for Charlie to get home.

The fish pie she had made that afternoon went down a treat. By the time bath time and bedtime were complete, with only minor protest from Max for a change, Tasha felt like a nervous wreck. She had drawn her bedroom curtains without so much as a glance across the street. Charlie had texted to say that he was on his way home. She turned on the television and watched whatever programme was showing without taking in a word. Eventually she heard Charlie's key in the lock. Her pulse quickened as adrenaline coursed through her veins.

'Hi, babe,' he said, loosening his tie as he came in, bending over to kiss her on the cheek and revealing an enormous bouquet of flowers in a dramatic flourish. 'These are to say thank you for taking the children to Aunt Marigold's yesterday. I realised I didn't thank you properly last night, I was on such a high from the business trip...'

He looked so pleased with his romantic gesture, standing there in front of her with eyes full of love. Bile rushed up her throat and she felt pure disgust at herself. She swallowed heavily and took the bunch of flowers.

'Thank you so much, Charlie,' she said. 'You didn't have to do that!'

Charlie shook his head. 'I think I don't always tell you just how grateful I am for your efforts. I know how much you do for us all – it never goes unnoticed even if I am rubbish at saying it out loud as often as I should.'

Tasha blinked back tears, desperately trying to stay in control of her emotions. She was unbelievably moved but it made her feel her betrayal even more acutely. She had to fight back the urge to blurt out her confession, knowing it would be another purely selfish act. Looking for forgiveness would only serve to cleanse her guilty conscience whilst plunging Charlie into a whole world of heartache. There was no way she could do that to him.

Trying to act normally, she said, 'Ha! Well, thank you. I'm touched!' She got up from the sofa, threw her arms around him and kissed him on the lips. She felt extremely self-conscious and was almost certain he would notice that she was acting strangely. 'I'd better put these in water,' she said, walking into the kitchen.

Charlie followed her through. 'What's for dinner?' he asked.

'Fish pie.'

'Delicious!'

'I hope so,' Tasha said. 'Are you going to shower first or do you want to eat now? It's ready when you are…'

'I'll jump in the shower first, I think. It's so clammy out there. That storm last night was unbelievable! Even the Tube station had flooded.'

'I know, it's very muggy, isn't it?' Tasha's mind flashed back to the similar conversation she had had with Javier that morning, and where it had led. While Charlie went upstairs to have a shower Tasha sat on one of the chairs at the kitchen table, staring at the vase of flowers. A vivid flashback of Javier kissing her stomach flickered unbidden into her mind. She felt a strong pang of lust at the memory and was furious at herself for indulging her salacious thoughts. How could she sit here feeling guilty and ashamed only to have flashbacks at the same time? She wished she could eradicate the whole episode from her mind but the truth was the sex had been incredible; she would have a hard job ever forgetting it. To distract herself she tried to think of the last time Charlie had bought her flowers. It must have been years ago. Why was she such a horrible person? She had been furious with him for not being grateful, for not appreciating her efforts, but he had clearly been noticing all along, he had just needed a bit more time to show her.

Tasha set the table and played some music through the speakers. She even lit a candle. She needed to make every effort with Charlie that she could, in an attempt to make amends. As Charlie thudded down the stairs fresh from the shower there was a knock at the door. Tasha's heart jumped into her throat as she heard him open it. Male voices echoed down the hallway. She strained to hear who it was, she was sure she could hear Javier's voice. She steadied herself on the island.

'That was Javier,' Charlie said, coming into the kitchen. Her heart skipped a beat. 'He said you told him about Ella and he's looked up a contact that he has remembered who works in a hospital in Port-au-Prince. He's written the number down for you with his below.'

'Oh, great!' Tasha said, turning away from him in an attempt to conceal the crimson flush she could feel rising up her neck and onto her face.

'What a nice guy!' Charlie said, reaching into the fridge and pulling out a chilled beer. 'Isn't that kind?' He flicked the cap off with a bottle opener and took a swig.

'Very,' Tasha said, trying to keep her voice normal.

'What's the latest with Ella? Have there been any updates?'

'Mum messaged us earlier. Apparently there have been further improvements and she is starting to feel a lot better, thank goodness.'

'Excellent news!'

'I'm going to try and call her tomorrow.'

'Is she planning on continuing with her trip?'

'Apparently. I'm not surprised. She's been looking forward to it for so long I can't see a setback like this stopping her. And so long as she is given a clean bill of health by the doctors it should be fine.' Tasha could feel herself talking too fast.

'Poor old Ella.'

'I know. It's been a terrible week but hopefully the worst is over.'

'Let's hope so. And at least you have this doctor's contact details if anything else happens.'

'Exactly,' Tasha said. She went about serving up the fish pie on autopilot. Her pulse was racing at the thought of Javier and Charlie talking at the door. How could Javier have been so brazen to come over like that? To look her husband in the eye mere hours after sleeping with her... She suddenly worried that she was trusting him to keep quiet when she barely even knew him. She could hardly vouch for him keeping his word, yet she had entrusted him with the future of her marriage. She looked at the Post-it Charlie had stuck on the fridge, held in place with a heart magnet Max had given her for Mother's Day. How ironic. She wondered whether she should get in touch with Javier to reiterate the importance of his silence. Or maybe she should wait 'till she next ran into him...? She suddenly realised Charlie was talking to her, but she'd been too lost in her thoughts to hear.

'Sorry, what did you say?'

'I found out today that we won the new business. The clients from the weekend...?'

'That's brilliant!' Tasha smiled enthusiastically. 'So it was worth it in the end,' she said as she put two steaming plates of fish pie and broccoli in front of them.

'Absolutely. And thank you. This looks delicious!'

'You haven't tasted it yet.' Tasha laughed.

Charlie devoured his plate quickly, his blue eyes sparkling as he talked animatedly about work. She loved seeing him in such high spirits and realised just how stressed his job could make him when it wasn't going well. The sick feeling in her stomach was growing more and more intense. If only she could wind back the clock to this morning. It seemed impossible sitting here with her husband that she could have even contemplated doing such a thing. She had never kept a secret like this from Charlie before. It felt so wrong, so deceitful. A moment's madness and she would be paying the price in guilt forever. The fact that he was so totally oblivious made it all the worse. As she listened to him she prayed that he would never find out what she had done.

Chapter Seventeen

Tasha lay on her Pilates mat seeking refuge from her rampaging thoughts. She had been tormenting herself all week, running through what had happened with Javier over and over again, chastising herself repeatedly for having broken her marriage vows so carelessly. Listening to the teacher's instructions, she tried her best to stay in the moment, concentrating on each position, pulling her attention back to the present when her mind wandered. She desperately needed a break from her thoughts but there seemed to be no escaping them.

'Are you OK?' Flo asked, taking a bite of her chorizo omelette as they sat having lunch after the class. 'You look a bit peaky.'

'Yeah, I'm all right. I've just been feeling a bit under the weather this week.'

Flo was peering at her suspiciously. Clearly, she could tell there was something amiss. 'Are the kids behaving themselves?'

'The usual. Flora is still ten going on fifteen. Though actually Max has shown signs of improvement recently, thank God.'

Flo nodded. She didn't pursue her line of questioning,

for which Tasha was grateful. 'I can't actually believe it's the last day of school tomorrow. Jake made a chart weeks ago with the number of sleeps to go. Each morning as they cross off another day my anxiety levels increase.'

'I know what you mean. The kids are beside themselves with excitement but the thought of it is killing me. It's enough to make me want to sack it all in and get a job.'

'Really?'

'Yup.'

'That bad, hey?'

'Actually, I've been thinking about it for a while now. Not necessarily as a GP either. Maybe something new… working for a charity, doing something useful…'

'What would you do for childcare?'

'I'd have to find a wrap-around nanny or something.'

'Have you started looking?'

'Not really. I don't know where to begin!'

'You could sign up with a temping agency. They would do the hard work for you and you could try a few different things to see what might work.'

'That's actually a really good idea.'

'What does Charlie say? Is he supportive?'

Tasha thought back to their recent conversation. 'Yes, he was when I broached the subject. Do you know, I think it'd be good for me – it would get me out of the house, make me feel like I've got more to talk about than just my children...' Stop me from making hideous mistakes like shagging the neighbour...

'I think it's a great idea,' Flo announced.

'What about you? Would you ever consider going back to work?'

'As much as I complain, I do kind of like being a stay-at-home mum.'

'That's all right, then. I have done up until now... but something feels like it's missing for me at the moment and I think having a job might just fill the gap.'

'Well, I'll watch this space with interest. Though you better not work Thursdays. Who will come to Pilates with me? And more importantly, who will come for lunch afterwards?'

'Don't worry. I won't be abandoning you anytime soon.' Tasha laughed.

'You had better not!'

*

A few hours later the doorbell rang. Tasha's heart jumped into her throat and a flush of adrenaline rushed through her veins as it had done every time the bell had rung since Monday. She had scurried in and out of the house as quickly as possible without raising her gaze just in case Javier was around. So far, she hadn't seen him since their passionate encounter but his number was still stuck to the fridge and every time she saw it, it burnt a hole in her conscience. She pounded down the stairs and opened the door. It was Nina, arriving to babysit.

'Hi, Nina, thank you so much for coming!' Tasha gushed as she realised with relief that it wasn't Javier.

'No problem,' Nina said cheerfully, slinging her rucksack down at the foot of the staircase.

Max was in the sitting room watching *Paw Patrol*. 'Right, Max, it's bath time,' Tasha called. 'You've had your reward time, now turn it off, please.'

'But, Mu-*um*, I'm watching something,' Max moaned.

'I know but you can press record and finish it tomorrow. It's time for your bath and Nina is here to help you get ready for bed.'

'I don't want a stupid bath!' Max folded his arms and stamped his foot. Tasha bit her tongue, trying to remain calm and not push him over the edge into a tantrum. She came over and wrestled the remote out of his tightly clenched hands, turning off the television and placing the remote on the top shelf out of reach.

'Come on, Max,' Nina said. 'I'll read you *Aliens Love Underpants* if you are good.'

Tasha tried not to mind that Max capitulated immediately to the young Danish girl – why was it that the children listened to a virtual stranger more than to her? She supervised bath time, much quicker without Bella, who was at a sleepover, then got herself ready for dinner while Nina read to Max. She called down to

Flora to come and get in the bath water.

'Coming!' Flora yelled up the stairs.

'Thanks so much, Nina,' she said. 'Make sure Flora doesn't stay up too late reading, won't you?'

Nina nodded. 'Where are you off to?' she asked. 'Somewhere nice?'

'We're going out for dinner in Kensington.' Becca and Andrew were up in London for the night and the four of them were going out for a meal to celebrate Andrew's birthday.

Tasha looked in the mirror one last time to check her make-up. She had ringed her dark blue eyes with liner in a similar hue to her irises, dabbing concealer under her eyes to cover the signs of her disturbed sleep the past few nights. She was nervous that Becca might notice something was up.

'Right. I'm off!' she said, 'Night, darlings. Behave yourselves!' She smiled at Nina. 'I hope they're good. My phone will be on so just give me a call if there are any problems.'

As she stepped out of the front door she risked a quick glance across the road. The lights were on in Javier's house; he must be home. Her heart pounded in her chest at the thought. She quickened her pace and walked as fast as she could down the road towards the Tube. She knew she would have to see him sooner or later but she didn't feel strong enough quite yet.

They were meeting at a restaurant called Scott's, one

of Andrew's favourite places. He had declined a big celebration this year having thrown a full-blown fortieth bash the year before.

'Sorry I'm late!' Tasha was the last to arrive. 'Happy Birthday, Andrew!' she said as she kissed him, then Becca and finally Charlie.

'Champagne?' Charlie asked, pouring her a glass without waiting for her response.

'How are our gorgeous nephew and nieces?' Becca asked, looking glamorous in a black sequined top.

'Our amazing babysitter seems to have them under control – though she only has Max and Flora, which helps. Bella is at her friend's house. Who has got Daisy and Ferg?'

'My mum,' Becca said.

'Luckily Granny loves babysitting,' said Andrew. 'I don't know why we don't take her up on her offers more regularly. She's so close by…'

'To freedom from the wee bairns.' Charlie laughed and held up his glass. 'Happy birthday, bro!' They toasted Andrew, polishing off the bottle of champagne in record speed, clearly all determined to make the most of their night of freedom.

As they ate Tasha couldn't stop looking at Charlie. Her actions on Monday had had the most transformative effect on the way she saw him. All of a sudden, she realised just how much she had been focussing on the negative with him, ignoring his humour, his kindness and his good looks. She was hit with the full force of what a catch she had and she berated herself all the more for her stupidity. She tried to keep her mind in the present and concentrate on the conversation but she kept losing herself in her thoughts.

She zoned back in to hear Charlie talking about Max. 'We thought we had parenting nailed – first Flora and then Bella, these lovely, quiet, angelic little children...'

'Until Flora developed her mood swings, you mean,' Tasha added.

'True!' Charlie agreed. 'But then Max came along and proved us completely wrong!'

'Bless him!' Becca laughed. 'He is a little monkey.'

'I seem to remember you being rather similar as a child, Charlie. It's hardly a mystery where he got that cheekiness from.'

'He was actually pretty good last weekend, considering what happened to the poor thing,' Tasha said.

'After the lunch?' Becca asked.

'Yup! The hottest day of the year... On the way home Bella vomited all over herself and Max in the car!' Tasha winced at the memory.

'Did she?' Charlie asked, aghast. 'You never told me!'

'Oh, God, how disgusting! I can't think of anything worse!' shrieked Becca. 'What did you do?'

'I pulled over as soon as I could and whipped them into the nearest toilet. They were both covered in sick and only in their pants.'

'Why no clothes?' asked Charlie.

'The children were all playing in the sprinklers,' Becca explained.

Tasha continued. 'The worst bit was the rest of the journey back into London in a car smelling of sick, and to top it all off the air-conditioning was broken too. Max was surprisingly good considering.'

'Oh, my goodness, you poor thing!' Becca said.

'That sounds pretty revolting,' Andrew agreed.

'I can't believe you didn't tell me!' Charlie laughed. 'I mean, I'm sure it wasn't funny at the time...but-'

'I suppose I can begin to see the funny side now – not so much when I was scrubbing sick from the car after being stuck in it for a total of six hours!'

'Awful!' Becca agreed. She paused. 'You know Andrew and I have been talking about trying for number three recently...'

'Really?' Tasha gasped. 'How exciting!'

'Maybe when I get back from my next tour,' Andrew said. 'Obviously it does help if I'm in the country!'

'That's amazing news,' Charlie said.

'I guess the leap from two to three isn't as big as three to four?' Andrew asked. 'At least you can still fit them in a normal car...'

'It's not too bad,' Tasha assured them. 'There's definitely a lot more juggling required, and a lot more laundry, but overall I'd say it's definitely worth it.'

'I certainly can't imagine life without Max,' Charlie said. He reached under the table and squeezed Tasha on the knee.

'Me neither,' she said. Her heart swelled with emotion and she felt her eyes brim with tears as she considered once again how selfish she had been to jeopardise the happiness of the family she loved more than life itself.

'I guess we'll see!' Becca smiled.

'Well, fingers crossed!' Charlie said.

'I'd love to have another baby around,' Tasha added. 'I was just thinking the other day how much I miss having a newborn. They are so unbelievably sweet and cuddly.'

'They make me so broody,' Becca agreed.

After dessert and coffees, they ordered taxis to take them home. On the way back, Tasha's thoughts turned to Andrew and his work in the SAS. It always amazed her how they never discussed it, as close as the four of them were.

'Do you think Andrew really has been in Northern Iraq training the Kurds?' she asked.

'Probably not.'

'Would you ever talk about it? You are his brother, after all.'

'No. He's very strict about it,' Charlie said. 'It's just not the done thing.'

'Do you think Becca knows what he actually does

when he is away?'

'Not necessarily. He isn't meant to tell her much and many people don't tell their other halves more than the bare essentials.'

'It's terrifying when you see them so happy together to think how he is risking it all, isn't it?' She realised how ironic her words were.

'It really is the ultimate sacrifice – for the safety of our country and the greater good.'

'Amazing really...' She tailed off, lost for words in admiration for her brother-in-law. She dreaded to think what he had been through, what awful things he must have seen. She suddenly remembered her conversation with Flo at lunch. 'Flo suggested I sign up with a recruitment agency to look for some temporary work, so I could try out a few different jobs in different industries, see what I might enjoy...'

'That's not a bad idea,' Charlie said. 'Are you going to?'

'I think so. There's no harm in seeing what they might come up with for me,' she said. 'Who knows what the future holds?'

That night as they lay in bed, Charlie took her in his arms and made love to her. She tried to put all thoughts of Javier out of her mind, tried not to compare them. Afterwards she told him she loved him as he held her close. Her head was spinning as she tried to fall asleep. She wondered if there would ever be a day when she didn't have to live with the regret that was currently consuming her.

Chapter Eighteen

The following day was the last day of the summer term for Flora, Bella and Max. They woke up in the best of moods, overexcited and champing at the bit for their holiday to begin.

'I'm *so* happy!' Max sang as he bounced on his bed.

'Come on, you need to get dressed. It's still a school day today,' Tasha pleaded, trying to ignore her hangover.

'I'm *too* happy to go to school. I want the holidays to start *now*!'

Tasha couldn't help but laugh. He looked positively angelic in his dinosaur-print pyjamas. 'Today will be over before you know it. And you need to say goodbye to all your friends, say thank you to your teachers…'

'I can't wait to give Miss Newman my card! I hope she likes it.' Max jumped off the bed and over to his desk, where he picked up a heartfelt home-made thank you card.

'How sweet!' Tasha hadn't seen him make it and her heart melted at the sight of the wobbly felt-tip hearts covering the folded piece of paper. 'I'm sure she will love it, and we've got her a present too that you can give her.'

Tasha had organised presents for all the children's teachers, as she did at the end of each school year. They traipsed down the road laden with an assortment of bags, each labelled with the appropriate teacher's name and ready for distribution.

'I wonder who is going to look after Gomez over the holidays,' Bella said. Gomez was the class hamster.

'I'm sure Mrs Pumphrey will.'

'I'm going to miss him *so* much!'

'I can't *believe* I'm going to be in Year Six in September,' Flora said. 'It's *so* scary!'

'*I* can't believe I'm going to be in Year Two!' said Max. They chattered animatedly all the way into the school building, where Tasha helped them deposit their gift bags around the various classrooms before making a quick escape as the school bell rang. As she walked home she distracted herself by planning activities to keep the children amused over the next five and a half weeks. She knew come two o'clock that afternoon she was on her own in terms of childcare. How the teachers coped with thirty-plus children at a time she would never know. To her, three seemed taxing enough.

That evening Charlie came home in time for the children's dinner, a tradition that they kept each year to kick off the summer holidays with a bang. They always went to their local Italian, a child-friendly pizzeria up the road where the children gorged themselves on margherita pizzas and ice cream sundaes piled high with marshmallows and fudge sauce. They had a whole weekend of family fun planned out ahead of them.

On Saturday Charlie drove them all to Chessington World of Adventures. They went on a river ride, visited a haunted house, ate lunch at a burger shack, sailed through the air on a Ferris wheel, clambered through the monkey park and soared through the skies on various roller coasters. Tasha's guilt was amplified: she couldn't remember the last time she had seen the whole family look so happy, the sound of the children laughing and squealing was music to her ears, but all she could focus on were the ringing accusations from her conscience.

On Sunday they spent the afternoon at Water World, a giant swimming pool full of water slides, wave machines and rapids to float around on in rubber rings. They accompanied the children on an endless round of trips down the fastest slide possible: a plastic tube that twisted and turned like the roller coaster they had been on the day before. Both places were so hectic and all-consuming Tasha had little time to retreat into her thoughts, a welcome relief after the previous week. But each time she stopped, even for a moment, Tasha felt the now familiar rush of panic course through her at the thought that at any moment she could be found out. If Charlie discovered what she had done that could be it for their happy family. One word from Javier and the precious balance of trust that was the lynchpin of their happiness could be irreversibly damaged, never to be the same again. She tried to stop herself from imagining what life would be like should the unthinkable happen, but her mind kept escaping into a future that might never exist. By the end of the weekend she had made a decision. It was clear what she needed to do. She had to do everything in her power to keep her secret hidden, and that meant ensuring that Javier was not going to break his word.

Chapter Nineteen

The following morning Tasha answered the door to reveal Chloe, her younger sister, on the doorstep, dressed head to toe in her usual mishmash of patterned, bohemian clothing. Tasha was nervous that her sister might see right through her false cheerfulness, but at the same time she was desperate to see a friendly face.

'Yay!' Tasha squealed, hugging her tightly. 'How lovely to see you!'

'Hey, sis!' Chloe said, following Tasha into the house. 'Where are the little ratbags?'

'In the garden. They're so excited to see you.'

'Well, it's not every day I get to come up to the Big Smoke and hang out with my favourite mini relatives.'

'We are honoured that you're spending one of your precious holiday days with us. How was the end of term?' Chloe was a secondary school Geography teacher and she, like the children, had just broken up.

'Fine, thanks. As soon as I finished my reports I started winding down. I am bloody glad the holidays have arrived though, that much is for sure. I'm exhausted!' She slung her bag down and came through into the kitchen.

'The opposite of my sentiments! Apart from the exhaustion.' Tasha laughed. 'You'll stay for lunch, won't you?'

'Yes please, I'll head back this afternoon. I'm leaving tomorrow for Bali!'

'Oh, how amazing! How long are you off for again?'

'Five whole blissful weeks. And I cannot wait!'

'Is it going to be hot?'

'Hopefully. I keep checking the forecast and it's looking pretty good so far.'

'God, I'm so jealous.' Tasha sighed. If only she could run away from her problems and lie on a sun-drenched beach in the middle of nowhere. 'Have you had your vaccinations? You don't need malaria pills, do you?'

'No, I don't, thank goodness. And yes, I'm fully immunised, don't worry. Mum's been on at me ever since she found out about Ella.'

'It's great news, isn't it?' They had heard from her that morning; she had finally been discharged from hospital and was feeling a lot better.

'Such a relief. She certainly won't be making that mistake again!'

At that moment three little voices squealed as they charged into the kitchen. 'Auntie Chloe!' The children were already covered in dirt, their T-shirts and shorts wet from squirting each other with water pistols.

'Hello favourite nieces, hello favourite nephew!' Chloe replied as she hugged them all tightly.

'Do you want a coffee?' Tasha asked.

'I'd love one, thanks,' Chloe replied as the children pulled her outside into the garden, chattering furiously as they told her all about their weekend activities at Chessington and Water World.

Tasha slotted a capsule into the coffee machine and pressed the button. It churned loudly as it clunked into action. At that moment Tasha's phone vibrated in the back pocket of her jeans. Her heart leapt into her mouth as she pulled it out. She breathed a sigh of relief. It was only Rosie, confirming their plans to meet later. Charlie had a quiet few weeks at work ahead and Tasha was planning to make the most of going out without having to pay for childcare, he had promised he'd be home in good time. Her heartbeat returned to normal as she replied confirming their dinner plans. Having pressed send, Tasha scrolled down her messages to make sure she really had deleted her text to Javier.

After much deliberation, lying awake all night deciding what to write, she had finally taken his number from the Post-it on the fridge and sent him a message that morning. It had said:

> Hi Javier, I have been panicking all week and just want to make sure that you meant what you said about not telling Charlie. It would be the end of our marriage if he found out. Please keep your word and never say anything to anyone about what happened on Monday. Thanks, Tx

Her nerves were a-jitter as she thought about him receiving her text. Maybe he was at work and his phone was in his locker? Maybe he hadn't even read it yet? She wondered whether he would reply.

Pushing thoughts of Javier to one side, she took the coffees into the garden and sat down. The children had started a competitive game of garden Jenga. They were soon engrossed in the removal of carefully balanced bricks, allowing Tasha and Chloe to have a long overdue catch-up.

'Right, what do you fancy for lunch?' Tasha asked a short while later as the tower collapsed for the third time, sensing it might be time for a change in activity before an argument broke out.

'Can we have bangers and mash?' pleaded Max.

'Bangers and mash it is, then,' Tasha said. She went into the kitchen and raided the fridge, sure she had some sausages somewhere. Having checked the freezer, she realised she was out of stock.

'Chlo, are you happy to stay with the kids while I nip out to the shops?' Tasha asked.

'No probs,' Chloe replied as she chased Max around the flower bed. To the children's intense delight, she had picked up one of the abandoned water pistols and was attempting to squirt them.

Tasha laughed at the sight. It was lovely to have someone else to entertain the children. 'I'll be back in five,' she called, grabbing her bag and heading out of the house.

She heard someone calling her name as she shut the front door. She recognised the voice instantly.

'Javier,' she said, blushing furiously as she looked up to see him standing by his motorbike in front of her.

'Hi.' He looked even more handsome than usual in his black leathers.

'Hi,' she replied. Memories of him kissing her flooded her mind as she stood, awkward and speechless, in front of him. She turned her head to glance back at the house, checking the windows. Chloe and the children were nowhere to be seen. She knew they would still be in the garden playing.

'I just got your message,' he said. 'Don't worry. I promise you have nothing to panic about.'

Tasha breathed a sigh of relief. She spoke quietly, just in case anyone she knew was somehow within earshot. 'Thank you so much. I know it's silly, you already told me. I just worked myself into an absolute state…'

'Relax!' Javier smiled his most charming smile as he got onto his bike. His eyes were slightly shadowed, his stubble longer than usual. 'I'm off to the hospital. They've called me in early; one of the registrars has gone home sick. I desperately need a coffee – one thing I can't be is tired in my line of work as you know.'

'Of course!' Tasha said. 'Well, I won't keep you.'

'Have a lovely day!' he called, revving the engine and turning his bike around before driving off down the street.

Tasha stood glued to the spot; she felt relieved but also unnerved. It was the first time she had seen him since she had slept with him. It hadn't been as awful as she had thought it would be. He was so completely unfazed by the whole situation that it made it less awkward than she had anticipated. But she still couldn't believe she had actually done what she had done with him. She tried to stop the flashbacks from popping into her mind but it was impossible to wipe them out completely. Shaking herself, she carried on down the road, her mind whirling as she walked, on autopilot, to her local shop, choosing a couple of packets of sausages and some extra milk.

She told herself that she needed to trust him. She had no reason not to. After all, it was hardly in his interest to tell Charlie. That would make life more difficult for him and, if anything, she was convinced Javier was the kind of guy who wanted an easy life, without complication. That was presumably exactly why he was single. Tasha decided she had no choice but to accept his word and try her best to move on.

She had a lovely lunch with Chloe and the children before taking the kids to the park and then rustling up chicken goujons, chips and peas for dinner. Charlie took over at bath time, having arrived back early as promised.

'Thanks so much for getting home,' she said, coming into the bathroom to kiss him goodbye.

'No problem.' Charlie smiled as he checked the temperature of the water. 'Have fun with Rosie. Send her my love.'

'I will.'

Tasha kissed the children goodnight, grabbed her handbag and went out. They were meeting near Tottenham Court Road so she headed straight for the Tube. She glanced up at Javier's house. There were no lights on, unsurprisingly – he would still be at work.

'I ordered a bottle of rosé.' Rosie got up from the table to hug Tasha. They were at a small new restaurant on Greek Street opposite the Prince Edward Theatre.

'Good idea!' Tasha said, trying to act as normal as possible. She knew Rosie, just like Chloe, would be on to her in a flash if she let her guard down even for a second. 'I could do with a few drinks. We had a rather hectic weekend to celebrate the start of the summer holidays.'

'Oh, yes? What did you get up to?'

'Chessington World of Adventures followed by Water World.' Tasha laughed. 'I know, I know – just up your street.'

'Maybe one day!' Rosie laughed. 'I bet the kids loved it though.'

'They did. And so did we. It's so cute seeing them in seventh heaven like that.'

'Gorgeous.'

'So? What's the latest with Josh?' Tasha asked,

determined to steer the conversation away from herself.

'Well... it's funny you should ask,' Rosie said rather coyly.

'What do you mean? Have you got news?' Tasha was suddenly excited for her friend. Rosie beamed a huge smile and looked as if she were about to burst with happiness.

'We're officially a couple!' she exclaimed.

'No! You're kidding? When did *that* happen? How?'

'After our last phone call, I decided to write him a letter. I wanted to show him how serious I was.'

'I love it! There's nothing like an old-school love letter to show your intentions are genuine!'

'Exactly! It was a bit cringe but I basically wrote him a note saying that I really liked him, that I would never write about him without his permission and that I wouldn't date anyone else or write any dating blog posts for the foreseeable future if he would just give me a chance.'

'Hang on... so you're actually suspending the blog? Can you even do that?'

'I can do what I like really. I've decided I am going to write a series of posts on dating-related topics like "Top tips for flirting", "Top tips for online dating profiles" and stuff like that... I'll make it up as I go along, I guess. I have no idea how long this will last...'

'So, what happened? How did you give him the note?'

'I just slipped it on his desk in a sealed envelope and waited to see what would happen.'

'And what did he do?'

'A few hours later he came sidling over to my desk, clutching the letter. I felt like a teenager, I was so nervous to see his reaction.'

'What did he say?'

'He thanked me and asked me what I was doing that evening. When I said I was free he told me he'd book somewhere. We went to a lovely French restaurant near work and have been seeing each other ever since!'

'Oh, my God!' squealed Tasha. 'This is *so* exciting!'

'I think I might actually have a boyfriend!' Rosie laughed. 'For the first time in God knows how long.'

'Someone has finally persuaded you to give a relationship a go! This is *huge*! He must be incredible!'

'I know! He is. I *really* like him. He's smart, intelligent, funny… and what is more he seems like a thoroughly nice guy. A Charlie type. Not to mention the fact that he is also incredibly fit and amazing in bed too…' Rosie raised an eyebrow.

'I'm glad to hear it! Cheers to Josh!' Tasha laughed, raising her glass and masking the internal angst that had erupted at the mention of what a nice guy Charlie was. As if she needed reminding… At the thought of Charlie, she stuck her hand in her bag to find her phone and see whether Javier had been in touch. She didn't think he would reply to her text having seen her face to face earlier that day, but she wanted to check anyway just in case. She rummaged around trying to locate it whilst talking to Rosie about Josh, but it was nowhere to be found.

'Sorry, I think I've lost my phone,' Tasha said, explaining why she was rootling through the contents of her bag, tipping most of them out onto the table.

'Is it there?'

'No, it definitely isn't...' Tasha's heart was starting to race slightly as she scanned her memory to recall where she was when she last had it.

'Where did you last have it?' Rosie echoed her thoughts.

'I'm just trying to work that out. I don't think I actually looked at it on the Tube...'

'But surely you used Google Maps to find this place?'

'No. I know how to get to the Prince Edward Theatre: we only came recently and it's just opposite.'

'Maybe you left it at home?'

As soon as Tasha heard the words she realised that was exactly what she had done. She had left it on her bed. It had been in her hand when she had decided to change her flip-flops and put on some slightly smarter sandals. She must have left it lying there on the duvet. Suddenly her pulse raced as she realised that she had no control over Charlie seeing it. Her palms started to sweat. She felt herself flush with panic as adrenaline coursed through her veins. She had deleted that message, hadn't she? She assured herself that she had – she remembered double-checking earlier that day. But what if Javier had texted her?

Tasha had to fight the urge to get up and leave the table right that second and race home. She reassured herself once again. Javier had seen her earlier – there was no need for him to message after that. But he might, there was no denying that. She should never have texted him – now he had her number and there was nothing she could do about it. Rosie was still talking to her, oblivious to the inner turmoil that was spiralling out of control within her mind. She nodded and smiled but Rosie's words fell on deaf ears. Their food arrived but Tasha was so distracted, so desperate to get home and find her phone that she couldn't enjoy it. She wished she could feign illness or some kind of crisis she needed to rush off for but Rosie knew her too well. Maybe she should just tell Rosie the truth? But Tasha was too ashamed even for her best friend to find out. She was embarrassed; she didn't want to be judged. The only person who could *ever* know what she had done was Javier.

'Do you want pudding?' Rosie asked as the waiter offered them the dessert menus.

'Do you know what, I'm actually feeling pretty stuffed and exhausted after the mania of the weekend. I might make a move.' Tasha yawned loudly, spying an opportunity to beat a hasty retreat.

'No problem. I'm actually staying at Josh's tonight...' Rosie looked sheepish.

'You should have invited him! Oh, my goodness – you're probably *dying* to get over there!' Tasha laughed.

'No way was I going to invite him to a girly dinner. But we should have supper, all four of us, soon though. That is for sure,' Rosie said. 'I need you to vet him for me, to make sure he gets your seal of approval.'

'I'd absolutely love to meet him.' Tasha smiled. 'Let's definitely do that.'

They paid the bill and walked to the Tube. Tasha had to force herself to keep a natural pace rather than sprinting home as fast as she could. When she and Rosie had gone their separate ways, she ran for the Tube carriage as the train pulled in to her platform. As she sat in her seat she tapped her feet and drummed her fingers nervously against her thigh. Her stomach fizzed with nerves. She prayed that Javier hadn't sent her a reply, and that if he had that Charlie hadn't seen the message. She kept on talking to herself; the rational part of her brain reassured her that more than likely Charlie hadn't even noticed that she had left her phone behind. He was probably in the sitting room watching television. He might not have even been up to their room since she'd left. Plus, even if he had found it, he probably would have just left it on the bed. She trusted him not to look through her messages. He was the least nosy, least jealous guy. There wasn't a possessive bone in his body.

She trusted him completely. Which was ironic, seeing as he clearly shouldn't trust her.

Tasha willed the train to speed up, to get her back to Putney faster, but it trundled along at its usual pace, unaware of her desperation. As her stop approached she stood ready to get off, bolting through the doors as soon as they opened before racing along the platform to reach the turnstile and the exit as fast as possible. She went out of the station and rushed home as quickly as she could, pounding the pavements, determined not to let another second pass unnecessarily where her phone was unattended and potentially the catalyst of a chain of events she had absolutely no intention of letting come to pass. The unthinkable simply could not happen.

As she turned onto her road her heart pounded; she tried her best to catch her breath so that Charlie would not suspect she had been rushing home. She forced herself to stand still on the doorstep for a moment or two, letting her breathing return to normal. She took a final, deep breath in and exhaled slowly. Butterflies stormed inside her and she felt sick with nervous anticipation.

She turned the key in the lock, telling herself that Charlie would be on the sofa watching television, that she would act completely normal, come in and say hi, have a quick chat about Rosie and Josh and then casually say she was desperate to go to the loo, walk upstairs, pick up her phone and put it safely out of harm's way in her pocket. She pushed open the door and took a step inside.

Chapter Twenty

Time stood still. Charlie was sitting on the bottom step of the stairs, facing her. He held her phone in his hand. One look at the expression on his face told her all she needed to know. A cold chill shot down the length of her spine.

'Hi,' she said, trying to keep her voice normal. Maybe she was wrong, maybe it was just her paranoia.

'Hi,' he replied. His voice sounded strangely impassive. 'You left your phone.'

'Yes,' she said. She was watching him closely, trying to gain some control of the situation, to somehow regain the upper hand.

'You got a message.'

'Oh yes?' she said, trying not to show her panic.

'The number wasn't saved. But I recognised it. The same number that has been stuck on the fridge this past week.'

The blood turned to ice in her veins. Still, she was determined not to give anything away. After all, she had no idea what the message had said. 'Javier? Yes, I thought he might get in touch about Ella...' She tailed off somewhat sheepishly.

'About Ella?' Charlie repeated coldly, his voice bitter with sarcasm.

Tasha stood still. She had run out of words. Charlie stood up and came towards her. 'I heard a beep and picked it up. The message flashed up on your screen. Let me read it to you.' Tasha couldn't breathe as he unlocked her phone and opened the message. He cleared his throat. His voice sounded tight and strained. '*Nice to see you earlier, beautiful Tasha. Don't worry. Our secret is safe with me. I will never tell Charlie. Maybe one day I will tempt you once again. Kiss.*'

As she listened to him read Tasha's world imploded. She knew she had mere seconds to try and salvage this situation. She needed to think of a story that would somehow explain it. Her mind raced at a thousand knots but it was no use. It was completely blank. Tears welled in her eyes as she saw the hurt in his. She *had* to think of a way out of this. Quickly. But time was passing and there was nothing she could think of to say or do. A tear spilled down her cheek as she realised there was nothing left but to tell him the truth.

'I'm sorry,' she whispered.

'So, it's true?' Charlie swallowed. 'You have had an affair.' His voice was heavy with disbelief. 'With Javier?'

'I'm so sorry,' she repeated. 'It only happened once...' More tears trickled down her cheeks.

She could see her words were wounding him, each one a poisoned dart.

'Only once...' he repeated softly, shaking his head as if he couldn't take it in. He looked completely stunned. He walked into the sitting room and sat heavily on the sofa. Tasha followed him in and closed the door behind her, dropping her bag and her keys to the floor. Her heart was pounding in her chest.

'When?' he asked.

'Last Monday,' she said. 'I'm so sorry, Charlie. It meant nothing. It happened so quickly. The second it was over I regretted it. I don't know what I was thinking. I've been feeling sick at the thought all week. My mind has been tying itself in knots trying to understand how I could do something so stupid, how I could hurt you like that, how I could risk our family's happiness for something so completely inconsequential, so totally pointless, so selfish—'

Charlie interrupted her with a single, piercing question. 'Why?' It was all she had been asking herself for the past seven days. He looked at her and she saw that his beautiful blue eyes were brimming with tears. She hadn't seen him cry for years, and she couldn't bear the thought that she was the reason for the hurt he was so clearly feeling.

'I don't know,' she whispered, shaking her head fervently. 'It was nothing... honestly.'

'How *could* you?' he asked.

'I don't know. I'm so sorry...so, *so*, sorry... I told him it meant nothing. I saw him this morning and I begged him to delete it from his memory, never to tell you because I didn't want this to happen and I never wanted to hurt you. I love you *so* much, Charlie.'

'Oh, I don't think so,' he said. He shook his head; he seemed almost shell-shocked.

'I *do*. I love you. I *love* you...' She knelt in front of him and took his hands in hers, showering them with kisses amongst her tears. 'If I could turn back time I would *never* have done it. I think I was out of my mind. I haven't been feeling myself lately, I've been so down, so depressed.'

'*You've* been down? Like that's some kind of excuse?' Charlie shook his head again in disbelief. '*I've* been the one working all hours to provide for this family. You have no idea the stress I am under at work. You have *absolutely* no idea.'

'I know and I'm so sorry.'

'I don't want to hear it. If you had your way I wouldn't even know about this. You have betrayed me in the worst way possible.' His voice was cold, each word steeped in anger. He seemed to be retreating into himself before her very eyes.

Suddenly his face flickered with rage. 'That *bastard*!' he shouted through gritted teeth. He strode down the corridor and flung open the front door. Before she could stop him, he had stormed across the street and was hammering on Javier's door, calling his name. Thankfully the lights were not on and he was still at work. The last thing Tasha wanted was a scene in front of the neighbours; it would be much better if Charlie had some time to calm down before he saw him. Right now his emotions were running about as high as was humanly possible.

'Charlie, stop. He is not in, come back inside!' Tasha pleaded. 'Let's talk. We don't want people to hear us...'

Realising Javier was not home, he crossed the street and went back inside. He couldn't even bring himself to look at her. She begged him to talk to her but he pushed past her and went up to their room. She ran after him, keeping her voice as low as possible to avoid waking the children. Without saying a word, he grabbed a bag and started stuffing it with clothes. He packed his charger, his laptop, his wash bag. Every time she stood in his way he pushed past her, his jaw rigid with anger and hurt. Before she knew what was happening he was downstairs grabbing his keys and his phone.

'Don't!' she cried. 'Charlie, *please!* We have to talk about this. Don't just leave. I am begging you... please...'

'Get out of my way, Tasha,' he instructed. His eyes were emotionless; he had shut down. She knew there was no way she could change his mind. She moved to one side and within seconds he was out of the door, leaving her sobbing in the hallway. Tasha picked up her phone and reread the message from Javier. She wailed and threw it to the floor, collapsing onto her knees, tears streaming down her face. She ran onto the street but Charlie had already disappeared. She wanted to scream his name, but she didn't want to risk waking the children. Instead she came back inside and scrabbled on the floor for her phone once again. She hadn't even had a chance to explain what had happened. She pressed the speed dial for Charlie and it rang and rang. It was no good. She knew him well enough to know he wouldn't answer.

Her breath wasn't coming easily. She put her head between her knees and concentrated on her breathing. Hysteria bubbled up within her. What had she done? Oh, God, what had she done? She picked up the phone again. This time she called Rosie.

'You found it!' Rosie laughed down the line.

'Rosie...' Tasha's voice was desperate as she burst into hysterical sobs.

'Tash? What's happened?' Rosie asked, realising immediately that something was seriously wrong.

Tasha tried to catch her breath, to regain enough composure to speak. 'It's Charlie,' she sobbed. 'He's left. I don't know what to do. The children...'

'What do you mean?'

'He's left. He found out... I've cheated on him...'

'*What?* What are you talking about?' Tasha could hear the astonishment in Rosie's voice.

'It's true...' Tasha didn't know what to say. She shook her head. She couldn't stop crying.

'Right, I'm coming over.' Rosie hung up the phone.

Tasha didn't move a muscle. She knelt on the floor, letting the tears roll down her cheeks. Her mind kept racing ahead to the worst possible conclusion. Charlie would never forgive her. He would never come back. Loyalty was the one thing he valued above everything. His ex-girlfriend, Chessie, had cheated on him at university with one of his best friends and it had affected him deeply. He had been left broken-hearted, unable to forgive either Chessie or his friend. All the old wounds would have reopened. She knew he would not take this betrayal lightly. With one moment of lunacy she had ended it all. Fourteen years flashed before her eyes and she suddenly thought she might vomit.

Tasha didn't know how long she'd been sitting there, when out of the silence there was a knock at the door. She got up from the floor and opened it. Rosie came in. 'It's going to be OK,' she said as she hugged her. Rosie took her into the kitchen, closed the door behind them, made them a cup of tea and got Tasha to tell her the whole story. She listened as Tasha explained what had happened, step by step.

'He will come around,' Rosie reassured her. 'You just need to give him time to think. It will have been such a shock, that's all. But eventually he will calm down and you will be able to talk to him about it. About how you've been feeling, you can tell him what a stupid mistake it was, how you weren't in your right mind, how you love him more than life itself. You can beg him for forgiveness and I am sure he will understand.'

'But what if he doesn't?' Tasha whispered. 'What if he can't forgive me?'

'He will. It's Charlie, Tash. He loves you more than anything in the world. He loves your children – you are a family. He won't let that disintegrate. I promise.'

'God, I hope you're right,' Tasha said. 'How could I have done this to him? I am the worst person in the world.'

'You aren't the first person to make a mistake like this, Tasha, and you certainly won't be the last. I know right now it feels like the end of the world but it *will* be OK.' Rosie stroked her hair as Tasha rested her head on her shoulder, tears continuing to stream down her cheeks.

Eventually Rosie put Tasha to bed, making a bed up for herself in the spare room so that Tasha wouldn't have to be by herself. Tasha tried calling Charlie again and again but his phone went straight to voicemail each time. She sent him a message saying how much she loved him, pleading with him to talk to her, to let her explain, begging him for forgiveness. She lay awake staring at the empty space beside her. She couldn't even remember the last time he had slept away from her without her knowing where he was.

Chapter Twenty-one

Tasha didn't sleep a wink. She tried to get some rest but her rampaging emotions got the best of her. Harrowing remorse competed with terror for the future as she contemplated the possible consequences of her actions. She tossed and turned. At some point she heard Javier's motorbike signalling his arrival back home. She wanted to run outside and scream at him for texting her, but she knew the only person to blame in this situation was herself.

As the early hours of the morning ticked by, she began to dread the dawn of a new day. What would she tell the children if Charlie didn't come home that evening? They wouldn't miss him in the morning, but surely they would notice if he didn't come home at all? What if he never forgave her? What would happen to her, the children, the house? Her head spun as she followed the chain of thought, imagining the reactions from her parents, his parents, their siblings, their friends, the other school mums… It was too awful. The worst thing of all was how completely and utterly to blame she was. There was no one else she could pass the buck to; this whole situation started and ended with her, with her selfish, impulsive behaviour.

As the first crack of light began to stream through the curtains she got up. She checked her phone for the thousandth time – still nothing from Charlie. She called him again, still no answer. What would he be doing now? Probably going into work like the reliable, dependable guy he was. Her heart swelled with emotion as she imagined him putting on a brave face in the office, acting normally and holding it together despite the enormous hurt he was feeling inside. She texted him again, another pleading message, begging for forgiveness, asking him to come home that evening so they could talk.

Tasha opened the curtains and forced herself to look across the road. Javier's house was still in darkness, his curtains closed. She looked in the mirror. Yesterday's make-up was smudged all over her cheeks. Her eyes were puffy and swollen. She showered and brushed her teeth, knowing she had to pull herself together, to try her best to appear normal in front of the children. Taking a deep breath, she got dressed and went downstairs.

Tasha made herself a cup of coffee, stronger than usual to make up for her lack of sleep. She tried to stop herself from thinking about the look in Charlie's eyes as he realised what she had done but she knew it would be forever emblazoned on her memory. Blinking back a fresh bout of tears, she looked up to see the neon-pink

Post-it note stuck on the fridge. Furious with herself, she marched over to it and threw it in the bin. Why had she been so stupid as to text him? If she hadn't done that then Charlie might never have found out. Today would have been just another normal day.

Yet in some strange way she was glad that he knew. Keeping the secret from him for the rest of her life would have been just as big a betrayal as sleeping with Javier in the first place. At least now he knew exactly what kind of person she was. It was only fair that she should pay for her actions.

Tasha went out into the garden and sat at the table on the terrace. The sight of the barbecue and all the memories that it evoked of Charlie and his little helper Max caused a new wave of self-loathing to bubble up inside her. She sipped her coffee and tried to stem the torrent of self-abuse that rushed through her mind.

A few minutes later the sliding door opened and Rosie stepped out to join her.

'Morning,' she said, coming over to sit on the chair beside her.

'Morning,' Tasha replied. 'Are the children still asleep?'

'I didn't hear anything. How are you feeling?'

'Rubbish. I didn't sleep a wink.'

'You do look rather tired,' Rosie admitted. 'I've called in sick to work. I'm staying here today – I think you could do with the moral support, if nothing else.'

'You don't have to do that...'

'I know. But I've done it already.'

'Are you sure?'

'Absolutely. Did you hear back from Charlie?'

'No. I've sent him messages, I've tried calling... but no luck.' Tasha sighed.

'Give him time.' Rosie leant across and squeezed her knee. 'He will be in touch soon enough, I'm sure of it.'

'Oh, God. I hope so. I just can't believe what I have done. I feel so completely stupid.'

'We all make mistakes, Tasha.'

'Not mistakes like this. This has changed everything, in an instant.'

'It'll be OK,' Rosie said firmly, clearly determined to stay positive for Tasha's sake. 'Now, I'm dying for a cup of tea. Can I make you another coffee?'

They went back inside and pottered around the kitchen, waiting for the children to wake up.

Max was the first to make an appearance.

He came plodding in, wearing his dinosaur pyjamas.

'Good morning, darling!' Tasha said, fixing a smile on her face.

'Morning.' He rubbed his eyes sleepily.

'Did you sleep well?' she asked.

Max nodded and pulled himself up onto the chair next to Rosie.

'Hi, Max.' Rosie smiled.

'Hi,' he replied, yawning loudly. He was entirely

unsurprised by Rosie's presence.

Flora was next up. She was much more excited by their unexpected visitor. 'Godmother Rosie!' she cried, rushing over to give her a hug. 'What are *you* doing here?' she asked.

'I thought I'd surprise you!' Rosie said. 'I'm spending the day with you all!'

'Oh, *brilliant*!' Flora squealed. 'This is going to be the best day *ever*!' She clearly couldn't believe her luck. In Flora's eyes, Rosie was just about the coolest person on the planet. At least with Rosie around Flora would be at her most charming: she saved her mood swings for relatives alone.

When Bella came downstairs they all sat down for boiled eggs and soldiers for breakfast. The day passed in a blur. They went to the park and had a picnic lunch before going to the cinema to watch a film the children had been desperate to see for ages. Tasha was so grateful to have Rosie with her. She felt completely discombobulated, as if she were watching herself from a distance.

When the children had finished their dinner and had their baths, Rosie offered to read Max a bedtime story. He scampered down the corridor into his bedroom and jumped into bed in eager anticipation. Rosie was clearly a wonderful influence on Max: he had behaved like an angel all day, as had Flora. While Rosie read with Max, Tasha read Bella a chapter of her *Famous Five* book.

Then they both went into Flora's room to check on her and kiss her goodnight. When they were all settled they went downstairs and ate the rest of the chilli they had given the children earlier.

'Thanks so much, Rosie,' Tasha said when they had finished their food as well as several much-needed glasses of wine. 'I honestly don't know how I would have survived the day without you.'

'It's a pleasure. Are you sure you don't want me to stay again tonight?'

'I'm sure. You've done more than enough already.'

'Keep me posted on any news from Charlie, won't you?'

After Rosie had left Tasha called Charlie once again. She knew he wouldn't answer but she had to keep on trying.

Much to her surprise, he picked up. 'Tasha,' he said.

'Oh, Charlie, thank God. I'm so glad you are speaking to me.'

'Are the children OK? What did you say to them?' he asked.

'I just told them you were working late. They didn't realise you weren't here last night. Are you coming home?'

'No.'

Tasha's heart sank. Her eyes filled with tears. 'Where are you?' she asked.

'In a hotel.'

'Please come home, Charlie. Please. For the children...'

'Don't guilt-trip me, Tasha.' His voice was cold and distant. 'I have no idea if I will ever want to be in the same house as you again, and as for being within a stone's throw of that bastard...' Charlie tailed off. He sighed heavily down the line. 'One thing is for sure – right now I need some space.'

'I understand,' she said quietly. 'I'm so sorry.'

'Tell the children I'm away on business if they ask. Say I'm sorry that I didn't say goodbye. I'll phone them tomorrow evening and pretend I'm in Zurich.'

'OK,' she said. She knew she shouldn't push him, that she should give him time and space. 'Charlie?'

'Yes?'

'I hope one day you will be able to forgive me...'

She could picture him sitting on the edge of his hotel bed, all alone. It was so wrong. He should be here with her, with his family. She felt consumed with guilt.

'Bye, Tasha,' he said, hanging up the phone.

'Bye,' she said, but he had already gone. She sat on the sofa and stared numbly at the floor.

Chapter Twenty-two

'Mum, Dad wants to speak to you,' Flora said, passing Tasha the phone. It was Thursday evening and, as agreed, Charlie was pretending he was abroad.

'Hi,' she said, conscious to make her voice sound as normal as possible in front of the children.

'Hi. I just want to talk to you about this weekend.'

She walked out of earshot. 'Right. Will you be coming home? We miss you...'

'I want to take the children to my parents'. Without you.'

'Oh.' She took the handset into the sitting room, not wanting the children to notice that her eyes had filled with tears.

'I'm not ready to see you. To be honest, Tasha, I'm not even ready to talk to you. I just can't stop thinking about...' He couldn't even finish his sentence. The unspoken words hung heavily in the air.

'I'm sorry,' she whispered. 'I really am.'

His voice broke. 'Christ!' There was a long pause. 'Anyway. I want to see the children.'

'I understand.'

'I'll tell my parents you're on a girls' weekend with

Rosie.'

'OK.' Tasha swallowed. 'I'll tell the children the same thing. When do you want to leave?'

'I'll leave work early and come over at around four. I'll grab a few things and then we'll set off so we're there in time for dinner.'

'Right.' Tasha was trying very hard not to cry.

'I'll bring them back on Sunday.'

'What about Sunday night? Will you stay here?'

'I doubt it.'

'OK,' she said. 'When you're ready.' She hoped to God that day would be soon.

*

The next day she watched the clock nervously as the hours ticked by. 'Daddy is taking you to Granny and Grandpa's house this afternoon,' she had explained to the children that morning. 'You need to pack a bag each for the weekend.'

'Are you not coming with us?' Bella had asked.

'No. I'm afraid not. I'm going to stay with Rosie for the weekend. She has arranged lots of things for us to do and I can't really say no… she'd be very sad. Though obviously I would much rather be with you all…'

The children had seemed completely unfazed at the thought of spending the weekend without her. It was a good thing, she reassured herself, though it didn't exactly make her feel great. Tasha had made sure they had everything they needed: toothbrushes, pyjamas, clean clothes, raincoats and wellies.

At four on the dot, Charlie let himself in through the front door.

'Daddy!' Bella squealed as she jumped into his arms.

'Daddy!' Max hurtled down the stairs at the speed of light, joining Bella.

'Hi, Dad,' Flora said, more self-conscious than her siblings but coming over to join the group hug nonetheless.

'It's good to have you home.' Tasha smiled. She wanted to give him a kiss but knew from the way he was struggling to make eye contact with her that it would not be a good idea. Her heart wrenched at the sight of him. He was wearing a smart navy suit and a blue shirt, which made his eyes look even brighter than usual. His tie, covered in pink elephants, had been one of the ties she had given him for his anniversary present. She knew how hard it must be for Charlie to be right opposite Javier's house. She remembered his pure anger on Monday night as he had stormed across the street and hammered on the door. He must be finding it so difficult to bottle up all his emotions and remain calm in front of the children.

It didn't take long for Charlie to pack a bag and before she knew it they were all traipsing out to the car and loading the boot with their suitcases. She kissed the children goodbye, plastering a false smile on her face. 'Have a lovely time with Granny and Grandpa!' she said.

Charlie got in the car.

'Wait, Dad, you forgot to kiss Mummy goodbye, silly!' Bella scolded.

'Silly me indeed,' Charlie replied. He almost winced as he wound down the window. He glanced over to Javier's house where mercifully there was no evidence of anyone home. Tasha came over to the open window, bent through, and pecked him on the lips.

'Bye!' she said, trying to appear bright and breezy.

'Have fun with godmother Rosie,' said Flora. 'Say hi from me!'

'I will!' Tasha called as she waved goodbye.

They drove off without further ado, leaving Tasha standing on the pavement, furiously blinking back tears. She had nothing to do. She could hardly call up her friends and make plans without explaining why Charlie and the children were away without her. Rosie and Josh were in Paris for the weekend. She had offered to cancel but Tasha had adamantly refused. She looked at Javier's front door and rued the day she had stepped through it. She glanced up at the bedroom window. The curtains were open. In her mind's eye she could see the room, she could see the two of them lying naked on his bed. She turned around and walked inside. Closing the door behind her, she let out a deep sigh. She looked around her family home. What would it be like to live here without Charlie? Suddenly overwhelmed, she howled in despair. She didn't want to find out. She'd never wanted this. How could she have let this happen?

Tasha spent the evening drowning her sorrows in red wine and watching reruns of *Friends* on the television. It was about the only thing she felt she had the mental capacity to do. She stared mindlessly at the screen, mostly lost in her thoughts. When she eventually went up to bed she found one of Charlie's jumpers lying in a bundle of discarded clothes and held it close, breathing in the familiar scent of his aftershave. She cried herself to sleep clutching it tightly.

When Tasha opened her eyes again her bedside clock informed her it was 10 a.m. She couldn't remember the last time she had slept in that late. The emotional stress of the previous weeks had clearly taken its toll. She was grateful that she had finally managed to catch up on some sleep but the house felt horribly empty without the patter of children's feet and the constant babble of chatter that usually filled it. It was a family home, not designed for one person, and by herself it felt awfully big and lonely. She checked her phone: nothing from Charlie, the only person she ever wanted to hear from these days. She imagined them all at Caroline and Stephen's house. They had probably been up for hours; maybe they were playing in the garden or taking the dogs for a walk. She wished she were there with them but she knew this was the price she had to pay. She scrolled down to the message from Javier that had started it all and pressed delete.

It occurred to Tasha that she should warn Javier that Charlie knew. Charlie would never make a scene in front of the children, but he might well confront him at some stage. She dreaded making contact but knew it was probably better to get it over and done with, especially while she was alone. It would happen sooner or later, after all. Having showered and dressed, she summoned the courage to cross the road and ring Javier's doorbell.

A couple of minutes later, the door opened. Javier stood in front of her looking quite dishevelled, as though he had only just woken up.

'Tasha!' he said in surprise, his brown eyes twinkling warmly. 'To what do I owe this pleasure?'

'Hi, Javier. Do you mind if I come in for a moment?' she asked.

'Of course!' He opened the door and gestured for her to go inside, closing it behind him as he followed her.

'Before you say anything, I-I'm not here for the reason you might expect…' Tasha stammered rather awkwardly.

'Right!' Javier laughed. 'Can I pour you a coffee? I just made a pot.'

'No, thank you,' she said.

'So, what's up?' he asked, obviously realising she had something to discuss.

'It's Charlie. I was out on Monday night with a friend. I'd left my phone behind... your message popped up on my screen and he saw it.' Realisation dawned on Javier's face as she spoke. 'He knows what happened between us...'

'Oh.' Javier winced. 'I'm sorry, Tasha.'

'It's my fault.' She shook her head. 'I'm the one who is married.'

'Where is he?'

'He's gone to stay with his parents. He's taken the children. They don't know anything. He hasn't stayed at home since... They think he's been away with work.'

'OK.' He nodded.

'I just thought I'd better warn you. He was pretty furious when he found out, as you can imagine.'

'Yes.'

'It's probably best to keep your distance, if you can avoid him.'

'Right. Well, thanks for letting me know.' It was suddenly extremely awkward between them. Javier was looking very uncomfortable, the opposite of his usual relaxed demeanour. She didn't know what else to say. In fact, she wanted to get out of there as quickly as she could.

'Right, well, I'd better be off...'

'OK.' Javier nodded. 'Have a good weekend.'

'Yes.'

'Bye, Tasha.' He held the door open again. She

avoided contact with him, ducking awkwardly around him to get outside.

'Bye,' she replied as he closed the door behind her. She crossed the street, again looking to see whether anyone might have noticed her movements. No one was around. She went back home, retreating to safety, and returned to her spot on the sofa. She didn't leave it again all day.

By Sunday Tasha was feeling extremely claustrophobic, trapped within the four walls of her house. She decided to get out, aiming for the river and the Thames pathway that ran alongside it. She bought herself a coffee from the vending truck at the start of the old towpath and set off towards Hammersmith Bridge and beyond. The sky was heavy with charcoal clouds, the water absorbed their reflection. She walked for hours, lost in her thoughts, trying to come up with a plan of action. She knew Charlie well enough. She knew that if she pushed him to come home he would retreat further away from her. He needed time to process what she had done. When he was calm he would decide whether he wanted to talk, to try and work things out. But she knew she had to let him come to her. She had to leave the ball in his court.

When she got home she sat at her desk and wrote him a letter.

My darling Charlie,

I hardly know where to start, what to write, but I know I need to try – to somehow explain myself, and to ask, beg, for you to somehow find it within your heart to forgive me. My actions have been desperately wrong. Javier meant, and still means, absolutely nothing to me. I regret what I did, that moment of insanity, more than anything else I have done in my life. I keep hoping this is all some kind of horrific nightmare, that I'll wake up and you'll be here.

I know I promised you I would never betray you, that you have suffered enough in the past and I meant it... There are no excuses, I just feel I have lost myself these past few years. I don't even recognise myself right now. I just felt like I've been moving blankly from one day to another, drowning in the repetitive monotony of daily life staying at home, running the house. I'm not trying to make excuses for my behaviour but I haven't been able to get my feelings out in the open to you as I should have and when I tried it always seemed to end up in an argument...

I love you, Charlie, I love you so much. I will wait for you, for as long as it takes you to find a way to forgive me. I will do anything for us to be together, as a family, again.

Yours, always and forever,
Tasha

She put the letter in an envelope to give to him when he came back that afternoon.

*

'Mum!' Max hugged her as she opened the door to greet them. She had been waiting by the window for them to arrive. It felt as though they had been away from her for weeks.

'Hi, darlings,' she said, hugging them one by one as they came through the door. 'Did you have a lovely time?'

'It was so fun.' Bella beamed. 'We went to the village fete!'

'There was a tombola,' Flora said. 'I won a bottle of wine, but I gave it to Granny and Grandpa.'

'That was very kind of you!' Tasha smiled.

Charlie was hovering by the door, looking awkward, as if he would rather be anywhere else than in her presence. She wanted to give him a hug, but he was looking grateful that none of the children had noticed their lack of physical contact this time.

'Dad won me this!' Max exclaimed, holding up a huge cuddly monkey. 'He knocked all the coconuts off their sticks in the coconut shy.'

'Clever Daddy!' Tasha said. 'How was the traffic?' she asked Charlie.

'Fine,' he replied, clearly not in the mood for a chat.

'I've got a roast chicken in the oven for your dinner,' she said, turning to face the children.

'Oh, Mum! We had roast chicken for lunch!' Flora laughed.

This threw Tasha. Why hadn't she thought of that? 'Silly me, of course you did…'

'Can't we have bacon and eggs?' Max pleaded.

'Well, we don't want to waste the food. Maybe you can all have a little bit and we can use the rest up tomorrow?' The children charged into the kitchen, tummies rumbling. 'Would you like some dinner?' she asked Charlie quietly.

'No, thanks. I'd better be off.'

For a moment he looked as though he wanted to say something but then he hardened his features, as if mentally clamping down on his emotions.

'But… what shall we tell the children?' she whispered. 'I can always sleep in the spare room, if you'll stay?'

'I'm afraid that's just not an option for me. I've told them I'm very busy at work, that I am staying at the office for a while.'

'Did they believe you?'

'They've got no reason to doubt it.'

'I suppose not…' She swallowed. 'Charlie, I've written you this.' She presented him with the letter. 'Please read it.'

He took the letter and looked at it. For a moment she thought he was going to refuse it but then he folded it in half and put it in the back pocket of his jeans.

'Right, kids, I'm off,' Charlie called. They came back to say goodbye.

'When will you be staying at home again?' they asked.

'When this big deal at work is over,' Charlie said. 'I will miss you but it's very important that I'm in the office in case someone needs me.'

'Do you really have to sleep there?' Flora asked. She was looking at her parents somewhat suspiciously.

'Yes, I'm afraid I do… and I'll be having lots of meetings late at night so it's easier for me that way anyway.' Thankfully Flora seemed to accept this response.

They said goodbye and Tasha saw him out. 'Are you staying at the same hotel?' she asked quietly.

'Yes,' he replied.

'Will you read my letter?' she asked.

He nodded. 'Bye, Tasha.' He turned and walked towards the Tube. She noticed that he didn't look up though she imagined he was using all of his self-restraint not to look over at the house across the road. She closed the door and gathered her strength before turning around and immersing herself in the children's dinner, bath and bedtime routines. At least being busy with a houseful of children was better than being alone with just her thoughts for company.

Chapter Twenty-three

It had been over a week since Charlie had found out about Javier. Tasha hadn't heard from him since he had left the house on Sunday. She had hoped that he might get in touch after reading her letter, having realised how genuinely remorseful she was, but maybe her words hadn't expressed her feelings accurately enough. Besides, Charlie had always preferred actions over words. It was wishful thinking on her part that a heartfelt letter could do anything to rectify the damage her actions had caused. She had never felt so powerless.

On Wednesday evening the house phone rang. Hoping it would be Charlie, Tasha practically fell over herself in her rush to pick up the receiver in the kitchen.

'Hello?' she said.

'Hi.' Charlie's voice echoed down the line. *God, how she missed him.*

'Hi, Charlie, how are you?' she asked, cringing at the formality between them.

'I'm OK.' There was a pause. 'I read your letter,' he said.

'Oh...'

'I think we should talk.'

Tasha's heart skipped a beat. She felt a wave of relief flood through her. 'I'd love that,' she said. 'When?'

'I'm away this weekend – in Zurich, remember?'

'I know,' she said. It was in their shared calendar. 'How about tomorrow?'

'I can't do tomorrow. Next week though. Tuesday?'

'OK,' she said, immediately wondering why he couldn't do the following day, what he might be doing, who he might be seeing. 'Do you want to come here?'

'Not really.' She knew he wouldn't want to run the risk of bumping into Javier.

'How about I come to you, then?'

'We can make a plan next week.'

'I'll see if Nina can look after the children.'

There was an awkward silence. She couldn't bear how different their attempts at communication were these days.

'Are the kids around?'

She took the handset back into the sitting room and passed the telephone to Flora, who chatted to her father before passing him onto Bella and then Max. As she listened to their conversations, Tasha tried to take comfort from the fact that he wanted to meet up. *Perhaps all was not lost after all?* She was praying that he would find it within him to forgive her enough to come on their family holiday the week after next. The thought of staying at their little rented cottage in Dorset without him was unbearable. They had first gone four years ago when Max was only two-years-old. Each summer since they had returned to the same place, building new layers of memories, getting to know the area better and better each time. Tasha hadn't allowed herself to contemplate what she would do if he told her he didn't want to come. The children would be heartbroken, and so would she. Once again, her stomach lurched with guilt and the by-now-familiar panic that there was no way she could undo what she had done.

'I wish Dad didn't have to stay at work,' Bella said later that evening as she tucked her in.

'I know,' Tasha said, feeling even worse than usual as she kissed the top of her head. 'It's rubbish, isn't it?'

'And he said he's on a business trip this weekend.'

'Poor Daddy. He's working very hard.'

'I think we all better be extra good next time he comes home,' Bella said. 'Maybe we can make him breakfast in bed?'

'That's a lovely idea.' Tasha felt overwhelmed with emotion. 'What a kind thought.' She could only hope that Bella would get the chance.

Chapter Twenty-four

Tasha attempted to zone out as she lay on her mat in Pilates, moving from plank to side stretches, all fours to standing poses. Every muscle in her body seemed to ache with tiredness.

'You're child-free today, aren't you?' Flo asked as the class came to an end.

'Thank God! Mum's got them for the day.' It had become a tradition in each school holiday: Lizzie would take them off to a different museum or landmark to give Tasha a break. 'Who has yours?'

'Hortense, the French exchange.'

'Oh yes. How's that going?' Tasha asked as they rolled up their mats.

'Not bad. She is very quiet, which isn't a bad thing if you ask me. She's eighteen but she looks about twelve.'

'Quite nice having an extra pair of hands for the summer?'

'Exactly. All under the pretence of learning English. It's basically like having a free au pair.'

'Sounds great! Does she have any friends?' Tasha laughed.

A short while later they were sitting down for lunch.

'I actually took your advice and signed up with a recruitment agency this morning,' Tasha said. She had arranged the meeting a while ago and had almost cancelled before realising she needed something new to focus on now more than ever.

'Oh, really?' Flo looked impressed. 'Amazing! Good on you… What did you have to do?'

'It was surprisingly straightforward. I filled out an application online and they arranged for me to go in and meet them to go through my CV and discuss what I was looking for, or not looking for as the case may be!'

'And what happens now?'

'They'll send me possible jobs and we'll see if anything interesting comes up, I suppose.'

The waitress came over and Tasha ordered a coffee, her third of the day. She still wasn't sleeping well and caffeine was the only thing keeping her going.

'Late night?' Flo asked. 'You look quite tired, you know.'

Tasha laughed weakly. If only she knew. 'Something like that,' she said. 'I'm not sleeping well at the moment.'

Suddenly her eyes filled with tears. Flo immediately leant across the table, grabbed Tasha's hand and gave it a squeeze. 'Tash, what is it?' she asked. Her face was full of friendly concern.

Tasha shook her head; she couldn't possibly tell her. She tried to stop the tears from coming but it was impossible now that they had started. Flo's sympathy was making it harder for her to pull herself together.

'What's wrong?' Flo asked again, her eyes searching Tasha's.

She had to say something to explain her tears. 'It's Charlie...' she said.

'Is he OK?'

'Well... not really.' Tasha took a deep breath. She looked at Flo and decided she would come clean. If Flo judged her it was nothing more than she deserved. At least she knew that Flo was trustworthy. She wouldn't tell anyone if Tasha asked her not to. 'I've really messed up...' Tasha wiped the tears from her eyes. 'I... I slept with someone else.'

Flo's eyes widened with shock but she didn't say anything. The hand that had been holding Tasha's flew up to her mouth. 'Who?' she asked.

'No one you know, no one anyone knows...'

'Oh, my God.' Flo was clearly more than surprised at this news. 'When?'

'A couple of weeks ago. Charlie found out.'

'Oh, Tasha. Holy shit. How? What happened?'

She told Flo a shortened version of the story. 'Obviously I don't need to say this but please don't tell anyone.'

'*Of course* I won't. God, I can't believe it. How's Charlie now?'

'He hasn't spoken to me much since. I can't exactly

blame him. He's staying in a hotel.'

'What have you told the kids?'

'We've said he's busy working late and needs to be in the office.'

'And the weekends? Do they think he's working then too?'

'Last weekend he took them to his parents'. We told everyone I was with Rosie on a girls' weekend. This weekend he is on a genuine business trip.'

'Oh, my God. Do you think he's going to be OK? Do you think he'll come around?'

'I have no idea. I hope so. I can't imagine what will happen if he doesn't.' The tears were rolling freely now. 'I just feel so stupid. I can't believe I could have screwed things up like this... and for what? A quick shag?'

Flo shook her head. She could tell Flo was thinking exactly that. She knew she would be just as shocked by her behaviour as Tasha herself was.

'Look, I don't want to make you feel worse, but I can see it might take him a bit of time to get his head around all this.'

'I know.' Tasha sighed. 'Last night he asked to meet up on Tuesday to talk.'

'That's a good sign, isn't it?'

'I hope so. We're meant to be going to Dorset the following week.'

'Of course!'

'God knows what we'll tell the children if he doesn't

feel he can come. Maybe he should go and I should stay behind? But how would I explain that to the kids?'

They talked through the various options. It felt good to have someone to share her turmoil with other than Rosie. Apart from Becca, who Tasha was adamant could never find out what she had done, Flo was the only other friend she felt close enough with to talk to about all this. She had been worried that Flo would judge her, that she wouldn't understand. And she probably didn't, but rather than telling her off and making her feel guilty she was trying her best to support her. Listening and trying to give advice rather than preaching. She could probably tell that Tasha felt guilty enough already without needing any help from her.

After lunch she had a couple of hours to herself before Lizzie was due to bring the children home. She stripped and remade the beds, hung the washing out and loaded the machine with dirty sheets. Then she sat down to check her emails. She scrolled through some of the initial job specifications that had come into her inbox from the agency following her meeting that morning. Nothing looked too appealing. She closed the laptop with a sigh and went out into the garden to deadhead the roses. The air was heavy with their musky scent. As she snipped each stem she watched the velvet petals fall to the ground in a delicate pirouette. As always, she was able to draw peace from the presence of nature and its intricate, mesmerising beauty.

Tasha was immersed in the task when the doorbell rang. Her pulse quickened slightly in case it was Javier but the voices she heard as she went inside reassured her that it was not. She opened the front door.

'Hi, Mum!' chorused the children as they charged inside.

'Hi, darling!' Lizzie said. 'What a day!' She looked completely worn out.

'How was it?' Tasha asked.

'Wonderful, thanks!' They had gone to the Natural History Museum to visit a new exhibition about whales.

'Did you know the blue whale is the largest animal that ever lived on Earth?' Max was clutching a new book of whale facts and beaming with excitement.

'I didn't! How incredible! Did Grandma buy you that lovely book? That was very kind of you, Mum.'

'Did you know their tongue can weigh as much as an elephant?' Bella asked.

'And their heart can weigh as much as a car!' Flora added.

'Gosh, how amazing! It sounds like you are all budding whale experts!' Tasha laughed. 'I'm so glad you had such a lovely time.'

'I am dying for a cup of tea,' Lizzie gasped. She had collapsed onto one of the kitchen chairs. Her dark grey hair was escaping from the tortoiseshell clips that rested an inch or two away from each temple.

'I'm not surprised! Thanks so much for entertaining

them all day, Mum. I'll put the kettle on. And I've got some brownies for tea.' This elicited squeals of excitement from the children.

'I hear Charlie has been staying at work this week,' Lizzie said. 'I didn't realise that was even possible!'

Tasha had no idea how to handle this. She stupidly hadn't thought through what to say to her mother. She should have known the children might bring it up.

'Yes, they have some facilities,' she said vaguely. 'There's a mad deal on at the moment and everyone is there around the clock.'

Luckily her mother knew very little about the world of asset management and the ways of the City. She seemed to accept this without question, moving the conversation on swiftly. 'I'm meeting Sandra at ten o'clock tomorrow morning.' Sandra was an old colleague from when Lizzie had worked at Sotheby's. Tasha's mother had given up her career when she had had her but was still a fanatical art lover.

'Where are you going with her?'

'The National Gallery.'

'How lovely!'

'I'm determined to make the most of my time in London.'

'Well, it's a real treat for us,' Tasha said, looking fondly at her mother, grateful to have her with her. 'You should come and stay more often.'

Chapter Twenty-five

After another whirlwind weekend and a total of two weeks without Charlie, Tasha was beginning to get a taste of what single motherhood must feel like. She missed him so terribly and was absolutely desperate for him to come home. All of her hopes were pinned on Tuesday evening's meet-up. She was more nervous than she had ever felt. It was worse than going on a first date with a complete stranger. As Nina arrived for the handover Tasha felt as if she might be sick from the butterflies in her stomach.

Charlie had asked her to meet him in Victoria in a pub called The Crown. She was early so she ordered herself a gin and tonic for Dutch courage before sitting at a table in the corner. She fixed her gaze on the door, waiting.

Ten minutes later Charlie walked in. Her heart swelled with love as she watched him approach her table. She half stood to greet him but he didn't kiss her, he just sat down opposite her. She sat back down, unsure of what to do or say.

'Hi,' he said before getting straight back up. 'Actually, I need a drink. Do you want another one?'

'Yes, please.'

'G and T?'

She nodded.

'So... how have you been?' she asked when he came back from the bar. He looked different: dejected and tired.

'Busy,' Charlie replied. 'Zurich was exhausting but successful.'

'Good, I'm so glad,' she said.

He looked down at the table. 'How are the children?'

Tasha gave him an update on their trip to the Natural History Museum and their weekend's activities, but it was impossible to ignore the elephant in the room. She couldn't stand it for a second longer.

'Charlie, do you think you can forgive me? Will you come home? Please...? We can't go to Dorset without you. The children will be heartbroken. I will be...'

Charlie took a deep breath and held her gaze. She could see how much he missed her, despite the hurt he was clearly suffering. For a moment she was filled with hope. Perhaps all was not lost after all.

He fiddled with a coaster on the table. 'I can't get the thought of the two of you out of my mind. In fact, I have been thinking of nothing else for the last two weeks. I just can't believe you could do something like this. You *know* how I feel about cheating... Call me naïve, but I thought we meant our wedding vows.'

'I did. I still *do*... It was a *stupid* mistake. The most

stupid mistake I could *ever* have made and I regret it more than anything I've done in my life.'

'How could I ever trust you again?'

'You *can*, Charlie, *I promise*. I'm so sorry I've given you reason to doubt it. But there is absolutely no way I could ever do something like that again. I have come so close to losing you, to losing *everything* and I just can't bear it. Please just give me the chance to prove it to you.'

'I'm sorry, Tasha…' He looked so upset. She couldn't bear the hurt she had caused him.

'Please…' she begged.

He was silent. He stared into his pint of beer, seemingly lost in his thoughts.

After several minutes he sighed and slowly nodded his head.

She held her breath, hardly daring to hope.

'OK,' he said quietly.

Relief coursed through her. 'Thank you,' she whispered, reaching out to take his hand. A tear trickled down her cheek. 'Thank you, Charlie. I'll sleep in the spare room. I-I'll think of something to tell the children.'

He nodded, withdrawing his hand from hers.

They went back to his hotel and collected his belongings before getting a taxi home. Tasha felt so grateful to him for giving her a chance to fix things. She just couldn't contemplate the alternative. What would she have done if he had said no? It didn't bear thinking about.

Charlie was very quiet in the taxi. Neither of them knew what to say. When Nina had gone Tasha turned to face him. 'Would you like some curry? I made some for the children and there's plenty left.'

'Thank you.' He nodded. The atmosphere was thick with tension. 'I'm going to check on them,' he said.

'Hopefully they are all asleep,' she called after him as he went up the stairs. She didn't know how to act; she couldn't pretend nothing had happened yet she was desperate to restore some sense of normality.

'I might do some unpacking...'

Tasha nodded and left him to it while she sorted out two plates of food. She called up to him when it was ready. They sat in their usual seats on the sofa and watched TV. Even though they had done exactly the same thing a thousand times before, tonight it felt completely different. It was like starting from square one. Tasha knew she had to regain his trust but she had no idea how to. She was willing to do whatever it took, to take it as slowly as Charlie needed.

When the programme they were watching finished she made up the spare bed for herself. 'Night,' she said as she took her charger, water glass and book from her bedside table.

Charlie was just getting into bed. 'Night,' he replied. She wanted nothing more than to climb under the duvet and snuggle up to him but she knew that that was out of the question.

'Thank you for coming home,' she said, closing the door behind her. She rested her forehead against the door for a moment before making her way down the landing to the spare room.

Chapter Twenty-six

'Can we have a made-up story tonight?' Bella pleaded as she got out of the bath and into the towel Charlie was holding out for her. He'd left extremely early that morning but had made it home in time for bath time, much to the children's delight.

'I'll see what I can do,' Charlie said, wrapping her up in it like a parcel. Max was already rubbing himself dry vigorously with his *Lion King* towel while Flora sat on the loo in her dressing gown.

'How come you don't have to sleep at the office any more?' Flora asked.

Tasha listened to their conversation as she sorted through a pile of laundry at the top of the stairs. She wondered once again whether Flora was more astute than they gave her credit for.

'It's calmed down a bit for now,' Charlie said. 'Thank goodness.'

'That's lucky! Just in time for Dorset!' Bella said.

'I can't believe it's *this* weekend!' Max squeaked, racing past Tasha into his bedroom to perform several celebratory jumps on his bed.

'Dad, can I show you my poetry book I've been

writing?' Bella asked, taking him by the hand.

'Put your pyjamas on, please,' Tasha said as she brought a pile of washing into Max's room and started to put it away in his chest of drawers. 'Then it's time to do your teeth.'

As she took some more neatly folded clothes into Bella's room Bella was showing Charlie the first two poems she had made up for her home-made anthology. 'Wow, darling, these are brilliant!' Charlie said.

'I want to make up stories like you when I'm older,' she informed him.

Soon they had all piled onto Max's bed for their story. As Tasha continued pottering about she listened to Charlie speak. She reminded herself just how lucky they all were to have him and vowed never to do anything to jeopardise the family's happiness again. She knew their marriage needed work but they both had to be willing to work at it together. The first step was having him back home; their relationship could be dealt with at a later stage.

That evening Tasha cooked him his favourite meal, steak and chips with Béarnaise sauce. She was determined to make every effort, even lighting a candle and laying the table.

'Did I overcook it?' she asked as he prodded his meat unenthusiastically.

'No, it's fine. I'm just not particularly hungry.' He pushed his plate to one side and looked at her, rolling the stem of the wine glass between his thumb and forefinger back and forth, watching the red liquid swill around the fragile balloon of glass. He raised his gaze to meet hers. 'You know a nice meal isn't going to fix things? It's not as simple as that. You can't just pretend everything is OK, Tasha.'

'I know,' she said. 'I'm not pretending it is. I am just trying to make an effort, to show you how sorry I am.'

'Sorry doesn't even *begin* to cut it.' She could hear the anger in his voice. 'The fact I have to sit here knowing that *bastard* is right across the road from me... that I might see him at any moment. That I can't even confront him in case the children overhear...'

She nodded, her appetite now completely lost.

'I know I can't undo what I've done but at least going forward I can try to improve things, we both can.'

'Why did you do it?' he asked. He was looking directly at her, searching for some kind of explanation.

'I don't know,' she said.

'Well, you'd better come up with some kind of reason. If I'm going to find a way to move past this I need to understand exactly what happened.'

'I was upset...'

'About what?'

'It's hard to pin it on anything in particular. I guess it was more a build-up of frustrations, resentment, boredom, loneliness – loads of emotions that I was doing a terrible job at dealing with. We haven't exactly been in a good place recently...'

'And that... *smarmy* bastard was the cure, was he?'

'No!' she said. 'Not at all.'

'Then what?'

'He was just... there. That's all.'

Charlie looked as if he might cry. She tried to explain herself, to somehow excuse her behaviour. 'That Monday, after the awful lunch at Marigold's and you having been away for the whole weekend, I was feeling annoyed with you for not asking a single question about how it had gone.'

'But I bought you flowers to say thank you.'

'I know. I felt terrible. I can't excuse myself... but by then it was already too late.'

'How did it happen?' Charlie looked pained at the thought. 'Actually, I don't want to know.'

'OK.'

'No. I do. Tell me.'

Tasha took a deep breath. 'I bumped into him in the morning and told him about Ella. He said he'd give me that number. I went inside to get it and—'

'Stop.'

They sat in silence for a few minutes. Tasha stared into her glass of wine. She could hear the clock ticking on the wall behind her. She couldn't bear the look in his eyes.

'Why did he bring the number around? Does he have no fucking morals showing up here like that? He just chatted to me as if nothing had happened. How can anyone be so brazen? And to think I was saying what a nice, helpful guy he was...' His jaw was clenched in anger as he thumped his fist against the table, causing the cutlery to rattle on his plate.

'I'm so sorry.'

'I must have looked so stupid.'

'You didn't. Of course you didn't, Charlie.'

Charlie looked at her. 'Was he better than me?'

'I—'

'Don't answer that.'

'He wasn't.'

'I just can't believe that I'm back here again. Though I suppose this time at least you haven't fucked off with my best friend.' He laughed bitterly.

'*No!* I would never leave you.'

'You'd never leave me but you'd shag the neighbour in a blink of an eye.' His voice was cold.

'Never again...' Tasha didn't know what else to say.

'It *never* should have happened in the first place.'

Charlie suddenly stood up. His chair scraped across the floor. 'I've had enough of this conversation.'

He took the bottle of wine and his glass, leaving his plate of food barely touched, and left the room. The sitting-room door slammed shut behind him. Tasha fought back tears as she cleared up their dinner. She went up to the spare room. She wanted to stay out of Charlie's way before he said something he might regret.

All of a sudden, the house felt too small for them both.

Chapter Twenty-seven

Charlie came back from the office much later for the rest of the week, trying to wrap up as many loose ends as possible before their holiday, which by now Tasha was dreading. He ate at work, avoiding any similarly painful conversations over dinner. Tasha enlisted the children's help as she began to pack up the house for Dorset, enjoying the threat of cancelling the holiday, which seemed to put an effective end to the usual arguments.

By Saturday morning a mountain of luggage was piled by the front door, ready to be loaded into the car. Quite how Charlie managed to get it all into the roof box and the boot she would never know, but, sure enough, by mid-morning they were on the road with three overexcited, grinning children in the back seats. Tasha thanked her lucky stars that they were all together, knowing just how close it had come.

'Can we have *The Lion King*?' Max asked. It was his favourite Disney movie and listening to the soundtrack on the way to Dorset had become a Hargreaves family tradition. Soon they were all crooning away to *Circle of Life* at the top of their lungs. Tasha handed out the picnic she had made at carefully timed intervals throughout the journey in an attempt to keep the children quiet. Thankfully the iPad and its selection of films worked wonders in terms of peacekeeping, as did the functioning air-conditioning unit, having been dealt with at long last by Tasha earlier that week.

Several hours later Bella cried out that she had spotted the sea, signalling their imminent arrival in Burton Bradstock. As they drove through the village they all strained their necks to take in the familiar surroundings. Before long Charlie was turning down the long and winding road that took them out of the village towards the beach and their rental house. The little blue sign saying Scuttle Cottage hung at a jaunty angle from the ivy-covered gate post.

'We're here!' Charlie announced as he pulled into the drive.

'Hooray!' squealed all three children, champing at the bit to get out and explore.

The car had barely come to a standstill before the children flung themselves out of it, scrambling up the steps and into the gently sloping garden. The white pebbledashed cottage was a welcome sight.

'Thanks for driving,' Tasha said. 'At least the traffic wasn't too bad!'

'Probably our best run yet,' Charlie agreed. They seemed to be just about OK as long as they stuck to suitably inane topics of conversation.

Tasha inhaled deeply as she got out of the car, filling

her lungs with salty sea air. It felt so good to be back.

'Mum, Dad! I've got the keys!' Flora shouted, having retrieved them from their usual hiding place under a loose rock in the garden wall. Soon the children were in the house, darting in and out of every room, reporting back their findings to Charlie and Tasha: a new TV, different tiles in the bathroom, a new carpet in the hall.

They chuckled at the sight of them. It was always their favourite week of the year. If only she could shake the dark cloud hanging over them and allow herself to relax and enjoy it. So much rested on Charlie's capacity to forgive and move on. She knew that just because he had agreed to come with them, there was no guarantee he would be here to stay and the thought terrified her. Trying her best to put worries about the future and regret of the past out of her mind, she set about unloading the car with Charlie.

*

'Can we go down to the beach now?' Max asked as he unpacked the last of his suitcase under Tasha's supervision.

'As soon as everyone's ready,' she replied.

'Can I take my fishing net so we can go rock-pooling?'

'Fishing net, buckets and spades, the whole shebang!' She laughed.

'I've already got my swimming costume on,' Bella said, appearing at the door with Flora, both dressed in T-shirts and shorts. They were sharing the attic bedroom at the top of the house.

'Me too!' Flora grinned. Her knobbly knees were still bruised from a recent roller-skating party.

When everyone was ready Flora, Bella and Max raced down the sandy path that cut from their back garden across the dunes to the beach. It was warm but windy, the sky an empty canvas of white cloud. It could have been torrential rain and thunder and lightning: nothing was going to stop the children from getting in the water. Tasha and Charlie walked behind. Despite the friction between them they couldn't help but laugh as they watched the children strip off their clothes and sprint into the sea, shrieking and splashing each other with ice-cold water. It was a blessing that they had the distraction, otherwise the unresolved tension between them would be unbearable.

'I feel bad! We should be in there with them,' said Tasha.

'Have you not got your costume on?'

'No!' Tasha shivered at the thought. 'It's nowhere *near* warm enough for me to get in!'

'Well, I'm braving it!' he said as he added his T-shirt to the pile, slipping off his flip-flops and sprinting into the sea. He was in surprisingly good shape considering that he rarely got to exercise. As she watched him run towards the water she longed for the time when he might hold her in his arms again, thinking of the thousands of hugs he had given her in the past and how she had taken them completely for granted, along with everything else he offered her.

'*Da-aad!*' shrieked three little voices, returning his splashes as he bombarded them with spray. Soon they were all completely soaked through, running back to Tasha to find towels from her beach bag with shivering bodies and chattering teeth, salty wet hair plastered across their faces.

'I'm freezing!' Bella trembled with cold. 'Can we go back to the house?'

'We've only just got here!' Max said. 'No way!'

'How about some races to warm you up?' Tasha suggested. 'First to get to the big rock gets to choose what we have for dinner!'

All five of them sprinted across the sand to the rocky outcrop at the far side of the beach. Charlie slowed his pace to ensure that he was last, trying not to drop the fishing nets, buckets and spades that he was carrying.

'I won!' Flora screeched, panting as she sat on the rock with Bella and Max close behind.

'What'll it be, then, darling?' Tasha asked, leaning forward and resting her hands on her thighs to catch her breath as she joined them.

'Fish and chips obviously!' Flora grinned.

'Fish and chips! Fish and chips!' chanted Max and

Bella in delight.

Feeling slightly warmer, they traipsed around the rocks catching shrimps and searching for crabs before building a sandcastle. Flora got a stick and wrote Hargreaves House in the sand beneath their castle, carefully decorated with shells, stones and seaweed. It stood proudly, a transient work of art ready to be swept away by the incoming tide.

A coral blush tinted the sky as dusk fell. Worn out from their exertion, they walked back to the house for warm baths and hot Ribena.

Later, Charlie drove to the fish and chip shop, returning with newspaper swaddles of battered cod and salty chips. They devoured their food hungrily; the sea air having worked up a healthy appetite. After the children had fallen asleep Tasha and Charlie watched a movie. She decided she would wait and see if and when Charlie brought up Javier, that it was better not to mention it or try and talk to him unless he wanted to. She knew she had to keep the peace between them as much as she possibly could.

'Do you want me to sleep on the sofa?' she asked as they turned off the lights and locked up.

'I will,' he said.

'No, Charlie... that's unfair.'

'It's fine,' he repeated. 'You take the room.'

'What if the children come down?'

'I'll say I woke up early.'

'If it's the middle of the night?'

'They won't come down. If they do, I'll say I wasn't feeling well. They're more likely to come into you...'

She nodded. 'I'll just say the same thing. That you weren't feeling well so you went downstairs to get a drink.'

'Fine.'

'Charlie...' Tasha wanted to say so much yet when he looked at her she felt lost for words. 'I love you,' she said.

He returned her gaze but he didn't say anything. He just nodded, following her upstairs to change into his pyjamas and brush his teeth before going back down to the sitting room with a blanket. Tasha got into the bed feeling guiltier than ever. It should be her having an uncomfortable night on the sofa, not Charlie. But he was too much of a gentleman to let it be the other way around. Realising she hadn't checked on the children, she got out of bed and tiptoed into their rooms. Reassured that they were all sleeping peacefully, she slipped under the covers and closed her eyes, willing her exhausted mind to stop its incessant chain of thought and sleep.

Chapter Twenty-eight

The weather remained muggy and overcast for the whole week but they refused to let the odd spatter of rain dampen their spirits. They pulled on cagoules and headed off for bracing walks along the coastal paths, they ate picnics on the beach, looked for shells and went crabbing, rock-pooling and kite-flying. Despite Charlie's best efforts Tasha was worried that the children might have noticed a change in their relationship, especially Flora. Surely they would pick up on the lack of physical contact between them? They were both making valiant attempts to keep things as normal as possible, focussing as much attention as they could on the children, doing their best to ignore the huge elephant in the room. But each evening when the children had all gone to sleep and it was just the two of them left alone the silences became longer and the awkwardness grew even more unbearable.

Despite her promise to herself that she would wait for him to initiate the conversation, by the last night, Tasha couldn't take it any longer.

'Charlie, please can we talk?' she asked, turning to face him on the sofa. 'I can't bear feeling so distant from you. I know I deserve everything I get, but can we please discuss what's going on?'

Charlie continued to stare at the television.

She tried again. 'If we're going to move past this you need to let me back in.'

With a sigh he picked up the remote and turned the television off, turning to face her.

'I don't know how to,' he said.

'Just talk to me.'

'I feel like I don't even know you any more.'

'I'm exactly the same as I've always been.'

'But that's precisely the problem, Tasha. You are not. The Tasha I knew and loved would never have done something like that.'

'I wish I hadn't.'

'So do I.'

'It's still me though, Charlie. I screwed up, I know. I completely screwed up, but I'm still the person you married. I made a mistake, that's all...'

'You *promised* me when we met you would never cheat on me.' Charlie looked so forlorn; he was gazing into the distance as though reliving the heartbreak she had helped him overcome.

'I know,' she admitted sadly.

'I told you how important that was to me. After Chessie... I swore I would never love again.' He took a deep breath. 'I promised myself that I would never get my heart broken like that. The thought of going through that for a second time was not an option. But you came along and gave me your word. And I believed you. When we got married you vowed to be faithful until death parted us. And yet you did the one thing you *swore* you would never do. You *know* how I feel about it, and you did it anyway. And seemingly without stopping to think for one second how I might react if I found out. You just thought I'd be fine, that I'd forgive you. Good old reliable Charlie… Well, it's not as simple as that, Tasha.'

'I know. I am not expecting it to be simple. But you do *have* to forgive me, Charlie. You have to at least try. We can't carry on acting like strangers. We have been through so much. Surely you don't want to throw it all away? Please… *Please* forgive me. I will never do anything to break your trust in me again…' Her eyes brimmed with tears as she looked at him, trying to convey just how much she meant what she said.

'But how am I supposed to believe a word that you say? You've said that to me before and look what happened.'

'I mean it this time.'

'You *mean* it this time? So, you didn't mean it before?' Charlie laughed bitterly.

'No, that's not what I meant.'

'Well, what did you mean, exactly?'

'God, I *wish* I'd never met that stupid man!' She felt desperation rise within her as she tried to somehow claw back Charlie's affection. 'He means *nothing* to me, Charlie. Nothing. I love you, no one else has even come close. I have loved you since the moment I met you. It was nothing but complete and utter madness. I was out of my mind! I am so disgusted with myself I can barely even look at myself in the mirror. Trust me, I couldn't feel worse than I already do.'

'Trust you...' Charlie ran his hands through his hair and rubbed his temples. He looked so exhausted. Sleeping on the sofa could hardly have helped. 'That is the problem. I don't think I can.'

'But—'

'Look, I'm going to stay at the hotel tomorrow, Tasha. I'll tell the children I've got to catch up with work.'

'No, Charlie, *please*.' Tasha could feel the panic rising within her. 'Don't go to the hotel again. Stay with us. I'll stay in the spare room...'

'I'm sorry, Tasha. I need to think.'

'Let's just try to move on and look to the future instead.'

'It's easy for you to say.'

'No. It's not. But we *must*.'

'I've made up my mind,' he said, firmly.

Tears coursed down Tasha's cheeks. She shook her head. 'Please,' she whispered.

Charlie looked at her. She wanted to hug him but she didn't know how to cross the gap between them; she was terrified he would shove her away if she did. She wiped her eyes and took a deep breath.

'Please,' she repeated once again. 'I'll do *anything*...'

His eyes were full of sorrow as he looked away. 'We'd better set off in good time tomorrow,' he said, trying to change the subject, to signal that there was no point continuing this conversation.

Tasha couldn't bear it for a second longer. She had to leave the room before she broke down completely. She stood up and walked out, climbing the stairs up to their bedroom with a heavy heart. She had hoped that his agreeing to come back, to come to Dorset, was a good sign. She couldn't believe he was leaving them again, that he needed more time to think. To distract herself from the panic that was welling inside her she packed her belongings into her bag. Charlie's clothes were on the other side of the wardrobe, hanging neatly beside her own. She folded his clothes and laid them in his suitcase, waiting in vain for him to come upstairs to get ready for bed.

Eventually the door opened. Lying in bed, Tasha kept her eyes shut as she listened to him creak across the floorboards. He brushed his teeth and changed his clothes. She waited for him to go back downstairs but instead he got into the bed, careful not to wake her. No doubt he wanted to get a good night's sleep before driving them back the next morning. He kept as far away from her as possible as he pulled the covers over himself. It dawned on her that this could be the last time they ever shared a bed and more tears slid across her cheeks. She turned around and stared at his back. She reached out and put her hand on his shoulder but he shifted his weight slightly and lifted her hand to move it off. She pulled it away. He couldn't even bear for her to touch him. As she closed her eyes and allowed the tears to trickle onto her pillow she could hardly believe that they had come to this point. She would never have dreamed it possible.

Chapter Twenty-nine

'A colleague has offered me his flat in the City.' Tasha looked at Charlie as he sat opposite her. He had been staying at the hotel for the last four nights. During his phone call with the children the night before he had asked her to meet him. He took a deep breath and continued. 'He's posted long term in Zurich and he only comes back for the odd weekend. He said I'd be doing him a favour if I house-sit for him while he is away. It's just lying there empty at the moment. I think I'm going to take him up on the offer…'

Panic erupted inside her. 'No. Charlie, *please*, don't do this. I am *begging* you…'

'The thing is, Tasha, I don't want to be in the same house as you any more. Since Dorset I've been doing some serious thinking. I want…' He paused. 'I need some time apart.'

'No,' she whispered. 'Please…'

'I'm sorry.'

Her eyes filled with tears. 'But what about the children?' She barely dared ask.

'I think we need to tell them what is happening. It's not fair to keep lying to them like this.'

She felt sick to her stomach at the thought. Her mind spun as she tried to think of something she could do to put a stop to it. 'No... we can't...'

'I don't see how we can avoid it.'

'But—'

'I know. It's hardly what I want either, but I don't see that we have a choice.' He clenched his jaw tightly.

Tasha couldn't think of anything to say. Her mind seemed to have gone completely blank.

'I wish I could change things.'

Charlie looked at her but said nothing.

'What do you want to tell them exactly?' she asked.

'The truth. Well, a version of the truth anyway.'

Tasha swallowed. Her mouth felt unbearably dry.

'I think we should say that we are having some time apart, that we've been together a long, long time and that sometimes couples need a break from each other.'

'But they'll be heartbroken,' Tasha whispered.

'So am I,' Charlie replied, his eyes brimming with emotion.

At this her eyes welled up.

'Then change your mind,' she begged. 'I'll do *anything*. Anything...'

But she could tell it was no good. His mind was made up.

'We have to tell them it has nothing to do with them,' he continued. 'That we still love them just as much as we always have. I've been doing some reading about the best way to talk to children about stuff like this.'

'When do you want to talk to them?'

'This weekend.'

'So soon?'

'I can't keep lying to them.'

Tasha nodded sadly.

'I'll come over on Saturday morning.'

'We should do it together.'

'That's better for them. Then I'd like to spend the weekend with them.'

'I'll see if I can stay with Rosie.'

'Thanks.' Charlie cleared his throat. 'I just hope I don't bump into…'

She nodded. He didn't need to finish the sentence.

'Charlie…'

He looked at her. She held his gaze, trying desperately to think of anything to say that might stop this from happening. Once they told the children it was real. There was no way out. Everyone would find out. Her palms began to sweat.

'Are you sure we can't try and make it work? Can't we give it more time… before we say anything?' she asked.

'I need space. It's not that easy.'

'I know. And I'm not trying to simplify it. I am just so desperate for this not to happen…' She tailed off. 'I know things weren't right between us, but we can work on it. We can get back to how we used to be…'

'Well, perhaps you should have thought about that before you jumped into someone else's bed.'

'I'm so sorry...' She felt like a broken record.

'I know you are sorry. But it doesn't change anything, Tasha. You can't undo what you've done.' With that, Charlie pushed back his chair and stood up. 'Look... I'll see you on Saturday,' he said. 'I'll call the children tomorrow.'

She looked at him as he stood across the table from her; his suit was crumpled and his eyes dark and shadowed.

'Goodbye, Tasha,' he said.

He turned and walked away.

She sat back down on her seat at the empty table and choked on an alarmingly loud sob. She didn't care who was watching; she let the tears stream down her cheeks, staring at the chair he had just vacated, trying to take in what had happened.

When she had regained some composure, she got out her phone and ordered an Uber home. There was no way she could hide the fact that she had been crying from Nina, who was babysitting, but luckily Nina was far too tactful to say anything. She accepted the cash Tasha offered her and left. Tasha went up to bed with a heart like lead. She had no appetite. She climbed under her duvet and rested her head on the pillow, staring at the other side of the bed, where Charlie should be.

Chapter Thirty

'Charlie wants to tell the children we are having some time apart,' Tasha said as she poured herself and Rosie large glasses of wine. Rosie had come over for dinner the following evening. Tasha was in desperate need of some moral support and encouragement having spent the day furiously fighting back tears, trying to quell the sheer panic that relentlessly pulsed through her.

'Oh, Tasha. I'm so sorry.' Rosie gave her a hug. 'Was Dorset a complete disaster?'

'It was so awkward, like being on holiday with a stranger, not my husband. We had a bit of an argument on Friday night but I didn't think it would come to this.' She shook her head. 'He's been staying in a hotel. He said he can't bear the thought of being in the same house as me.'

'I guess it's all still a bit raw.'

'More than a bit. He is so hurt. I just can't believe I was capable of causing him so much pain. What was I thinking?'

'I think that's the problem when things like this happen. If you had all your wits about you and knew the consequences you probably wouldn't have done it in the first place. It's just hard to think of the bigger picture in the moment. I can completely understand how it happens.'

'There's no way Charlie will ever see it like that. Especially after everything that happened with Chessie. I don't even expect him to. It's my fault. I know how he feels about cheating but I did it anyway. I keep thinking how I would feel if it was the other way around.'

'Look, Tash, it's happened now so there is no point torturing yourself.'

'I can't help it.'

'You have to look to the future, not the past.'

'The future looks pretty shit from where I'm standing.'

'Well, you just have to do your best to change that, Tash.'

'How?'

'Firstly, you need to give Charlie this space right now. That much is for sure. If he has made his decision, which it sounds like he has, then you need to respect his wishes, as hard as that may be. He needs to get over it and if the best way to do so is to be away from you then that is how it must be. At least that gives him the chance to miss you, to realise how lonely life would be without you and the kids.'

'You're right.' Tasha sighed and took another sip of her wine.

'I'm sure he will come back eventually. But in the

meantime, you have to get on with your life as best you can, for the children's sake. You're just going to have to take each step as it comes. So, the next thing to face is telling the children?'

'Yup.'

'Saturday, right?'

'That's what Charlie wants...'

'OK. So, you have until then to prepare for that. You can make sure you have done your research so you know you are doing the best you can for the children in terms of supporting them through this.'

'I've already started. It's all so depressing.'

'That's great! And in the meantime, you can continue to make sure they have a wonderful end to their summer holidays, as you always do.'

'What about my family? I'll have to tell them. I'm sure Mum must be suspicious – the kids told her Charlie was staying at work when she came up.'

'Did she say anything?'

'No, but she might be thinking it.'

'Are you going to tell them what you did?'

'I guess I'll have to.'

'Well, maybe that's another conversation to have with Charlie.'

'Oh, God. They're going to be so disappointed.' Tasha thought of her parents, her sisters, Becca and Andrew; her spirits plummeted.

'Don't even think about that until after you've told

the children. One thing at a time, remember?'

'You're right. Thanks so much, Rosie. What would I do without you? Speaking of which, I've got another favour to ask. Charlie wants the house to himself this weekend. Do you mind if I stay at yours on Saturday night?'

'Not at all. I'll tell Josh that I am busy with someone far more important...'

'You don't have to do that. I could always stay without you?'

'No way. I'll make us a nice meal if you don't feel like going out, or we can have a takeaway. We can even go wild and paint the town red if that's what you want.'

'I'll probably be having an emotional breakdown. You might be better off leaving me to it.'

'As if!' Rosie squeezed her hand.

'God, this is so miserable. I keep thinking "what if?" – it is driving me insane!'

'That's why it's pointless. What does it achieve? You can't change the past so you might as well stay in the present.'

'I know. I just can't bear it. I literally hate myself.'

'Tash,' Rosie reprimanded her. 'You mustn't think like that. We are all human. We all make mistakes – Charlie included. It takes two people to let a relationship get to the point where somebody strays.'

'I'm not so sure...'

'It does. You said it yourself, you didn't feel like he

was listening to you, you weren't that happy.'

'I suppose. Anyway, God, this is so horrendously boring for you, not to mention depressing.' Tasha took a deep breath. 'Tell me about Josh.'

'Tash I am hardly going to bang on about my new relationship at a time like this!' Rosie rolled her eyes.

'Please. I am dying to hear all about him.'

'No!'

'Come on! Seriously, Rosie. I need the distraction. How is it going?'

'It's going well...' Despite herself Rosie couldn't help the soppy smile that spread across her features.

'I'm so happy for you. Tell me more! What's he like?'

'He is a gentleman. He's got lovely manners.'

'I love that in a man.' His good manners were one of the things she had always loved about Charlie.

'I think you'd really like him.'

'Maybe I can meet him this weekend?' Tasha suggested. 'If I can pull myself together.'

'Let's see. We won't plan anything, but he'd love to meet you at some stage. I've told him all about you.'

'Oh, God. He's going to think I'm awful.'

'I've painted you in a very sympathetic light, don't worry.'

Tasha couldn't help but laugh. What a pitiful state she had caused herself to end up in. 'How is the blog coping without your usual dating antics?' Tasha asked.

'I've actually had really good feedback from my last

post.'

'That's brilliant. Perhaps this could be a new direction for you?'

Over dinner they brainstormed more ideas for Rosie's blog and the possible advice she could dole out to her followers. Afterwards, Tasha waved her off in an Uber as she headed over to Josh's flat. Tasha was extremely grateful to have such loyal friends in her life. Both Flo and Rosie had been brilliantly supportive, always ready to talk and to cheer her up when she needed them. If only she could tell Becca too; she hated keeping it all a secret from her. But the thought of her reaction when she found what Tasha had done terrified her. Becca's loyalties lay with both Charlie and Tasha, she had no idea whose side she would take and the thought of losing her friendship as well as Charlie, was heartbreaking.

Having cleared up their dinner and tidied the general detritus a day with three children on school holidays resulted in, Tasha went upstairs and ran herself a bath, pouring generous amounts of lavender bath oil into the hot water. She thought about what Rosie had said. She knew that living in the moment was her only option. If she allowed herself to live in the past she would be swamped by guilt and regret; if she spent too much time thinking about the future she would be overcome with panic. The answer had to be to stay mindful and present in each passing moment. She tried to quieten her mind and enjoy her bath but the voices in her head were clamouring for attention. She definitely had a long way to go before she achieved any form of mindfulness but she was determined to try her best.

As Saturday approached and with it the deadline for telling the children, Tasha began to feel increasingly anxious. She continued researching the impact of separation and how best to minimise the damage. On Friday afternoon she caught a glimpse of Javier as she ushered the children and their scooters inside on the way back from the park. He waved and she nodded before scurrying inside as quickly as possible. She half thought about warning him that Charlie would be spending the weekend but she couldn't face talking to him.

The house phone rang late on Friday evening. 'Tasha?' It was Charlie.

'Hi,' she said.

'I wanted to talk things through.'

A dart of hope shot through her. 'Have you changed your mind?' She couldn't hide the desperation in her voice.

He sighed down the line. 'No.' There was a long pause. 'I just thought it would be a good idea to discuss how we are going to do this.'

Tasha swallowed. 'Me too. If you are sure that this is what you want...'

He ignored her. 'I'll come over at about nine. They should have finished their breakfast by then. We can have a chat with them, you can stay for as long as they need to talk with us both, and then you can leave us to it. Will you stay at Rosie's?'

'Yes.' There was silence down the line. 'I can't believe this is actually happening.' Her voice wobbled with emotion.

'I can't either. But I don't see how we can avoid it. I can't change the way I feel.'

She nodded her head and bit back tears. 'I know.'

'Let's just try our best to explain it in the simplest terms possible.'

She swallowed hard, trying to keep her voice from breaking. 'The advice I've seen says we shouldn't go into any detail.'

They discussed the various articles that they had read and came up with a few key lines to use. They both agreed that they should appear united in the decision, that Charlie wouldn't blame Tasha in front of them and that they would reassure them that they both loved them, that they would still see Charlie at weekends and sometimes in the evenings too.

'Are you going to tell your parents what I did?' Tasha asked nervously. 'And Andrew and Becca?'

'No. I'm not going to give them any details. I don't want them to judge you and risk someone saying something that the children might pick up on. And I don't think you should tell your family what happened either.'

Tasha felt relief course through her. 'What shall we say?'

'Just say we are separating and we don't want to discuss why.'

'Becca will never let it go. Neither will Chloe. They'll want to know exactly what happened.'

'You'll just have to stick to the same line. That we don't want to discuss it and that's that.'

'OK.' Tasha paused. 'Can we say we are separating temporarily?'

'I wouldn't set a time limit on it, Tasha.'

Her cheeks were damp with tears. She dabbed at them with the sleeve of her jumper and nodded to herself.

'I just wish there was something I could do to change your mind. If only I could turn back the clock I would *never* make the same mistake again.'

'Does Javier know that I know?' Charlie interrupted her, reminding her once again exactly why this was happening in the first place.

'I've told him. I thought it for the best so he can avoid you.'

'So, you've seen him?' She could hear the anger in his voice at the thought.

'I just went around for a few minutes to tell him that you knew. Then I left as quickly as possible. I haven't seen him apart from that.'

'Right.' Tasha hoped fervently Javier would make

himself scarce for the weekend. 'Or at least I certainly hope that's the truth.'

'I wouldn't lie to you, Charlie.'

He laughed acerbically. 'You say that now... you didn't exactly volunteer the information in the first place. If I hadn't seen that text...'

'You *can* trust me.'

'I can't. That's precisely the problem.'

'I know. But I *promise* you can now.'

'They are just words, Tasha. Sadly, your actions speak far louder.'

Tasha could see she was digging herself in deeper so she decided to end the conversation before it took a turn for the worse. 'I'll see you in the morning, then,' she said, sadly. Perhaps overnight he would do some thinking and change his mind? She could only pray that might happen.

'Yes. See you then.'

'God, I hope the children will be OK.'

Normally he would be the one to reassure her, the calming voice of reason, but not today. 'So do I,' he said. 'Whatever happens, they must know just how much we love them.'

'I love you too, Charlie.'

'I'll see you tomorrow.' He hung up the phone.

Tasha tried to concentrate on her breathing, to stay in the moment and not race back in time or forwards to the dreaded conversation that would have to happen in the morning, but it was impossible. She was terrified that the children would completely fall apart, especially Max. He had been so good lately, she hoped against hope that this wouldn't set him back. Bella was such a quiet, calm child, she would probably internalise any upset. And Flora already had a tendency towards anxiety; this could be disastrous for her. She was so mortified that she was hurting the children she loved more than anything, that she would do anything to protect. In her heart of hearts, she knew there was no changing Charlie's mind at this point. If only she could be punished for her actions alone, rather than dragging everyone else down with her.

Chapter Thirty-one

Tasha dug her nails into her palm to stop herself from crying. She looked at the three little faces sitting opposite them at the kitchen table and her heart broke. They were so expectant: three pairs of rosy cheeks, three pairs of round blue eyes looking from her to Charlie and back, waiting to hear what it was that they had to say. They were the picture of innocence. To think that because of her their blissful, stable family life was about to be ripped from underneath their feet... She couldn't cope with the guilt that coursed through her.

Charlie cleared his throat. 'Darlings, Mummy and I have been talking,' he began. 'You know I've been spending some time in the office recently because I have been very busy at work?'

'Yes,' Flora said. Max and Bella nodded.

'Well, it's been quite nice for Mummy and me to have some time apart. Sometimes when grown-ups are married they like having a little break to spend time without each other. We still love you more than anything and want to spend time with you whenever we can, but we also like having our own places to live.' Charlie took a deep breath. 'From now on Mummy is going to keep living here and I am going to live in a flat near the office.'

The children looked blankly at them. 'Why?' Max said.

'Why can't we live together like we always do?' Bella asked.

They all looked so confused. 'Are you getting a divorce like Samantha's parents?' Flora asked.

'No, we're not, darling,' Tasha said, crossing her fingers under the table. 'We are just having a little break. Sometimes grown-ups decide that it is a good idea for a while.'

'I don't understand. Don't you love each other any more?' Flora asked. The expression of angst on her face was heart-wrenching.

'We do. Of course we do,' Tasha said. 'It's tricky to explain but you don't need to worry at all. We love you, and we are always going to be your mummy and daddy. It's just that for a while we will live in different places. Sometimes Daddy will stay here with you, and sometimes he will stay at his flat.'

'But I don't want you to live in different places,' Max said, his voice sounding very small.

'Neither do I,' Bella added. 'I like it when we all live here.'

Flora had gone very quiet. She was looking from Tasha to Charlie and back, as if trying to work out what was really going on.

'Is it something we've done?' Max asked, his voice wobbling.

'Not at all, darling.' Charlie got up and gave him a hug. 'It has absolutely nothing to do with any of you. You are all perfect.'

'It's nothing anyone has done, I promise,' Tasha said. *Except for me,* she thought bitterly. She dug her nails in even deeper, concentrating on the painful sensation in her palm to stop herself losing control. She knew how important it was that the children didn't see the raw emotion that was threatening to erupt from her at any moment. She glanced at Charlie. His jaw was tense and she could tell just how hard he was finding this conversation.

'What about the weekends?' Flora asked. 'We'll still be together at the weekends, won't we?'

'No, darling,' Charlie said. At this his voice broke slightly. He cleared his throat loudly. 'It'll be more like taking it in turns…'

Tasha took over. 'Some weekends with me and some with Daddy.'

'During the weeks I'll be working so it won't be much different,' Charlie said. 'I don't always see you before bedtime normally anyway.'

'But we know you're here if we need you,' Flora said.

'I'll *always* be here if you need me,' Charlie assured her. 'And I will call you every day to find out exactly what you have been up to and you can call me whenever you want.'

They answered the children's questions patiently and calmly, each time reassuring them that they were not at fault, working together to come up with non-accusatory and responsible answers, doing their best to handle what was without doubt an extremely difficult conversation. At the end of it Tasha told them that this was going to be a Daddy weekend, so she was going to stay with Rosie.

At this Bella suddenly burst into tears. Flora soon joined her and Max jumped up from the table and ran around to hug her. 'I don't want you to leave us,' he cried.

'I'll be back tomorrow, darlings,' she said. 'Then we will have a lovely day together. And on Tuesday you'll be back at school and you can see all your friends!'

'But it won't be lovely because we won't be together, will we?' Flora said, her voice getting louder and more emotional with every word. 'Daddy won't be here. It's never going to be lovely again!'

Charlie attempted to distract them with fun suggestions for the rest of the weekend while Tasha snuck off upstairs to grab her overnight bag. She came back to kiss the children goodbye, trying her best to stay cheerful as she did so.

Charlie walked her out to the door and stood briefly on the doorstep with her.

'That was awful,' she whispered, her eyes filling with

tears.

'I know,' Charlie said. She wanted nothing more than to wrap her arms around him and hold him tight.

'I'm so sorry,' she said. 'I just wish I could make this all go away.'

Charlie nodded and swallowed. He glanced across the road. His jaw tightened. Tasha followed his gaze and saw that the lights were on.

'I'd better go, then,' she said. 'I hope they're going to be OK.'

'I'll be here if they aren't.'

'See you tomorrow, then.'

Tasha turned and walked down the street. Her heart was breaking. She could barely summon the energy to take each step. She felt emotionally exhausted and utterly drained. Mindlessly she made her way to Rosie's flat near Bermondsey Street, texting her to let her know she was en route. She rang the bell and Rosie answered the door, her face a picture of concern. Tasha finally let her guard down. She burst helplessly into noisy sobs as Rosie hugged her.

Chapter Thirty-two

It took a while for the floodgates to begin to close and for Tasha to regain some of her composure. The emotions she had been doing her best to repress in the past few weeks in a valiant effort to hold things together came spilling out. She couldn't stop crying, shaking uncontrollably at the horrendous turn of events that had resulted in her sitting here, on Rosie's sofa, away from her family. It didn't matter how many times Rosie reassured her that it was not completely her fault, Tasha knew that no one had forced her into Javier's bed. It had been entirely her decision.

Rosie put a steaming mug of tea and a packet of chocolate Hobnobs in front of her. 'It was so much harder than I could have anticipated,' Tasha gulped through her tears.

'It must have been horrendous. It sounds like you both handled it as well as you possibly could have.'

'Charlie was amazing.' At this a fresh wave of tears came gushing out.

'He'll look after them this weekend, and you'll be back with them tomorrow. You can reassure them and put their minds at rest. Children are so adaptable, they will get used to the idea more quickly than you think.'

'I hope so. They just looked so confused. As if they couldn't understand why on earth we would do such a thing.'

'It's a bit beyond their reasoning. I suppose they only know what they are used to, what they have experienced so far. When they realise that the reality is actually OK they will be fine.'

'But will the reality be OK? That's what I worry about. I just hope to God that somehow Charlie decides to forgive me. I'm hoping that he might miss us so much that he comes around and gives me another chance.'

'Exactly. He might surprise you. He might surprise himself.'

'The problem is the trust issue. You know his first love cheated on him with his best mate at uni? He was completely devastated. It took him years to get over it. The stupid thing is I *know* that about Charlie. I know him inside out. But it wasn't enough to stop me from putting him through this all over again.'

Tasha buried her head in her hands and Rosie put a comforting arm around her shoulders. They sat on the sofa talking for a long time, eventually deciding to go for a walk along the river to get some fresh air. The golden light of the late-afternoon sun gilded the water as the daylight began to seep away. Tasha always found being by the river extremely calming. She tried not to let her imagination run away with itself thinking of the children and Charlie at home without her.

To take her mind off things they spent the rest of the day watching movies, ordering pizzas for dinner. She got several missed calls from Becca, all of which she ignored. She knew Charlie must have told her and Andrew about the separation, but she couldn't face speaking to her just yet.

The next morning Tasha was in desperate need of coffee after yet another sleepless night. They went out for breakfast across the road. She checked her phone and saw that she had received a text from Charlie.

> Children all fine, asked some more questions but generally OK – Bella woke in the night. I told my family last night. They wanted to get in touch but I said best to give it some time as neither of us really want to talk about it, that we are both OK and agree it's for the best

'There's no kiss at the end,' Tasha said sadly. 'I can't help but think this could be for real, Rosie.'

'It's still so soon after he found out, Tasha. It all happened so recently. It's far too early to tell.'

'I suppose I'm going to have to tell Mum and Dad, and Chloe and Ella. And call Becca. Oh, God. I'm just not sure I'm up to it. What are they going to think? They'll be so shocked... It's so completely out of the blue.'

'You'll feel better once it's out in the open,' Rosie

assured her. 'And at least then they'll be able to support you through this.'

'Charlie doesn't want us to tell anyone about Javier. He just wants us to say we are separating without explaining why. I'm sure everyone will jump to their own conclusions. I feel bad – like I should own up to what I have done, especially to Becca.'

'What is his reason for not telling them?' Rosie asked.

'He's worried someone might say something to the children, even accidentally. He doesn't want them to think badly of me.'

'Well, that's sensible. There is no need for anyone to know what goes on behind closed doors. Your relationship is between you and Charlie, so it really isn't anyone else's business. If you tell Becca she'll undoubtedly tell Andrew and then he may tell his parents and before you know it the secret is out.'

'I suppose. Though I can't help but think that if it were him I'd be shaming him publicly for what he had done out of spite.' Tasha sighed. 'Charlie is such a good person, he always does the right thing.'

'I'm sure you wouldn't have,' Rosie countered. But Tasha didn't have such a strong faith in her own moral compass.

When Tasha felt suitably fortified by coffee and pastries they went back to Rosie's flat. She left Rosie typing away at a new blog post while she settled down to make the dreaded calls.

'Hi, darling!' Lizzie's cheerful voice came down the line. 'How are you?'

'Fine, thanks, Mum. Any news from Ella? I haven't had any new emails for a while.'

'We FaceTimed her last night. She is in Cuba! Having a wonderful time and feeling much better still, thank goodness.'

'Great!'

'How are the children?'

'Fine, fine... I'm not actually with them at the moment,' Tasha said.

'Oh, how so? What are you up to?'

Tasha considered her next words carefully. She knew she couldn't wimp out. She took a deep breath and said, 'They are with Charlie. I'm staying with Rosie for the weekend.' She paused. 'Mum, I have something to tell you which is going to come as a surprise. Charlie and I have separated.'

'Separated?' Lizzie's tone of voice conveyed her confusion.

'We are taking some time apart from each other.'

'But... why? What do you mean?'

'It's complicated, Mum. I don't really know how to explain it. Charlie is moving into a colleague's flat in the City for a while.'

'Has he had an affair?' Lizzie asked bluntly.

This made Tasha reel with guilt that Lizzie should immediately assume her daughter was the innocent party.

'No!' Tasha replied quickly. 'Nothing like that.'

'Then why on earth...?' Her mother tailed off. She was clearly completely nonplussed, as Tasha had predicted.

'As I said, Mum, I don't really want to go into detail. It's between me and Charlie.' She heard Rosie's voice echoing in her mind and tried her best to follow her advice. 'The main thing is that we both agree it's a good idea. And hopefully it will just be temporary, to give us some space... Things have been... tricky recently.'

'Have you been arguing?'

'A bit.'

'God, this is awful, Tasha!'

'I know.'

'I'm afraid I've no idea what to say.' There was a pause. 'And the children? I suppose this explains why they said he was sleeping over at the office.'

'They're OK... I think. We only told them yesterday.'

'And how is Charlie?'

'Upset, as am I.'

'Then why?' Tasha could all too clearly picture the exasperated look on her mother's face. 'Surely you can talk things over, patch things up? Gosh, the amount of times your father and I have come to blows over the years. If we had separated every time we would have barely spent any time in the same house! It's a bit drastic, don't you think? And it can't be good for the children.'

'Thanks, Mum. Rant over?' Tasha bristled.

'Sorry, darling. I'm just very shocked.'

'I can tell. Look, it hasn't been an easy decision and obviously if we had thought it possible we would have avoided it, but we think it is for the best. Hopefully the space will make us realise how important our marriage is.'

'By us you mean Charlie, I take it?'

'Well...'

'Mmmm...' She could tell her mother wasn't quite convinced. She passed the phone over to Bertie and Tasha had to repeat herself all over again. Her father sounded even more perplexed than her mother. Tasha could tell they didn't buy her story. They must suspect some kind of infidelity or betrayal but she stuck to her guns, part relieved that she didn't have to confess her adultery and part guilty that she had got out of doing just that. After she had finally hung up the phone, she sent an email to Ella, Chloe and Becca. She knew that all three would ring her as soon as they read it but she explained that it was easier for her to put it all in writing, that having just talked it through at length with both parents she felt completely drained. Sure enough, Becca called her straight away.

'Tasha?' Becca's voice sounded full of concern. 'Are you OK? What's happened?'

Tasha burst into tears at the sound of Becca's voice.

'Sorry. I'm OK,' she said through her sobs. 'I just had quite a difficult conversation with Mum and Dad.'

'I'm sorry. I know you probably don't want to talk to me, but I just had to check you are all right?'

'I'm OK, considering...'

'And the kids? Charlie?'

'They're all right. We all are. It's just hard. It's so new...'

'I just don't understand what can possibly have happened. When we saw you for dinner the other day everything seemed absolutely fine between you.'

'I know. It's really hard to explain.'

'Charlie told us you don't want to talk about it, as you said in your email.'

'Exactly. We've agreed it's for the best.'

'I hope he hasn't done something wrong. To hurt you?'

Everyone seemed to assume it was Charlie's fault. 'He hasn't. It's just... tricky, that's all.' Tasha was at a loss for words.

'Don't worry. I understand, you don't have to say anything. I just want to be here for you, and so does Andrew. And for Charlie too... Is there anything we can do? Help with the kids? Give you guys some space, some time together?'

'Sadly, I don't think that's an option at the moment. Thank you though. I'll call you if there is. And I'd love to see you soon. Perhaps when things have settled a bit?'

When she had managed to convince Becca that she was just about holding on and not about to have some kind of nervous breakdown she ended the call and collapsed back onto the bed, completely worn out.

'So?' Rosie asked, coming into the bedroom.

'So...'

Rosie sat down next to her.

'They know?'

'Yup. I haven't spoken to Ella and Chloe yet, but they will be calling me as soon as they check their email, I can guarantee.'

'How were the others?'

'Shocked. Surprised. Confused. Just as I expected really. None of them are satisfied with my lack of explanation but they are just going to have to accept it, I suppose. I can tell they all think Charlie has cheated, even Becca. It makes me want to tell them it was actually me – to protect him.'

'Just as he is trying to protect you.'

Tasha yawned. She had never felt so exhausted in her life. Mental exhaustion was so much harder to handle than physical exhaustion. She had certainly had her fair share of sleepless nights with three babies, but this felt completely different. Her brain felt overloaded, every cell in her body hurt and she felt unbearably sad, as though her very soul ached.

'What do you want to do?'

Tasha pulled herself up to sitting. 'I think I'll go for a

walk.'

'Do you want company?'

'Do you know, I think I'd actually like to go by myself. I need to think. And I need to prepare myself for seeing the children later, and Charlie...' Tasha sighed.

'I understand. If you change your mind just call me and I'll come and find you.'

'Thanks, Rosie. You really are the best.' Tasha hugged her.

She walked up to London Bridge and looked out across the city. The familiar skyline with its high-rise buildings gleamed in the sunshine. The famous landmarks: The Gherkin, St Paul's Cathedral, The Shard, stood proudly like majestic beacons. Tasha walked along the Thames path, using the time to align her thoughts, to try and process some of what had happened and to make a plan for moving forwards in this time without Charlie as she waited for him to come back to her. She couldn't contemplate any other ending. He just *had* to come back. They had to become the happy family they always had been once again. But it all rested on him. She honestly couldn't say if she would be able to do what she was asking of him had it been the other way around. She hoped he was a better person than she was if that were the case. Tasha had never realised just what a powerful gift forgiveness was until it was her that needed to be forgiven.

By the time Tasha arrived back in Putney on Sunday

afternoon she felt just about able to retain her composure and face her family.

'Darlings!' she cried as she opened the front door to find a pirate, a fairy and a Disney princess hurtling down the stairs.

'Hi, Mum!' they chorused, momentarily pausing their game to greet her.

'They've been raiding the dressing-up box,' Charlie said, coming down the stairs behind them.

'What fun!' Tasha crouched down to admire their costumes as they pirouetted and curtsied for her. 'Have you had a lovely weekend?'

'It's been brilliant!' Flora informed her. 'We made fajitas. And last night we had pizza and watched a movie!'

'We climbed the biggest tree on the common!' said Max.

'And we tried to fly our kite but there wasn't enough wind,' added Bella.

'Wow! You *have* been busy!' Tasha laughed, feeling unbearably left out.

'How was godmother Rosie?' Flora asked.

'Oh, she is very well, thank you, darling. She sends you lots of love,' Tasha said.

'I've put some fish fingers and chips in the oven for their dinner,' Charlie said.

'Thanks,' she replied. She didn't know what else to say.

The children had charged back into the sitting room to continue acting out what appeared to be a mash-up of *Peter Pan* and *Frozen*.

Tasha followed Charlie into the kitchen.

'This feels so wrong,' she said.

'I know. It'll certainly take some getting used to.'

'I hope we don't have to get used to it for long.'

'I saw Javier,' Charlie said, ignoring her previous comment.

Tasha's heart skipped a beat. 'What?'

'We were going out to the pizzeria last night for dinner. He pulled up on his motorbike.'

'Oh, God, Charlie. I'm so sorry. What did you say?'

'Nothing. I had to restrain myself from going up to him and punching his lights out. He saw me. He was clearly watching me to see what I'd do but I had the kids so I had no choice but to walk away.'

Tasha winced. She knew how hard that must have been. 'I'm sorry I put you in that position.'

He looked at the floor. 'I packed up some stuff last night,' he said.

'OK.'

'I'll leave you to it, then, I suppose.'

'Were they OK today?'

'Pretty much. Keep an eye on Bella though. She seemed a bit quiet earlier.'

'I will.'

Charlie ordered an Uber. He said goodbye to the

kids, who were thankfully still engrossed in their game. They didn't notice him hauling several suitcases out to the taxi, and they didn't hang around to say goodbye or watch him and Tasha's awkward parting. She closed the door and took a deep breath, gathering her energy to plunge back into the unrelenting chaos of family life. At least there wouldn't be much time for soul-searching and feeling sorry for herself while the children were around.

Chapter Thirty-three

'What has he done?' Chloe asked. It was late on Monday evening. She had arrived back in the UK hours earlier, just in time for the start of term. 'You might have fooled the others but you can't fool me. I *know* something must have happened.'

Tasha was sorely tempted to tell Chloe exactly what she had done but she managed to resist the impulse. 'It... it's complicated,' she said. 'I really don't want to talk about it. But, it's not what you think.'

'And there's no way you can work it out?'

'I'm hoping that we will.'

'God, Tash, you poor thing. Are you OK?'

'I'm just about holding things together.'

'And the kids?'

'They're OK. Telling them was awful, but you know what kids are like... They don't really understand. And it's only been a couple of days. I'm not sure that it's even sunk in yet.'

'Where's Charlie now?' Chloe asked.

'He's staying at a colleague's flat in the City.'

'Alone?'

'Yes, the colleague works abroad. Charlie is house-sitting.'

'How were Mum and Dad?'

'Confused. Very shocked. As everyone is, I suppose.'

'I've already had a barrage of texts from her asking if I know anything.'

'Well, I'm not surprised. You know what Mum's like.'

'She might be a pain in the arse at times, but you know she'll be there for you no matter what.'

'I know. In fact, she just called to tell me she is coming up tomorrow.' Tasha felt a rush of sadness. She knew she was lucky to have such an amazing family around her, but Charlie was her true family. He had been for fourteen years. She felt unbearably lonely without him.

Ella had also called her the previous evening. They had had a stilted conversation thanks to the unreliable Wi-Fi. Having now explained the sorry story multiple times, Tasha was fed up with talking about it. She wanted to retreat into peace and solitude, away from prying eyes and awkward questions. Unfortunately she knew the latter were unavoidable. The new term started the following day. The children would no doubt tell their friends and the school grapevine would soon be thrumming with gossip.

Tasha had made an appointment with the children's headteacher to inform the school of the separation. She felt it was better to be open. In a way she was grateful that it was the start of a new year. She hoped that the children would be so busy they wouldn't have time to think about what was going on at home. Tasha, on the other hand, would have plenty. She was glad her mum was coming up to stay; at least she would have some company for a few days.

*

Tasha had broken down in tears during the meeting. She had arrived somewhat frazzled after overcoming a monumental meltdown from Max, who had been unable to locate his summer holiday project. Mrs Hemmingway had been sympathetic and full of assurances that the school would keep a close eye on all three children but Tasha had felt like an enormous failure as a mother nonetheless. When she arrived home, Tasha was extremely relieved to find her mother waiting on the doorstep.

A short while later she was sitting in the kitchen with a steaming mug of tea and a plate of chocolate biscuits.

'So, darling,' Lizzie said. 'Are you going to tell me what is really going on?'

Tasha had been expecting this. 'It's out of bounds, Mum. I told you – it's not up for discussion.'

Her mother paused; her green eyes peered at her daughter over the rim of her glasses. 'OK,' she said slowly, clearly sensing just how fragile Tasha was and not wishing to pursue a line of enquiry that might send her over the edge completely.

'How are the children?' she asked. Tasha filled her in on the morning's events.

'I'm not surprised. I'd expect them to be a bit out of sorts for a while. Molly's daughter just divorced her husband and the children were absolutely distraught.' Molly was a member of Lizzie's book club. Tasha couldn't help but wonder how exactly this information was meant to help her.

'So, what do you want to do while you are here?' Tasha asked, trying to change the subject.

'I'll help you with the children. I might not be much use in the kitchen but I can do the shopping, help with the laundry, keep you company. But first things first,' Lizzie said as she looked around the kitchen. 'This place needs a jolly good sort-out.'

When they had finished their coffees, they set about tidying up the house, which, Tasha had to agree, did look as though a bomb had gone off inside it. She just hadn't had the energy to keep on top of the housework lately. It had been messy enough before the four of them had turned the contents of the house upside down in their search for Max's project book earlier that morning. It had eventually been discovered underneath the *Oxford English Dictionary*. Charlie had apparently suggested Max use something heavy to press a four-leaf clover that he had found in the park. He had wanted to show it to his new teacher. When the clean-up was complete Lizzie and Tasha loaded the machine with washing and packed away some of the beach paraphernalia from Dorset that was still cluttering up the back garden.

After lunch they went for an invigorating walk along the river to get some fresh air, buffeted along the way by dancing gusts of wind. By pickup time they were both standing in the playground as the clock ticked half past three, ready to receive the children and hear all about their first day back. Tasha reached down and gave her mother's hand a squeeze. Despite Lizzie having invited herself to stay, Tasha had never been more grateful to have her mother with her.

Later that evening she went into Bella's room to tuck her in. Lizzie was with Max, reading him a bedtime story.

'Mummy, please can I have a made-up story?' Bella asked. 'Like Daddy's?'

The children had FaceTimed Charlie earlier and were clearly missing him not being around for their first day back at school. 'I'm not as good as Daddy but I can certainly give it a try,' Tasha said, stroking Bella's hair as she bit back tears.

'I really miss him,' Bella said. 'I wish he could tell me one. I wish he wasn't living somewhere else.'

'I know,' Tasha said. She wanted to promise her that it wouldn't last forever but she had no way of knowing what the future might hold.

Instead she tried to replicate one of Charlie's stories. He always ensured that the children took the starring role and she did the same. She kept talking until Bella's eyes closed, her long curly lashes resting gently on her cheeks. When she was asleep Tasha tiptoed out of the bedroom; she could hear Max and Lizzie talking. She paused outside the door to listen.

'I told my teacher that Mummy and Daddy aren't living together any more.'

'Oh?' Lizzie said. 'And what did she say?'

'She said that I could talk to her if I ever feel sad about it.'

'That's good.'

'She was really nice,' Max said. His voice was so small, it sounded as though he had been crying. 'Is it our fault?' he asked.

'What do you mean, darling?'

'Is it our fault Daddy isn't here any more?' Max repeated.

'Darling, of course not,' Lizzie said emphatically. 'It's got nothing at all to do with any of you. It's just something that happens sometimes. It's between Mummy and Daddy and no one else.'

'Do you think Daddy will come home?' Max asked.

'I'm not sure,' Lizzie said. 'Try not to worry about it, darling. You just concentrate on school, on your lovely friends, and having fun. We all love you very much, especially Mummy and Daddy.'

Tasha bit her bottom lip to stop herself crying. She waited for a moment or two before going into the bedroom to kiss Max goodnight. He asked Tasha to stay with him until he fell asleep, something he hadn't done for a long time.

Chapter Thirty-four

The first week of the new academic year did not pass by as smoothly as Tasha had hoped. Despite the distraction of school, the consequences of the separation were clearly beginning to take their toll. Max's behaviour regressed; he was asking for more cuddles, more stories, and more time with Tasha. He had even appeared in her bedroom in the middle of the night asking to sleep in her bed. Bella seemed all right, though she was always so quiet and measured it was hard to tell exactly what was going on in her mind. Flora, on the other hand, seemed to be venting all her sadness and frustration at her mother. Slamming doors, huffing and puffing, eye rolling and sarcasm were her weapons of choice. She clearly thought Tasha was to blame for Charlie's departure from the family home; her father could do no wrong – in fact, she seemed to idolise him more than ever.

Tasha was due to hand over parental responsibility to Charlie on Friday afternoon, and, after the week she had had, she found she was actually looking forward to the break. She was due to stay with Rosie until Sunday and she was fed up with moping around feeling sorry for herself, wallowing in regret. She needed to take responsibility, both for her actions and for her own happiness. She knew that it was her fault Charlie had left her but she acknowledged that he had been less than perfect himself. Besides, she knew it was not good for her to spend every waking moment fighting off tears. She felt as though she had used her quota for a lifetime in the past few weeks. Instead, for this weekend at least, she was determined to put her family drama to one side and enjoy herself.

'Have fun with Daddy,' she said, bending down to kiss and hug each child as she said goodbye. Max clung onto her, reluctant to let her go, but she peeled herself away with promises that she'd be back before he knew it. In contrast Flora didn't seem nearly so upset at her departure; she stood almost protectively in front of Charlie, clearly delighted to have him home.

'Be good,' she called, giving Charlie a cheery wave. Her determination began now – she fixed a smile on her face and tried her best to mean it.

'Bye,' he replied. 'I hope you like Josh.'

'I have a feeling I'm going to!' She smiled, slinging a small overnight bag over her shoulder and closing the front door behind her. She was going to meet Rosie and Josh at a Lebanese restaurant in the City. She couldn't wait to meet the famous apple of Rosie's eye.

Soon she was taking the lift up to what felt like the very top of an enormous skyscraper. As she ascended

Tasha looked at herself in the lift's mirrored walls. She was feeling pretty good in her outfit of teal silk shirt, black jeans and heeled ankle boots. While the children were at school that morning she had had her roots touched up at the hairdresser and she was happy with the results. Never more so than when Charlie had commented on her hair upon arriving at the house earlier that evening, asking if she had done something new. She wondered whether a bit of distance was all he had needed to notice her more clearly. She certainly felt that the lens of their separation was showing Charlie in a whole new light. He seemed less familiar and more appealing; she found herself appreciating just how good-looking he was. They had even managed to have a relatively normal conversation when she had filled him in on Rosie's new relationship.

The restaurant was famous for its views overlooking the City; the walls were mostly made of glass to allow diners to see as much as possible of the panorama below. The evenings were getting darker now as the autumn rolled in and the lights from the buildings below glowed softly in the twilight. Tasha headed over to the bar, spotting Rosie perched on a bar stool next to an extremely handsome, bearded man in a smart navy blazer and a crisp white shirt.

'Tasha, this is Josh,' Rosie said, unable to disguise the pride emblazoned across her face.

Josh stood up and kissed Tasha on the cheek. 'Tasha,

it's great to meet you,' he said with a broad smile.

Tasha was impressed. He was every bit as good-looking as in the pictures she had seen, if not more so in the flesh. 'You too! I've heard so much about you!'

'All good, I assume?' Josh winked at Rosie.

'Of course!' Rosie laughed. Tasha ordered a gin and tonic from the barman and sat down.

'This place is amazing,' she said. 'I don't know why I have never been up so high – the view is astonishing!'

'It'll get even better when it gets darker later and the City properly lights up,' Josh promised. 'And the food here is pretty incredible too.'

'I can't wait!' Tasha said.

'How are you feeling? Was it OK leaving the kids?' asked Rosie.

'It was better. I'm slowly getting used to it, though obviously I would rather be leaving them by choice rather than necessity. But I'm determined to have some fun this weekend and take advantage of the break from motherhood!'

'Good for you!' Josh said, raising his glass and chinking it against hers.

After a couple of rounds of drinks at the bar they moved to their table by one of the vast windows. They ordered mezze sharing platters full of hummus, tabbouleh and baba ghanoush, as well as an assortment of meat dishes, selected by Josh.

'How do you know so much about Lebanese food?'

Tasha asked.

'I used to live in Beirut.' Josh explained how he had worked as a correspondent in Lebanon earlier in his career.

'What was that like?' Tasha asked. He told them stories about his time there, describing trips to tiny fishing villages on the coast and the spectacular stalactites and stalagmites in the caves at Jeita Grotto that spun miles and miles deep into the mountains. By the end of the night Tasha had decided that she thoroughly approved of Rosie's new boyfriend. He was fascinating company, interesting and observant, and despite his good looks there was no air of arrogance detectable. He was also clearly as besotted with Rosie as she was with him. It was heart-warming for Tasha to see one of her best friends so in love.

After dessert, taking advantage of Josh's disappearance to the bathroom, Tasha grabbed Rosie's hand and whispered, 'I *love* him! He is so perfect for you in every way.'

'I'm so glad you like him!' Rosie was beaming from ear to ear. 'I can tell he likes you too.'

'Let's hope so. I have a feeling I'll be knowing him for a long, long time!' Tasha laughed.

They all clambered tipsily into a taxi back to Rosie's after their meal. Tasha collapsed into bed and fell asleep within moments. It was the first time she hadn't obsessively checked her phone to see whether Charlie had been in touch, or to find out when he had last been active on WhatsApp.

The following morning dawned clear and bright, in crisp autumnal perfection. Josh was busy with a deadline so he went back to his flat to work, leaving Rosie and Tasha free to do whatever took their fancy.

'How about we go to my gym for a spa day?' Rosie suggested as they devoured stacks of pancakes and blueberry jam for breakfast.

'Now that sounds like a fabulous idea!'

'I can give you a guest pass. They have a pretty good café we can get some lunch at too.'

They spent the day ambling from the pool to the Jacuzzi, the steam room to the sauna, chatting and relaxing. Tasha felt some of the tension slowly ebb away from her. She realised she had been living on pure adrenaline for the past month and it felt good to give herself a treat.

That evening they met Josh in the West End to see a show before drinking cocktails at a trendy Soho bar. On Sunday they went for a long walk along the river and Tasha collected a few conkers for Max. She was looking forward to getting back home and seeing them all.

She waited until around five to get back to Havers Street. She hesitated as she stood on the doorstep, key in hand. It suddenly occurred to her that perhaps she should ring the bell. She told herself not to be so stupid and let herself in. It was her own house, after all. She called out and heard a response from down the corridor. The children were all sitting in the kitchen ready for tea. Charlie was serving out a pasta bake. Her heart filled with love as she watched him, and she was overcome with a sense of missing him so strong that it felt completely overwhelming.

'Don't get up!' she called, coming around to kiss them all on the cheeks where they sat. 'Did you have a lovely weekend?' she asked. Flora was silent while Max and Bella chatted away to her as they ate their pasta. Tasha pulled up a chair and devoted her attention to them, trying to make up for the time she had lost in being apart. She aimed several questions at Flora, forcing her to talk to her. She had read that it was common for a child to blame one parent, and knew that she needed to do everything she could to help her adjust to their new circumstances as patiently as possible.

'The pasta looks yummy,' she said to Charlie.

'I made enough for your dinner too,' he said, gesturing over to the serving dish. He had filled a Tupperware container for himself. Her heart wrenched as she thought of him back in an empty flat eating pasta out of a plastic tub later that evening. She thanked him and told him all about Josh and what she had been up to that weekend.

'Sounds like you had a rather more relaxing weekend than we did!' He laughed. He looked pretty exhausted. 'I must say, I now realise just how much you do... It's hard work looking after you ratbags,' he said, ruffling Max's hair as he did so. His tone was light but she could see he meant it. Perhaps it would help him understand how she had been feeling.

'Yup, I'm not going to argue with that one!' She laughed. 'As much as I love you all dearly,' she added, noticing the three little faces that had lit up with righteous indignation.

Later, as Charlie was leaving, she walked with him to the front door. 'Anything I should know?' she asked.

'Nothing in particular came up. Flora and I had quite a long chat at bedtime, the same questions about us, nothing new. She seems OK.'

'With you at least.' Tasha nodded. She didn't want him to leave. 'Charlie...' she said.

He looked at her expectantly, but yet again she couldn't find the words so instead she smiled.

Then he did something completely unexpected. He put down his bag, pulled her into his arms and hugged her. Tasha's heart stopped beating for a moment. It felt incredible to be back in his arms, to feel his strong, warm body against hers, to smell his familiar scent. She pressed her cheek into the soft fabric of his jumper, trying to savour every second of his embrace.

All too soon he let go and said goodbye, turning to walk off down the street. She watched him go, lost for words. As she shut the door she allowed herself the briefest smile. *Could that have been a good sign?* she wondered. Was he missing her? Maybe he would change his mind and give them another chance? She told herself not to get her hopes up, despite wanting nothing more.

Later that evening Tasha sat on the edge of Flora's bed. 'Is everything OK?' she asked.

'I'm fine,' Flora replied without lifting her eyes from her book.

'Are you sure?'

Flora's eyes filled up with tears.

'What is it, sweetheart?'

'I just miss Dad when he's not here.'

'I know you do, darling.'

'I don't see why he has to go!' Flora's cheeks flushed pink with the injustice of it all. 'What did you do to make him want to leave?'

Tasha's heart sank. It was just as she suspected. The accusation stung; she worried her daughter could see right through the lies they had spun.

'I don't want you to get divorced like Samantha's parents. I *hate* you for making him leave!' Flora burst into angry sobs.

'I haven't made him do anything, Flora. I know it's really difficult for you to understand, and that you feel sad and a bit cross, and I am so, so sorry for that.'

'Just leave me alone, Mum,' Flora sobbed, turning to lie on her side facing the wall. 'I just want to be by myself.'

Tasha sat on the bed for a few moments trying to

decide whether she should persist with the conversation, to try and alleviate some of the blame Flora was so clearly apportioning to her. In the end she decided it was probably better to leave her be. 'OK, darling,' she said. 'But, please, try not to worry. Everything will be OK, I promise. We will all get used to things soon, and we still love you... so, so much.'

Tasha went back downstairs and sat on the sofa. The brave face she had been wearing all weekend crumpled away and she burst into tears. She replayed the hug with Charlie over and over in her mind, relishing every second of it. It had been an all too bittersweet reminder of just what she had thrown away.

Chapter Thirty-five

The heavens opened during the second week of September. Leaving the house without every item of clothing becoming immediately water-logged became impossible. Tasha insisted that all the children wear wellies to school and the house was soon filled with damp garments hanging up to dry. The weather suited Tasha's mood. Try as she might to lift her spirits and look on the bright side, she found it harder than ever with the continuous onslaught of rain. The children were all extremely fractious, having been cooped up at school with no outdoor play, indoor games and no fresh air. She tried to encourage them to go out in the garden in their wet-weather gear but they were less than enthusiastic. To make matters worse Max was continuing to wake, up to several times a night, appearing in Tasha's room complaining that he couldn't sleep.

'I'm sure it's because of Charlie moving out,' Tasha said as she took a gulp of red wine. It was Thursday and she was having lunch with Flo after Pilates. 'He's much more clingy and wanting to be near me all the time.'

'It could be that,' Flo agreed.

'Last night I caved in and let him sleep in my bed. It's just so exhausting!'

'I don't blame you. I would do the same. How are the girls?'

'Bella seems OK. Flora is behaving more like a moody teenager than ever.'

Flo laughed. 'Oh dear. A glimpse of things to come?'

'God help us!'

'And how are things with Charlie?' Flo asked hesitantly.

'Not too bad considering...' Tasha didn't want to go into much detail. 'He's still talking to me. He's been amazing actually.'

'That's good. Though it must feel incredibly strange living separately after so long.'

'It's horrible. I realise now that I took him completely for granted. Now I'd give anything to have him back, with all the habits that used to drive me up the wall included. It's awful that it takes something so drastic to make you realise what you had.'

Flo nodded. There was silence for a minute or so until Flo moved the conversation on, telling Tasha about the mind-boggling summer holidays that Mrs Perfect and her family had apparently enjoyed – abseiling in the Alps, amongst other pursuits. Tasha laughed at the thought, grateful for the distraction.

The following day Tasha was aching all over. It had been her first Pilates class in quite a few weeks, having been unable to leave the children over the holidays, and she was feeling the repercussions of her time off. Having dropped the children at school she detoured via Sainsbury's Local, making a mental list of all the items she had failed to buy in her weekly online shop. As she turned onto Havers Street she clocked Javier coming out of the house and getting on his motorbike. Deliberately slowing her pace, she pulled her mobile out of her pocket, pretending to be in the depths of an interesting conversation so he didn't try to stop and talk. He zoomed down the road, giving her a cheery wave as he zipped past her. Her heart rate had gone into overdrive. She would do anything to get away from having him so close by. It was not only painfully awkward but also a constant reminder of what she had done. She thought once again about moving to the country, remembering the house near Andrew and Becca's that they had looked at on the way back to London a few months before. It would have been one thing doing that with Charlie by her side, but quite another moving away all alone; another dream that now lay in tatters.

Having cooked a lamb stew for dinner, she opened her laptop to get some much-needed admin done. As she scrolled through her emails a message from the recruitment company caught her eye. A well-known hedge fund had been let down by a new recruit who was meant to be covering a maternity-leave position. They wanted to know whether Tasha would be interested in the job temping as a PA. The start date would be October 1st. It was worlds away from medicine, but the thought of being in the City appealed to her somehow. It would certainly be completely different.

Tasha stared blankly at the screen for several minutes, made a split-second decision and reached for the telephone to call them before she could change her mind. She explained that she was interested and before she knew it had arranged to go in for an interview the following Monday while the children were at school. Nervous anticipation fluttered in the pit of her stomach at the thought. Part of her wanted to wimp out immediately and cancel the appointment, but a larger part of her was excited about the opportunity. It could be perfect, and if she didn't like it she could just leave at the end of the maternity cover. No harm done. She probably wouldn't get the job anyway but it would be good to get the interview practice if nothing else. She tried to quell the critical voice within her that was doing its best to persuade her not to try, saying she wouldn't be able to cope. Instead she reminded herself of just how capable she was. She was a qualified doctor, for God's sake. She had always been good at multitasking and had ample experience with the administrative side of general practice.

Luckily there wasn't much time to be nervous. Charlie was in Geneva for the weekend and Tasha had decided to take the children to Surrey to stay with her parents, realising Bertie hadn't seen much of his grandchildren for a while and keen for an extra pair of hands, or two. It was lovely to enjoy the country air for a couple of days and she was able to take advantage of their babysitting services to sneak upstairs, go through her CV and mentally run through potential interview questions that might come up.

Bertie cooked up a storm all weekend, culminating in a very impressive roast beef with all the trimmings for Sunday lunch. Max slept through on Saturday night for the first time all week, which was a huge relief to Tasha, though Flora was still a bit temperamental, chatting normally to Lizzie and Bertie but monosyllabic with her mother. Tasha had been twisting herself in knots with guilt at the impact the separation was having on her children. It felt odd being at Lizzie and Bertie's house without Charlie, despite the fact she had stayed there with just the children many times before. She noticed his absence now more strongly than ever. They FaceTimed him on Saturday and Sunday evening before the children's bath time, his slightly pixelated face as handsome as ever on her iPhone's screen. She wondered which colleagues were out there with him, imagining some successful young businesswoman in a power suit flirting with him over one of the corporate dinners he would no doubt be attending later that evening. The thought of him there with a hotel room at his disposal and every reason to repay her adultery made her feel nauseous. Perhaps she was being naïve to think he hadn't already done so. He was, for all intents and purposes, single. And she had absolutely no one to blame for that but herself.

Chapter Thirty-six

Tasha's nerves were jangling furiously as she sat opposite Amanda from Human Resources at the offices of Pearson Gregory on Monday morning. She had travelled into the City on the Tube after dropping the children off at school. She had been questioned rigorously about her career to date, what skills she had that she felt would be transferable, and what her strengths and weaknesses were. Whilst it was nothing too challenging she was grateful that she'd found time to prepare over the weekend. She was happy with the way she had handled most of the questions, despite knowing she could have done better with one or two. They had discussed her salary and the hours she would be expected to work, then Amanda had left the room, returning a short while later with one of the other PAs Tasha would potentially be working with.

As the interview came to an end Amanda thanked her for coming. She explained to Tasha that they would be making their final decision by the end of the day. They were trying to move things along as quickly as possible due to the rapidly approaching start date. Tasha couldn't be sure but she thought she was in with a good chance of success. Rebecca, the PA who had joined in the interview towards the end, seemed like a friendly, competent person, and she felt they had established a good rapport.

Tasha had a spring in her step as she walked out of the rotating glass doors and onto the busy street. If they offered her the job she would have proved to herself that she was still worthy of employment. A shiver of excitement ran through her at the prospect. She would have plenty of things to think about other than the needs of her children and running the household. Yes, those would all still be there, but she would have a whole batch of new concerns to deal with on a daily basis, and it would all be so different from the norm. She told herself not to get her hopes up, just in case, though she now felt sure that if this role was not for her she would find one that was.

Tasha listened to the sound of her heels tapping against the pavement as she walked down the road to a nearby coffee shop. She was wearing one of her old work outfits, which she had been rather amazed to find still fitted her. She had weighed herself for the first time in ages that morning and the scales confirmed that she had indeed lost half a stone. It seemed even heartache had some small silver lining. It would certainly save her a lot of money if she could use all her old work clothes rather than buying a whole new wardrobe. She ordered herself a coffee and soaked in the hustle and bustle of being in central London during a busy working day. Deep in her core she knew this was just what she needed. A sense of purpose other than being a mum, a reason to leave the house, get dressed up in a smart outfit, try something new and rediscover the Tasha of pre-motherhood once again. Pulling out her mobile phone, she decided she had better call Charlie to let him know about the interview. She wasn't far from his office. The thought occurred to her that she might be able to see him and her stomach lurched at the possibility.

'Charlie?' she said as he answered the phone.

'Hi, Tasha. Everything OK?'

'Yes, yes. Fine, don't worry. Are you free? I'm actually near Bank.'

'Bank? What are you doing there?'

'I just went for an interview. It was all a bit last minute. Can you meet for a coffee?'

'I'm about to go into a meeting. What was the interview?'

'It was with Pearson Gregory.'

'The hedge fund?'

'Exactly.'

'Really? What for?' She could hear the surprise in his voice.

'A maternity cover has fallen through and they're looking for a replacement. I would be a PA.'

'A PA? That's quite different from a GP! Are you sure you'd like it?'

'Not really. Maybe. It might be worth a try.'

'I didn't actually know you were looking. I mean, you did mention it a while ago, but...'

'I know. I met with a recruitment agency in August. They sent me the job specification and something about it felt right. I've no idea if I'll get the job but I think it might be good for me. I wanted to speak to you about it either way.'

'To me?'

'To make sure you are OK with it?'

'Right. Well, when would it start?'

'Really soon. The first of October.'

'OK. What would we do about the children?' Even the use of the word 'we' was music to her ears.

'I'm going to look into childcare options now.'

'To do school drop off and pickup?'

'Yup, that's all I'd need.'

'Sounds good. I can ask around at the office, see what agencies my colleagues have used?'

'That'd be great. I'll put my feelers out too. Though let's wait and see if I get the job first! After all this talk I'll probably find that they've said no!'

'Well, if they offer it to you I think you should go for it, if that's what you want. If you don't like it, you can always leave.'

'Thanks, Charlie. I appreciate the support.'

'Right, I've got to go. Let me know what they say.' He ended the call all too abruptly. He had been unexpectedly supportive. It made her question why she always doubted him.

*

Later that evening her telephone rang. She ran into the kitchen to escape the racket the children were making before accepting the call.

'Is that Natasha speaking?'

'It is,' Tasha said.

'Oh, good evening. It's Alice calling from Time Recruitment.'

'Hi, Alice.' Tasha caught her breath.

'I've just had a telephone call from Amanda at Pearson Gregory, and I am delighted to inform you that they would like to offer you the job!'

'Oh, that's wonderful!' Tasha sighed as relief coursed through her, coupled with a bubbling of excitement that she hadn't felt for a long time. This was really happening!

'They need to know as soon as possible whether you are in a position to accept.'

Tasha told her that she would be delighted to accept, and Alice explained the next steps, leading up to a start date of October 1st. Having hung up the phone, Tasha called Charlie, leaving a voicemail with the news that she was soon to be gainfully employed, and explaining that she would start looking into childcare as soon as possible. She sent out a message to various local groups of friends and fellow mums, explaining that she was on the lookout for wrap-around childcare starting from October.

The following evening, having made several phone calls to follow up various leads in response to her cry for help, she arranged to interview a friend of a friend's daughter. She was called Emily and she was a student at University College London. All her lectures were late morning and she was looking for tutoring or similar work to earn some extra cash. Tasha spoke to Emily on the phone and decided that she sounded ideal. On Wednesday evening Emily came over to the house for her interview. Charlie had arrived earlier, in time for the children's bath time, making the most of being at the house on a weekday. He had insisted on a joint interview, not wanting to be left out of the decision-making process.

Both Charlie and Tasha warmed to her immediately, deciding then and there that she would be a perfect fit. She was bubbly, intelligent and seemed full of common sense, asking all the right questions. They agreed an hourly rate and went through exactly what would be expected of her. It was all happening so quickly but it felt as if it was falling into place exactly as it was meant to.

*

'Bloody hell!' Rosie exclaimed as Tasha informed her that she was going back to work. 'Good for you!'

'I know!' Tasha could hardly believe it herself. 'I'm so excited. I've just been going through my wardrobe salvaging all the long-lost outfits from the back of the cupboard. I'm terrified, don't get me wrong. But it feels like the right time.'

'How awesome that you'll be in the City, too. Do you think we'll be able to go for lunches?'

'Hopefully. Unless I'm so busy I only have time to eat a sandwich at my desk. I guess it all depends on my boss, Katherine. I hope she's normal.'

'Fingers crossed. Perhaps I can get you a PA job here at the paper if not?'

'God, now you're talking. Wouldn't that be fun? I've suddenly realised there's a whole world of different industries out there I'd like to explore.'

'Endless opportunities!'

'How's Josh?'

'He's great, thanks! He loved meeting you. He thinks you're amazing.'

'I'm glad to hear it. That was a lovely weekend.'

'When is your next weekend off? You are always welcome to stay, you know.'

'Thanks, Rosie. You are a legend. Charlie's got them this weekend, but they've begged to stay at his flat. He's picking up a camp bed for Max on Friday. Apparently the two girls are going to share his bed and he's going on the sofa.'

'Sounds squashed!'

'It's Bella's birthday on Sunday and her one request is that we all spend it together.'

'Is that going to be OK?'

'I hope so. We're going to Harry Potter World. The tickets have been booked for months. It'll be nice to spend the day as a family, for once.'

'Do you think Charlie will be all right with it?'

'He's usually pretty good at putting on an appearance of normality in front of the kids. Perhaps he'll realise just how much he misses me and come home.'

'I hope that's exactly what happens.'

'Wishful thinking.'

'You never know. There's no way he doesn't miss you. He just needs to let the Javier thing go.'

'Hmmm. That's the problem. He's never going to forgive me for that.'

'Never say never.'

'I know him.'

'There's always hope,' Rosie reminded her before making her apologies and ending the call. She was running behind on a deadline for an article on psychic matchmaking; apparently it was the latest trend. Her blog was doing better than ever having taken its new turn and her paper had even jumped on the bandwagon, commissioning articles off the back of blog posts. It seemed likely that she would never have to write her singles column again, which was lucky given how well things were going with Josh.

*

As always it felt strange waking up to an empty house on Saturday. Tasha spent the day catching up on laundry, changing the sheets, tidying and sorting through the endless piles of clutter that always seemed to accumulate no matter how much she tried to whisk things into their rightful place during the course of the week. She got sidetracked from her task mid-afternoon, finding herself knee-deep in a pile of photo albums. She had always been efficient at making albums, originally sticking photographs in by hand and lately creating big photobooks online. She poured through them, pausing at particularly fond memories of the children, of her and Charlie. Her eyes filled with tears of happiness swiftly followed by tears of heartache. Tearing herself away, she set about baking Bella's birthday cake. She tried not to think about the fact that, for the first time, her little girl would wake up on her birthday without her mother.

The next morning, she met Charlie and the children outside the entrance to Harry Potter World.

'Happy birthday, darling!' she cried as Bella ran over and jumped into her arms. Tasha laughed and spun her around. 'Has it been a good one so far?'

'Amazing, thanks!'

'Hi, Mum.' Flora hugged her, closely followed by Max. Tasha tried not to show her surprise at this show of affection from her eldest daughter. Perhaps she was slowly coming to terms with the separation? Or maybe she had decided to stop blaming her mother quite as much? Tasha wondered whether Charlie had said something to her the night before.

'Dad cooked us pancakes for a birthday breakfast!' Max announced.

'Sounds yummy!' Tasha smiled at Charlie. He was wearing a chunky-knit navy jumper that she had given him a few years ago. Dark stubble shadowed his jaw; he obviously hadn't shaved since Friday. His bright blue eyes crinkled as he smiled at her. Only she would notice that it wasn't a truly happy smile, see the shadows under his eyes and know how rare it was for him to have troubled sleep. The photographs she had been looking at flicked through her mind like a slideshow, all the wonderful memories they had shared. She wished she could show them to him.

'Right, who is ready to go in?' he asked.

The children responded with a chorus of 'Me!' as Tasha produced the tickets from her handbag. They filed in through the gate. Bella was in seventh heaven as they visited the magical sets, admired the props and costumes, and learnt about some of the special effects that had been used in the *Harry Potter* films.

Later that afternoon they arrived back at Havers

Street with arms full of *Harry Potter* merchandise from the gift shop. Bella was amazed at the incredible cake Tasha had baked. It was a beautifully iced golden snitch, complete with rice-paper wings and a sprinkling of edible gold dust.

'Mum, you are so clever!' Flora announced, no sarcasm detectable. It seemed she was still on her best behaviour. Tasha was beginning to suspect that it might have something to do with Charlie's presence.

'You do make the *best* cakes,' Max agreed.

'We are so lucky to have you,' Bella declared.

Charlie nodded. Feeling awkward, Tasha declared it was time for Bella to cut the cake. She opened her presents and they watched as she jumped around the room in excitement with the revelation of each new gift. There was nothing quite like watching your children's sheer joy as they celebrated each birthday and Christmas. Tasha reminded herself to treasure each second. There would be a time when such innocent abandon was a thing of the past.

'Daddy, please will you stay for bath time and bedtime?' Bella asked. 'I want a birthday story.'

Charlie agreed and, after their bath, he sat on the bed with the children piled around him. Tasha, at the birthday girl's request, sat on the end of the bed too. He told them a wonderful story about a beautiful princess called Bella whose parents, the king and queen, threw her a magnificent birthday ball. The story had the desired effect as the children's eyes began to close; they were exhausted from their busy day. Soon enough they were all tucked up in bed, dreaming of Harry Potter.

'Do you want to stay for some dinner?' Tasha offered as they went downstairs.

'No, it's all right. I'll find something,' Charlie said. He was hovering awkwardly in the hall, his hands thrust into the pockets of his jeans.

'Seriously, it's no bother. I've got some left-over lasagne in the fridge.'

Charlie looked as though he was contemplating his options. 'Actually, a quick bite would be great,' he said. 'Thanks.'

Tasha's heart soared as she went into the kitchen. She told herself not to get her hopes up. It had been a long and exhausting day, and he probably just wanted an easy dinner, rather than her company. They sat at the kitchen table, drinking red wine and eating lasagne, laughing at the children's antics earlier in the day.

'I was looking through some old albums yesterday,' Tasha said. 'Do you remember that holiday we had in Mykonos?' she asked.

'Of course I do.'

'That old taverna overlooking the sea?'

'God, that was amazing, wasn't it?'

They looked at each other, each one lost in their memories.

'Right,' Charlie said, standing up and taking their

plates over to the dishwasher. 'I'd better get going. I've got an early start tomorrow.'

A wave of disappointment settled over Tasha.

'Thanks for the lasagne, it was really good. And for making such an effort with the cake. You always do. It must have taken you ages.'

'It's nothing.'

'You're a great mum.' He smiled at her and, as she held his gaze, she felt the air tighten with tension.

'I miss you,' she said.

'I miss you too,' Charlie said as he took a step towards her. His eyes shone with love and sorrow. She wished she could do something to take the hurt she had caused away. He tucked a strand of stray hair behind her ear and traced his fingers gently down her cheek. Her stomach flipped at his touch. She reached out and took his hand, holding his fingers softly in hers. It had been so long since they had had any physical contact, just that one hug. She didn't want it to stop. A thousand unspoken words passed between them.

Tasha took a step closer. Slowly, she brushed her lips against his. He was still for a moment. She thought he might recoil and push her away, but then he closed his eyes. As if overwhelmed with longing he pulled her firmly towards him and kissed her. It was as if they had never kissed before. The familiarity was still there but there was a renewed passion, a new urgency that had not existed between them since the early days of their relationship. He kissed her hungrily, as if making up for every lost second of their separation. Unwilling to risk being seen, they went up to their room, locking the door behind them. Safe in the knowledge they could not be interrupted they made love with an almost desperate intensity. Tears rolled down Tasha's cheeks as he kissed her over and over again.

Afterwards she lay in his arms, listening to the sound of his heartbeat as their breathing returned to normal. She ran her fingers through the dark hair on his chest and breathed in the dizzying smell of his aftershave. It felt incredible to be back in his arms. She would do anything to stay trapped in that moment for the rest of time.

'I'd better go,' Charlie said, the words slicing through her like a knife.

'Really?' Tasha asked, completely thrown. 'But—'

'I'm sorry, Tasha. That probably shouldn't have happened...'

'It was wonderful. I thought—'

'I know. And it was. But it doesn't fix anything.'

He didn't need to explain himself. They had talked about it so many times already. She sat up and stared at the floor, unable to watch him dress. All too quickly he was fully clothed. The intimacy that they had shared well and truly broken.

He looked at her awkwardly and cleared his throat loudly. 'I'll see myself out,' he said. She nodded. As the door shut behind her she lay back on the bed, still warm from where their bodies had lain intertwined mere moments before. She stared blankly at the ceiling, tears burning in her eyes. She could scream with frustration. Trust was such a precious thing: so fragile and delicate. Once broken, it was almost impossible to repair. Charlie's trust should have been her most treasured possession, but she had recklessly thrown it away.

Chapter Thirty-seven

'Tasha!' Becca cried as she enveloped her in a warm hug. 'It's *so* good to see you.'

'And you,' Tasha replied, holding her sister-in-law close before ushering her inside the house.

'I've been so worried about you,' Becca said as she followed Tasha into the kitchen. She pulled a big box of salted caramel chocolates out of her bag and gave them to Tasha. 'You look like you need fattening up!'

'Oh, thank you! You didn't have to do that!' Tasha turned to face her. 'I'm so sorry I haven't seen you. I just needed some time...' She tailed off, not knowing what to say. She had put off meeting up with Becca so far, making excuses when Becca had offered to drive straight up to London and see her. She was so close to both Tasha and Charlie that Tasha knew she had to make sure she was feeling strong enough to face her. She was terrified of blurting out the truth, but she had promised Charlie she wouldn't and she knew she needed to do everything in her power to keep the last fragile shreds of trust between them from dissipating altogether. She could do nothing else to go back on her word.

'It's OK. This is all so sudden, it must be taking a

while to get your head around,' Becca said. 'It is sudden, isn't it?' she added, clearly wondering whether there had been some deeply buried trouble between Tasha and Charlie that they had somehow expertly disguised.

'Yes. It is quite, I suppose.' Tasha was determined to be as vague as possible. She poured them cups of freshly brewed coffee.

'I know you both said you don't want to discuss it but we are desperate to know what's happened so we can help you fix things...'

'I know you are. I'm sorry, it must seem really strange, but we just need some time to figure things out, that's all.'

'Do you think he'll come back?'

'I hope so. I really don't know.' Tasha felt her eyes well up with tears. Becca's face shadowed with concern and she reached out and squeezed Tasha's hand.

'Oh, Tash.'

'I'm sorry.' Tasha tried to plaster a smile on her face.

'Stop apologising. You haven't done anything wrong.' She seemed so sure of it, just like the others. It amazed Tasha how everyone assumed she was so innocent.

'But I have,' Tasha whispered. 'It's not just Charlie's fault.'

'Has he had an affair?'

Tasha shook her head. 'No, I promise.' She almost wanted Becca to ask the same question about her, daring her to tell the truth. But she didn't.

'OK. So, it's something else...' She didn't seem as if she was going to drop the subject.

'I know it's really hard, that you want to hear everything so that you can help us through this. And I would want to do the same if it were you and Andrew, but we've agreed that we just want to keep our problems between the two of us, for the children's sake. We really think it's for the best.' Becca nodded. 'Obviously all I want to do is tell you every last detail and get your advice,' Tasha continued, 'but I can't.'

'I understand. I'm sorry I've asked you so many questions. I suppose it just seems to us that there *must* be a solution. You are such a perfect couple, so completely meant to be. We seem to be having a hard time coming to terms with it, so God knows how you two must be feeling.'

'It is really hard,' Tasha admitted. 'But at least I've got something new to focus on now: I am going back to work next week.' She hoped this would be a satisfactory change of subject.

'What? That's exciting! When did this happen?'

'Last week, it's all come out of nowhere.'

'What will you be doing?' Becca asked, intrigued.

'It's a maternity cover as a PA at a hedge fund called Pearson Gregory. Completely random, I know, and the polar opposite of being a GP, but I just wanted to try something new.'

'That sounds interesting. And it'll definitely be completely different!'

'Exactly. I'm so glad I'll have something else to think about other than Charlie.'

'It'll probably do you the world of good.'

'I think it will. At least I hope so.'

'Are you nervous?'

'I'm terrified. I have to stop myself from calling them and saying it's all been a huge mistake.'

'Well, I'm proud of you, Tash.' Becca smiled. 'You are amazing, and I'm sure it'll be easier than you think once you've actually started. The thought is probably much more daunting than the reality.'

'I hope so.'

'What will you do with the kids?'

'We interviewed someone called Emily last week. She seems perfect. She'll do before and after school and then I'll take over as soon as I get back home.'

'That sounds good.'

'She met the children yesterday. She came with me to the school to pick them up and stayed for tea and homework so she could see the whole routine.'

'And what did the children think of her?'

'They seemed to like her. They like all their babysitters. Anyone but their own mother!'

'That's not true!'

'I know. Though it can feel like it at times, especially with Max and Flora.'

'Were they on their best behaviour?'

'I had hoped they would be. The girls were all right but Max was at his petulant best, refusing to do his homework or eat his dinner. It took me all my powers of persuasion not to end up with Max in full-scale tantrum mode.'

'Oh dear!'

'Luckily, Emily didn't seem too bothered.'

'That's definitely a good sign.'

'She'll need to be strict if she's going to get their homework done every night!'

'What do the children think about you going back to work?'

'Bella and Max haven't really said much. Flora has been more inquisitive, wanting to understand what I am doing, and how it's going to affect her. I feel bad that it's yet another change for them all.'

'They'll get used to it.'

'I feel like I've been saying that a lot recently. They're still getting used to Charlie being away.'

'It's true, though. They are adaptable little things.'

'Speaking of getting used to people being away, when is Andrew going back to Iraq?'

'Next month,' Becca said.

'And how are you feeling about it?'

'I'm trying not to think about it too much. It has come around so quickly. I feel like he's only just come back and now he'll be off again.'

'God, you poor thing. I really mustn't complain about my situation. At least Charlie isn't in danger.'

'It is what it is.' Becca smiled. She was so strong. 'And he does love it,' she added.

'He does, doesn't he?'

'The good news is he has got a few days' leave over Christmas – we found out yesterday.'

'That's brilliant! The children will be over the moon.'

'It's just not the same trying to celebrate when he isn't around.'

'I'm so glad you'll all be together. Maybe you can get on the case for baby number three?'

'I'm not sure I'd be up for that quite yet. Imagine having morning sickness with Andrew away!'

'God! You are right. Definitely not a good idea!'

'It's going to be weird having Charlie and the children without you this weekend,' Becca said. 'Do you think we should cancel?'

'Not at all. Charlie wants to see Andrew before he goes off again, and there's no point in the whole weekend being disrupted because of us.'

'Are you sure?'

'Absolutely. It's been in the diary for ages and the kids are really looking forward to it. Flora and Bella are so excited about their girls' dorm with Daisy!'

'I don't want you to feel too left out though.'

'I have to get used to it,' Tasha said. She was taking a leaf out of Becca's book and trying to be stoic. It made sense for Charlie to go, she knew that he wanted to spend time with his brother while he had the chance. Hard as it might be for her knowing that they were all having a lovely time without her, she had made her bed, and now she had to lie in it.

Later, when Tasha had waved Becca off, she decided to make a run for the shops. She had a list as long as her arm of bits and bobs for the children and she needed to buy a new pair of work shoes too. Her start date was approaching rapidly and she felt quite nauseous with anticipation.

Just as she was browsing the shoes in M&S Tasha's mobile phone rang. She was surprised to see that it was the school calling, and even more surprised to hear Mrs Hemmingway's voice echo down the line.

'Good afternoon, Mrs Hargreaves,' she said. 'I was wondering if you might be able to pop in this afternoon before you pick up the children? Say two forty-five? Nothing to worry about, there's just something I'd like to talk over with you.'

Tasha agreed to meet only to spend the rest of the afternoon worrying about what Mrs Hemmingway might want to discuss.

When the time came for their meeting, Tasha was shown into Mrs Hemmingway's office by the school secretary. She beckoned Tasha to sit down, smiling kindly at her over the top of a pair of reading glasses perched on the bridge of her nose. Her grey hair curled softly onto the collar of her lavender floral blouse.

After a few minutes' small talk Mrs Hemmingway explained the reason for their meeting. 'Flora has told her teacher that she thinks the separation might be her fault.'

'Oh,' Tasha said, slightly surprised. 'I see.'

'Has this come up at all at home?'

'To be honest, no. Max had mentioned something similar to my mother but other than that...' Tasha shook her head. 'Flora has actually been quite tricky with me, a bit temperamental and angry. She told me she thought it was all *my* fault... She never mentioned she thought she might be to blame.'

'It's perfectly normal to see a difference in behaviour between home and school,' Mrs Hemmingway said, passing Tasha the box of tissues as she failed miserably to maintain her composure.

Tasha nodded, sniffing inelegantly.

'They often don't want to rock the boat,' Mrs Hemmingway continued. She suggested various strategies that Tasha and Charlie might consider using at home to encourage Flora to open up, assuring Tasha that they would continue to keep a watchful eye on all three children during this 'challenging time', as she put it.

That evening Tasha phoned Charlie to talk things through with him.

'Right. I see,' he said. 'What can I do?'

'I think you should probably try and get her to talk to you this weekend. Perhaps you could leave Max and Bella with Becca and Andrew and go for a walk just you and Flora?' Tasha suggested.

'That's a good idea. Poor Flora. It's typical of her to blame herself.'

'I feel awful. I'm the one to blame.'

'I'm not entirely innocent either,' Charlie said. 'You clearly weren't happy and that was largely down to me.'

Tasha was pleased to hear him acknowledge the part he had played in their relationship breakdown.

'The important thing is that we are there for Flora,' he said. 'I'll let you know how I get on. Keep me posted on anything else that comes up, if she talks to you between now and then.'

'I will,' she promised.

Later that evening Tasha brought the subject up. She was lying on the bed next to Flora, Flora's head resting on her shoulder. Tasha stroked her hair as she spoke. 'Darling, Mrs Hemmingway mentioned that you might be feeling a bit to blame for Daddy and me not living together any more. Is that true?'

Flora looked up at her; tears glazed her eyes. 'I do sometimes feel like that,' she admitted.

'I know, it's really hard for you to understand. I am so sorry that you feel confused by the whole situation, darling. I wish there was a way of helping you understand better, but I promise it really hasn't got anything to do with you, or Max or Bella. It is definitely no one's fault, especially not yours.' Tasha explained the separation again, without going into detail.

'I just don't believe you, Mum. You can't be happier without Dad. None of us are.'

Tasha felt slightly lost for words. Pretending that she thought it was the best thing for them all was such a lie that she wondered whether Flora could sense her dishonesty. It wasn't the best thing for herself or Charlie, Tasha was convinced of that, but she knew there was nothing else to say. She had to stick to the story no matter how much she wished it weren't the case.

'I just wish things could go back to how they were before,' Flora said. 'I wish we could be a normal family again.'

'I know, darling. I'm sorry.' Tasha hugged her and kissed her pale forehead. She tucked her into bed and listened as Flora read her a few pages of her book. 'Sweet dreams,' she said as she closed the door behind her.

She texted Charlie to tell him about their chat and he replied.

> Thanks for letting me know.

Later as she lay in bed she replayed what had happened on Sunday night over and over in her mind, trying to work out what Charlie had been thinking, what his motivation had been and what he might be thinking now. In a way she wished it had never happened. She felt more acutely aware than ever now of just how much she missed him. She tried to imagine a time where she would be ready for a new relationship, should Charlie never come back, and she knew it was impossible. She couldn't even contemplate it. No one would ever live up to him. No one could even come close.

Chapter Thirty-eight

'So, how's it all going?' Rosie asked after having placed their orders with the waitress at their chosen brunch place.

'We slept together,' Tasha confessed.

'*What?*' Rosie squealed.

'I know.'

'This is huge! When? How?'

'It was completely out of the blue. Last Sunday, we spent the whole day together for Bella's birthday. He stayed for dinner and the next thing I knew we were having sex. Then he left, just like that.'

'Oh, Tasha…'

'I shouldn't have got my hopes up. But it was so amazing. I just feel worse than ever now.'

'Well, I think it's a good sign. It shows that he is still irresistibly attracted to you, otherwise he wouldn't have done it.'

'Maybe. Or maybe it had just been a while and he was desperate for a quick shag?'

'Tasha! You know that's not true!'

'It could be. Though I agree I think there was probably more to it than that. One thing is for sure, nothing about this situation is straightforward. I feel like I'm treading on eggshells most of the time. I'm so conscious of trying not to make things worse in the desperate hope he'll somehow come back to me.'

'Has he said anything about the future?'

'Not a word. Except that nothing has changed. He still doesn't trust me enough to be with me like that.'

'I wish there was something we could think of that would prove you wouldn't do it again.'

'Me too,' Tasha sighed. She decided to change the subject. 'How's Josh?'

'He's great, thanks.'

'Any news?'

'A bit... we talked about moving in together yesterday.'

'That's amazing! What did you say?'

'Nothing in particular, just a vague discussion about whether it might happen some time in the future.'

'And?'

'We both want to. So I guess it may happen sooner rather than later!'

'That's so exciting!'

'I know. The very first time I would let someone into my flat.'

'Would it be your flat?'

'Actually I don't know. He has an awesome place too. I suppose we'd have to draw straws!'

They were interrupted by the arrival of two

cappuccinos, complete with heart-shaped dustings of chocolate. 'How are the children?' Rosie asked.

'Bella and Max are both doing well, Flora not so much. The headteacher called me in last week. Apparently she has told her teacher that she's worried me and Charlie separating is her fault.'

'Oh, poor little thing.' Rosie's beautifully groomed brow furrowed with concern.

'Charlie is going to have a talk with her this weekend. We've had a chat too. I think we just need to keep reassuring her that it is nothing to do with her, and hopefully sooner or later she'll accept it.'

The waitress brought over their smashed avocado and poached eggs, accompanied by rounds of sourdough toast. They were going to the National Gallery afterwards so they needed some energy. To stop herself from feeling miserable without the children Tasha had drawn up some touristy things she'd like to tick off her list, things she had always wanted to do but never quite got around to. She wanted to make the most of her newly acquired free time, and she hadn't been to the National Gallery for years and years. Of course, she had done lots of galleries, museums and landmarks with the children, but it was completely different taking three small people along for the ride. Without them, she and Rosie wandered around at their own pace, uninterrupted. Tasha relished the peace and quiet.

Before she knew it, it was Monday morning and the

first day of her new job. Dawn unveiled a bright, clear day as Tasha sipped her coffee in the garden. She had barely slept. The nerves had really set in and her mind had whirred all night, dreaming about her return to the world of work.

Emily came over at the agreed time of 8 a.m. and Tasha ran through her instructions for one final time. She had risen earlier than usual to shower and dress before rousing the children, giving them breakfast and beginning the process of getting them ready for school, to be completed by Emily. Closing the door on the noise and chaos behind her, having wished Emily the best of luck, she took a deep breath in and tried to quell the nervous butterflies that were fluttering wildly inside her. She glanced at Javier's front door. The lights were on; he had probably just got home from a night shift. Focussing straight ahead, she walked briskly towards the Tube, her stomach churning.

It felt unbelievably strange to be one of the many commuters surging down the steps and onto the platform once again. There was a buzzing energy that felt almost palpable, the cumulation of so many people with a shared sense of purpose. She stood in the crowded carriage and read the paper as the train took her into the City. Emerging into the outside world once again, she walked to the offices of Pearson Gregory. Gathering her strength, she took a deep breath and pushed through the glass doors, heading for the reception desk to introduce herself.

There was so much to take in, from the telephone system to the computers, the photocopier to the coffee machine. She was grateful to Deborah, the PA she was replacing, who, despite being the exhausted owner of an eye-wateringly large bump, did an excellent job of showing her the ropes.

'So, what's Katherine like to work for?' Tasha asked.

'She is actually very reasonable, in comparison with some people I've worked for,' Deborah replied. This was music to Tasha's ears. 'So long as you're efficient, and an excellent multitasker, you should be fine.'

'Great!' Tasha smiled. She felt slightly out of her depth and way outside her comfort zone yet at the same time she felt a renewed sense of energy and purpose. It was completely different from her previous job, yet she found this new world strangely appealing. She knew that in a matter of time all the new information she was struggling to absorb would become second nature. She just had to get through the first few weeks without collapsing into tears, then she would be fine. She tried her best to maintain an exterior of calm competence, even as she scribbled notes all over the comprehensive handover file Deborah had prepared for her. 'Fake it till you make it' was the phrase that kept popping into her mind.

When five o'clock finally arrived, Tasha joined the throng of commuters heading away from the City. She felt thoroughly worn out. Her feet ached in her heels and her head spun with information.

'So how did it go?' Chloe asked.

Tasha had called her as soon as she came above ground from the Tube, desperate to talk to someone about her first day. 'All in all, I'd say it could have gone a lot worse. I think I bluffed it well enough.'

'That's brilliant. Well done! Are you exhausted?'

'Absolutely shattered.'

'Did it feel weird not being with the kids?'

'Not too bad. I can't wait to see them now though.'

'Good for you, sis,' Chloe said. 'I'm proud of you. What's your boss like? Did you meet her?'

'Yup, I met her this afternoon. She actually seems nice. Quite normal. She's got kids of her own so hopefully she'll be reasonable if there are any childcare issues.'

'That's a relief.' They talked as she walked, discussing Ella's recent email home and Chloe's new cohort of geography students.

Tasha hung up the phone as she turned the key in the lock at precisely 5.45 p.m. She was relieved to hear the sound of happy chatter coming from the kitchen. Emily seemed to be running a military operation. Neatly completed homework was laid out in three piles on top of the children's bookbags along with reading diaries open at the correct page so that Tasha could check the comments. The children were eating pasta and pesto with peas for their dinner.

'Wow!' Tasha exclaimed, as she surveyed the scene. 'It looks like you've had a good afternoon,' she said, a note of question in her voice aimed towards Emily.

'It's been fine, thanks! I think!' Emily laughed. She did seem a touch frazzled.

'The pasta bag spilled all over the floor,' Max informed her.

'We decided to cook it anyway because Emily said the germs would be killed in the hot water,' Bella said.

'Sorry,' Emily apologised, wincing slightly. 'I hope that's OK with you.'

'Of course!' Tasha smiled. 'It's good for the immune system.'

'We were learning about germs in science today,' Flora said. 'Did you know there are over ten thousand types of bacteria?'

'And I got my finger trapped in the loo door at the end of PE.' Max showed her his bandaged index finger with pride.

'Mrs Nicholson said I've got to practise the recorder more, Mum,' Bella added.

'We've got to do an assembly on Friday on evacuees,' Flora continued.

They were all so keen to fill her in on their day, Tasha couldn't help but laugh.

'One at a time!' she begged. 'I can't concentrate if you all talk at once!'

'Right, I think I'll head off now if that's OK?' Emily asked, no doubt desperate to make her escape.

'Absolutely. Thank you so much,' Tasha said. 'You are an absolute superstar. I mean it. See you tomorrow. Say goodbye,' she instructed Max, Bella and Flora.

'Bye, Emily,' they chorused as she picked up her bag and gave them a cheery wave.

'And thank you,' Tasha said.

'Thank you!' they chanted.

'See you in the morning!' Emily called as she walked out.

Tasha turned her attention back to the children for a full debrief. She didn't have another moment to herself until about eight o'clock, when all the children were finally settled. Comatose with exhaustion, she sat on the sofa with a bowl of soup. Emily hadn't cooked enough pasta for her to have leftovers and she had no energy whatsoever to come up with anything more ambitious than tipping a tin of Heinz tomato soup into a pan. She flicked on the television and settled back to watch the *Great British Bake Off*.

Halfway through the programme Charlie rang. As always when she saw his caller ID her heart leapt into her throat as if it were the first time he had ever called her.

'How was it?' he asked.

'Exhausting but good,' she said. 'I just hope I didn't make any cock-ups. There's a lot to learn.'

'I bet. And were things OK with Emily?'

'She seems amazingly competent. I think it's going to work out really well with her.'

'Great! Sorry I didn't get a chance to talk to you last night.' When he had dropped the children off Tasha had hoped that he'd be able to stay and tell her about his talk with Flora but he had had to rush off.

'No problem,' she said. She wanted to ask where he had been in such a hurry to get to on a Sunday evening but didn't quite have the nerve. What if he said something she didn't want to hear?

'Did you have a good weekend?'

'It was great. Nice to see Andrew before he goes.'

'And did you manage to have a chat with Flora?'

'Yes. I did as you suggested and we went for a walk, just the two of us.'

'Good, I bet she loved that. So how did she seem?'

'I think she is OK. But she is definitely anxious.'

'I did some more research over the weekend. Apparently it's a very common reaction for children to blame themselves. It seems we are doing the right thing. Consistency and continuous reassurance is crucial.' There was a clatter in the background. 'Is everything OK?' she asked, wondering what the noise could have been.

Charlie cleared his throat. 'What? Oh, yes, something... fell over. It's nothing.'

'Are you at home?'

'Yes. Look, Tasha, I've actually got to go… I'll call the children tomorrow, OK?'

'Oh, right. OK.'

Within seconds Charlie had hung up the phone. A feeling of discomfort spread throughout Tasha's body, prickling at her skin. Had there been someone else in his flat with him? Hot tears sprung into her eyes as her imagination went into overdrive. Was he seeing someone? Was that why he'd had to rush off yesterday? She couldn't bear the thought. The idea of another woman being anywhere near him made her panic. She had been hoping that he was pining after her, taking his time to process what had happened, working towards coming back to her. But what if she was completely wrong? What if he had been preparing himself, not to give their relationship another chance, but to start a new one? What if he had meant what he said? The trust was gone… Why would he stop himself meeting someone else? God knew he was eligible enough to be snapped up. Tasha knew more than anyone just how lucky any woman would be to have him.

Dread and nausea churned in her stomach as her mind stormed with thoughts. She tried to calm them by reasoning that she had no proof whatsoever that this was the case. It could have been a precariously balanced pan on the sink, and nothing more. Or a friend who had come over for dinner. Besides, she had given up her right to be privy to the goings-on in his life the moment she had broken their wedding vows. She had to let it go.

'What can I do to get him back?' she asked Rosie, half an hour later. She had lost the battle to remain calm, deciding to call Rosie to seek her advice instead. 'I can't risk him meeting someone new, Rosie. I just can't bear it.'

'I know. That would be unbelievably shit. But don't worry. We'll think of something...'

'But what?' Tasha was panicking. 'The more pressure I put on him, the further he is going to withdraw. I need to persuade him somehow that I am still the one, that even though I fucked up massively I am worth coming back to. But how? When *I* don't even believe that it is true.'

'Come on, Tasha. You have to believe it!'

'But I'm honestly not sure that I do. Maybe he would be better off with someone else.'

'You can't possibly think that. You are the mother of his children. There is nowhere better for him to be than with you.'

'I feel like it's all slipping away. Or that it already has... that I'm too late. I should never have let him leave in the first place.'

'You couldn't have stopped him. It was his decision to separate, remember?'

Tasha sighed. 'I feel as though I'm trapped in a nightmare.'

'We'll get you through this,' Rosie said. 'I promise.'

'So, what shall I do?'

Rosie was quiet for a moment or two. 'You know, the *best* thing you can do, as far as I can see, is work on being happy yourself. Take care of yourself, embrace your new job, your new life away from the family home. Work on fixing all the problems that brought you here in the first place. Try to make yourself as happy as you can possibly be. When Charlie sees the change, he might be drawn back to the Tasha he first met and fell in love with all those years ago.'

She nodded her head. 'I guess so,' she said. Rosie's advice rang in her ears as she tidied up the kitchen and laid out the breakfast things ready for the following morning. She was right. What other choice did she have? But for now, it was about all she could manage to climb up the stairs, check on the children, and crawl into bed. She would get on with being the best version of herself in the morning.

Chapter Thirty-nine

Tasha's phone vibrated in her pocket just as she was doing her best to arrange a complicated conference call across multiple time zones. Her heart sank as she saw the caller had been the children's school. Not wishing to be seen using her mobile phone at her desk, she scurried out to the ladies and listened to the message. Sure enough, Mrs Hemmingway's kindly voice echoed down the receiver. She was being summoned. Again. Only this time, it wasn't Flora Mrs Hemmingway was concerned about. It was Max.

She called the school and was put through to Mrs Hemmingway by the secretary.

'I'm afraid I can't make it in to see you this afternoon,' Tasha explained. 'I've actually gone back to work, so I'm no longer doing drop-off and pickups.'

'Ah, I see.' Mrs Hemmingway's less-than-enthusiastic reaction made her worry that she should have informed the school about this additional change in her circumstances.

'I'm sorry,' she added hastily. 'I probably should have told you. It's just that it all happened so quickly!'

'Not to worry, Mrs Hargreaves.' Tasha felt sure that,

despite this reassurance, she was being judged as an incompetent mother.

'Is Max OK? Could we possibly discuss whatever's happened over the telephone instead?' Tasha asked.

'Yes, it's not a problem. Though if we have any more incidents then we might have to have a chat in person.'

'Gosh. It all sounds rather serious. What is it that he has done exactly?'

'I'm afraid he's been acting a little... forcefully, shall we say, with his peers. He's been getting into trouble rather frequently, especially at playtimes. And today he pushed another child in the lunch queue.'

Tasha's heart sank. 'Oh dear,' she said. 'I'm so sorry. I'll talk to him when I get home.'

'It is important that Max knows we're all "singing from the same hymn sheet", so to speak,' Mrs Hemmingway continued.

'I quite understand.'

'It would be very helpful if you could have a general chat about how violence is unacceptable no matter how he is feeling inside, that taking it out on another person is never the way to deal with his emotions.'

'Of course.' Tasha felt as if she was the one being told off.

'We've suggested that he writes down any feelings and puts them in the teacher's worry box. Perhaps you could start a worry box at home too?' Tasha had no idea what a worry box was. No doubt she probably should know already.

'Absolutely,' Tasha said. 'What is a worry box, exactly?'

'Just an old tissue box or something will do. He can decorate it himself perhaps. And a notepad by the side. The idea is that when he feels upset he can write down whatever is bothering him and put it away in the worry box. That way you can read it and talk to him about it, whilst at the same time he can relax knowing that it is "off his chest", if you see what I mean? We'll see how it goes but it usually helps children who are going through... a tricky time.'

Tasha hung her head in shame. 'That sounds like a great idea. I will get onto it this weekend, when we have some time together.'

Mrs Hemmingway seemed pleased with Tasha's response to the problem, ending the call with the usual pleasantries. Tasha wanted to phone Charlie straight away but her to-do list seemed never-ending and the minutes were ticking by alarmingly quickly before her scheduled five o'clock departure. She ploughed through as many tasks as she could manage: filing, binding, printing and photocopying, all the while trying not to worry about the mental state of her children.

At a quarter to five she got stuck on the phone trying to rebook a cancelled flight for Katherine later that evening, resulting in her running late to get back to relieve Emily, who had plans of her own and had already reminded Tasha that she needed a prompt handover so as not to be late herself.

She called Emily as soon as she came up from the Tube. 'I'm so sorry. I'll be there as quickly as I can,' she said, running as fast as her heels allowed her. She turned into Havers Street and rushed towards the front door. She could see the children peering out of the window. Emily flung open the front door, coat already on, handbag over her shoulder, clearly relieved to see Tasha at long last. As Tasha crossed the road the heel of her shoe suddenly broke, her foot twisted and the ground flashed up to her face as she fell forwards onto the pavement. The contents of her handbag flung themselves all over the place.

'Bugger!' she said under her breath. 'Don't worry!' she called as Emily rushed over to help her. 'I'm OK!'

'Are you sure?' Emily asked.

'Yes, yes, I'm fine... my silly heel.' Flora, Max and Bella raced out of the front door to her aid. 'Please go,' Tasha said. 'You're late enough already.'

'I can't leave you injured!' Emily protested.

'I'm fine, honestly. I'll feel much worse if you are late. Go. It's nothing, really.' She tried not to wince as she inspected the grit that was embedded in the palms of both hands.

'Hi, darlings,' she greeted the children, who had crouched by her side.

'Are you OK, Mummy?' they asked, concern

plastered across their stricken faces.

'Absolutely. I'll be fine. Now GO!' she instructed Emily. Finally persuaded, Emily ran down the street, calling 'Thank you!' behind her as she went.

'Here, Mum, let's get you inside. Now what have you done?' Flora asked, dropping her favoured sulky-teenager attitude and taking on the mantle of responsibility that came hand-in-hand with being the eldest child.

Tasha tried to get up but her ankle was so painful she couldn't face moving just yet.

'Mum, can't you stand up?' Bella asked.

'I'll help you!' Max said, offering his shoulder for support. 'I'm really strong.'

'Thanks, darlings, I'm sure it's fine. I just need to take my time, probably.'

'You need a doctor,' Bella announced. 'Even doctors need doctors sometimes...'

'Good idea!' Flora smiled at Bella. 'Shall I get the doctor who lives opposite?' Flora asked. 'The lights are on so he must be home.'

'No, don't worry,' Tasha said. She shifted her weight, wincing. It really was painful. She probably did need some help.

'Come on, Mum. I think you need help,' Bella echoed her thoughts.

'Yes, let's get the doctor,' Max insisted.

She had to agree it wasn't a bad idea. If only it

weren't Javier though. He was the last person she wanted to rely on for help.

'OK,' she said, admitting defeat. 'Flora, why don't you go and knock on the door?'

Javier opened the door after a minute or so, quickly assessing the scene in front of him.

'Mum's hurt her foot, we think,' Flora said. 'Will you please come and help us get her inside?'

'Tasha!' Javier rushed over and knelt by her side. 'Are you OK? What happened?'

'I'm fine. I think. My heel broke and I've gone over on my ankle. It's pretty sore, it's probably just a sprain...'

'Here, let me help you,' he said, offering her his hand.

'Thank you,' she muttered as he hauled her up to sitting.

'Does this hurt?' he asked, gently examining her ankle. She nodded, wincing as her ankle throbbed in pain. He was so handsome, the classic hero rescuing her in her moment of need. She knew most women would love nothing more than to be in this position, but she couldn't feel anything other than awkward embarrassment, not to mention dread at what Charlie would think when he found out that they had had further interaction. Despite all this Tasha found herself wishing that she had shaved her legs, telling herself off immediately for caring. 'It does look like a sprain,' he said. 'We need to get some ice on it. And you'll need to rest it.'

'That's what I thought,' Tasha said. 'At least a sprain should heal relatively quickly.'

'Poor you, Mum,' the children said. There was nothing they loved more than a good injury to fuss over.

'Oh, God, this is the last thing I need,' Tasha groaned. 'I've just started a new job.'

'Oh, really? Did you apply to retrain in the end?'

'No... nothing like that. It's completely new,' Tasha continued. 'I'm temping at a hedge fund.'

'A hedge fund? That is different!'

'Tell me about it!'

'Do you like it?'

'So far...'

'Well good for you,' Javier said, helping her to her feet. 'That's fantastic.'

She tested her weight gingerly on the offending ankle. 'Ouch.' She winced.

'Here.' Javier pulled her arm around his shoulder and supported her as she hobbled towards the front door.

'Thanks,' she said. 'It's really kind of you.'

At the door Tasha turned to him, having transferred her weight onto Flora's proffered shoulder. 'We'll be fine from here. Thank you.' She smiled, communicating with her eyes just how inappropriate it would be if he came in, given the circumstances.

He nodded, signalling that he understood exactly what she meant. 'Right, kids. You need to make sure

Mummy sits down and raises her leg up high with a packet of frozen peas to stop any swelling. Doctor's orders. And you need to be very good and very helpful,' he instructed. Bella had scooped up the contents of her bag and was carrying it inside.

'Are you a real doctor?' Max asked, clearly impressed.

'I am indeed, just like your Mum, so you'd better do as I say.' Javier winked.

'That tactic doesn't always work for me, does it darling?' Tasha laughed. Max smiled and shook his head sheepishly.

'If you need anything, just give me a call,' he added, looking at Tasha. 'I hardly need to tell you this but ice, rest, elevation,' he repeated as he walked back across the street.

'Thanks!' she called after him. She hobbled into the sitting room and lowered herself onto the sofa.

'Is it really painful?' Bella asked.

'It's not too bad,' Tasha replied. 'It'll be much better with some ice on it.'

'Ta-da!' Flora arrived back into the sitting room flourishing a bag of peas. 'I found some.'

'Thank you, darling,' Tasha said. 'Max, would you be an angel and put a couple of those cushions in a pile for me, please?' Her team of young nurses soon had her resting her leg in an elevated position as Javier had instructed.

Just as she got settled her phone started to ring.

'It's Dad!' Max said excitedly, answering the call.

'Hi, Dad!' The children crowded around the screen.

'Hi, darlings!' Charlie replied.

'Guess what's happened to Mum!' Max spun the phone around to show Tasha prostrate on the sofa. The children certainly loved a bit of drama.

'Hi!' Tasha said.

'She's sprained her ankle,' Bella announced gravely.

'But it's OK. The doctor helped her,' Max informed Charlie.

'Which doctor?' Charlie asked. Tasha could immediately hear the change in his tone of voice.

'You know, the neighbour opposite,' Flora explained.

'Oh, that one!' Charlie said. 'How kind of him.' His voice was laced with sarcasm only Tasha could detect.

'Flora asked him to help. I was out on the street and couldn't get up,' Tasha explained as Max angled the screen towards her.

'I see,' Charlie said, suspicion shadowing his face, and irritation. 'Is it definitely a sprain?'

'Apparently so.'

'How can you be so sure?'

Tasha paused. 'Er... Javier examined me.'

'You needed another doctor's opinion, did you?'

There was silence. Tasha wanted the ground to open and swallow her. She felt so awkward. 'It's fine now.'

'It's not fine,' Flora said, peering closely at the ankle

in question. 'It's very swollen.'

'Poor Mum.' Bella came over and stroked her forehead before kissing her on the cheek.

'We'll look after her, don't worry, Dad,' Max said. Tasha doubted he was too worried. 'We'll be extra good at bath time and we'll go to bed without a fuss.'

'Good,' Charlie said. 'I'm glad to hear it. So, how were your days?' he asked as the three children sat on the other sofa to have their nightly catch-up.

As Tasha listened she noticed that Max didn't say anything about getting into trouble at school. She watched him closely; he seemed happy enough. Of course it was true; just because he seemed all right at home didn't necessarily mean he'd be the same at school. As the children said goodbye to Charlie she told him she'd call him later, that there was something she needed to discuss with him. He didn't exactly look thrilled at the prospect. She could tell he was still annoyed about Javier helping her.

She relied on Flora to help her up the stairs to supervise bath and bedtime, deciding to stay upstairs rather than go back down again. She hoped that by putting no strain on it at all and keeping up the ice packs the swelling might reduce in time for tomorrow. Flora brought her up a bowl of risotto, cooked by Emily, who had luckily made enough for leftovers, and she also brought in a large supply of disposable ice packs from the first-aid box.

Later, when the children were in bed and while Tasha lay propped up with pillows under her throbbing ankle, the doorbell chimed. There was no way she was going to attempt the journey downstairs to answer it. *Maybe it was Charlie coming to make sure she was OK?* But if it was he would just let himself in with his key. A minute or so later her phone bleeped with a text message.

> Hope your ankle is OK and you are resting. I've left an old crutch by your front door, I broke my foot a few years ago in a bike accident. Try to keep the weight off it for the next couple of days. Hope you are all right? Javier x

How kind of him, she thought. She might have royally screwed up her marriage because of him but she could still see why he had been so irresistible to her. He was such an alluring mixture of mystery, confidence and charm. She typed a reply:

> Can't make it to the door but thank you. I really appreciate it. Tasha

She hesitated about whether to reciprocate the kiss, knowing how Charlie would feel if he could see it. She pressed send then deleted both messages, just in case they could somehow come back to haunt her at a later stage. After last time, it just wasn't worth the risk.

She decided to call Charlie. She would tell him about the crutch, knowing there was no point in concealing the truth from him with three extremely informative children around.

'Are you angry?' she asked.

'What do you think?'

'I'm sorry. It was just that he happened to be there.'

'Of course, I don't like the idea of that man being anywhere near you, or my house, or my children. You can hardly blame me!'

'Of course not.'

'I don't want you to give him the time of day.'

There was silence.

'You wanted to talk?' Charlie asked, his voice clipped.

'Yes. I got a phone call from Mrs Hemmingway again today asking me to come in.'

'Flora again?' His voice immediately softening with the change of subject.

'No. It was Max this time.'

'Oh. Why, what's happened?'

'Apparently he's been acting up, being too rough with the other children.'

'Have you spoken to him?' Charlie asked, sounding concerned.

'School has. I said we would too. I didn't get a chance this evening, but I thought maybe this weekend we could?'

'I'll definitely talk to him,' Charlie said. He was very strict about violence and Tasha knew that he would take it seriously. She explained about the worry box and told Charlie she'd make it with Max on Saturday morning, ready to take to Charlie's flat when he picked them up before lunch.

'Well, I suppose it's not a bad suggestion,' he said.

Tasha began to feel a bit better about things as they talked it all through. She loved the feeling of support that came with co-parenting, and was thankful that they had always managed to keep their children a priority throughout all the upheaval. She had to give Charlie credit: no matter what he was feeling about her he had, as far as she knew, never given the children a single inkling as to what was going on inside his head.

Chapter Forty

A roaring fire crackled and hissed in the hearth at the pub Becca had chosen for lunch. They sat at a table nearby to warm themselves from the frosty October air outside, placing their orders with a passing waiter and asking for a couple of glasses of Merlot.

'So how was the fortieth last night?' Tasha asked, slightly jealous having spent the evening alone defrosting the freezer.

'Fun, thanks, though I'm feeling a little worse for wear this morning. I probably overdid it a bit.'

'Was it weird without Andrew?' He had returned to Iraq the previous week.

'I'm actually quite used to it. Though obviously I'd rather not be on my own.' Realising that Tasha might not have much choice in future, Becca added, 'Sorry... that was insensitive.'

'Not at all. And you're right, going to parties and stuff must be hard. I haven't actually been to anything yet without Charlie. I keep making excuses so I don't have to.'

'Ah... hair of the dog!' Becca said as she sipped the wine that had just arrived. 'It's so nice to come up to the city and have some time without the children.'

'I bet. I imagine the next few months are going to be pretty manic for you.'

'Don't remind me!' Becca laughed.

'How did Andrew seem when he left?'

'Riled up and ready to go but obviously sad to leave us at the same time, especially the kids.'

'And how did Charlie seem the other weekend?'

'We didn't really talk about you two. It didn't seem right to bring it up in front of the kids, and at dinner on Saturday night I couldn't get a word out of him. He seemed tired though. I can tell he isn't as happy as he always has been with you.'

This made Tasha feel the tiniest bit better. Their plates of food arrived, piled high with roast pork and all the trimmings, including huge strips of golden brown crackling.

'This is absolutely delicious!' Becca said as she devoured her food. 'The perfect hangover cure.'

'Isn't it?' Tasha agreed. 'And how does Daisy seem to be coping with it all?'

'She's drawing lots of pictures of Andrew, she constantly makes him presents and cards for us to send him or give him when he gets home. Apparently it really helps children deal with their emotions if they write things down, or draw.'

'That makes sense. Did I tell you about the worry box we have for Max?'

'I don't think so. What is it?'

Tasha explained how it works. 'He hasn't used it much. I keep checking it before bed and telling him that it's there if he wants it.'

'Perhaps even knowing that he can use it helps him feel less worried. What about Flora? Is she still up and down?'

'Not too bad at the moment. She goes through phases of thinking she is to blame. Even Bella has been a little quieter than usual lately.'

Becca was the ideal person to talk to. She had a lot of experience with children missing their father's presence, after all. She shared a few ideas that she'd tried with Daisy, like keeping a journal for him to read when he got home. They treated themselves to sticky toffee pudding for dessert with their coffee, before paying the bill and heading back to their family homes, ready to welcome their various children back for a cosy Sunday afternoon in front of their own fireplaces: Daisy and Fergus back from Becca's mum, and Max, Flora and Bella back from a weekend at Charlie's.

That evening Tasha checked inside Max's worry box as she tucked him into bed. There was a note inside covered in his spiky writing and she asked him if she could read it.

'I am worried about Christmas,' it said. She read it aloud with a lump in her throat and asked Max what he meant.

'Where will we be?' he asked. 'Will we be at Daddy's or here? Will Santa come to Daddy's? Will he know where we are? Will we all be together?'

Tasha couldn't bear it; he had obviously been thinking about it a lot. Her heart swelled with emotion as she tried her best to answer each question.

'Darling, part of the magic of Santa is that he always knows how to find children. He knows exactly where each child in the world is. Otherwise, if you were to stay with friends or go on holiday you might not get any presents, and that wouldn't be fair, would it?'

Max seemed relieved to hear it. 'OK.' He nodded.

'And even if we are not all together at Christmas, we will always be together in our hearts. It's like Uncle Andrew. Even when he is away he always stays with Auntie Becca and Daisy and Fergus, right in their hearts.'

He seemed somewhat comforted by this, but not entirely. Tasha tried her best to reassure him, giving him extra stories as she tried to settle him down to sleep. For Tasha, seeing the children struggle was hands down the worst part of it all. She just couldn't bear to see the price they were paying for her mistake.

Chapter Forty-one

In November the boiler broke down just as the icy tentacles of winter unfurled and the temperature plummeted. Unwilling to spend longer than necessary without hot water or central heating, Tasha was forced to take a day of holiday to wait in for British Gas. Bath time the evening before had been cancelled and they had all spent the night huddled together in Tasha's bed, each child having woken from the cold.

Tasha filled the machine with load after load of washing. She found it impossible to keep on top of the laundry now she was back at work and the laundry baskets were all overflowing. While she was waiting she decided to make a start on Flora's birthday cake, for which neither heating nor hot water was required. Much to Tasha's disbelief, Flora was turning eleven on Saturday. She had decided to attempt a replica netball for her cake. Following in Bella's footsteps, Flora had asked for a family day out ice-skating as her birthday present. Thankfully Tasha's foot had mostly recovered over the last few weeks. She had relied heavily on the crutch for the first few days until the swelling had gone down, hobbling around the office trying her best to maintain her productivity levels despite her injury. She knew ice-skating wasn't the best idea but at least the boots should be sturdy enough to support her ankle. That reminded her – she needed to give the crutch back to Javier. And she also needed more eggs for the cake.

Keeping an eye out for the British Gas van, she darted to the corner shop at the end of the road to buy eggs and milk. She came back via Javier's, took a deep breath and rang the bell. She waited anxiously but there was no answer. Somewhat relieved, she rummaged in her bag for a pen and paper, scribbled a thank-you note and propped the crutch against the doorframe. She turned around just as the British Gas van pulled up. Several hours later, much to her relief despite the vast expense, the boiler was repaired, hot water was flowing from the taps once again and the central heating was cranking and groaning back into life.

Realising she was now free for the rest of the day, Tasha called Emily to give her the afternoon off. She nipped into Putney to buy a couple more presents for Flora's birthday, making it to the school gates just in time for pickup. It was actually lovely to have the chance to greet the children as they came into the playground; the fact that it was a novelty rather than a daily occurrence changed it into more of a treat for Tasha. She really was glad that she had gone back to work. It was making a big difference to her mental state. She found she looked forward to the time she spent at home with the children at the end of the day, just as she looked forward to her time away from the home and housework when she was at work. She thought back to what Javier had said about the power of change and realised how right he had been. A change really was as good as a rest.

*

Flora's birthday dawned clear but freezing cold, appropriate weather for ice-skating. Tasha was definitely not a natural skater. It seemed to her that trying to balance oneself on two thin metal blades defied the laws of physics.

She shrieked as she stepped onto the rink. As always, she had been the last to get her skates on, having fastened everyone else's for them before starting to do her own. 'Come on, Mum!' Flora laughed, skating over to take her hand, as if it were the easiest thing in the world.

Max was also completely fearless, pushing straight off from the wall and zigzagging his way into the centre of the rink. If he fell down he just stood straight back up again, his low centre of gravity serving him well. Charlie was making his way around the edge with Bella, who always needed some time to gain confidence before letting go of the wall. She probably took after Tasha in terms of ice-skating ability, while Flora and Max were as co-ordinated as their father.

'I'm so wobbly!' Tasha shrieked, clutching onto Flora for dear life.

'It's so fun, isn't it?' Flora was beaming. 'I *love* it!'

Tasha wasn't so sure. She skated slowly around the rink with Flora as her guide, keeping a close eye on Max as he skidded about.

After a while her ankle began to throb so Flora skated her back over to the side. Tasha clambered over to a bench to sit down and remove her boots, happy to watch the rest of her family enjoying themselves. By now Bella was much more confident. Charlie was teaching Flora and Max how to skate backwards. God only knew how Charlie could skate so well. He had never been taught. It was the kind of thing that just came naturally to him.

When the children had finally run out of steam they went to the American-style diner that was attached to the rink and ordered chicken nuggets and chips. Tasha produced the perfectly iced netball from the enormous cake box she had brought with her, much to Flora and the children's delight, and they ate cake for pudding before going back to Charlie's for a sleepover. Tasha made her own way home, trying not to feel too upset at the thought of missing yet more precious birthday time with her children.

As she got back she noticed that the lights were on in Javier's house and she wondered if he was home alone.

A tiny part of her was tempted to knock on the door, knowing that he was in and would offer her company. She was so lonely; she missed Charlie so desperately. But she wasn't in the mood to fight off any advances. She knew perfectly well that if there was even the tiniest shred of hope that Charlie might forgive her and come home, she had to cling to it. If she were to go anywhere near Javier, then she would be stamping out that flicker of hope for good. And there was no way she could do that.

Chapter Forty-two

'Our house has been like a sick bay this week,' Flo moaned as she sat at the kitchen table bunged up with cold. Her nose was bright red and she looked rather peaky. 'All the kids were off school on Monday.'

'Eurgh! I'm not surprised you've caught it, then.'

'I think I've passed the contagious stage now,' she added, aware that Tasha was probably keen to reach for her Dettol.

'I'm glad to hear it!' Tasha laughed.

'The kids are all back at school but my house still absolutely stinks of Olbas Oil. I've had them all doing inhalations morning and night!'

'And salt gargles?'

'Oh, yes. That's how I can tell if they're really feeling ill. If they'll agree to a salt gargle it's definitely genuine.'

'Sounds like you're through the worst of it? It's definitely doing the rounds. Bella has had a bit of a cold this week and apparently the school is rife with it.'

'Better than the v and d of last winter...'

'Don't remind me!' Tasha balked at the memories.

'Though there's still time for that, I guess.'

'Right, that settles it! I'm going to the chemist

tomorrow to stock up on Vitamin C and echinacea.'

'Good idea. I might do the same.'

Tasha had invited Flo over to make up for missing their weekly post-Pilates catch-ups. She felt as though they hadn't seen each other for ages. When they had finished the pizzas that Tasha had picked up on the way home from work, and most of a bottle of wine, declared by Flo to be 'purely medicinal', Flo brought up the separation. Tasha filled her in on the latest developments. 'I've developed a strange paranoia that he might be seeing someone,' she admitted.

An uncomfortable look flickered across Flo's face, instantly fanning the flames of Tasha's suspicion. 'What is it?' Tasha asked, immediately on high alert. 'Do you know something?' Mark and Charlie worked for the same company, albeit in completely different departments. It had been through Mark that Charlie had heard about the job in the first place.

Flo looked torn. Tasha's heart rate quickened.

'Tell me if you do,' Tasha implored. 'I'd *much* rather know.'

Flo sniffed and took another tissue from the box beside her. She blew her nose. 'Sorry. I didn't know whether I should say anything. It could easily just be gossip...'

'Come on, Flo,' Tasha pleaded, desperate to hear whatever it was Flo was hiding from her.

'Are you sure? You might not like it...'

'I'm sure.'

'Well, Mark heard through the grapevine that Charlie might be dating someone,' Flo admitted.

Tasha's heart plummeted. 'Oh,' she said, completely shell-shocked. A shiver ran down her spine and she broke out in a cold sweat. She had absolutely no idea how to handle this information.

'I'm so sorry.' Flo winced. 'I didn't know whether to tell you. It may not even be anything serious.'

'It must be if word has got to Mark?'

'You never know – it's probably just office gossip.'

A flurry of questions hurtled through Tasha's mind. 'When did he tell you?'

'Last weekend.'

'Do you know how long it's been going on?'

'No, I'm afraid not. Look, Tasha, I'm sure it's nothing but hot air, people jumping to conclusions...'

Tasha gripped the edge of the table as if to steady herself; the room seemed to spin as she processed the news. She shook her head. 'Oh, my God. I just can't believe this! This is my worst nightmare.'

'I'm so sorry.'

'Honestly, Flo, it's better that I know.'

Tasha felt utterly sick. Charlie, seeing someone else. The thought of it: him sleeping with someone else, kissing them, holding them... Suddenly she could see him falling in love, moving on from her completely, introducing the children to his new girlfriend, even remarrying. She let out a panicked sob as the tears began to flow.

'Shit, now look what I've done,' Flo said as she passed Tasha the box of tissues. 'It's probably not even true,' Flo tried to reassure her.

'Did Mark mention a name?' Tasha asked. She could tell Flo had more information to spill.

Flo nodded slowly. 'But remember, it's just a rumour. It could be complete bollocks.'

'I doubt it. What is her name?'

'Sophia.'

'Sophia,' Tasha repeated softly to herself.

When Flo eventually left, clearly riddled with angst as to whether she had done the right thing in telling her, Tasha sat on the sofa with the rest of the bottle of wine. She opened her laptop and searched for any Sophias she could find on Charlie's company website. There was only one result. It had to be her. Tasha's heart was pounding as she pressed on the thumbnail and waited for the page to load. Soon enough a picture of a breathtakingly gorgeous young brunette opened on her screen. Tasha let out a slow exhalation, trying her best not to panic. This was who Charlie was dating. *Oh, my God*, she thought. *I could never even begin to compete with that.* She had shiny, long dark hair and a dazzling smile, revealing a perfect set of pearly white teeth. Tasha felt as if she might throw up. She took another gulp of wine and peered closer. She noted her name, Sophia

Beauchamp, and typed it into Google. She spent a good couple of hours searching for her profiles on Facebook, Instagram and LinkedIn, trying to find out as much about her as she could. But despite her best efforts she didn't learn much. Sophia was obviously clued up on privacy settings, preventing random strangers like Tasha from spying on her.

Tasha almost called Charlie several times to confront him, but she stopped herself. If he confirmed it then she would know it was true. At the moment it could just be gossip. She had a sneaking suspicion it was genuine, but she was no way near ready to hear from Charlie that he was seeing someone. The longer she could try and kid herself that it might not be true, the better. Her head spun. It just couldn't be. He couldn't be anywhere near ready to start a new relationship yet, could he? But if someone as beautiful as that should appear on the scene, someone new, exciting and young, basically the opposite of her, then why would he say no? Especially if she had set her sights on him and was going out of her way to catch him… Eventually, she couldn't bear it a second longer. She closed her laptop and went up to bed. Tasha tried to shut off the images of Charlie and Sophia that continuously flooded her imagination, but it was useless. She cried herself to sleep, taunted by her thoughts.

Chapter Forty-three

'Apparently Charlie is seeing someone,' Tasha said. She had called Rosie on her lunchbreak for an emergency debrief, exhausted after yet another restless night.

'No!' Rosie gasped.

'I know!' Tasha shook her head. She still couldn't believe it.

'How do you know?' Rosie asked.

'Flo told me last night. I just don't know what to do with myself! I can't bear the thought of it. He'll never come back to me if he's dating someone else...' Tasha could feel the emotions she had tried so hard to repress all morning spill out of her.

'OK, OK, slow down,' Rosie instructed. 'First of all, where did Flo get this information from?'

'Mark. He works in the same company, remember?'

'Right. And what exactly did she say?'

'He's heard that Charlie is dating a colleague called Sophia Beauchamp.'

'Is it definitely true?'

'Not definitely. She said it could be a rumour.'

'OK,' Rosie said. 'That's good. Have you looked online to see if she even exists?'

'Of course! I jumped straight on my laptop after she left and spent ages looking her up.'

'Did you find her?'

'There's only one Sophia in the whole company. And, to make matters worse, she is ridiculously stunning.'

'OK, well, let's try not to jump to any conclusions. It could be bollocks.'

'As Flo said. But equally it could also be true.'

'Maybe. Or maybe wires have been crossed, they might have been at a work engagement together or having a business lunch and someone's seen them and the rumour mill has kicked into action...'

'That would be the best-case scenario but somehow I doubt it.'

'Are you going to ask him?'

'I don't know. What if he admits that it's true?'

'What about Becca? Do you think she might know something from Andrew?'

'Andrew's in Iraq... so no. I doubt it.'

'Maybe she could try and find out for you?' They spent the rest of her rushed lunchbreak talking about what Tasha should do, until she realised she was meant to be back in the office taking minutes for a meeting and had to dash.

The rest of the day was so incredibly busy that Tasha didn't have more than a couple of spare moments to think about Charlie. On the way home, she stopped at Waitrose to buy some supplies for dinner. Chloe was staying the night. She was up in London for a rare training day and was taking the opportunity to check in on Tasha.

Chloe arrived after the children had gone to bed. Tasha could tell she had spent the day cramped up in a stuffy conference room: she demanded a large, stiff drink as soon as she got through the door.

Tasha poured them both gin and tonics. 'So,' Chloe said, chinking her glass against hers, 'are you still enjoying being a city slicker?'

'I am actually loving it. It's not the most thrilling work in the world but there's so much to do that the days absolutely fly by.'

'That's great!' Chloe smiled. 'What are your colleagues like?'

'Nice enough. It's just so fun being in central London. And I'm enjoying having something else going on other than housework and childcare.'

'I bet. I think it's a good idea, especially now the kids are all at school.'

'It feels like the right time,' Tasha agreed.

'Are you missing being a GP?'

'In some ways. It feels like a lifetime ago... I think it's good to be doing something so completely different. It's very hard to compare. And it's only temporary. Who knows what the future holds?'

'Exactly. Ella seems to be getting on well,' Chloe said. 'Have you heard from her lately?'

'We've FaceTimed a bit. Thank God she'll be back next month and we can all stop worrying about her at last.'

'I can't believe it's already November. Are you all still coming to Mum and Dad's for Christmas?'

'That's the plan.'

'Will Charlie come?'

'I don't think so.' Tasha took a deep breath. 'I just don't know what to do... Max is already worrying about it.'

Chloe looked concerned. 'Perhaps you'll have worked things out by then?' she suggested, ever the optimist.

'It sounds like I may have been naïve to think that was ever on the cards. I've heard Charlie might be seeing someone.'

'*What?*' Chloe was clearly angry on her sister's behalf. 'It's a bit soon, isn't it? What is he thinking?'

'It might just be a rumour, but I wouldn't be totally surprised if it were true.'

'Tasha, what exactly happened? Are you sure you still won't talk about it?'

'I'm sure.' Tasha was determined to stick to her ground.

Chloe looked at her searchingly and nodded. 'Well, are you going to ask Charlie if it's true?'

'I don't know. Do you think I should?'

'Maybe. It's good to have all the facts in a situation like this, don't you think? If he is, then it might help you move on.'

'That's the problem. I really don't want to move on. I just want to fix things.'

It was hard for Chloe to give her advice when she had no idea what had happened. Tasha could tell she thought Charlie had cheated on her, probably with the girl he was rumoured to be dating. It upset her that Charlie had undoubtedly plummeted in her family's opinion, but she couldn't do much about it without telling them the whole story. It was more important to protect the children, at any cost. Realising that pursuing her relationship woes wasn't going to get her very far, she changed the subject, talking about Chloe's love life and school instead.

They had a lovely dinner together; it was great having some company in the house again. As she went to bed Tasha felt the extra sense of security that came from having another adult around, from not being the only responsible person present. Unlike the previous night she actually managed to get a few hours' sleep. She woke feeling a fraction more human and with a fraction more energy to face the day, though she was extremely grateful that it was Saturday and she didn't have to go to work. Charlie was having the children for the night. She wondered if she would be able to tell if he was dating someone from their interaction at handover time. She was going to watch him like a hawk in case he gave anything away, even just in his body language.

*

'Hi,' Tasha said as she opened the door. She had made a special effort, choosing one of his favourite tops and putting make-up on despite the fact she had no plans to leave the house. Chloe had left earlier that morning to meet a friend in Brighton and today was moving day for Rosie and Josh. All her other friends would be spending time with their families, and the thought of joining them and being the subject of their pity was hardly appealing so she would be flying solo once again.

'Hi,' Charlie said as he smiled at her. Her heart soared. He really did have the most incredible smile, so full of warmth. 'How are we all this morning?' he asked. As she talked him through the handover she scrutinised his face to see if she could pick up on any clues, any traces of Sophia.

Charlie stifled a yawn as he listened to her. 'Late night?' she asked.

'It was quite.' Charlie smiled, clearly not wishing to elaborate as to why.

'What were you up to?' Tasha asked, determined to try and suss out any awkwardness.

'Oh, just a work thing,' Charlie said. Tasha's heart lurched with a rush of adrenaline. That could definitely be code for Sophia. She wanted to find out more, but she couldn't figure out how to ask without revealing her suspicions.

'Oh. Right, of course,' she said somewhat awkwardly. 'Well they're all packed up and ready to go.' She lowered her voice to a whisper. 'They are hiding in Max's bedroom. They want to scare you!'

Charlie played the game perfectly, mock searching for the missing children. They jumped on him with their loudest 'Boo!', collapsing in hysterics as Charlie faked his shock. Tasha laughed along with them, all the while trying to quell her panic that one day this family scene could play out with another woman in her place.

Before she knew it, she was alone once again in an empty house. The laughter of a few moments before seemed to reverberate around the rooms, like a distant echo. She found the weekends without the children much harder now that she was back at work. It gave her the vaguest taste of how hard it must be for Charlie not seeing them every day. At least she always saw them all first thing and was always able to do bath time and bedtime. He must miss them so terribly. Maybe the loneliness was to blame for his new relationship. Determined not to mope, Tasha set about the mammoth list of chores that she hadn't had time to get around to in the past two months. There was enough to keep her busy all weekend, a blessing in a way, seeing as the alternative was to drink the entire booze cupboard dry whilst staring at photographs of Sophia Beauchamp.

Chapter Forty-four

Tasha was sorting through an enormous pile of clean laundry at the top of the stairs. It was nine o'clock on Friday evening, the children were finally asleep, and she was almost ready to drop. As soon as this last chore was finished she was planning on going downstairs and flopping on the sofa for some mindless television escapism. As she folded and sorted she went through her ongoing mental checklist of jobs, adding retrieving the Christmas decorations from the loft to the top of the list. She couldn't believe it was December already. They were going to get a tree the following morning, with Charlie, who had kindly offered to carry it in and set it up in the heavy weighted stand, as he always did. Another job she needed him for. Tasha had chased Flo for further news about Sophia but it seemed there was nothing more to tell. Mark had no more information; no further digging had thrown anything else into the light. Tasha felt herself well up with tears, as she did each and every time she pictured Charlie with Sophia.

With a heavy heart she picked up the laundry basket to take it downstairs. She paused to listen, sure she had heard a gentle tap at the door. Sure enough, there was another light tap. *Who could it be at this hour?* she wondered. *Javier? It had to be. What could he possibly want?* Her mind darted over various reasons for a late-night visit as she walked down the stairs. She opened the door a crack, expecting Javier to be waiting expectantly on the doorstep.

To her surprise, it wasn't Javier waiting for her, but Charlie.

'I didn't want to wake the children,' he said. 'And I didn't want to let myself in... in case you had company.'

She could see instantly that he had been crying. 'What is it?' she asked, her pulse quickening in expectation of bad news as she held the door open for him to come in. He looked deathly pale.

'Charlie, what's happened?'

'It's Andrew,' Charlie croaked, his voice breaking. He looked at Tasha and his eyes filled with tears; the pain in them said it all.

He shook his head.

'He's dead.'

His voice was barely a whisper.

'*What?*' Tasha's mind reeled. 'No!' she gasped, as her eyes widened in shock. Her hand flew up to her mouth.

'Becca rang... He was killed early this afternoon.'

'Killed? Andrew's dead?' The meaning of his words just couldn't seem to sink in.

Charlie nodded. He stepped closer and wrapped his arms around her. He hugged her tightly, as if she could somehow help take the pain away. In his embrace it suddenly hit her. Tears coursed down her cheeks and she broke into noisy sobs as she thought of Becca, Daisy and Fergus, of Andrew's body lying somewhere: lifeless, broken, cold.

'I can't believe it,' she whispered, pulling away and looking up at Charlie.

'I know.' He was clearly still in shock.

'Oh, my God, *Becca*... your parents... Do they know? Do you know what happened?'

Charlie shook his head. 'Becca didn't go into much detail. She was so upset she could barely talk. Her mum had to take the phone in the end.'

'I just can't bear it.'

'She had phoned Mum and Dad straight before calling me. Mum is absolutely devastated, they both are. I'm going to drive up there now. But I had to tell you first.' Charlie had to stop talking. Tasha had never seen him so upset. It broke her heart.

'They've asked me to pass the news on to certain people, so I've been making some pretty horrendous calls.'

'Oh, Charlie. I'm so unbelievably sorry,' Tasha said. 'I just can't get my head around it.'

'He was in Syria, not Iraq, as I had suspected. He was hit by an IED.'

'Oh, my God. Poor Andrew.' Tasha wiped the tears from her cheeks with her sleeve. She felt shocked to the core and completely shaken. All the angst she had been experiencing over the last few months, the self-pity, paled into insignificance in the face of sudden death's brutality. How could Andrew be dead? He was such a vital part of all their lives, such a force of nature, such an incredible person. How could it be that he was no longer alive? Just like that?

They went through to the sitting room and sat on the sofa, both numb with shock. Charlie was quiet and Tasha didn't know what to say. There were absolutely no words for a situation like this: the abrupt, cruel waste of Andrew and everything he had to offer, all the life he had left to live. There was nothing she could say that would offer any comfort. She couldn't stop thinking about Becca. How would she go on living without him? She would have to raise the children on her own... Tasha's heart wept for her dear friend. 'Poor Becca,' she whispered, shaking her head in disbelief.

'I know,' Charlie said. Deep frown lines creased his forehead, his eyes were bloodshot and swollen with grief. She knew just how devastated he must be. Andrew was not only his brother but his best friend. How was it possible that they would never see him again? That no one would? She just couldn't accept that it had really happened.

'How did she find out?' Tasha asked.

'Some officers went to her house.'

Tasha nodded, picturing the scene, the knock on the

door. The fear in Becca's eyes as she saw the officers approach. Dread taking its ice-cold grip around her heart.

'She's got one of them there with her now. He'll help us arrange the funeral.'

'Oh, God, the funeral…' Tasha's eyes filled with tears once again at the thought. 'I just can't believe this is real. It feels like a nightmare.'

'I know.' A solitary tear rolled down Charlie's cheek. He was normally so stoic, rarely displaying much emotion. It made his grief all the more heart-rending to see. Lost for words, Charlie turned towards her. She put her arms around him. His shoulders heaved as he finally broke down. She held him tightly until his sobs subsided.

'Shall I come too? To your parents'?' Tasha asked.

'No, don't worry. You stay here with the kids.'

'What about Becca? Shouldn't we go to her?'

'If she wants us to. She'll need some time…'

'When will the funeral be?'

'Fairly soon, I imagine.'

'God, the thought of it… the coffin.'

'I know… *Jesus!*' Charlie stood up and walked over to the wall. He thumped his fist against the door frame, angry with the world for being so unbearably cruel, unable to accept what had happened. They talked about Andrew while Charlie gathered his strength for the drive to Norfolk. He was dreading seeing the look in his parents' eyes, knowing just how upsetting it would be to see them so heartbroken. They reminisced about some of the amazing times they had all shared, laughing and crying. It was as if the earth-shattering news had drawn a temporary veil over their recent issues. Tasha was too stunned to give her obsession over Charlie and Sophia a single thought. Charlie needed her, and she needed him. Right now, nothing else mattered.

When he felt ready to leave she waved him off in their car, knowing how much Stephen and Caroline needed him to be with them. It was at times like this when family became the most important thing there was. She picked up her phone and called Becca on her mobile, sure that she wouldn't answer but wanting her to know she was there if she needed her. She spent a long time composing a message of condolence. It was so hard to decide what to say, she knew full well that no words could bring even the slightest comfort to her. She couldn't even begin to imagine the state of confusion, panic and despair that Becca must be in. How she would have handled telling Daisy... Fergus would be too little to understand. Selfishly she wished she could have Charlie by her side as she lay in bed later that night, staring at the ceiling, still trying to process the news, to adjust to a world without Andrew in it.

The next morning Tasha bit back tears as she showered, trying to stop her face from giving away any signs of the news she had agreed not to share until the afternoon, when Charlie arrived back. He had texted her first thing to tell her he was driving his parents straight to see Becca and the children that morning, at Becca's request. She wanted them all to be together while they organised the funeral. Charlie would return to Becca's house again later that evening, but he wanted to be there with Tasha when they told the children.

Their reaction was heart-wrenching. It was the first time the children had had to deal with someone they knew dying. As they tried to understand what it meant they asked more and more questions, each as impossible to answer as the last. 'Why did Uncle Andrew have to die? What happened to his body? What will Daisy and Fergus do without a daddy? Who will look after Auntie Becca? Will he be an angel in heaven now?'

Tasha was so glad that Charlie was with her. She needed his strength and reassuring presence to pull herself together and keep strong for the children's sake as they answered each question as best they could. It felt as if they had had too many serious talks with the children of late. She hated how much they had been through these past four months. Though it was nothing, she reminded herself, in comparison with what Fergus and Daisy would be experiencing now and in the years to come. There was nothing like the death of a loved one to give you a much-needed reality check.

She had called Becca again that morning, but she hadn't got through. Becca had sent her a message.

Thank you dearest Tasha, for your kind words. We're doing OK. I'll speak to you very soon, Bx

Every time she read the text she welled up with tears. Becca always seemed so strong, but Tasha knew what must lie underneath that brave outward appearance.

'Can we make Auntie Becca, Daisy and Fergus a card?' Max asked.

'That's a lovely idea,' Tasha said, moved by his thoughtfulness.

'It might be nice if you can draw a happy memory to help cheer them up a bit,' Charlie suggested.

'I'm going to draw us all in the swimming pool playing Marco Polo,' Bella said. 'Do you think they'll like that?'

'They'll love it, darling.' Tasha smiled.

'I'm going to draw a picture of us all at Fergus's christening,' Flora said as she fetched the tub of felt pens. 'That was the best day ever!'

Later, as they waved Charlie off on his way to Becca and his parents, Tasha thanked God from the bottom of her heart that her family were all there in front of her, healthy and safe. Even if they were never a traditional family unit again, she could accept that if she had to, so long as they were all OK. Though she knew she would never stop loving Charlie, not even for a moment.

Chapter Forty-five

On Sunday Charlie had called Tasha to tell her the funeral would be taking place the following Wednesday. It had all happened so quickly, organised with the typical quiet efficiency of the military. In the tradition of the SAS there would be no pomp and ceremony, no parade, just a quiet local service in their village church. Charlie had stayed with Becca and his parents, offering them his support, helping with Daisy and Fergus, generally being there for them all. He had also been working on the eulogy, which Becca had asked him to give. Tasha knew how much he hated public speaking. This would be without a doubt the hardest thing he had ever had to do; so much raw emotion. Tasha was beside herself with nerves on his behalf. What if he lost control and couldn't get the words out? It would be too heartbreaking to see. And she knew how important it would be for him to feel as though he'd done Andrew proud.

On Wednesday Tasha got the train to Surrey, having left the children in Emily's care. The journey passed by in a total blur. She was lost in her thoughts, still trying to come to terms with what had happened. When her taxi pulled up outside the church, memories of Fergus's christening came rushing back. It had been the last time they were all gathered there: a truly happy occasion, the opposite of what they were all about to face.

The grey stone offered calm sanctuary from the cold wind that nipped at its walls. One of Andrew and Charlie's cousins greeted Tasha at the door, offering her an order of service. Her heart leaped into her throat as she saw the photograph of Andrew on the front page, so handsome in his uniform, so full of life. Fighting to control her emotions, she was shown to a pew near the front, behind Becca, Caroline and Stephen. Daisy and Fergus were at home, both far too young to witness such a harrowing sight. Tasha slipped into the pew, reaching forward to squeeze Becca on the shoulder. She turned to greet Tasha, giving her a glimpse of the faintest smile behind the tightly clamped mask of pain. She looked fragile and lost; a shadow of herself. Tasha kissed Caroline and Stephen, offering her condolences, furiously blinking back tears in the face of their brave smiles. They looked as though they hadn't slept in days. A family gathering missing one vital piece.

The church was packed to the rafters with Andrew's loved ones. The pungent scent of white lilies lingered in the air. Half-smiles of greeting flickered across faces heavy with sorrow as they caught the eye of long-lost friends. The overwhelming weight of grief was palpable.

A hush amongst the congregation announced the

coffin's arrival in the church. The pall-bearers, led by Charlie, were some of Andrew's closest friends. As the solemn procession made their way up the aisle silent tears streamed down Tasha's cheeks. Charlie's eyes brimmed with tears, pain etched his features. She knew she would never forget the sight as long as she lived. Becca broke out into sobs as she saw the coffin, the Union Jack an emblem of the cause for which Andrew had so selflessly given his life, his beret and belt the poignant reminders of the beloved man to whom they had belonged. Having placed the coffin down Charlie took his seat between Becca and his parents. He turned around and smiled at Tasha, deep purple grooves under his eyes. She could feel his agony with every fibre of her being.

Soon the space was filled with voices singing, defiant, determined to give Andrew the send-off he deserved. When the time came for Charlie to give the eulogy, Tasha could barely breathe as she watched him take his place at the pulpit. He was so like his brother in so many ways, those deep blue eyes, the kindness in his face. Her heart went out to him; she was willing him on with every cell of her body. His hands trembled as he looked around the congregation, causing the paper he held to tremor against the polished wood.

He cleared his throat, took a deep breath, and began to read. His touching words echoed around the church. It was beautiful, every word heartfelt. He described his brother through a series of stories, covering each stage of Andrew's life, eliciting several laughs amongst the multitude of tears, never more so than when he talked about Becca: how complete she had made his life, how his children were the best gift he could ever have been given, how much he adored them.

Tasha had never felt so proud of Charlie as she did in that moment, watching him standing up there, so vulnerable yet so strong. She had never felt so completely full of love.

All too soon they were standing out in the bitter cold at the freshly dug graveside, watching the coffin as it was slowly lowered into the ground. A gentle drizzle of rain drifted down as if heaven itself were weeping. Tasha reached out and took Charlie's hand in hers, he squeezed it tightly. She looked at Becca, clutching hold of her mum; the anguish on her face was so agonising it broke her heart. She watched Stephen and Caroline, arm in arm, so frail themselves. She couldn't begin to imagine what it must feel like to see your child buried; no parent should ever have to witness such a thing.

After the wake they drove back to London with the heaviest of hearts. Charlie was needed back at work the following day. Tasha had offered to stay instead of him but Becca had assured them she would be all right, that she wanted some time with just her and the children. Becca had been brave beyond imagination at the wake, smiling and greeting Andrew's friends and family as if offering them comfort when it should have been the other way around. Daisy had joined them for a while, dressed in the fuchsia-pink dress Andrew had always said was his favourite, a much-needed splash of colour, resplendent in her childish innocence, unable to quite comprehend the enormity of what had happened or the loss she would suffer without her father.

'It was a beautiful ceremony,' Tasha said quietly as she drove. The rain had begun to fall more heavily, the wipers swept across the windscreen, back and forth in a rhythmic beat. 'Your eulogy was perfect. Andrew would have been so proud.'

'Thank you,' Charlie said. 'It was definitely the hardest thing I've ever had to do. God, it all happens so bloody quickly, doesn't it?'

'One moment they are here, the next they are gone.'

'Life can be so tragic.' He shook his head, still finding it hard to believe that his brother was really dead.

'It's amazing how we forget just how mortal we all are.'

'Isn't it?' Charlie said, staring blankly out of the window.

When they pulled up on Havers Street Tasha glanced across the road, noticing the lights were on. Back inside they paid Emily, thanking her for looking after the children, who were all tucked up in bed. She left, telling Tasha she would see her in the morning.

'Right, I guess I'll be off,' Charlie said. He looked

comatose with exhaustion.

Tasha's heart fell. She couldn't bear the thought of being on her own after the harrowing events of the past few days. And she didn't want Charlie to be alone either. Part of her had been hoping the total agony of Andrew's death might have brought Charlie back to her. That he might stay with her that night. She swallowed and nodded. He was probably going to meet Sophia, who would no doubt be waiting for him with open arms. At this the tears welled up once again, but she fought them back.

He looked at her and she turned away, not wanting him to see just how desperately she still missed him, when he was so clearly moving on. 'I'll call tomorrow,' he said, 'to speak to the kids.'

She nodded again.

They checked on the children, who were all fast asleep, and then Charlie left, closing the door quietly behind him. Tasha walked into the kitchen. She opened a bottle of wine, poured herself a glass and sat down. She stared at the wall, at a framed photograph of them all, taken two years ago in Dorset. She felt numb from pain and loss. She howled as she let the tears fall freely, crying for Andrew, for Becca, for Daisy and Fergus, for Charlie, and for their children. In that moment she knew that Charlie had truly gone, that he was never coming back.

Chapter Forty-six

Tasha didn't know how long she had been sitting there. She felt as if her heart had been ripped from her body. She didn't know how she was going to continue, how she could possibly rebuild her life without Charlie by her side. She wiped her tear-stained cheeks and marvelled at the power of love, how it could make you feel the dizzy heights of elation and joy whilst also, when taken away, the very darkest despair. She felt quite light-headed. Looking at the bottle of wine, she realised she had drunk over two thirds without really noticing. And she hadn't eaten anything since breakfast.

A storm was brewing. Tasha listened to the sound of the wind as it whipped against the window, lost in her thoughts. The windows rattled. There was a light tapping sound. She strained her ears. It came again, just as it had on Friday night. Tasha got up from her chair and walked into the hallway. Suddenly her heart was pounding. Maybe Charlie had changed his mind? She stumbled to the front door and pulled it open, adrenaline coursing through her veins.

Javier was standing there. 'Oh!' she said, trying not to show her disappointment. 'Hi.'

'Tasha. Are you OK?' he asked. She had clearly been crying: her eyes were puffy and swollen, her face blotchy and red. 'I saw the children earlier on their way back from school. They told me about your brother. I'm so sorry.'

'Thank you.' She wiped her eyes with her sleeve. 'It was my brother-in-law actually, Charlie's brother.'

'What a terrible tragedy. I saw Charlie leave...' He paused. 'He doesn't live here any more, does he?'

Tasha suspected he had wanted to know the answer to that particular question for some time. She shook her head, unwilling to elaborate.

'I thought I'd come over to see if you were all right. If you want some company? I know how it feels to lose someone close to you...'

Tasha wondered what he meant, who he had lost. She took one look at the sympathy in his eyes and collapsed into tears once again. He took a step closer to her and embraced her in a heartfelt hug.

The hum of an engine approaching caught her attention. She opened her eyes.

Charlie's face was staring at her through the rain-spattered window of a taxi. He had come back! As she broke away from Javier's arms, realising with utter panic how it would look to Charlie, she saw him say something to the driver, who pulled away, driving off down the road. The hurt in Charlie's eyes had been unmistakeable.

'CHARLIE!' she shouted, running down the street. But it was too late. He had gone. How would she ever explain what she had been doing in Javier's arms? 'Shit!' she shouted.

'Charlie?' Javier repeated, his voice revealing his confusion as he followed her out onto the street.

'He just pulled up... he's driven off. He must have seen us hugging. Oh, for *Christ's* sake!' Tasha put her head in her hands in exasperation. How typical that he would turn up at that bloody moment. She took a deep breath. 'Look, Javier, thank you for coming to see if I'm OK. I am fine. I promise. But, I've got to go...'

She ran up the steps and into the house, closing the door behind her, leaving Javier looking at her somewhat bewildered. She sprinted into the kitchen and grabbed her phone, calling Charlie on speed dial. It rang straight through to his voicemail.

'Look, Charlie, it's me,' she said. 'I promise that wasn't what it looked like. Please, you *have* to believe me. He rang the bell, I thought it was you. I was praying it was you. I opened the door and he was just standing there. He asked me about the funeral – the kids had told him about Andrew. Before I knew it, I'd burst into tears and he had hugged me... The next thing I know I open my eyes and you are right there in the taxi. I *promise* nothing happened! He's gone now. Please, come back...' She ended the call, pacing around the kitchen. She could scream with frustration. Of all the things to have happened, that was the worst possible scenario she could imagine. What had he been coming back for? What if that really had been him deciding to give her another chance? There was no way he would now he'd seen her with Javier. She crumpled onto the floor and stared at her phone, willing Charlie to call her back. She sent him messages and called him again and again but there was no answer. It was too late. She had ruined her last chance. Perhaps it was no more than she deserved. After all, if Becca and Andrew couldn't have a happy ending, why should she?

Chapter Forty-seven

The next evening Charlie called to speak to the children. He hadn't replied to her voicemail, or any of her texts that day. 'Did you get my messages?' she asked, having raced to pick up the landline before one of the children got there first. 'I've been trying to explain about what happened.'

'I did. It doesn't matter.' Charlie's voice was clipped and curt. It was as if he had finally given up caring.

'I promise, what I said in the voicemail was all true... It was nothing, just the worst possible timing. What were you coming back for?' she asked.

'Nothing. Like I said, it doesn't matter.'

'But it *does*!' She felt desperate for him to tell her.

Charlie interrupted her. 'Look, Tasha. Can I speak to the children? I haven't got long.'

She realised it was no use. She went into the sitting room and passed the handset to Flora, who was in the middle of building a tower out of matchsticks for a DT project. Tasha slumped on the sofa next to Max, who was watching *Paw Patrol*. Bella was dutifully practising her recorder, the slightly wobbly notes of *Silent Night* echoing down the stairs from her bedroom. Tasha knew she had blown any chance she had of getting him back. He was probably in a rush to go and meet Sophia. Seeing her in Javier's arms would have pretty much given him the green light to pursue his new relationship without so much as a backward glance. She felt sick to her stomach. Now she would never know what he had been going to say to her.

'Mum, Dad says he'll get our Christmas tree this weekend,' Flora said, turning away from the receiver. 'He wants to know if that's OK?'

'Tell him I say thank you,' Tasha said. She didn't feel particularly festive, but she knew that she needed to at least attempt some seasonal cheer for the children's sake. Perhaps once they had decorated the tree she would start to feel a tingle of Christmas spirit once again. Everything just seemed so depressing. First her marriage break-up and then Andrew's death. She couldn't imagine how their lives had got to this point.

Before she knew it, it was Saturday morning and she was standing in an empty house staring at a six-foot tree, undecorated and taking up a large proportion of the sitting room. They had all walked to the park first thing to choose it. Charlie had carried it home, installed the tree in its stand, and then disappeared promptly with the children. There had been minimal conversation between them; the intimacy that they had shared in the wake of Andrew's death seemed to have evaporated. Tasha had promised the children fervently that she would wait until they got back the following afternoon to decorate the tree. She trudged upstairs to locate the Christmas decorations that were tucked away somewhere in the loft, before spending the rest of the afternoon in a mountain of wires on the sitting-room floor trying to detangle the fairy lights.

In the evening she went for a Christmas drink with Rosie and Flo, an annual event that had started twelve years ago when they were her bridesmaids. They had treated Tasha to champagne at the Ritz, deciding it was such a wonderfully festive experience that they would maintain the tradition each year, taking advantage of the huge tree and the live music to plunge themselves into Christmas spirit. Tasha hoped it would have the desired effect and lift her out of her gloomy mood. Perhaps everyone else's festive cheer would somehow rub off on her. She wore a sparkly black top and some bright red lipstick, in an attempt to bring some colour to her pale face. She dabbed concealer under her eyes in a bid to disguise the bags. She hadn't slept much since Andrew had died. Part of her felt it was wrong to go out and celebrate so soon after his death. But another part of her knew both he and Becca would want life to carry on as normal. And she knew how much Flo and Rosie were looking forward to their annual catch-up. Tasha was the middle link between them; they wouldn't see each other without her there.

Surprisingly, she found she really enjoyed herself.

There was something uplifting about being in such opulent surroundings, with so many joyful people out for Christmassy cocktails after a busy day shopping. Flo and Rosie were both in remarkably high spirits. Rosie was just high on life full stop these days, thanks to Josh, and Flo was making the most of an evening out of the house, having left Mark in charge of the kids. They raised their champagne glasses in a toast.

'Cheers!' Rosie said.

'Cheers!' Flo and Tasha replied.

'To Andrew,' Rosie added. They chinked their glasses again, pausing for a moment to think of him, and Becca.

'How was the funeral?' Flo asked. Tasha filled them in, telling them about the funeral, the wake, and the incident with Javier and Charlie upon their return.

'God, that is just typical,' Rosie said.

'Isn't it?' Tasha laughed in bitter disbelief at the bad timing.

'I wonder what Charlie was going to say?' Flo asked.

'I know. I'll never know, now. That's for sure. He's clammed up again. I really thought we were beginning to get somewhere after Andrew…'

'Such bad luck, Tash,' Rosie sympathised.

'Has Mark heard any more news about Sophia?' Tasha asked Flo.

'Still nothing. Look, the more I think about it, the more I'm sure it was just a rumour,' Flo said.

Tasha knew she was just trying to make her feel

better.

'Mmmm,' Tasha said. 'He always seems to be dashing off somewhere or other. It would certainly explain a lot if it was true.'

'What are you going to do for Christmas?' Rosie asked.

'We'll be at my parents'. Charlie is going to stay with Becca and the kids, with Caroline and Stephen. On Boxing Day he'll come and pick them up and take them for a few days, so I'll be at home with Chloe and Ella. At least I won't be on my own...'

'Thank God for that,' Flo said. 'When is Ella back?'

'Tomorrow!' Tasha said. 'She's been away for so long, I can't believe it.'

Tasha steered the conversation away from herself and onto Flo and Rosie. She didn't want to wallow in her misery, knowing the best way to avoid it was to focus on their news, their happy lives instead. They ended up finishing the bottle of champagne and then ordering all sorts of weird and wonderful cocktails. The bill was extortionate, as always, but they declared it worth every penny as they stumbled onto the Tube home, Flo and Tasha heading west, and Rosie heading east.

The next day, Tasha hit the shops to get some much-needed Christmas shopping done, trying her best to ignore her throbbing head. She piled up the boot of her car with bag after bag of gifts, stocking fillers, wrapping paper and ribbon. Normally she was much more organised than this, but her return to work seemed to have made her woefully behind schedule. She stood by the car with her shopping list and pencil, crossing off all the purchases she had made: gardening gloves for Caroline, golf balls for Stephen, a cashmere shawl for Becca, stacking blocks for Fergus, a *Frozen* doll for Daisy, a saucepan for Bertie, an art book for Lizzie, a frame for Ella and pyjamas for Chloe.

The last item on the list read 'Charlie?' She had left it blank, having no idea what she could possibly give him. She wasn't even sure if it was appropriate to get him anything at all. Did separated couples buy each other gifts? Suddenly an idea sprang to mind. An album. She could choose a selection of her favourite photographs of the children, of the family altogether, from the past ten years, and make him an album. It might seem odd if she chose photographs of them as a couple, especially from before Flora was born, but he couldn't think it strange to be given pictures of his family, could he? Perhaps it would make him miss their life so much he would come home? It was a long shot, she knew, but it must be worth a try. Pleased with her idea, she darted back to Paperchase to find something suitable.

Back home with her laptop in front of her, she scrolled through hundreds of photographs, searching for her favourite snaps. Her mobile rang, interrupting her search. As always, she hoped it was Charlie, and was disappointed to see her mother's caller ID on the screen.

'Hi, darling!' Lizzie's cheerful voice sounded in her ear as she answered the call.

'Hi, Mum,' Tasha said. 'How are you?'

'All well here, thanks, darling. We're just on our way to collect Ella from the airport. The flight was delayed by three hours so we're much later than we would have liked to be, but at least if we go and pick her up we can make sure nothing else can possibly go wrong! Otherwise you never know, she'd probably catch the wrong bus or miss her train station and end up in Land's End!' Lizzie laughed in exasperation.

'Good point. I can't believe her trip is finally over.'

'Thank the Lord!'

'It'll be great to see her.'

'That's what I want to talk to you about,' Lizzie said.

'Ah… Christmas?'

'Well, yes, that, and exactly what you need from me in terms of the children…'

'Right.' Lizzie had kindly offered to help with the children for the few days between the end of term and Tasha finishing work. Emily was going to Rome with her boyfriend, so was unable to take on full-time babysitting duties.

'The kids break up next Friday, so they're fine for the first two days as it's the weekend. Then I'll need your help from the Monday to the Wednesday when I get home from work. If that's still OK?'

'OK. I'll see if I can persuade your sisters to come and

help!' Lizzie said. 'All three of them for three days might be a bit much for me. And Bertie needs to stay with the dogs so he's no use.'

'They'd love to see Chloe and Ella, great idea,' Tasha said. 'I'll send a WhatsApp on the family group now.'

'OK, darling. And then you'll be with us from the twenty-second on?' Lizzie asked.

'Yes.'

'What about—?'

'Charlie? He's going to be at Becca's with his parents. He'll pick the kids up on Boxing Day and they'll spend a few days with him.'

'Right. So... you're definitely spending Christmas apart?' Lizzie confirmed.

'It certainly looks that way,' Tasha said.

'OK.' Lizzie was being as supportive as she could be given the circumstances and the little information she had been given, and Tasha was grateful for the fact her family had stopped trying to find out every detail of their separation. She no longer had to fend off the endless invasive questions; it seemed that her family had finally accepted the separation as the new norm, even if she hadn't.

Chapter Forty-eight

It was a strange, unsettling Christmas without Charlie. He was notable in his absence every second of the day. He hadn't been there with the children to put treats out for Santa and the reindeer, he hadn't helped her hide the stockings bulging with presents at the foot of their beds, he wasn't there on Christmas morning sporting his musical tie and festive socks, nor was he there by her side in church. She could feel the rest of the congregation's stares as they gossiped about her, the space next to her conspicuous in its emptiness.

Her heart went out to Becca. If she dared feel sorry for herself for even one second, she thought of her friend and got a healthy dose of perspective. Charlie might not be with them, but he was still alive. And he was offering Becca some much-needed support. She just wished she could be there with her too. She hadn't seen Becca since the funeral, having been busy at work before plunging into Christmas activities with the children. When she had suggested meeting up the day before Christmas Eve Becca had been meeting the solicitors to discuss Andrew's will, and the accountant to go through their finances. There was so much to face, so much to deal with, it must be impossible for Becca to feel as if she was keeping on top of it all. She knew from her messages how grateful Becca was for Charlie's help. He was never more than a phone call away, offering his advice and trying to take as much of the burden off her shoulders as he could.

Christmas lunch was cooked to absolute perfection by Bertie. They pulled their crackers, laughed at the terrible jokes, and gorged themselves on Christmas pudding and champagne. They opened their gifts in front of the Christmas tree before wrapping up warm and taking the dogs for a long walk. By bedtime the children were absolutely worn out, as was Tasha. When they were down for the night, in matching Christmas onesies from Chloe, she collapsed onto the sofa with her sisters and parents, cradling yet more champagne, and watching the Christmas specials on the television. She missed Charlie with every fibre of her being.

The next morning Charlie came to pick the kids up as planned. 'Dad!' they squealed as they raced out to give him a hug.

He spun each of them around crying, 'Merry Christmas!' in his best Santa impersonation. 'Did Santa come?' he asked. 'Did you get lots of presents?'

'We got *so* many!' Bella cried.

'Look at my Spiderman costume. Isn't it cool?' Max did an elegant twirl to show off his suit.

'Very cool. What about you, Flora?' Charlie asked,

his eyes twinkling at the children's enthusiasm. 'What was your best present?'

'A make-up set!' she replied, sounding very grown up.

'Make-up!' Charlie cried in mock horror, raising an eyebrow at Tasha.

'From Auntie Ella.' Tasha laughed apologetically. Ella, Chloe, Bertie and Lizzie came out to greet Charlie. She watched as they all wished him a happy Christmas. The usual camaraderie between them had gone, so it was actually quite painfully awkward despite everyone putting on a good show for the children's sake. Charlie politely refused Lizzie's offer of a cup of coffee.

'We'd better set off. Thank you, though,' he said, opening the car doors for the children to pile in. He had come over in a taxi and was taking the car back with him. She had left Becca, Daisy, Fergus and Charlie's presents in the boot with the children's suitcases, carefully wrapped and labelled with cards. He hadn't given her anything, she noticed, but she didn't mind. She was still glad that she had made the gesture. Tasha kissed the children goodbye and waved them off, tears stinging her eyes as she watched Charlie turn out of the drive, Max's nose pressed up against the window as he blew her kisses.

Chapter Forty-nine

A few days later Bertie dropped Tasha off outside Andrew and Becca's house. He had decided not to come in, worrying that a visit might be too much of an intrusion for Becca at this early stage of mourning. It was bitterly cold. A diamond frost clung to every surface, sparkling with all its might in the bright light of the sun. The icy gravel crunched underfoot as Tasha walked across the drive to the front door, her breath like puffs of smoke in the air.

Becca smiled bravely as she opened the door. 'It's *so* good to see you,' she said, hugging Tasha warmly and ushering her inside. There was no wreath hanging on the front door, no Christmas tree occupying its usual place in the entrance hall.

'Mum!' Max scampered over to give her a hug. Daisy raced into the hall, out of breath, as was Max. As his only junior she had clearly been commandeered to play some sort of 'baddie' for Spiderman to chase.

Bella and Flora were in the sitting room playing Twister. Charlie was supervising the game while Fergus merrily bashed a selection of pots together at his side. 'Hi, darlings!' Tasha called.

'Hi, Mum!' Flora and Bella replied from their contorted positions on the floor.

'Don't get up!' she said. 'You'll spoil your game.'

'Hi,' Charlie said.

'Hi,' Tasha replied. 'Everything OK?'

'Great, thanks.'

'Would you like a cup of tea?' Becca asked, looking from one to the other. She was clearly still intrigued as to what had come to pass between them.

'I'd love one,' Tasha replied gratefully. 'But I'll make it. Charlie?'

'I'll come and get mine in a minute,' he said.

Tasha followed Becca into the kitchen. Tasha could see her shoulder blades jutting out through her cardigan. She must have lost about a stone in weight.

'How are you doing?' Tasha asked, having made three cups of tea and taken the lid off the tub of homemade flapjacks she had brought.

'As you can imagine,' Becca said, tears welling up in her eyes. 'Not very well.'

Tasha reached out and squeezed her hand, smiling sympathetically.

'I honestly don't know what I'd have done without Charlie. He's been such a great help, as has my mum, of course, and Caroline and Stephen…' Tears spilled down her cheeks. 'Sorry,' she whispered, reaching for a tissue.

'Please, don't apologise,' Tasha said. Becca smiled and nodded. Words were almost redundant. Nothing could convey the feeling of loss that hung so heavily between them. Tasha didn't want to offer trite condolences, to attempt to make her feel better when such a thing was impossible. Only time could begin to heal the wounds, and time could not be rushed.

'How is Daisy?' Tasha asked. 'She was amazing at the wake. As were you…'

'I can't even remember it, to be honest, it feels like such a blur. Daisy is so wonderful. I am not sure if she understands that she will never see him again…' Becca shook her head in disbelief as more tears rolled down her cheeks. 'But then… I am not sure I can believe that either…'

'I know,' Tasha said. 'It seems impossible.'

'And Fergus is the best comfort. He doesn't understand. He just carries on as normal. At least I can pick him up and cuddle him whenever I need to…'

Tasha could see how exhausted Becca was. Her eyes were swollen and ringed with dark shadows. Charlie brought Fergus into the kitchen and joined the conversation. The game of Twister had apparently ended with Max launching himself on top of his sisters like a human torpedo. His tactic had worked; all four children were now playing his game.

They ate the flapjacks and sipped their cups of tea, talking about the funeral, more details that had emerged about Andrew's death, how much support Becca was receiving from the army and whether there was anything more Tasha and Charlie could do to help.

'Do you know what? There is something. It would be an enormous favour...' Becca looked almost hesitant to ask.

'Anything,' Tasha said.

'Whatever you need,' Charlie echoed.

'I am desperate for some time alone,' Becca said quietly. 'I just need some space to process everything, to gather my strength.'

'Of course,' Tasha said. 'I'm sure that would do you the world of good. Do you want us to have the children?'

'That would be the favour. I just feel at the end of my tether.' At this Becca started to cry. Tasha got up and went over to her, holding her tightly. 'As long as I have the kids with me I keep trying to put on a brave face. I don't feel like I've really had the chance to just cry, sleep and stare into space. To figure out what the hell I'm going to do. To even begin to get my head around all this. It's all I want... just for a couple of days. To think about him, uninterrupted, to draw some strength for this next year without him... for every year after that...' Charlie passed Becca the box of tissues from the centre of the table and she wiped her tears.

'Becca, absolutely. Of course we will. You need to do whatever helps you feel better. And if it's time alone you need, that's exactly what we will give you,' Charlie said.

'I'd feel too bad to ask my mum. She's by herself

too...' Becca tailed off.

'Why don't we take Daisy and Fergus with us now?' Tasha suggested. 'We could pack their stuff up – we've got everything they could possibly need at home already. It would be too easy.'

Becca looked tempted at the thought.

'Could I borrow your car, perhaps?' Charlie said. 'I could drive them back to London and Tasha can drive ours. They can stay with us for a couple of days. Then I'll bring them back on Sunday? In time for New Year's Eve? Would that work?'

'Are you sure?' Becca asked. 'It wouldn't be too much for you both?'

'Of course not, Becca.' Tasha smiled. 'We're so happy to do anything at all. Honestly, whatever you need, you only have to ask.'

'I'm so grateful. I really don't know what I'd do without you all. Everyone's been so amazing.'

'It's the least we can do,' Charlie reassured her.

They confirmed the plan. Charlie rang up the insurers and made sure he was covered to drive Becca's car. Andrew's car would still be there for Becca to use so she wasn't stranded in the house. Tasha organised the children with enough clothes and supplies for a couple of days away and they loaded the cars up with all five children, everyone's suitcases, coats and wellies and set off.

Leaving Becca alone with just the dogs for company

seemed like a cruel thing to do, but it was what she wanted and Tasha could understand why. It had been such a whirlwind: Andrew's death and the funeral, then Christmas. Having so many visitors, her parents-in-law to stay... She could imagine a couple of days just being alone in the house, not having to look after the children, just being with all her memories, all Andrew's things, would do her the power of good.

*

Back in London, it quickly became apparent to Tasha and Charlie just how overwhelmingly chaotic life would be had they produced two more offspring. The difference between three and five mouths to feed, bodies to fit in the tub, bedtime stories and the like was quite dramatic. Tasha and Charlie were both run off their feet: unpacking, cooking, taking the children to the park, watching over Fergus, finding pyjamas, erecting the travel cot, making a camp bed up for Daisy and supervising bath time. By the time they'd got all five children settled for the night they were both ready to collapse with exhaustion.

'Do you mind staying here tonight?' Tasha asked as they slumped onto chairs in the kitchen. 'Just in case there's some kind of emergency. I'd feel much better having someone else in the house.'

'You mean you'd rather my help than Javier's?'

Charlie asked. 'Surely he'll be around to come to your aid at the first opportunity?'

Tasha had been waiting for him to finally bring Javier up. '*Of course* I'd rather your help. I have literally seen Javier once, for about five seconds, since I hurt my ankle. I don't see him. I hardly speak to him if I can help it. I told you, he just turned up out of the blue that evening, offering a sympathetic ear and a really badly-timed hug, which I know I should have refused. I was really upset...'

Charlie looked at her searchingly, trying to work out whether to believe her. Having someone doubt her every word was so infuriating. Tasha knew the reason he didn't trust her, but it didn't make it any easier. If only there was some way she could prove to him that she was telling the truth.

'Please, Charlie. We can't go on like this. You can't doubt every word I say. You have to decide, once and for all, whether you can trust me. You trust me with your children every day, after all. For Christ's sake!' Tasha suddenly felt at the end of her tether. 'I made *one* mistake. One, huge, unbelievably stupid mistake. You can't punish me for it for the rest of my life!'

Charlie was quiet for a moment or two. He nodded slowly. He sighed, running his hands through his hair. It was as if he was resolving some internal battle. Perhaps he would finally let it go? 'I'll stay,' he said. 'But in the spare room.'

'Of course.' Tasha was just grateful that she wouldn't be alone.

'Do you want a drink?' Charlie asked.

'I'd bloody love one!' Tasha smiled. 'The biggest glass of red wine on offer, please.'

'Thank you for the photograph album, by the way,' Charlie said as he opened a bottle and poured her a glass. 'I loved it.'

'No problem!' Tasha said. She didn't want to make eye contact in case he was embarrassed by the unreciprocated gift. Instead, she concentrated on warming up the bolognese she had made that afternoon. She added some of the wine from the bottle and set the pan to simmer. They collapsed with their bowls of pasta in front of the television, both of them shattered from the day, not to mention the sheer emotional roller coaster of the last few weeks.

Saturday was equally exhausting. To occupy the children, they wrapped them all up warm and set off for a long walk along the tow path, Fergus tucked up in his pram. They went to Pizza Express for lunch on the way back, always a safe bet to accommodate groups of children, the combined decibels of all their junior diners enough to drown out the contributions from their own gang. In the afternoon they watched a movie under the twinkling lights of the Christmas tree. It was all too bittersweet for Tasha, having Charlie home, especially that evening. She knew that it could be the last time she spent the night under the same roof as him. She tried to stay strong, thinking of Becca. She didn't want Charlie to see how totally dependent on him she still was. Besides, she knew she could lose the plot completely the following night, when she was all alone again, by herself for the first time in her life on New Year's Eve. When the children were in bed they watched television, side by side but distant. It was still so awkward between them. The ease and camaraderie, the ever-present banter of before nowhere to be seen.

The following day Charlie loaded up the car and drove Daisy and Fergus back to Becca. They had called to make sure Becca was ready to have them back and she had thanked them profusely for taking them off her hands, assuring them that she felt much better after some time alone and that she was looking forward to having her children home for some much-needed cuddles. Tasha waved them off, once again trying not to cry as Charlie left her, knowing that she might not get to spend time with him like that ever again. No doubt he was spending New Year's Eve with Sophia. He would be getting the train back to London that afternoon. If only he were coming back to her...

'Are we still having our New Year's Eve dinner, Mum?' Flora asked.

'Of course we are,' she said.

Charlie and Tasha usually said that the children weren't allowed to stay up until midnight, knowing how much of a write-off New Year's Day would be with three overtired, grouchy children. Instead they were allowed to play party games all afternoon and have a special New Year's Eve meal, with their chosen menu. They had a wonderful time despite Charlie's absence, bobbing for apples, playing board games, charades and a competitive game of musical statues. Tasha laughed so much tears came into her eyes as she watched the children dance around the room. It was a delightful sight, and one she wished Charlie were there to share with her. Their chosen menu consisted of chicken and chips with beans, and jelly and ice cream for pudding. By ten o'clock, the children having stayed up beyond their bedtime as an extra treat, she had finally managed to get them all tucked up in bed and off to sleep.

With a peaceful household once more, Tasha went back downstairs to tidy up the sitting room. *What a way to spend New Year's Eve,* she thought. She couldn't stop the tears from filling her eyes as she went into the kitchen to clear away the dishes. She stood at the sink, tears streaming down her cheeks, lost in her thoughts as she washed the pans in the soapy suds. Elbow deep in dishwater, she suddenly looked up as she heard a knock at the door. She wiped her eyes with the sleeve of her jumper, drying her hands on the back of her jeans as she walked towards the front door.

Chapter Fifty

Charlie was standing on the doorstep. He stepped inside and pushed the door shut behind him. Without saying a word, he pulled her towards him and kissed her. He held her tightly, his body pressed firmly up against her. Tasha felt as if she could melt into his arms; the comfort of his embrace was like nothing else. Her head was spinning in confusion. He pulled away, looking into her eyes with such tenderness and love that her heart skipped a beat.

He traced his thumb gently down the side of her face. His eyes glistened with tears. 'Tasha,' he said.

She barely dared to breathe.

'Leaving Becca all alone, with the children… All the way home I couldn't stop thinking. There *has* to be a way for us. Andrew's death has made me realise just how much you mean to me, how much our family means to me. Nothing else matters. I have to forgive you. I love you so much. I have never stopped loving you, not even for one second. Being apart from you, the lonely nights, seeing the children without you – I feel like I've been missing a limb.'

'Oh, Charlie.' Tasha's voice was choked with emotion. She could hardly believe her ears. She fell back into his arms and kissed him again. 'I love you so much. I promise you I will never let you down again, I swear it.'

'I know,' he said. 'I have been thinking about what you said on Friday. You are right. I can see how hard this has been for you, and I have to accept responsibility too. I wasn't making enough effort with you. I was so wrapped up in work I stopped listening, I wasn't a good enough husband to you, and for that I am sorry.'

'But... what about Sophia?' Tasha asked, dreading to even bring up her name in this moment, for fear of spoiling it. But she just had to know.

'Sophia?' Charlie looked confused.

'Flo told me you were seeing someone...' Tasha said. 'A colleague...'

'Oh,' Charlie said, looking slightly awkward. 'Right. I did see her a few times, but...' he cupped Tasha's face in the palms of his hands and shook his head '... she wasn't you, Tash. You are the one. You always have been.'

Tears were rolling down both of their cheeks now. He kissed her again, making up for all the time they had been apart. Eventually, they found their way upstairs to their bedroom. Tasha felt completely overwhelmed as Charlie made love to her. As she lay in his arms all the heartache gradually began to ebb away. She felt a deep sense of peace begin to return.

Chapter Fifty-one

'I can't believe you're here.' Tasha smiled as she cuddled up to Charlie in bed. It felt amazing to wake up next to him again.

Charlie pulled her towards him and kissed her.

'The children are going to be so happy!' Tasha pictured their faces when they told them the news.

As she lay in his arms Tasha felt the most extraordinary happiness alongside the bitter sadness of Andrew's death. She almost felt guilty at her elation about having Charlie back when Becca was faced with such deep and permanent loss. However, she knew that Andrew would have been the happiest of all to hear that they were giving their marriage a second chance, and she clung to that.

Tasha could hear the children stirring. She crept out of bed to investigate, finding them in Flora's room.

'I've got something to show you,' she said. 'Come with me!'

They followed her into the bedroom, intrigued. 'Dad!' they squealed with delight as they saw Charlie.

'What are you doing here?' Flora asked.

'It's a surprise!' Charlie said. Tasha laughed as she

saw the happiness spread over their little faces. This was how it should be, the family all together. He looked at Tasha for approval. She smiled in return and nodded. 'Mummy and I have decided to live together again,' he said. 'We just missed each other too much to be apart.'

'Oh *yay*!' squeaked Max.

'That is the best news I have *ever* heard!' Bella cried.

'Really?' said Flora. 'Starting from now?'

'Yes!' Tasha said. 'Starting from now!'

They threw their arms around Charlie and Tasha. 'This is the best day of my life!' Bella declared solemnly.

'Can we tell all our friends?' Flora asked.

'Of course you can, darling,' Tasha said.

'Hooray!' the children cried as they hugged their parents again and again. Charlie ruffled their hair and laughed. He leant over to give Tasha a kiss.

Later they went to Wimbledon Common for a walk, wrapped up in their warmest winter clothes. They tramped through the damp woodland, cheeks red from the chill in the air, grins plastered across the children's faces as they stamped on icy puddles with their wellington boots. Tasha had to keep pinching herself in case she was dreaming, to be sure that Charlie had really come back. She had been so close to losing him, she could hardly believe that he was truly there.

*

The next day Tasha was back at work. She phoned Rosie on her lunchbreak. 'I *knew* he would come back!' Rosie cried. 'I just knew it. He loves you so much, there is no way he could live without you.'

'I am so happy!' Tasha couldn't keep the smile off her face. 'I am never going to complain about anything he does, ever again.'

'Ha,' Rosie laughed. 'I'll hold you to that one, shall I?'

'Well, we'll see!' Tasha had to admit that it was an unlikely promise.

'So, what now?' Rosie asked.

'I think we need to have some chats, once we're used to being back together, to re-evaluate everything and see if we can make any changes going forward.'

'Have you talked about Javier?'

'Not really. Charlie says he doesn't want to.'

'Maybe he'd rather just forget about it and move on.'

'Maybe. The main thing is that I don't want to take our marriage for granted ever again, and neither does Charlie. Losing Andrew has made us realise that more than anything.'

Afterwards Tasha called Becca; she had wanted to be the one to tell her, rather than Charlie. Becca was even happier than Rosie had been at the news, declaring it the first time she had really smiled in weeks. She reiterated what Tasha had suspected: that Andrew would have been the happiest of them all to hear it. 'If we can learn anything from his death,' Becca said, 'it has to be to just love each other as much as we can while we still have the chance.'

'You're right,' Tasha said. 'And we will, I promise.'

By the time Tasha had called her family and Flo to tell them the happy news her lunchbreak was well and truly over. She headed back into the office. She texted Charlie.

> My family are over the moon, as are Becca and the girls. They all send lots of love xx

She paused to look at her screensaver. It was the photograph of Tasha, Charlie and the children that someone had taken in Richmond Park all those months ago. She smiled at the memory.

That evening they shared a bottle of wine in front of the television, cuddled up next to each other on the sofa. She felt so close to him again, physically and emotionally, remembering all the times she had felt so completely disconnected from him, and she was so grateful that they had somehow managed to bridge the divide. They both knew there was a long road ahead, but for the first time in a long time it felt as though they were in it together, on the same team. Javier's presence across the road was the remaining elephant in the room, the constant reminder of just what they were trying to forget.

Later that night as they lay in bed, Tasha's head

resting on Charlie's chest, Tasha asked a question that had come somewhat out of the blue into her mind. 'How would you feel about moving away from here?' she said, looking up at him.

'You mean selling the house?' Charlie asked.

'Yes. Selling the house and moving to the country.'

Charlie was quiet for several minutes as he thought about it. They both knew it would be a good idea to move away from Javier, though neither of them said it.

'That's always been the dream...'

'I know. But really, what is stopping us?'

'It just feels like such an enormous decision.'

'Well, we could start to think about it,' Tasha said. 'We don't have to make any decisions to begin with.'

'Agreed.' Charlie was quiet for a few moments, stroking her hair. After a while he said, 'Do you remember that house that Andrew told us about?'

'Hazeldown? Do you think it's on the market yet?' Tasha asked.

'It could be.'

'It would be the ideal location. Near my parents, near Becca, it's near a station so we could both commute...'

'God, wouldn't it be nice to wake up to the countryside each morning? And the weekends... just peace and quiet, open fields...'

'It would be amazing!'

'A fresh start could be good for us, for all of us, the children included.'

'I think they'd love it. Though they'd be miserable leaving their friends...'

'They'd make new ones.'

'And Flora... she might actually be happier at a secondary school in the country...'

'I'd much rather that, in a way,' Charlie said. 'They'll grow up so fast in a city school.'

'Do you think we could really make this happen?' Tasha asked, hardly daring to believe it.

'I don't see why not,' Charlie said. 'We've always talked about doing it one day – maybe now is the right time?'

Tasha smiled and closed her eyes. It felt so good to be back in his arms; as she drifted off to sleep she dreamed of all the happy times they had ahead of them.

Chapter Fifty-two

Tasha's birthday fell on the thirteenth of January: a date no one would willingly choose. Everyone was always so bloated from their overindulgence, still coming down from the high of Christmas that they were never in the mood to celebrate. She never particularly looked forward to it.

The doorbell chimed at ten o'clock in the morning, just as Tasha was standing on a kitchen chair, straining to reach one of the overhead spotlights to change a bulb. Charlie still hadn't mastered the necessary technique, though Tasha was determined to teach him and add the task to his list of responsibilities. As part of their ongoing discussions they had agreed to redistribute household chores more fairly going forward.

Charlie answered the door. To Tasha's amazement, Lizzie and Bertie bustled into the house, having left the dogs at home with Ella.

'Surprise!' they cried as they hugged Tasha, Charlie and the children. 'Happy birthday, darling!' they said, handing her a present wrapped in floral paper.

'Mum! Dad! What are you doing here?' Tasha asked.

'Lizzie and Bertie have kindly agreed to babysit!'

Charlie explained. 'We're going away for the night. I've already packed your bag!' He looked extremely pleased with himself.

'Away?' Tasha asked. 'Oh, my goodness! Where are we going?' She couldn't remember the last time Charlie had planned a surprise weekend.

'You'll have to wait and see.'

'Have a wonderful time with Granny and Grandpa,' Charlie said to the children a short while later, having run through exactly what was required of Tasha's parents over the next twenty-four hours. 'And be good. Mummy and Daddy are going somewhere special for Mummy's birthday. And I'm afraid children aren't allowed.'

'Unfair!' they cried as Tasha and Charlie kissed them goodbye and made a run for the door.

It seemed that they were heading directly for Becca's house. No matter how many questions Tasha asked, Charlie remained resolutely tight-lipped. Soon they pulled up outside a Tudor house with a cockerel-shaped topiary hedge, Hazeldown: the house they had stopped to look at all those months ago. 'What do you reckon? Do you still fancy a look around?' Charlie asked.

'Can we? Is it actually on the market?'

'It certainly is! And I've arranged a viewing with Peter Cunliffe.'

'I can't believe it!' Tasha gasped, getting out of the car. 'It's so beautiful.' She looked at the whitewashed walls, the Tudor beams, the thatched roof. It really was the most charming house. And the setting was idyllic, surrounded by rolling hills and farmland.

An hour or so later, both Charlie and Tasha were completely in love with the place. Peter had given them a comprehensive tour of the property and grounds. Sweeping lawns were edged by beautifully-kept borders. There was an enormous farmhouse-style kitchen with an island and a huge green Aga, three big bathrooms, five double bedrooms, a dining room, sitting room, drawing room and a gorgeous conservatory stretching out onto the garden. It would need a bit of work, and more than a lick of paint, but its potential was undeniable. As they left Charlie promised Peter that he would be in touch very soon. Tasha and Charlie talked and talked about the serious possibility of a move for the remainder of their journey towards their second secret destination of the day.

An hour or so later Charlie parked outside a boutique country spa hotel. 'Here we are!' he announced as he switched off the engine. 'Our home for the night.'

Tasha squealed with excitement, jumping out of the passenger seat and flinging her arms around Charlie.

'It's got an award-winning spa. And we've got a dinner reservation in the restaurant this evening.'

They went into the hotel and checked in, looking around and admiring all the cosy seating areas complete with roaring fires, the twenties-style bar lined with bottles of different-coloured glass and the beautiful artwork that hung on the walls. Having dumped their bags in their suite, they went straight to the spa for a Jacuzzi and swim before returning to their room, where a bottle of champagne was waiting on ice.

'Happy birthday!' Charlie said as he poured her a glass. They toasted her birthday, soon falling asleep side by side in a champagne haze, luxuriating in the peace and quiet of being child-free. A while later Charlie woke her with a kiss, untying her white towelling robe and making love to her, taking advantage of their time together with no children to interrupt them.

That evening, after drinks in the bar, they ate a delicious meal in the hotel restaurant. The more they talked, the more time they spent together, the more Tasha felt they were reconnecting as a couple, repairing the damage they had caused one another stitch by stitch. As they lay in bed that night, Charlie produced a tiny velvet box from his bag. 'Happy birthday,' he said.

'Charlie!' she cried, opening the box to reveal a set of diamond earrings, each drop cut into the shape of a heart. 'They are absolutely beautiful! Thank you,' she said as she pulled him close and kissed him.

'I love you,' Charlie said, kissing her back.

'I love you too.'

In that moment, she felt the happiest she had ever felt, knowing just how far they had come and how much more of their journey together there was still to unfold.

The future seemed full of new and exciting challenges, full of hope and possibility.

Epilogue

'It's snowing!' screeched Max as he came bouncing down the landing and into their room, an impish grin fixed across his face. 'And Santa's been!' he squealed, depositing a bulging stocking full of gifts onto the bed, before bolting off to rouse the rest of the house with a 'Merry Christmas everyone!' Tasha laughed sleepily as she reached over to switch on her bedside table lamp.

'Happy Christmas,' she said, leaning over to kiss Charlie.

'Happy Christmas!' he replied. Tasha laughed at the sight of him in his reindeer pyjamas. She got out of bed and threw back the curtains. Sure enough, snowflakes were falling thick and fast, each one miraculous in its perfection, adding to the bright white canopy of snow that had already started to settle across the fields and hedgerows below. She still couldn't believe that this was her view: rolling countryside as far as the eye could see. She knew she would never get bored of it.

Seconds later Bella and Daisy, who were sharing a room, could be heard shrieking with delight as they looked out of the window and saw the snow for themselves. 'It really is snowing!' they cried, racing into the spare room to wake Becca and Fergus, who was in his travel cot by Becca's bedside.

Flora traipsed sleepily into their room with her enormous stocking. 'Happy Christmas, Mum and Dad!' She yawned.

'Come on!' Max squeaked, racing back into the room to retrieve his stocking. 'Let's go down and open our presents!' He looked as if he was about to spontaneously combust with enthusiasm.

They gathered around the tree, adorned with jewel-bright baubles. Carols played joyfully from the speakers and a fire crackled in the hearth. 'Look!' Max squealed. 'The carrots have gone!'

'And the whiskey is empty...' Daisy was beside herself with excitement. 'There's only a few crumbs where the mince pies were!' Their innocent disbelief was enchanting.

'You must have all been very good this year.' Becca smiled. 'Look at all these presents!' Tasha, Becca and Charlie couldn't help but laugh as they watched the children rip open the colourful paper and shriek in disbelief at the spoils that lay hidden inside. Max and Bella, who had joined Daisy at the local primary school, had written letters to Santa for their Christmas homework. Max was delighted to find Santa had granted his wishes, convinced more than ever that he was real. Bella played along despite the rumours flying around school that Santa didn't exist, clinging to the magical make-believe for one last time. Flora had settled in well to the follow-on secondary school, making new friends easily. She seemed much less anxious, much to both Charlie and Tasha's relief.

After a rushed breakfast, having managed to persuade the children to get dressed in their best frocks and Christmas jumpers, they piled into two cars to drive to church for the Christmas Day service.

Before entering the church, they walked over to the far side of the graveyard, where Andrew had been laid to rest, Becca carrying Fergus in her arms.

'Happy Christmas, Dad,' Daisy said, placing a card she had made on her father's grave.

'Happy Christmas, darling,' Becca repeated as she stepped forward to rest a wreath of holly at the foot of Andrew's gravestone. They paused, each of them taking a few silent minutes to pay their respects, before following Becca's lead and making their way into the church. No matter how much time passed it was still hard to accept that he wasn't with them.

After the service Stephen and Caroline were due to join them for their first Christmas in their new home. Never a day went by without Tasha thanking her lucky stars for their new life in the country. The space, the peace and quiet, the beauty of their surroundings: it was the stuff of dreams, and they both agreed it was the best decision that they had ever made. It was the perfect place to start the rest of their lives together, their own happily ever after.

Acknowledgments

Thank you to all of my wonderful readers for sharing this story with me. I really hope you enjoyed it. Writing this book has been rather a roller coaster journey! I started writing it when my daughter was three-months-old and finished the first draft seven months later. The following months were spent editing and copy editing, and, as I write these words and put the finishing touches to the manuscript, my daughter is now one. I remember reading an article by a fellow author while I was pregnant, saying something along the lines of 'you'd have to be mad to try and write a book on maternity leave.' With a contract already signed and a deadline agreed, I wondered whether I had bitten off more than I could chew! I am incredibly lucky to have such a wonderful support network of friends and family, all of whom, along with my editor and my agent, have enabled me to finish this book, whether through helping with childcare, the writing process itself, or offering moral support and encouragement.

It has been challenging but incredibly rewarding at the same time. The book is dedicated to my family: to my parents, Adam and Polly, and my siblings Sophie,

Emma and Robert, as well as to my husband Tom and our daughter Camilla. I'd like to thank my parents for everything they have done, and continue to do, for us all, and for being such wonderful grandparents. To my siblings, thank you for all the laughs, the camaraderie, and the support. Emma, Sophie and Mum, you are always the best sounding boards when I am plotting my books, thank you for all your help, for all the drafts you have read and for all your advice and ideas. Tom you have been my greatest support, as always, and Camilla, thank you for being the best baby we could possibly have wished for.

I would also like to thank my fantastic agent, Bea Corlett. You have been there every step of the way, always there at the end of the phone when I need you. Thank you for your unwavering support and belief in me. I would also like to thank my brilliant editor, Sarah Ritherdon, for challenging me to make this book a bigger, better version of itself. I would like to thank the rest of the team at Aria, my wonderful publishers, for all their hard work: Caroline Ridding, Sue Smith, Sue Lamprell, Camilla Lloyd, Nikky Ward and Melanie Price.

To Ben, Carice and Margs: thank you for all your help and advice and for answering all my questions so patiently. To the 'Grid Mummies' who helped inspire me with some of their stories about motherhood, thank you too.

They say it takes a village to raise a child, and it certainly takes a village to raise a child and write a book at the same time! So to my 'village' of friends and family, I'd like to thank all of you, wherever you are, for being there, for inspiring me, for all the wonderful times we have shared and for all the adventures yet to come.

A Letter from the Author

Dear all my lovely readers,

First of all, thank you for reading my book. It is just amazing to be able to share the imaginary world I have created with you for the hours it takes to read a novel, to know that you are following my characters on their journeys… wherever they may lead! You are invaluable and there is nothing more exciting than hearing from you as you spread the word and leave those much-appreciated reviews online. If you can spare the time then please do so, it really is the number one best way to help a writer out!

Please follow me on social media. My Twitter handle is @georgiecapron where you can find daily tweets from me, and I am also on Instagram @georgiecapronauthor. Please check out my website www.georgiecapron.com and like Georgie Capron Author on Facebook too.

I love hearing from readers so please message me on Twitter, Facebook or via the contact page on my website.

With love and thanks,

Georgie xx